I...

The Girl in th...

ROBERT J. CRANE

Ostiagard Press

INNOCENCE

The Girl in the Box, Book 43

Robert J. Crane

1st Edition.

This one is dedicated to Dan Prestegaard, a good man and a good friend, whose lifelong ambition was to be a character in a book. Congrats, pal, you made it!

CHAPTER ONE

"Fifty-eight votes for, fifty-one against."

My eyes were rooted to the television screen at the far end of our office, the sun shining bright through the panel of windows that stretched from end to end of the bullpen. I squinted against the reflected glare on the dark screen; dark because it painted a live view inside the state of Minnesota's House of Representatives chamber. State reps milled around, casting their votes in a icy-slow drip of progress, each cast vote sounding like the death knell of my damned life.

"Fifty-eight for, fifty-two against."

The dull, mechanical speaking voice of the daytime news anchor on the local station didn't help the mood in the bullpen. I sat on the edge of my desk, a ragged thumbnail clenched between my teeth. I'd never bitten my nails in my life, really.

Now every single one on both hands was sporting a ragged edge.

I hadn't had a drink in over twenty-four hours, and I was feeling it.

"They're calling this like a horse race," Reed, my brother,

said with utter disgust. His lips were still a pallid color after the events of last night, and specks of dried, fake blood still painted his tanned neck. He scowled at the screen, rumpled in a T-shirt and jeans, his long, dark hair tied back in a severely mussed ponytail.

"Well, it kind of is," Scott Byerly said. He, too, was tanned and covered in fake blood, but that was where the resemblance between him and Reed ended. His hair was dirty blond, short, with a waviness that bordered on the start of curls. He checked his phone and cringed; he'd put in a call to his dad to let him know about the destruction of their estate up north, but his father had not yet replied. Philip Byerly was an early riser, so the likelihood that he'd received his son's message was high. The probability he was ignoring him was higher still, and given that Scott's entire financial well-being rested on his father...

Well, it wasn't good.

"It's a horse race determining whether we get run out of town on a rail or not," Augustus Coleman chimed in. He was sitting in his chair, sullen, his dark skin matching his countenance in this case. He, too, was covered in dried fake blood, little dull spots on his ebony skin around the back of his neck.

"I doubt they'd use a rail," his brother Jamal said, drawling. He was a lot more relaxed than Augustus about this, his feet propped up, his new girlfriend in the seat next to him. That was probably what was relaxing him.

"I could change the vote tally on the screen if you'd like," ArcheGrey1819 said in her Eastern European accent. I truly did not know her name other than that. She glanced up at us, seeking approval, her brown trench coat an odd contrast; it was covering a flowery sundress. Her dark tresses were hanging partly over her face, hiding a set of eyes that were keenly watching the goings-on. From her, I got the sense of an animal ready to run.

"That's just the kind of trouble we need right now," Olivia Brackett offered. She was one of the few of us in the room not covered in fake (or, in my case, often, real) blood. She was also still wearing the same clothes as she'd been wearing yesterday, they just looked windblown as all hell from her time in captivity. "Getting caught altering the balance of votes when they're trying to ban us from the state for having powers."

"That's not exactly what the legislation does," came a crackling voice from the speakerphone on my desk. On the other end of the line was our lawyer, Miranda Estevez. "Essentially it criminalizes possession of powers without evidence of regular injections of suppressant. So if you want to remain in Minnesota–"

"Yeah, I don't think I want to take the neuter pill," I said, my arms folded tight in front of me. "Leave myself wide open to enemies and helpless against whoever wants to come after me."

Again.

No one said it. But the uncomfortable looks and dead silence in the room told me everybody was thinking it.

"Well, what's the alternative?" Angel Gutierrez asked. She was, of course, covered in blood, her light brown skin similarly flecked with the red spots, but only on one side of her face. Her own hair had been tucked back in a rushed ponytail. We all looked like we were living out of the trunks of our cars. Which, since the Byerly lake house had burned last night, technically we were. Not one of us had been back to the places we called home, drawn instead to this central gathering location in common, riven by the events unfolding before us.

"Uh, leave," Augustus said, getting up out of his seat and

draping himself over the edge of his cubicle wall to watch. It caught him just under the armpits and held him up as he stretched. "Personally, I don't want to be anywhere they don't want me. It's like going to a party of people who hate you. Why?"

"Spite...?" Scott offered, shrugging lightly.

"Spite is hardly a reason to inject yourself with neutering drugs and remaining in the presence of people who consider you their enemies," said the woman to my left. She didn't move much, her stillness in spite of these tense events a surprisingly calming influence on me right now. Her hair was curly and brown and hung free to just above her shoulders, the barest hints of gray starting to show at her roots. She had a no-bullshit expression on her face – or maybe that was just her face, actually – and stood a little taller than me, her arms wrapped around her slightly thinner (than mine) frame. The woman who'd been the first Valkyrie, daughter of the Goddess of Death, looked slowly around at us, and you could feel the deep well of her history in that moment. "In the days of old, it'd be a good reason to destroy them."

"Yeah, well, I'm not looking to go to war with the state of Minnesota right now," I mumbled.

"Thank God for small miracles," Reed said, a little sourly. He glanced behind him, into the window that opened to his office, and there, in the desk chair, a small woman with dark hair slept in his chair. Dr. Isabella Perugini, his slightly worse half. Fiancée. Hell on wheels. "I don't think I can handle any more wars at the moment."

I tried not to roll my eyes, because I could tell my brother was still a little raw about last night. Which was fair. I also withheld any snarky comments about it not being my fault, because...well...accepting responsibility felt like one of the twelve steps I was going to have to toddle my way through in the near future.

"Sixty-three for, fifty-eight against."

"Did I miss where it jumped up...?" Olivia asked, straightening her thin neck like a giraffe and focusing in on the TV.

"Whatever, we're five votes down now," Jamal said, leaning forward, Arche's hand on his shoulder. "Was six. Maybe..." He clenched his hand, his dark knuckles paling slightly.

"I think this one's in the bag, folks," Miranda said over the crackling phone line. "Governor Shipley wouldn't have called this if she didn't have the votes. Falling flat on her face would be awfully embarrassing after making a promise this big. And it already passed the state senate."

"We know, Miranda," I said, tense on the edge of my seat. "I think we're just hoping to hear a reprieve before the executioner's axe drops."

Reed eased a little closer to me. "If Minnesota's so important to you, you could just take the serum. Be a normal person. Hell," he said, looking around without much conviction, "maybe it'd make sobriety easier to achieve, not being in this job anymore."

"Walking around looking over my shoulder every day of my life, wondering if someone's going to walk up to me on the street and shoot me dead, without being able to do a damned thing about it?" I gave him a knowing look. "Yeah. That doesn't make me want to drink."

Reed smirked. "Fair point."

"Sixty-five for, fifty-nine against."

"Damn," Augustus said, letting out a breath I felt like we all were holding. "What do they need to pass it?"

"Sixty-seven." Miranda answered from over the phone.

"Sixty-six for, sixty-two against."

"Come on, come on, come onnnnnnn..." Jamal implored.

"Sixty-seven for, sixty-three against," the voice announced. "The Safe at HOME Act passes, and will move on to the governor for signature."

A long moment of silence followed. I stared at the TV, at that mythical number. Sixty-seven people, representing however many Minnesotans, had decided they no longer wanted me here.

Here in the place I was raised.

Here in the place I'd shed blood to defend.

Here in the place I'd nearly died to protect. Repeatedly.

"Sorry, guys," Miranda said. "Game over."

"Yeah," I said, a little hoarsely. Because it was, in fact, game over.

I'd lived in Minnesota for as long as I could remember. My parents had met here, lived here together, and I'd lived here my whole life, at least since I was a child. Ten years in captivity had been spent in Minneapolis. Eight years since I'd started plying my craft trying to save lives of Minnesotans, mostly spent here.

This was my home.

"Was" being the operative word.

I stared at the number sixty-seven, and a cold, trickling sensation down my spine told me it was all over now. All those years, come to an end.

Minnesota didn't want me anymore.

I couldn't stay.

"I guess it's time to leave," I said quietly.

Because it really was. The end of an era.

Time leave to my home behind.

CHAPTER TWO

"So...next steps?" Reed asked, looking around the room.

"Seems like, at least in the short term, we need to leave town," Augustus said. Then he made a show of wiping his brow. "I'm just glad I got my degree now, because at least I don't have to try and figure out how to transfer credits. What a nightmare."

"Truly no one is suffering as you are," Scott said acidly. I knew how he felt; his face was red, and I was sure he was contemplating deeply what this new ban meant for his family. Sure, they had means; they weren't having to figure things out while broke as a joke, but still...

This couldn't have been easy on him. His jaw settled into a tight line, and he looked to the side. Like me, Scott was a Minnesotan. This was bound to be hard on him.

"Can we even pick up and move?" Jamal asked, looking at Reed.

Reed stared back. "You mean financially? Not easily, no. But we have to unless we want to go to jail, so..."

"Can I recommend Florida?" Olivia asked. "The winters are a lot milder." Oh, right. She was from there.

"Texas," Angel chimed in. "Centrally located, unlike Florida. And they like us there."

"Florida likes us fine," Olivia shot back.

"Lots of places like us fine," Reed said. "Texas and Florida, sure. New York and California have also made bids to try and get us to come to them in the past."

I cringed. "Probably scratch California off the list." I let my eyes darted left and right. "Just...based on the LA thing last month...I'm not sure they'd want us anymore."

"Isn't New York chock full of heroes already?" Augustus asked. "Gravity, Cap'n Frozen Nuts..." Frost. He meant Captain Frost. But I had to concede his nickname for that turd was better.

"Everywhere is filling up with powered people," Reed said, pacing. "But I'd say we're likely to find an offer just about anywhere we care to look. Some will be better than others."

"Except Minnesota," I said. "Their benefits are generous, what with the three-hots-and-a-cot, but the pay is pretty shit."

"I know my opinion doesn't count, but I also vote for Texas," Lethe said, looking sidelong at me.

"I think you're all missing the point," Miranda said, weighing in over the speakerphone. "You don't have to decide right now. You have time."

Glancing at the TV screen, I interjected, "Nuh uh. You told us the bill goes into effect on Monday at midnight. It's Friday morning."

"It does go into effect Monday morning," Miranda said. "That's just when you have to be out of the state, though. Not when you have to have a new HQ set up. You can vacate the state and make your decision from any of the other forty-nine that don't hate you."

"I wouldn't suggest putting said decision off for long," Reed said sourly. "Sucks to be rootless, after all. Can we even get out of our lease, Miranda? Or leases, I guess, since we all have apartments and whatnot?"

Augustus cackled. "Mine's out at the end of the month and I was about to move out closer to here." He pumped his fist. "This timing is beautiful. Everything is coming up Milhouse."

Whatever that meant. Still... "I suppose I'll have to say goodbye to Ariadne," I said glumly. And try to find a new place to live. While being completely broke. Actually, in thousands of dollars of debt and collecting no paycheck, since now the struggling business that was putatively supposed to pay me was about to eat some unforeseen moving expenses.

"I'm on a month to month," Olivia said with a shrug. When she caught a stray glance from Reed she added, "When you got all axe-swingy last year, I figured it made sense to keep my options open in case you had to make more cuts."

"Same," Angel said. "I was going to move soon anyway. Just hadn't decided where yet."

"To answer your question, Reed," Miranda said, crackling through, "I think for business purposes, it's going to be best if you dissolve the company and declare bankruptcy."

"Shit," I muttered, putting a hand up to my head. The end was nigh, apparently.

"Don't let that panic you," Miranda said. "That doesn't mean the end of any of this, it just means this particular company goes away, and we form a new one. One that's not being besieged by constant lawsuits and motions from the State of Minnesota. In fact, this might solve a lot of your problems. It was tougher to argue that you weren't in the same business if you remained in Minnesota and continued doing the same things with the same owners, but given that they're forcing you out it actually opens things up for you quite a bit. You can just burn it down and start over."

"Maybe I'm channeling Friday here," Scott said, "but she

doesn't mean literally...?" He made a match-striking motion, then mimed dropping it brought his hands up, imitating flames rising.

"No, I mean when you declare bankruptcy for the company, the largest part of the debts that have been incurred over the last few years disappear," Miranda said. "All the back rent and damage disputes from your last office location, the credit card bills for the corporation – all the stuff that's been hanging around your neck the last few years? Gone. You start out at ground zero again, which, for a company that's been in the hole for several years now...means a fresh start."

Reed blinked a few times, his arms wrapped around himself. "You mean we can be free of all this financial bullshit?"

"Yes, but..." Miranda said, "...you're also starting at zero. No working capital to fund paychecks, or a new office lease."

"We might be able to get one of those states to fund that, though," Reed said. "A couple of them have offered some nice incentives for us to move."

"Actual cash with which you can fund lease of an office?" Miranda asked. "And make payroll?"

Reed sagged. "No."

I raised my hand. "Yeah."

He looked over at me. "...What?"

"I got an offer earlier this year that kinda fit that," I said. "Nashville wanted me to become their official superhero. There was a rather generous paycheck involved." I looked 'round the room. "Which could fund your paychecks, at least for the short term until we got money coming in."

Reed was shaking his head gently. "I don't want to put any pressure on you right now, Sienna. You need to get right first."

"I agree," I said, putting hand-to-heart. "But I'm not going to be 'right' if I can't work at all while I'm getting sober. I will literally go crazy. And probably start drinking again." I stood. "Let me reach out and see if they're still interested. If they are...maybe this is a bridge to getting things going for us again."

"Tennessee is centrally located," Augustus said, stroking his chin. I detected an ulterior motive, but I wasn't going to call him out on it.

"It's a bustling metropolis, Nashville is," Jamal added. Oh, yeah. They weren't even working very hard to hide it. "A growing city. Lots of cool things to do. Lots of opportunities. Growth."

"How far is it from Atlanta?" Scott asked, eyes heavily lidded.

"I don't know, like twenty hours' drive," Augustus said, looking out the window. Scott cocked his head, not buying that bullshit. "What? Atlanta traffic is *terrible*." After a moment, Augustus sighed. "Fine. Four hours. But it can be more in rush hour. Which is *always*."

"Uh huh," Scott said, rolling his eyes.

"What's your suggestion, rich boy?" Augustus fired back.

"South Dakota," Scott said, folding his arms. "It's close by. It's centrally located, you can get to New York, LA, Dallas, Atlanta, or Seattle in just a few hours. Either Sioux Falls or Rapid City are great locations, though I really recommend the western side of the state because the scenery is amazing–"

"I just spent a month in one of the Dakotas," Augustus said, shaking his head, "it's a big fat no from me, dawg. Also, Texas?" He pointed at Angel. "No. Just no. I will melt." He switched his finger to point at Olivia. "Same for Florida, except I'll sweat to death while melting."

"Can I suggest New York, then?" Arche asked. Her fingers

were rubbing Jamal's neck, little sparks seeming to jump back and forth, faintly, between her fingers and his skin. "Or San Fran? Both very happening places."

"None of us can afford New York," I said, "and I vote no on Scat Francisco, because if I want to walk through shit all the time, I'd rather we move to Montana and get a cattle ranch as our base. Cow shit smells better than people shit. Just my opinion."

"Is...is that an option?" Olivia asked. "Because I think I want the cattle ranch, too."

Angel turned her head slowly to look at Olivia. "...Why?"

"Cows are cute," Olivia said, her eyes getting all dreamy.

"They don't smell cute," Angel said bluntly. "Until they're butchered into the appropriate cuts and properly cooked."

Olivia grimaced. "Ew. No. So mean."

"What? You don't eat hamburger?" Angel asked, a light dancing in her eyes.

Reed was still holding his head. "We're not getting a ranch. I'm not even convinced we can successfully execute this move, since we have no money and I'm skeptical about this financing job offer of Sienna's." He rubbed his hair, successfully pulling some strands out of his ponytail. "Even if we were able to, we're going to be on a shoestring budget for months as we rebuild the company reserves."

"You said it yourself, Reed." I tried to fake a smile, make it reassuring. "The debt is what's been holding us back. Our caseload is great, and we'd be totally sustainable if we could get out from under all that other crap."

"Yes, but," he said, "we still have to be able to pay people." He gave a quick look around the room. "Unless there are any of you who'd like to work for free for the next several months?"

"Mmm, I kinda need money to eat and pay my bills," Olivia said, cringing.

"Same," Angel said. "But if you need to lay me off, I'll take the axe." When all of us looked at her, she shrugged. "I was thinking about getting back into the restaurant industry, honestly."

"Nooooo, don't go," Olivia said.

"You're trying to save those cows is all," Augustus quipped. "Also, let it be known: I need money as well."

"I could skip a few months of paychecks if I had to," Jamal said.

"Same," Scott said, reddening. "Or at least...I could until last night. Not sure about now." He drew a deep breath and looked at his phone. "Things might change after my dad gets back to me."

"Well, it sounds like you all have some decisions to make," Miranda said. "I'm going to have to jump off the call for a while. I'll start prepping the paperwork to dissolve the corporation and declare bankruptcy, because that seems like it's going to have to happen regardless of where you decide to go."

"Have at it, Miranda," Reed said. "Thanks."

"You're welcome." And then she was gone.

"Yo, how are we going to settle this?" Augustus said. "Sounds like we're all pulling in different directions."

"Texas," Lethe said.

"Well," Reed said, sighing, "I don't know that it's something we can even settle r–"

A clunking noise from out in the lobby drew him up short, a creasing line across his forehead. He started to open his mouth to say something, then stopped, cursing. "I forgot Madison's not out there anymore. Who's there?" he called.

Hard footsteps in the hall sent us all to red alert. Reed straightened quickly, his spine snapping into a straight line, lifting his palms to throw some wind. Scott turned, his own hands coming up.

I shoved them both aside. "Do you even have your powers back yet?" I squeezed my fist, and found the faintest aura of something moving as I did so, picturing Gavrikov all the while.

Fire at the ready. I guess we were re-empowered.

A woman in a dirty tank top came out of the narrow hallway into the bullpen from the reception area. She paused as soon as she hit the daylight exposure from the windows, squinting into the glare. Her hair was dark and hung lank in locks around her face, kinda short, almost buzz cut in the back, but with twin bangs that came off each side like spikes. It was as though her barber set a bowl on her head, but tilted it from the bottom of her chin to her crown and just whacked anything outside the cone of shame.

Her eyes were irritable and searching, and as soon as they found me through the harsh sunlight, she stalked over. There was no malice in her movements, and she looked like she hadn't slept in days. "You Sienna Nealon?" she asked, not harshly, but definitely with some purpose. The only thing in her hands was a crappy faux-leather purse that looked like it had seen a thing or twelve. She kept it, and her other hand, at her side as she came toward me.

"Slow your roll," Olivia said, stepping between us. Like I needed defense.

She took one look at Olivia and made a face that wouldn't have been out of place on someone who'd just stuck a skinned lemon in their mouth and bit down. "I need to talk to her," the woman said. "Get outta my way."

"Let's just chill a little," I said, leaning around Olivia to look this squinty lady in the eye. She had an aggressive number of tattoos on her shoulders and bare arms. I'd heard of putting your money where your mouth was, but she'd put her money where her skin was, and a lot of it, at that. "What do you want, ma'am?"

She ignored Olivia, looking right past her at me. "My boyfriend was arrested for murder. Metahuman-style murder. But he's innocent." She stared right at me, and I saw desperation wedded with determination in those dark eyes. "He says you're the only one who can prove him innocent."

CHAPTER THREE

I looked at the heavily tattooed, off-angle pixie-haircut woman with the burning eyes as she stared at me. Sure, she was a little...pissed off, really, but who wouldn't be, if their boyfriend had sent them on the crazy mission of trying to get my help to prove them innocent?

"I...don't really do...innocent...whatever," I said, struggling hard to figure out why I'd been dragooned into this particular case. "Provings? Whatever. I don't prove people innocent. I prove them guilty."

"So you don't care if someone's innocent when you send them to jail?" Her hackles went up, and so did her head, on a skinny neck. She kinda looked like a tattooed chicken, especially with the hair.

"No, I like to make sure the people I send to jail are guilty," I said. "What I'm saying is...I cannot recall ever taking a case where I've been forced to prove someone innocent." I snorted. "Actually...I might be the worst person to take that kind of case. I couldn't even prove myself innocent for, like...years."

"Who's your boyfriend?" Augustus asked, sliding his way into the conversation.

She hesitated. "Aaron Berry."

"Ooooh," Jamal said, cringing away. I noted a similar reaction from everyone around us, and heard a spitting noise behind me. I turned to find Dr. Perugini. I don't know if she woke up just to spit like that, but she was leaning against the door of Reed's office, arms crossed, and looking particularly spiteful at our guest.

"Okay, I missed something here," I said, looking around at the circle of judgment. "Who's Aaron Berry?"

"He's innocent," she said.

"He's guilty as sin," Augustus said. "They have the DNA evidence to prove it."

"How did you miss the Aaron Berry case?" Olivia asked, turning on me. "It's all anyone has talked about in Minnesota news for a month. Other than us. And sometimes, in concert with us, when they want to talk about why metahumans should be banned from the state."

"Aaron Berry was a teacher in a private school over in Stillwater," Reed said, thankfully, finally, telling me what the hell was going on. He was watching the girlfriend the whole time, though, like she was going to spring on one of us. "He was sexually abusing one of his underage students, then ended up murdering her to try and avoid the truth coming out."

"That ain't even how it happened," the girlfriend said.

"What's your name, miss?" I asked, trying to put a pin in the tensions around us.

"Paula Cunningham," she said, with violently sparkling eyes. Not metahuman sparkling, just angry as hell. "I'm telling you he ain't guilty. And he can prove it, if you're willing to meet with him."

I looked sideways at the TV, where the vote tally was still

on the screen. "I'm a little busy at the moment. Not sure I can really take on any cases just now."

"He needs your help something fierce," Paula said, and I felt like she was stabbing me accusingly with her eyes. "Everyone thinks he's guilty." She looked at my friends in a quick glance. "As you can see. 'Cept he ain't. My Aaron says he can prove to you he's not guilty, if you'll just meet him."

"Why not anyone else?" I asked, frowning. "Oh." I got it. "Ugh." I so desperately did not want to do any soul sucking right now, especially on an abuser and murderer. All I needed was Wolfe-like afterthoughts while I was trying to get sober.

Paula strode forward, around Olivia, and got right up to me, not in a threatening way. Her eyes had changed, going from hard to soft, pleading. "Ma'am...he ain't going to make it out before the deadline if you don't prove him innocent. And then...well, I reckon he ain't gonna make it out at all." She had a hard accent, midwestern with a little southern thrown in, almost, one of the weirdest I'd ever heard.

I looked to Reed, a little for guidance, a little to gauge his opinion of...well, any of this. He wore a slightly stricken look, his lips pulled tight. "What do you think?" I asked.

He seemed a little choked, but he got his answer out. "You should go." Then, straightening, "*We* should go." He drew a breath that inflated his broad chest. "Let's do this one together."

CHAPTER FOUR

"You think they're going to get any packing done while we're gone?" I asked, as Reed and I bumped along in his car along Highway 212 West toward the Cube. At least Aaron Berry had the virtue of being close at hand, being confined in the metahuman prison only minutes or so from our office rather than one of the other prisons in the state.

"I hope so," Reed said, muscles in his neck looking stiff as iron, his hands locked on the wheel, the midday sun shining through the windshield of his midsized SUV. "We're getting booted whether we like it or not, so it'd be better if they got a head start on the moving."

I imagined trying to shove the contents of that entire office into boxes and U-haul vans. Then I realized I wasn't going to have to imagine it, because we were going to be doing it, and soon. "Do we even get to keep that furniture and stuff if we're declaring bankruptcy?"

Reed's hands tightened on the wheel, his knuckles turning white. "I don't know."

My voice lowered almost of its own accord when next I spoke. "I'm responsible for all this, Reed."

He snapped a look over at me, bright green trees rushing by outside his window. "This isn't your fault."

"Isn't it?" I asked.

"No," he said, very firmly. "Look, you are going to have to make amends for some things you've done wrong in the course of your drinking, but this isn't one of them. Shipley has had it out for us since...well, at the very least since she greeted me on the tarmac at MSP right before the team got bushwhacked by that multi-power meta. You know, the one you suffocated in the computer storage facility?"

"'Allegedly,'" I said. "They were never able to prove it was me, or metahuman driven, so those folks got their insurance money to rebuild. But I forgot Shipley was there when you got off the plane." I shook my head as I looked out the window at the greenery going past. I'd made this drive what felt like a million times. Every mile of it was familiar to me.

"She was, and I think it got to her," Reed said. "Almost like she picked up a case of PTSD that day, and associated us with it. Even though we really got our asses handed to us there."

"No one said hatred had to be logical," I said, leaning on my hand. "Still...I can't shake the feeling that if I'd been a little less...me...things might not have taken the road they did."

"I think Shipley was always going to get the votes, eventually, whether you were here or not," Reed said. "It seems to me the Karens of Minnesota are winning right now, that they've hectored their representatives with every available public safety argument they have, from Wolfe's attacks back in the day to Gavrikov nuking Glencoe to Sovereign to...all points in between. Aaron Berry might have gotten Shipley closer to those last votes than you did." He shuddered. "This case..."

"You think he's guilty, don't you?" I looked in the rearview.

Paula was trailing behind us in a beat-up Chevy Aveo, which, as just about the cheapest car on the US auto market, seemed to be in my future. Maybe. Right now I didn't even have two nickels to rub together.

"I not only think he's guilty, the evidence is overwhelming," Reed said. "But..."

"Everything before the 'but' is bullshit."

"No, it's not," Reed said. "Everyone deserves their day in court, even the truly reprehensible." He looked at me and smiled. "If we're not going to apply our 'innocent until proven guilty' system of due process to everyone, including the worst, most heinous people, it won't stand for even those who aren't so accused. At least not for long." He didn't shudder this time, but his muscles tightened, especially in his neck, like he wanted to. "Aaron Berry did something so horrific I don't know if I could look him in the eye and keep myself from choking him to death." Now he looked at me. "But that doesn't mean he doesn't deserve every opportunity to present a strong defense."

"Plus, I can actually cut straight to the truth of if he's guilty or not," I said, glancing back out the window as a beautiful, green, open field of tall summer corn waved outside. When I glanced back at Reed, he was grimacing. "What is that face supposed to mean?"

Reed froze. "Ugh...shit." He looked like I'd caught him doing something really bad, like watching *Keeping Up With the Kardashians*. "It's just that...when you start to get godlike–"

"Goddesslike. But proceed."

"–and all-knowing about things, especially pertaining to dispensing justice..." He closed his eyes. "Usually bodies are about to hit the floor. Sometimes justified." He cringed and turned away. "Sometimes not so much."

"I can't help it if I know what guilt is, Reed," I said. "I

catch these people doing bad things, like trying to kill me, and it's not like I can just blow that off and ignore it–"

"I'm not talking about that," he said. "I'm talking about..." He looked to either side, as though someone were watching us. "...that fossilized Russian lady that was following you around...until she went missing."

I might have blushed a little. "Okay, when I have knowledge of a perpetrated atrocity that would never pass muster with court systems anywhere in the world, and I see a shot to...y'know...provide justice–"

"That's not justice," Reed said wearily. "Justice is twelve peers in a jury box, examining the evidence and–"

"Optimally, yes," I said. "But not always. Sometimes, especially when people have powers...things have a way of slipping through. I mean, we've been out of the meta closet for the better part of a decade and I'd argue that our justice system still hasn't fully adapted to the things we can do. I mean, seriously – you could murder someone walking across a bridge with a sudden gust of wind that sends them over. Splat. How does anyone prove that's you?"

Reed's lips drew back; he looked pained. "That doesn't give you the right to swoop in and administer your own justice, okay? That's what bothers me about your god...dess-like insight. No one truly 'knows' everything." He shuddered again. "There's got to be a way to adjudicate things like this. Yes, even someone like me blowing a person off a bridge to their deaths. There just has to be." He focused on the road. "It can't only be in our hands, because as you've recently proven...we are fallible, just as much human as anyone else except for the powers."

"Well, on that we agree," I said, feeling just a tiny bit stung by what he'd said. Of course he was right.

But it still hurt.

CHAPTER FIVE

We pulled down the long driveway to the Cube's expansive parking lot, and I found myself studying it with a strange sort of melancholy. Reed caught me looking as the trees passed, swaying in the wind along the paths of the grassy, woods-filled property, and he gave me a wan smile. "Thinking about all the memories you have of this place? From before it was the Cube?"

I nodded. Because before it was the premiere metahuman criminal storage facility on the planet...

It had been a tree-lined campus for a group known as the Directorate. My first contact after I left my home, and my first home after leaving my house. Here I'd met Scott and Kat and Ariadne, where I'd broadened my friendship with Reed and found out we were siblings.

Where I'd fallen in love under sunny skies and warm trees, been betrayed and cast out into the falling leaves and cold, wet snow.

I'd quarterbacked the war against Sovereign from this campus; imprisoned countless criminals, and done battle so often that the place still bore the scars of my last fight here.

In the distance beyond the main structure that now comprised the entry to the Cube, you could still see the concrete foundations of the old buildings. To one side was the foundation of the science building that had blown up multiple times, to another was the parking structure where I'd once fought off mercenaries intent on freeing the prisoners, and somewhere behind the Cube there was the last remains of the old dorm, where I'd lived so long and, fairly often, happily.

I stepped out into the warm, humid day, shutting the door behind me. The guards posted on the front doors were watching me carefully as I threaded my way over. The little Chevy Aveo cruised up and blocked my path. Paula rolled down the window, cigarette dangling from her lips. It smelled kinda good; another addiction I probably needed to overcome. "I'll wait for you out here," she said, and didn't wait for me to answer. She slipped the Aveo into a parking place at the end of the row.

"How about I wait out here, too?" Reed asked, plopping his ass down on his car's hood. "I hate going in there when I don't have to."

"I know the feeling," I called to him as I walked toward the entry. And I did know that feeling.

In more ways than one.

CHAPTER SIX

"You know the rules," Guard Kennebec said, hitting the button to buzz me into the visitor cell.

"Is that a question?" I asked as a klaxon honked in the distance to signal it was now unlocked. Kennebec held it for me, and in I went, preceding him to make the guy feel a little safer. "I've only been in here about a bajillion times now."

"Only a few since you left government service," Kennebec said tightly. He was tall, bald, built, and not a guy I'd want to mess with, meta powers or no. He had the suspicious look of a long-time prison guard, like he'd experienced every kind of bullshit pulled on him over the years. I'd hired him years ago, and here he remained, another ghost of my previous life come back to haunt me, apparently.

"Kennebec, it seems like I'm always working for the government, one way or another," I said. "Cut me some fricking slack, will you?"

Kennebec just shook his head, and it caught the glare of the overhead lights. "Look...if it were anyone else, I'd tell you to get lost. Especially with all the heat you've got on your ass right now."

"My ass likes heat," I said. "In fact, I might just take the opportunity afforded by Minnesota booting me out to go plant it on a Caribbean beach for a while, get this puppy some sun." I patted my rump. "Maybe I'll send you a postcard 'round January."

Kennebec's hardass facade cracked at that, and he smiled. "You suck, Nealon. Not all of us can afford to take Caribbean vacations." He mouthed some words into his radio, and another door klaxon honked. "You powered?"

"Yep. No thanks to BCA, but...yep."

"Noted. We just got your new friends from last night processed." Then he shook his head slowly. "I don't understand what Minnesota's thinking, but then, you're employment security for me."

"Yes, you have a vested interest," I said as he led me into a hall with a view I'd never seen before.

It was a circular corridor that overlooked a metallic, cell-lined courtyard below. Down there, tables were bolted into the ground, and male prisoners were congregating around them in small groups. I saw some familiar faces from last night – Emilio and Charles Custis, Chad Goodwin, Devin Fuller, and David and Nick Gustafson. A full boat, and they were all sitting together around a long picnic-style table, getting stray eyeballs from the rest of the inmates.

I saw some familiar faces among those orange-jumpsuit-clad clowns, too; Otto Oberhauser, Moose from new Omega, Jesse Daniel – a merc who'd been involved with the plot to kill the president – and sitting kind of alone by himself was Brance Venable, my personal vocal coach. Or at least the source of my ability to break glass with a song nowadays.

"Whoa, let's give way here," Kennebec said, and scooted aside as we started to enter another confined hallway. "Prisoner coming through."

I'd seen the prisoner who was coming through, and I said, "Hi, Chase. Long time no see."

Which was a lie, of course, I'd seen her literally hours ago, when they'd wheeled her off in an ambulance for emergency care before shipping her here. She limped along, off-balance, missing an arm, and studying me with hate-filled eyes. "Nealon," she nearly spat. Her bob haircut looked absolutely ragged.

"I'm sorry," I said, when she was almost past me, her cuffs clanking with every shuffling step. I tracked her with my eyes, and she acknowledged my gaze on her. "About your arm."

Her face tightened into a harder scowl. "But not the other ways you ruined my life?"

"No," I said honestly. "Your life was shit before we met, it was shit after you left the agency, and it's deepest shit now. I was barely involved in any of that. You chose who you worked for, you chose what you did. You got involved with people who had dirty schemes, who tried to assassinate the president...you made your bed, Chase." I shrugged. "But you're a big girl. You oughta know by now that life doesn't always deliver a hug and a kiss. It's all about bringing the pain."

"What do you know about pain?" She hocked one up and spat it at me.

I froze it out of the air with a wave of the hand before it touched me. Even though my immune system was incapable of being felled by diseases or bacteria, I was still a bit of a germaphobe, and being spat on was the ultimate insult to me. I'd rather be punched. "Nice try."

Her guard grabbed Chase by her remaining arm and dragged her off balance. No words needed to be spoken there; she started to twist, trying to get out of his grip, and I saw a light appear at her arm–

"Whoa!" Kennebec shouted, "we got a–!"

I crossed the distance between us and grabbed Chase by

the arm just before she flared her lightsaber and put my other hand over her throat. "Don't," I said simply, and she relaxed.

"Or what?" Chase sneered. "You'll drain my soul?"

"The rest of it, yeah," I said, and a little beam of light extended out of my skin just above my wrist, extending up to her throat. I had my own lightsaber now, but it was a pale imitation of hers. "A bit lacking in power, huh? Think I could shave my legs with it? Maybe give someone a slow, painful death? Like over the course of eight hours they go from a very slight tingle to a vague burning to–"

The guard at Chase's back pumped a syringe into her neck and she jerked, but didn't take her eyes off me. She'd probably known it was coming, but couldn't turn away from the threat at her front. Or she was engaged in self-preservation and allowed herself to be suppressed. It was coming, regardless of how she felt about it, from the moment Kennebec called out.

The glow at her sleeve faded away, and Chase relaxed. The guard took her down to the ground, onto her face, but not too hard. "Getting a little rowdy, Blanton," Kennebec said, easing up. He had a radio in one hand and his baton in the other. "This going to be a pattern with you?"

"No," Chase mumbled into the steel flooring. "She just brings out the worst in me, that's all."

"She's not wrong," I said. "We're definitely star-crossed. Take it easy on her. She's had a rough night."

Kennebec gave me a sour look. "You're lucky I don't dart you, too."

"Sorry," I said, and then, catching Chase's eye, I mouthed, "Sorry," to her as well. She kept her eyes on me as Kennebec led me away to the visitor chamber, and I could tell by the chilling look on her face that the bad blood between us was nowhere near settled.

That was fine. I was a big girl. I could take the heat if it came my way.

Except last night...I'd kinda proven that I couldn't take it. Not when it went hard against my weak points.

As I left Chase behind, her face mashed into the prison's steel flooring, I wondered how many more people like her in this joint actively despised me. It wasn't a small amount, that was for sure.

Oh, well. I'd just have to live with that. And always watch my back, a lesson I'd clearly forgotten in my drive to drink.

CHAPTER SEVEN

The visitors' rooms were not much to look at, not much to see, and I'd spent far more time in them than was comfortable for me. They often served as a transfer point where the prison guards took custody of prisoners from us, the law enforcement officers who worked on the outside of the Cube. Though, lately, Kennebec had made it a point to have me bring the threats all the way down to Gen Pop. I couldn't recall exactly when that shift had been made, but it had certainly happened. In fact, I couldn't recall the last time I'd been in one of these tight, octagonal cells.

I'd been searched, thankfully not stripped, though a female guard had touched me in places I hadn't been properly touched since Harry left me. She did it all with the most sour look on her face, too, like she was too good to be putting her hand all over my crotch without dinner and a movie first. When she pronounced me clean – a laughable proposition, since I hadn't showered in over a day, and I'd been through fire and water and ice and battle – Kennebec had brought me here and told me to wait. Which I was now doing, pacing the small room in a slow circle, wishing I could get this over with.

The door clanked open after I'd just about reached the end of my patience and was ready to call to be let out. Two guards waited beyond, along with a guy with exceedingly thin lips and disheveled hair that looked like it might have combed well but hadn't been touched with one in weeks. He had a couple bruises on his cheek, and he walked with a limp that was almost as bad as Chase's.

He came into the room under his own power, cuffed hands and feet rattling, the chain that joined the two and reduced his range of motion clanking when he made a longer step. He was probably north of thirty but looked older with the wear and tear his stay here had probably produced. His eyes were a little dulled and there were heavy bags beneath them, but they brightened when he saw me, his shoulders straightening. "Sienna Nealon," he breathed as the guards shut the door behind him. "Paula got to you."

"Persistent, your girlfriend," I said, drawing up to my full and unimpressive height and keeping my arms crossed in front of me. I was rocking the jeans and a T-shirt look, because technically I was supposed to be on vacation. "You're Aaron Berry, I assume? Otherwise you're in the wrong place, and I haven't talked to your girlfriend. I talked to someone else's, and she's a real spitfire."

"I am Aaron, yes," he said, breathing heavily, like he was just so pleased to see me. "Thank you so much for coming. It's, uh...a little tough to get someone out here who's not press, y'know?"

I grunted. "I hear you have an argument to make for me."

He shuffled his feet, rubbing his bound hands together. "An argument?" He shrugged. "There's no argument to be made. Everyone says I'm guilty. The evidence says I'm guilty."

I watched him carefully. "But you say you're not."

"I'm not," he said, "and I can prove it. But only to you."

"You realize, of course," I said, "that I'm not able to

testify in court to that effect. Whatever I were to see in your mind is not admissible evidence. I'm not even a great character witness. Assuming you're telling the truth."

"I don't want you to see the truth so that you can testify," he said, his shoulders slumped, the hangdog air about him pressing into me, that aura of hopelessness matching surprisingly well with my own current mood. "I want you to know the truth...so you can *save* me."

"I'm not particularly good at saving people lately," I said, looking at the smooth edges of the metal walls. They were bound tightly at the seams, bolts sunk in so that even metahuman strength wouldn't be able to pull them apart. "You might want to seek better counsel."

"I have counsel," he said. "And it's decent, too, because lawyers have this tendency to love the high-profile cases. But you know what my lawyer is talking about? A plea deal." His eyes were wild, desperate. "I'm not going to survive in here, okay?" He pressed his hand to his chest for emphasis, the metal clanking. "They haven't figured this out yet, but I'm not a meta. And apparently there's no simple test they can do that will allow me to prove I'm not, and get transferred to a non-meta prison. Where I might at least have a shot at surviving. Maybe. I hear they're not very kind to accused child rapists there, either, but at least the other inmates aren't coming at you with laser beams and shit."

"Wait." I raised an eyebrow at that. "You're saying you're not a meta. At all? Not even a weak one?"

He shook his head. "Not at all." He brushed his hand against the bruises on his face. "These are from a week ago. And I'm not suppressed."

"Hm," I said, frowning. I made a mental note to check with Kennebec on that. "That's not conclusive, at least not by itself. When you're injured before being suppressed, it doesn't always heal once you regain your powers."

"How does that work?" Berry asked, squinting.

"Like, I can cut my hair, for instance," I said, brushing it loosely back over my shoulders, "and if it gets burned off – which it has in the past – it regrows from my healing powers to the length it was after I cut it. There's a sort of 'set point' at work. Same with fingernails, toenails – if I lose a limb, they grow back to the same length they were before. Or rather, back to the most recently trimmed length." I shook my head. "It's weird. Anyway, point is you could have been wounded before being darted and it might not heal." I thought of Chase with her glowing powers and lack of an arm. Drusilla Cross, too.

"You can see inside my head," Berry said, leaning forward. All of his hope was on me, which was...disconcerting. "You can prove me innocent, at least in your mind. Then, maybe you can find the evidence that–"

"Proves you innocent? What if there is none?" I fixed him in my gaze. "Do you even know who framed you?"

Here he deflated, shoulders sagging down again. "I have no idea."

That was interesting. Usually the guilty parties I'd met were quick to shift blame to a very defined someone else, someone who was responsible for all their misfortunes. The fact that Berry had no idea who'd "framed" him was an interesting twist. That he wasn't positing wild theories as to how it happened was also interesting. He'd been behind bars for a while now; I would have thought his mind would have gone crazy obsessing over how he ended up in this mess. "Any idea how they did it, then?"

"I mean..." he kind of withdrew his neck, shoulders rising like twin crags on either side, like a turtle trying to get back into its shell, "...my DNA was...in my apartment."

I cringed. I didn't know much about this case, but this

was the skeevy bit. "As I understand it, they're talking about a very specific kind of DNA. Not skin follicles or hair."

"Well, they found those, too," Berry said, his neck and shoulders forming almost a W from the way he was scrunched up, like a hunchback. "Plus a little blood beneath her fingernails. And the..." He waved a hand in a circular motion; clearly he was uncomfortable saying it, too.

"Semen," I said, figuring it'd be better to break the ice on that one rather than dance around it all day. "They found your semen inside the victim."

His cringe was forceful, and I felt that instinct myself having said it. I wasn't the kind of person who delighted in, or even did well, with icky sexual conversations, especially with a suspected pedophile murderer.

But this was the evidence, and somebody needed to say it, and apparently that someone was me, even though it grossed me way the hell out.

"Yeah," Berry said, nodding slowly. "Like I said...that was in my apartment, too. Paula and I...we use protection. And I don't flush them, so..." He made an abbreviated motion like he was sinking a three-pointer, and I got it. He threw his condoms in the trash can after use.

"All right, well, this is all...hideously uncomfortable," I said, "so let's get down to brass tacks." I took a deep breath. "If I go through your memories in the depth it will take me to discern that they're real and unaltered...you will lose them. They'll be sucked into my head, never to return."

"God, please, take them," he said. "Hell, take everything for the last few weeks. Months, even."

I shook my head slowly. "No, I'm not interested in carrying all that weight, thanks. I'm only mentioning this because after I go through your alibi and the events around the murder...you will literally *not know whether or not you committed the crime*." I straightened up as tight as I could, because this was some serious shit. "All the certainty you feel right now? It's gone the moment I'm done. You're putting your life into my hands–"

"I'm in," he said, shoulders returning to their normal plane. His eyes were filled with quiet hope, and it shone through in his voice. "I'm all in. I trust you to take what you find and...and free me." He nodded again. "Hell...you're the only one who can at this point, because nothing I say in my own defense is going to matter."

Shit. I let out a long, slow breath. He was entrusting his life into my unsteady hands – willingly, hell, forcefully. And at maybe the worst possible time he could be doing such a thing.

"I'm not sure you know what you're asking for here," I said. "My hands are not the steadiest at the moment." That wasn't literally true; I didn't have the shakes or anything, thanks to Wolfe-healing. But it was, figuratively.

I wanted a drink more than almost anything I'd ever wanted in my life. I certainly wanted one a hell of a lot more than I wanted to be standing here, about to put my fingers on this guy's face and absorb his sad story, which I was already sure would feel like rubbing broken glass onto my raw, bleeding soul.

"I trust you," he said, taking a rattling step closer to me. "I know once you see inside my head, once you know I'm not guilty – you're going to do that thing you do."

I pursed my lips, squinting at him. "Kill a lot of people?"

He shook his head. "You're going to fight to get to the bottom of this. Until you find the truth."

I grimaced. "I'm about three days from getting kicked out of this state, lock, stock, and smoking hands. What you're asking me to do is take this on – along with all your memories – when I might not even be able to complete the investigation. Okay? That's the problem here." Along with the rampant desire for booze.

"I don't care," he said. "I know you can do it. You're the only one who can."

I closed my eyes. This guy was hanging on the edge of a cliff by his fingers, so desperate for help that he was pinning all his hopes on me in spite of everything I'd told him. And I was running away because of those, and...

...Because of that nagging little alcoholism problem I was going through that I hadn't told him about.

Still...innocent was innocent, and it'd be easy enough for me to determine whether he was. I could just pick at the surface of his memory and know pretty quickly whether he'd committed a murder or not. See for myself at a distance, without stealing memories. Then, if it looked clear...

...Well, I could go in and look a little closer. No harm, no foul if it turned out he was responsible. Maybe a little emotional scarring if I had to watch him kill that girl in his head, but what was a little more damage to my soul when it had already been mangled and dragged through the shit of life for years?

"Okay," I said, steeling myself for what had to come next and raising my fingers, flexing them to prepare for this. "I'll do it."

CHAPTER EIGHT

"You're just kind of...sitting there," Aaron Berry said, because I'd been hovering a few inches from him for a minute or two. He wore a perplexed look, a twisted, squinty sort of thing.

"Yeah..." I breathed, still cringing away from touching him. Why was this so hard?

Last night alone I'd absorbed four people – at least in part. That was four new shadows hanging around in my head, and I had barely given it a thought before diving in on them. Now that I was hanging over this guy, though, my palms a few inches from his face, I was having a sudden bout of reticence?

I took a few long, slow, deep breaths, steeling myself. Last night had been different. I'd intended to kill those people. Fully intended to absorb them right to death, then make full use of their captivity to torture the hell out of them for the rest of my life. This was different. There was no ill will here – unless he'd actually committed the murder. In which case...

Well, absorbing him to torture him would probably be bad, given he was a prisoner. But the thought lingered, because I obviously had self-control issues, and if I saw him murdering a young girl, there was a distinct possibility that I'd say to hell with the laws and he'd end up dead anyway.

"Okay," I said again, probably more to myself at this point than him. I flexed my hands, and eased a little closer...a shuffle step closer...and finally...

My hands were on his cheeks.

"This is going to burn a little. At first," I said, not closing my eyes. Cuffs aside, I just did not trust him enough to close my eyes.

"What happens after it burns?" he asked, holding stock still.

"It kinda starts to feel good. Now...shhh." I resisted the urge to close my eyes. Really, it felt a little like kissing with your eyes open.

The tingling along my palms started first. As expected.

Berry stood there, eyes squinted half-closed, and said, "I don't feel anyth – oh. Oh. OH!"

At the last he jerked, and I kept my hands planted on him as he tried, involuntarily, to pull away. There was no breaking this thing off now, though, and I held on tight as the fiery, sweet sensation in my palms tingled its way through my fingertips, and the world swirled around me as I entered–

The mind of a killer?

Well, maybe not.

Going into somebody's head is a strange thing. It's not what I might have expected before seeing inside one; it's not a jumble of synapses or neurons or cool sci-fi imagery like in the movies, the stuff they show you to let you know, "Hey, we're reading a mind!" Visual cues to tell you the world you've entered.

Me jumping into someone's head was a flash of images, and a strange sort of auto-guided tour of memory. All I had to do was think about what I wanted, and my powers seemed to immediately work toward that end.

I wanted to see the memory of the night his victim, Greta Oliver, was killed.

Pretty quick, I got my wish.

I was thrust into a dark memory, the world tilting around me. There was little light but that put out by a TV screen, its rectangular shape blurring in front of me. The bright colors were just a little too white for me to make out what was going on there; like I was looking into a baby sun.

My world tilted. Not completely; just a little. Then I swayed over to the other side, something metal and cold clutched in my – or rather, Aaron Berry's – hand.

It was a beer.

A look revealed more beer cans laid out across the end table at my left. All open, all empty, the whole surface was covered. A cooler rested next to my – his – leg, and with a last lift of the can in my – his – hand, the taste of that amber goodness swirled on my – his – lips.

I had never been a fan of beer, but I really wanted another one right now.

And Aaron Berry obliged. He reached down to that cooler, blue with a white lid, the surface grainy and plastic-y and lifted it, still swaying because...shit, the dude had gone through almost a twelve pack already tonight...and lifted out a cold, wet can, the droplets running down my – his – hand. I could feel every one of them like I was there, and when the can made that satisfying *crack!* upon opening...

A sense of deep guilt rushed over me, along with a craving I'd held at bay for less than twenty-four hours. Aaron lifted the can and poured it down his gullet, but I was the one enjoying the hell out of it.

He made it about halfway through when the memory started getting fuzzy. He tilted to the side again, so drunk he couldn't even sit upright, and then he lurched back against the couch–

Boom. Everything went black, and Aaron Berry was out.

He awoke to the thundering sound of knocking at the door, and I came back to consciousness with him. There was yelling and shouting, but he was still blitzed and barely able to push himself upright.

Didn't matter. The door came smashing down seconds later, and the cops came in full force. Cold cuffs found their way onto his drunken hands, and Aaron Berry found himself facedown in a carpet that still held the faint, rank aroma of spilled beer.

With a jerk, I pulled my hands from him and left that memory behind just as the sound of them reading him his rights started to play like a familiar refrain in the background.

Berry was gasping, hunched over, hands on his knees, the chains swaying. "That...that was...I don't know whether that was bad or awesome."

"It's kind of a combo platter, honestly," I said, backing up against the wall. I was a damned alcoholic, and the last thing I needed was to indulge another kind of addiction my family history suggested: absorbing souls. Because I really, really wanted to drink the rest of him, and not just because of the sweet, tangy nature of his alcohol memories being like sensory candy for me, a drink without taking one myself. I had my hand cupped against my chest, as if to hold myself back from temptation. "Do you remember what happened?"

Berry's forehand lines grew deep. "No...no, I don't."

"Like I told you." I managed to catch my breath. "Well, I've got your memories now. And I gotta tell you...getting blackout drunk the night of the murder? Not really a great alibi."

"Is...is that what happened?" Berry's face was a map of puzzlement.

"So it would seem," I said, threading my way around the circumference of the room, trying to keep maximum distance from him in the middle. I reached the door and gave it a good pounding, my palm slamming against the metal. "I'll look into your case. See what I can do."

He slowly turned to look at me, face utterly blank. "Thank you." He seemed about as absentminded as you might expect after getting his brain drained. "Did you see anything about powers for me?"

I had, but only a surface level look at a few dozen memories. "I saw that you don't have them. Or at least that you know of. Your strength certainly doesn't suggest anything metahuman about you." I harkened back to a memory of him struggling under the weight of a box of books the day before the murder. Doubt he'd miss that one.

"Oh, good," he said. "Thought I might have forgotten something."

"You have," I said, as the door clicked open. "Take it easy for the rest of the day. Soul drains are no joke. You'll be a little weak." I had some experience with this, having had my own brain turned to Swiss cheese by a vengeful succubus once upon a time. "Drink plenty of fluids, get some sleep, try not to trip on a shiv...all the usual precautions." Kennebec was holding the door for me, eyebrow cocked. "Maybe keep him out of gen pop for a few hours? He asked me to drain some memories for my investigation, and he's a little off."

Kennebec's lip curled in distaste. "Another favor, Nealon? Can I redeem these for cash value or are they just going to be an invisible chit sitting forever useless in my wallet like one of those coupons my wife gives me?"

"I'd think having the most powerful person on the planet owe you a favor or two would be worth a lot more than a buck off at your local buffet," I said, breezing my way out with a last look at Aaron Berry. "But I guess you could wait and see how well it works out for Mr. Berry before you decide."

Kennebec frowned. “Fine. I'll keep him out for a bit. But you owe me. Don't forget it.”

I smiled as I started to walk away. “I'm sure you won't let me. Because if the day comes when you need my help...I doubt there'll be anywhere else on the planet you can turn.”

CHAPTER NINE

Reed could see my face as I walked across the parking lot, and his grew tighter and more uneasy with each step I took toward him. His arms went from being wrapped tightly around him to slack, then to hanging at his sides, his hair blowing lightly in the warm, summer breeze. When I got close, he said, "So...we're taking the case, then."

"I know the timing's terrible," I said, launching straight into the speech I'd been rehearsing in my head since I'd gotten out of Berry's cell, "but–"

Reed waved a hand in front of him like a croupier spreading a deck out on a table. "No 'buts.' If you say he's innocent, we're doing this."

I eased to a stop next to him. "He's...well, I *think* he's innocent."

Reed's dark eyebrows crept up his forehead. "I usually like a little more certainty before I try and dismember the state's prosecution of a murderer."

"He, uh...got blackout drunk the night of the murder," I said, my own arms folded across my chest, trying to worm my hands deeper behind me, like I could turn this into the world's tightest self-hug. Which, with my strength, I probably could. "Woke up to the cops arresting him."

The cringe was strong with Reed. "Yikes. That's not much of an alibi. What if he did it in a somnambulate state?"

"The thought had occurred to me," I said. "But I think it's worth looking into. You know, with our three days remaining in Minnesota."

"Two and a half." He made a face. "And here I thought we might make time to do some touristy things one last time. State Fair's going on right now, don'tcha know?"

"Oh, you betcha," I sighed, because I, too, would have liked to see the Great Minnesota Get-Together one last time before being run out of town. "But I feel like saving his life is more important than hitting up Sweet Martha's for a pail of cookies and then drinking all we can stand at the milk booth."

Reed's eyebrow crept up again. "His life?"

"He's not a meta," I said. "But he's in Gen Pop, and he thinks he's gonna get the same treatment kiddie rapers get in any prison."

I swear, the cringe was starting to become a permanent fixture on my brother's face, and we'd only just taken this case. Well, it was that kind of story. "Yeah. That's not going to end well for him."

"Nope," I said, and the sound of a small engine revving turned my attention to the Chevy Aveo of one Paula Cunningham as she drove up the aisle toward us. She threw it in park in front of Reed's SUV and rolled down the window, a cloud of smoke threatening to billow out. "Mind if I bum one of those?" I asked, beating her to the punch of speaking with my metahuman reflexes.

Paula stared at me, then shrugged and reached into the center console. She came out with a pack of smokes and a lighter, offering them to me. I took a cigarette, begged off on the lighter, and lit the cig with my fingertip. She nodded, impressed, taking a drag off her own. "What'd you think?" she asked, now that we'd settled all that.

"I'm in," I said, taking a long puff of my own. As I blew it out, Reed subtly changed the air currents around my face, sending it up, up and away from us. I suspected based on the dispersal pattern – and the repulsed look on his face – he was doing the same to Paula's secondhand smoke. Either that or I had a wind current originating from somewhere around my navel.

"Thank God for that," Paula said, letting out another smoky breath that was carried away by the implacable upward wind. She looked at the end of her cigarette, watched the smoke blow up, then shrugged. "Where you gonna start?"

"Where'd the murder take place?" I asked, tapping a little ash off my tip.

"Down by the St. Croix River," Reed said, a little choked, like he was holding his breath. I don't know why; he wasn't even vulnerable to lung cancer.

"Yeah, they found her in the water on the morning of," Paula said, staring off into the distance. "I hear you could see her from the bridge. She got up in the reeds and grass and whatnot."

"Which bridge was that?" I asked.

"Stillwater," Reed said. "Wooded area just north of town."

"Got it," I made a mental note. "Since we're going over to the east side anyway, maybe we should check out Aaron's place? And his place of work?" I looked to Reed, as if for approval.

My brother frowned, still holding his breath. "Yeah. Sure," he said, sounding choked.

"I can let you into his apartment," Paula said. "Cops are done with it now. And his place of work is Stilloaks Preparatory Academy in Stillwater. Kids call it 'Stoaks' these days. Guess it's easier to text than the whole thang."

"I know where that is," Reed said, frowning. "That's that swanky school right on the Stillwater/Oak Park Heights town line."

"Thus the name, I assume," I said, paying attention to my cigarette more than the conversation.

"Yep," Paula said. "His apartment's just across the river in New Richmond, Wisconsin. Which do you want to hit first?"

"School, then apartment?" Reed asked. "Guessing the apartment is pretty much picked clean by the cops."

"Yeah, they had it closed up for a good while," Paula said.

"School it is," I said. "Then, after..." I looked at Reed. He knew what I was suggesting.

After...we'd need to talk to the parents of the victim. Also, friends, but that would hopefully be covered by the school visit.

Paula caught the shared look between us. "You ain't got to hide things from me. I get it, you need to talk to everyone, and I ain't gonna be offended that you need to have a conversation with the girl's parents. None of this is her fault, near as I can tell. No one goes out trying to get their ass killed, especially like that. And it damned sure ain't her parents' fault. So you talk to whoever you need to to get my Aaron free." She looked me in the eye, and hers were blazing like the tip of her cigarette. "You need someone's name, you let me know." She rustled around in the car's console and handed a business card to me.

I stared at the card; it was for one of those multi-level marketing companies that sold soap or widgets or something, but it had her name and cell phone number on it. "Thanks," I said, and the card went right into my jean pocket next to my cell phone. "I'll make sure we keep you in the loop if anything breaks."

She nodded, taking a hard pull on the cig. "Okay. I'm going to head on home. Aaron's place is like ten minutes from me, so you just let me know when you want me to be there." With a solemn nod at each of us, she drove off, her off-axis hair bobbling as she rolled the window up manually, her body rising and falling in the frame as she did so.

"She sure thinks he's innocent," Reed said, waving his hand one last time to blow the last of her smoke into the heavens. He looked really pained by the whole experience, and I noticed he was sidling away from me. Ah. Right. The smell offended him. As it had me back before I took up the habit.

"It's nice to have someone looking out for you no matter what," I said, looking at him only out of the very side of my eye.

He smiled, just a little bit. "It is, isn't it?" And then he blew the cigarette right out of my hand. "Let's go."

CHAPTER TEN

Stilloaks Preparatory Academy had a tree-lined driveway leading into a beautiful, expansive campus, the kind of thing I might have associated with a fancy New England private school. But this one was here, plopped into the founding city of Minnesota. I frowned as we looked upon the brick facaded splendor of the building, the trees all a deep green with summer's own fading glory.

We pulled up, the campus parking lot filled to brimming. "I didn't think Minnesota schools went back until after Labor Day?" I asked. "And the State Fair." High schooler labor powered the State Fair.

"This is a private school," my brother said, killing the ignition and unfastening his seat belt. His nose wrinkled, and I knew he was still sniffing that secondhand smoke I was carrying around, despite his best efforts to blow it off me. "They can go year round if they want."

As we were walking up to the wooden double entry doors, a couple security guards locked on to us. A subtle wind blew through behind us, and I wondered if that was Reed asserting his command over his powers so he could have them ready if he needed them.

I hoped not. I didn't plan to trespass here, and coming onto school grounds against the wishes of those in charge was the very definition of trespassing. Which was a sort of trouble I definitely didn't need right now.

"No press allowed on the campus," one of the guards, said pointing back up the driveway. "Didn't you see the sign?"

"Did you just call me *press?*" I asked, only having to feign outrage a little. "As in a *reporter*? Why, I've never been so insulted. You should have called me a whore, or a slag, or a c–"

"Okay," Reed cut me off, a humorless look on his face.

"Sorry," the security guard said, looking greatly abashed. "Didn't realize who you were. We've had a plague of reporters lately." He straightened slightly, and regained his tough look. "You working with the cops?"

"We're here on our Private Investigator license," Reed said, whipping out a card from his wallet that said, no shit, PI. He'd gone and done it. "Is there someone in charge we could talk to?"

The security guard hesitated, then reached for a walkie-talkie. "Someone here to see the headmaster."

A squeal over the open channel made Reed and me both cringe. It hit the perfect pitch to make dogs whine, right up there with long nails running hard over a chalkboard, and when I opened my eyes again, the security guard was looking at us quizzically. Then he must have realized his walkie-talkie hit a pitch that made us metas and dogs – hurt. "Sorry," he said, looking very genuinely so.

The walkie screeched to life again. "He says to send them back," a tart female voice said.

The guard looked, involuntarily, over his shoulder, where a black plastic dome security camera watched us from the eave just above the door. "Okay," he radioed back, then reached down to his belt for a key on a long metal chain pulley. He unlocked the door and said, "Sorry again. It's just the rules. Can't be too careful. Especially with all this going on."

"Honestly, I'm still just insulted you called me a reporter," I huffed, and he cringed again as he held the door for me.

I stepped inside, and into a whole 'nother world. I'd expected by the look of the place that I'd be entering a world of swank, but I had failed to realize exactly how swank we were talking here. Sure, I'd never gone to high school and had no idea what a public school was really like, save for TV and maybe the occasional, "Shape up, fly right, and don't do drugs, kids," sort of speaking tour that I got booked on as a superhero on the government dime.

None of them looked like this.

Reed whistled. "Welcome to Xavier's School for Extremely Rich Kids."

There was no doubt we were in a wealthy establishment. Instead of the white-painted concrete block walls I'd come to expect from every school I'd ever stepped foot in, here everything was wood-paneled and luxurious. The air had a crisp smell, like fresh apple cider was waiting down the hall, mingled with a hint of lemons. Which I followed my nose to the source of, a beautiful wooden trestle table with two water coolers – one with lemons floating in it, the other laced with orange peels.

"You thirsty?" I asked, easing over to the table. I picked up a plastic cup that looked a little like it was real glass – because I realized, belatedly, it was – and filled it with orange peel water. It was cool and refreshing, and a little citrus-y.

"I am now," Reed said, deigning to try the lemon water. His eyes flitted around the entryway.

There was (of course) a grand staircase leading up to the second floor. Banners with the school's academic and sporting achievements hung from every surface, letting us know we were in the presence of life's winners, and that if we weren't winners, too, we should probably GTFO. There was no sign of lockers, of school mascots, just the detritus of life's success stories stretching back generations in the form of team photos, golden trophies, and framed newspaper clippings celebrating the greatness of Stilloaks Preparatory Academy and all who dared to park their wealthy asses for a brief span of childhood within these hallowed halls.

"Office is over here," Reed said, jerking his head toward a rather obvious door that said OFFICE above it.

"Just a second," I said, "I'm not quite done basking in the fact that I'm a loser who's not worthy to walk these sacred grounds."

My brother snorted. "It's a bit of overkill, isn't it?"

I ran my fingers over a plaque declaring the Stilloaks Prep Debate team of 1998 State Champions. "Overkill is using a 9mm round on a cricket. This is using a nuke to kill an ant." I caught a glimpse of myself in the mirrored back of a trophy display. I looked absolutely terrible, even for me. The dark circles under my eyes made me appear to be kin to raccoons. The tangled hair made it seem like I hadn't bathed in a week. And the clothes...

Rumpled, smelled of smoke, and maybe a little BO, too. "Cumin," I muttered, getting a whiff of myself.

Reed was not looking at me, but he couldn't hide the cringe. He busied himself opening the door to the office, still studiously avoiding eye contact.

"You know, a good brother wouldn't have let me walk out of the office looking like this," I said, rolling right past him.

That pained cringe froze on his face, but he did nod, ever so slightly.

"Hello, hello," said a man as we came into the office. It, too, was decorated in the style of, "We're winners, so if you're not, you're in the wrong place." But it also possessed what I assumed were the standard accoutrements of a school office – a counter to separate the chosen employees from the rabble who deigned to tread upon their sovereign territory. A couple desks, scattered with papers and manned by harried-looking older women, their eyes fixed on me. Oh, and hallways hinting that their entire operation was not contained within this modest space.

"Hi there," I said, centering my attention on the man in the suit.

He was medium height, a little taller than me but less than Reed. He looked to be late forties-early fifties, with black, large-frame glasses and a clean-cut look. Thin, not a body builder but a guy who kept himself in shape. Light brown hair with the first hints of gray, and he wore a friendly smile with a trace of nervousness beneath it. "I'm the Headmaster, Dan Prestegaard." He waited by the counter, and shook Reed's hand briskly when he came around. "If you'll follow me, we can talk in my office."

Headmaster Prestegaard led us back into one of those corridors, past another desk filled with an older woman who watched us with something between interest and derision, and ushered us into a very nice office all his own. It had a little sitting area in front of the desk, light shining in on leather couches, and he beckoned for us to have a seat, which we did, as he took his own across a coffee table from us. "Get you anything to drink?"

"I just helped myself to some of your orange water out in the lobby, so I'm good," I said. "I assume you know what we're here about?"

Prestegaard's face fell. "Yes. It's all anyone's talked about for weeks, unfortunately." He shifted in his chair, crossing his legs at the knee. "I was given to understand, though, that the police had more or less wrapped up the investigation."

"Well, you know how it is," I said, before Reed could flash his PI badge. "The investigation goes on all the way up to the trial. We're forever dotting i's and crossing t's."

Reed gave me a barely-contained look of ire that I caught only out of the corner of my eye, and which might appear subtle to someone like Headmaster Prestegaard, who did not know him as I did. To me, it was not subtle, it was not restrained, and it said, quite plainly, "What the f– are you doing?"

I sat forward slightly in my chair. "Now, as I understand the case, it hinges on Mr. Berry's relationship with the girl in question, Ms. Oliver." My brain failed me. Had I even heard her first name?

Prestegaard waited, watching me intently. "Greta, yes." He hung his head slightly. "Such a bright student. Such a shame."

"Ms. Oliver, how old was she? And in which grade?" I asked.

"Uh, fourteen," Prestegaard said. "And in ninth grade. Just started, actually. We came back from summer break on August seventeenth."

"I see," I said. Shit. That was some dirty pool someone was playing, screwing around with a ninth grader. While I was certainly aware that such things happened, it still made my stomach turn over to contemplate it. "Had Mr. Berry had contact with Ms. Oliver before this year? To your knowledge?"

Prestegaard shifted uncomfortably in his seat. "Yes. We're a small school, only a student body of about 300, K-12. We pride ourselves on a first-class education with top-notch teachers who work with students over the course of many years. Mr. Berry's classes begin with seventh grade and extend up twelfth, so...yes, he'd been teaching Greta for a couple years now. World history, this year. American history last year."

"Interesting," I said, mainly because it kinda was to me. My mother's teaching had been comprehensive in the realm of history, and I could tell she had something of a passion for it. Less so, say, geometry, where she had to refer frequently to the textbook and work out the problems herself three or four times to arrive at the right answer. "I assume there was no hint of impropriety before now?"

"Absolutely not," Prestegaard said. "We take our students' safety very seriously. Any report of a relationship out of the ordinary between a teacher and a student would have been investigated. We didn't even get a whiff of something like that." Prestegaard looked fairly sedate about the whole matter; he was a cool cucumber, but if he was lying he was very practiced at it. And while I knew that these sort of things happened at schools, it'd take a dirty son of a bitch to try and cover it up if he knew about it in advance.

Which didn't mean he hadn't; but I was going to extend him the benefit of the doubt that he wasn't a sleazebag who'd hide a sexual relationship between one of his grownup teachers and a fourteen-year-old student. For now, at least.

"Did Berry show any obvious signs of being a metahuman?" Reed entered the conversation by clearing his throat first. "Did you have any inkling of him being a powered person?"

"No," Prestegaard said. "We had no idea. About anything. This has all been an enormous and unpleasant surprise."

"Did Ms. Oliver have any friends that we could talk to?" I asked. Reed, next to me, reddened slightly. Probably mad that I'd lied to get us in here and doing this, but...what was Minnesota going to do? I never cited being part of an actual police investigation. I'd let Prestegaard infer it, and away we went.

"She did," the headmaster said, standing. "If you'll excuse me for a second, I'll have them brought down. Obviously, they've been through this a few times before, and, uh..." He hesitated. "...Really, I should get their parents on the phone so they can–"

"Oh, this is completely informal," I said, just blowing right past that breach of protocol. "I don't want to put any pressure on them or anything. I'd be happy to talk to them all as a group, even. With you present, if that makes you more comfortable." Anything to avoid slowing the pace of things down enough to allow Prestegaard time to contact local police, or even my friends at Minnesota BCA.

"Uhhh." Prestegaard looked torn, protocol warring with his desire to be helpful. Such a useful human urge, and one I was definitely going to prevail upon here. "All of us, you say?"

"Sure, this is all background," I said, pretending to go through my pockets for something to write with. "I wouldn't even be here today, but I've been a little busy the last couple weeks, y'know. This is first chance I've had to dig into this case."

Reed's eyebrow twitched. But he said nothing, so credit to him.

"I suppose as long as I'm here, and this is informal, sure," Prestegaard said. "And short."

"Absolutely," I said with a charming smile. As charming as I could manage in my current condition, anyway. "Short. Sweet. To the point. I'm sure you have other things to do, and, this is mostly rubber stamp, follow-up stuff on our side."

"Right," Prestegaard said, nodding. "Give me a sec." And he headed out the door back through his secretary's office.

Reed let out a meta-low hiss of air. "Are you kidding?"

I answered in kind. Minus the hiss. "You really think he'd let us in if we told him we're working for Aaron Berry? Because my sense is that he's trying to move swiftly past the idea that Aaron Berry was ever in his employ."

"Of course he is," Reed said. "No school principal in their

right mind would put the fact that one of their teachers raped a student in their damned marketing materials, even if it was a public school!"

"This is probably our one and only chance to talk to the girl's friends," I said, keeping it meta-low, and trying to let Reed's apoplexy roll off my back. "So let's just keep cool and enjoy this goodwill while it lasts, okay?"

Reed clenched his teeth together. "You're posing as a law enforcement officer. That's a crime."

"I never said I was with law enforcement." I gave my brother an even smile. "If Headmaster Prestegaard came away with that impression, that's on him, not me."

Reed put his head down, laying it in his hands. "You got a little too comfortable with lying while you were away, and in my estimation it's only gotten worse since the Network and the alcoholism."

My smile faded, because my brother had struck true with that one. "I'll work on that when I get through some of my other...difficulties."

Reed looked at me sidelong from out of his hands. "You keeping a list of flaws to pound out of yourself?"

"No," I said, putting my eyes forward again, because I heard Prestegaard just outside the door. "Why would I waste time keeping a list of my own when I've got you to tell me everything I'm doing wrong?"

With that, we lapsed into an uneasy silence, my brother like a black hole of displeasure beside me, as we waited.

CHAPTER ELEVEN

Lucille was a nervous giggler, Ashleigh was the leader, and Syrena didn't say a damned word until the end of our little talk.

If I hadn't been interviewing these girls for leads, odds were good I would not have remembered their names five seconds after meeting any of them. They were the kind of forgettable early teens that populated malls on Friday nights in the days of yore. Now they probably spent their time making elaborate TikTok videos and...honestly, I couldn't even guess what else they got up to. Keggers, maybe? Or was that me projecting?

"Thanks for taking the time to speak to us," I said, looking first at Lucille. She had blond hair down her back, kinda slick, with hints of freckles at the cheekbones. Classic Scandinavian Minnesotan, exactly the sort you'd expect in a tony boarding school around these parts. She giggled, hand over her mouth, but there was no delight there, only nerves at play.

"It's just such an honor to meet you," Ashleigh said, a little haughty tone in her flat, midwestern accent. Her eyes were slightly wider than they had been before she'd noticed me upon entry to the headmaster's office. Her hand flapped back and forth around the vicinity of her chest, as though to signify that every word she spoke originated from her heart. She was dark-haired, tanned, and well made-up – for a ninth grader. Composed and well-spoken, too. It was obvious why she was the leader.

The last one...she was raven-haired, mousy, and her head seemed to be perpetually bowed. A flash of green eyes met mine once since she'd walked in the door. The rest of the time she seemed to be mostly interested in my scuffed-up, effed-up boots. That was Syrena.

"I don't want to take you away from class for too long," I said, catching the eyes of Ashleigh and Lucille, and getting a dry giggle out of the latter, "but would you mind – just real quick – telling me a little about Greta Oliver?"

"Sure," Ashleigh said, and I had to let her take the lead, because Headmaster Prestegaard was lurking behind them, hovering over their shoulders where they sat on the couch. "Greta was like...sweet," she began, clearly giving it some thought. "Just a really sweet girl. I don't think she really argued with anyone."

"She totally avoided drama," Lucille added, then – of course – giggled.

"Is there a lot of drama around here?" I asked, pretty sure I already knew the answer.

It was Ashleigh's turn to laugh. "We're in high school. It's *all* drama."

"That's a...really fair point," I said. "Um, in terms of friends...you were all tight with her?"

"Oh, yeah," Ashleigh said. "We were like...besties."

"So you all shot Tiktok videos together?" I asked. Reed frowned beside me.

"Of course," Ashleigh said, going for her backpack. Like,

duh. So natural. She pulled out a phone and messed with it for a second, then handed it to me.

It was a choreographed version of them dancing to...well, I didn't know the song, but it was filmed down by the river, in what looked to be downtown Stillwater. Then the music clicked for me. "Is that...Tina Turner's 'Proud Mary'?"

"Yeah, your generation has way better music than ours. The classics are like...amazing," Ashleigh said proudly. Headmaster Prestegaard looked like he was experiencing some bad chafing. Or maybe just age pains at being called "classic."

"Wow, I feel kinda old now," Reed said under his breath.

I watched the video; it was only twenty seconds or so, and the choreography was solid, camerawork was a B- at best, though. I avoided pointing out that the song was released before my birth. "Great. Do any of you know if Greta had a boyfriend?"

"Ummm, yeah, apparently Mr. Berry," Ashleigh said, oh-so-haughty. "But no, we didn't know then."

"Not even a hint?" Reed asked, clearing his throat.

Ashleigh just shrugged. "She was acting maybe a little weird? But not a lot."

"Had you ever heard any rumors that Mr. Berry dated any of his students?" I asked.

Ashleigh froze; Lucille had started a giggle which died in her throat.

And Syrena...

Syrena, already a model of stop motion non-animation, had somchow just about reduced herself to zero particle movement.

"Okay, I see we know a little something about that," I said. Mr. Prestegaard was frowning over their shoulders, but their attention was on me.

"We didn't know at the time," Ashleigh said quickly.

"No clue," Lucille said.

And then...they both looked at Syrena.

Expectantly.

"Girls...is there something you're trying to say here?" Mr. Prestegaard asked. "Because when you talked to the police, I thought you were pretty clear about–"

"I didn't tell them," Syrena said, her chin just about touching her breastbone, she was so slouched over.

Ashleigh and Lucille kept their eyes anchored on her. The atmosphere in the room grew thick; I didn't dare speak.

"Tell them what?" Mr. Prestegaard asked. His eyebrows were pushing tighter together, the relaxed look that had been present when first we'd met shot all to shit.

Silence. And everyone in the room now was focused on Syrena.

Finally...she spoke: "I was seeing Mr. Berry," Syrena said, the words barely squeaking out, through nearly clenched lips. She didn't dare look up, for the shame was all over her face. "I was...sleeping with...Mr. Berry."

CHAPTER TWELVE

The moments after Syrena's near-silent admission that her teacher had raped her were as the moments after a bomb has gone off, and you're looking around to assess the damage. Having been through that exact scenario on several occasions, I had to say I preferred it to hearing a fourteen-year-old make the kind of admission that Syrena had just laid out. Dealing with the gore and ichor of severed limbs and splattered blood was infinitely preferable to hearing what was, for all intents and purposes, a child, telling a tale of a trusted adult taking full advantage of them in the worst way...

Yeah. I preferred the blood and guts.

"Holy shit," Reed breathed. Everyone heard it.

Headmaster Prestegaard stood with his mouth open in pure shock. "I...this is..." He put a perfectly manicured hand against his face, and I wondered if he was experiencing any symptoms of a heart attack or stroke, because by the look on his face, he seemed to be. "...Dear God."

I was feeling a little like this room was entirely too small for me, or maybe like I was about to explode out in a gout of fire. I squirmed in my chair, and said the thing that was on my mind and driving me like a cowboy's spurs in his horse's flanks. "You're going to have to call the local police to file a report on this. And the girl's parents."

Prestegaard looked up at me. "I...you can't do it?"

"This has to be taken down by the proper local authorities," I said, shaking my head. "I'm sorry. They're going to need to involve–"

"Yeah, I know," Prestegaard said, shoulders falling in absolute defeat. "We've already been through it all once." He shuffled over to his door and opened it a crack. "Will you call the local police, please? We have to file a...a report."

I stood, looking at Syrena, who was not looking at me. "It was very brave, what you just did there, Syrena. I need you to be brave again, okay? Just for a little longer? And tell the story."

"Don't you want to hear it?" Ashleigh asked. Because of course she did.

"I'm not an expert at the kind of counseling and questioning your friend needs," I said. "It's a very sensitive subject, and it requires someone who's a little more prepared than me." Also, if I took one word down from her story, I was pretty sure it'd qualify as witness tampering, and I worried they'd be grounds for her parents to sue the shit out of me. My whole brain was tingling, a spider-sense warning that my little lie had produced a hell of a result. I needed to get out of here, fast.

"But you haven't even heard what happened," Ashleigh said. Her face was a crumpled mask of disappointment.

Reed, beside me, had also risen, and looked ready to beat a path the hell out the door. Still, struck by that, he bit. "Why? Did something happen that would suggest metahuman powers for Mr. Berry?"

Ashleigh and Lucille looked right at Syrena again, and I felt so embarrassed – for being here, for watching them take knowledge they had and use it to apply pressure to their friend. Also, I couldn't help but feel wildly out of place given that I'd come here to defend and investigate the man that they were now accusing of what I considered to be one of the most heinous crimes there was.

So there was that.

Syrena was now reduced to studying her own shoes, her head had retreated so far down. "He was...strong," she managed to get out. Barely.

I looked at Reed; he looked back at me, and I saw a mirror of my own discomfort at being here. "How strong?" I asked, trying to impose a mental countdown that would see me safely out the door before the first police cruiser showed up and started asking uncomfortable questions about why I was here and why I was asking questions that had turned up a rape investigation that they'd completely missed. Which would not put them in a charitable mood toward me.

To put it another way...if we were here when the local cops showed up, we were definitely getting darted. For sure.

"Strong like a normal man?" Reed asked, just going right on in where I feared to tread. "Or...stronger?"

Syrena took what felt like an eternity to answer. An eternity in which I swore the rattling, squealing air conditioner operating at the far corner of the building was a police siren for a good several seconds. Seconds in which my heart ceased to beat in regular intervals. "Stronger," she said.

Shit.

"We can't take this report," I said, giving Headmaster Prestegaard a quick nod, hoping to disengage us from this fiasco without undo suspicion. "I appreciate your cooperation, girls, and hope that you'll be as forthcoming with the local police as you have been with us, because this is an important piece of evidence." I forced a tight smile, which was entirely pained and entirely fake, and bolted for the door.

Reed, two steps behind me, said, "Thanks for your time."

"Feel free to come back if you have any other questions," Headmaster Prestegaard called after us. "Or if you need to tour the school looking for...evidence or anything." Helpful to the last.

I bolted past his secretary, then froze the moment I got into the main office. Outside the windows I could see a Stillwater PD car pulling up outside.

Turning to the nearest secretary, I asked, "There's another exit over here, isn't there?" And I pointed to the long hallway behind her. "Near the bathrooms?"

"Yeah." She looked slightly flummoxed. "How did you know there were bathrooms back there?"

"I can hear the plumbing," I said, tapping my ear and smiling. I couldn't; but the faculty had to go to the bathroom somewhere, and there was zero chance they'd go with the plebes. "I just need to nip to the loo real quick." I nodded at Reed, and he followed me as I plunged down the hall. "Thanks for everything."

"Please tell me you don't actually have to go to the bathroom," Reed said, hustling along beside me in the tight hallway. Behind us, I could hear the office door opening, and knew the cops were close at hand.

"Just trying to find a way out of this excellently constructed mess I landed us in," I said. The exit sign was ahead, and looming, just past a couple of bathrooms. Thank goodness for that. I pushed through the door and it gave, dumping us out into a parking lot at the side of the building filled with crappy cars that could only belong to the faculty.

I was about halfway out the door when I realized there was someone standing behind it, a cloud of smoke covering them like a small volcano puffing around their head. I sniffed; it made my fingers crave a cigarette to hold onto, and as Reed came out and made his sour face at the smell, I closed the door quickly and found a young girl in a school uniform standing there, cigarette in hand. "Whoops," she said, wearing a sly smile, "you caught me."

"Give me the cigarette and I won't tell anyone," I said, closing the door behind Reed, who was swiftly backing away from the smoke.

The girl stared at me for a second, then handed it over wordlessly. She had tightly braided dark hair, freckles, and a sly grin. "It's just a regular cigarette."

"Good, cuz I don't need to be taking up the devil's lettuce right now," I said, inhaling wonder and sweetness. "Got too many problems already without adding in reefer madness."

She snorted, covering her mouth. She wore the same navy sweater over a white collared shirt and school tie as the other girls, but she seemed a lot looser. "I've got some vodka under the seat in my car if you need a nip."

"My reputation precedes me, I see." I took another drag, and glanced at Reed. He was hanging by the corner of the building, peering around. At least one cop was probably loitering around out front, if I had to guess. He'd signal me once it was clear.

"Just internet rumors," the girl said. "I heard you went into a bar in Eden Prairie and drank all the big, bad biker dudes under the table." She hesitated, then her grin got slyer. "There was some other stuff that might have happened under the table after that. Sounded sketchy."

I froze, cig perched between my lips. "I...remember the drinking, but nothing hanky-panky-wise." Did that mean it hadn't happened exactly like she said? No. That was the problem with drinking to blackout levels. I had long stretches of time bereft of memory in the last months. "Anyway, I've turned over a new leaf. No more vodka." I tiptoed up behind Reed and glanced around the corner for myself. "Put that out on the internet for me, will you?"

"Yeah, I'll get it spreading to my five hundred followers on Socialite," she said. "Mom's going to really dig it. Probably share it to her three thousand yoga pants wine mom groups."

"Great, everyone will have heard it by morning, then," I said. Sure enough, around the corner, two cops loitered outside two different cars. Just hanging, shooting the shit.

"I'm Isolde, by the way," the girl said, now hanging behind me.

Reed turned around at that. "You have a mythic name."

"Clearly I am legendary," Isolde said with an easy grin. She reached into her sweater and pulled out her pack of smokes, grabbing a replacement for the one I'd filched. I lit it for her, sparing her the trouble of rummaging for a lighter. She nodded coolly at me. "Thanks for contributing to the delinquency of this minor."

"If you've got vodka under your car seat, my contributions seem minimal," I said. "Also, I'd ask you what you're doing here, but the answer seems self-evident."

"History is a drag now that Mr. Berry is gone," Isolde said, emitting a hell of a puff of smoke. "I'm just trying to manage my way through the dull days."

"Why won't these guys go inside?" Reed muttered under his breath. "What is this? Social hour?"

"You knew Mr. Berry?" I asked, keeping one eye on my brother and his rising blood pressure and the other on Isolde, who was calmly enjoying her cigarette.

"Everyone seventh grade and above knows Mr. Berry," Isolde said. "And loved him – until...y'know." She snorted, twin puffs of smoke drifting out of her nostrils. "Some of us more than others, apparently."

"Did you know anything about him sleeping with students?" I asked, deciding not to waste this chance to gather a little more on-the-ground feel for the state of Mr. Berry's rep at Stilloaks Prep.

"Uh, no," Isolde said, "because if I had known that was an option, I would have volunteered as tribute." She thrust her hand in the air. "Because Mr. Berry is a babe."

"Oh, God, what the hell?" Reed turned on us both, unmistakable disgust turning his face a darker hue. "He's a pedophile, if the allegations are true. I mean, seriously – fourteen-year-olds?"

"Yeah, that's gross," Isolde said, but she didn't seem too put off by it. "But that's...if you believe it." She shrugged. "Which I kinda don't."

"Do you know if he was sleeping with anyone else?" I asked.

"Uhm, well, his girlfriend," Isolde said, letting the cigarette burn in her hand. "I assume. But as to the girl, Greta? No clue. Couldn't have even placed the face until all this shit happened. Now she's famous."

"This isn't a very big school," I said, frowning. "But you didn't know her?"

Isolde shook her head, venting smoke calmly. "Nope. In the Who's Who of Stoaks...she was a no one."

"Where do you rate in the Who's Who of Stilloaks?" Reed asked, casting a look at her suspiciously.

Isolde flashed an impish smile. "Top of the class, bay-bee." Then she let a long puff out of her nose, which looked painful to me.

"Guessing you've achieved extra cool points for sneaking out of class to smoke," I said, taking my last drag and putting out the cigarette beneath my boot. "You want to tell me anything else I should know about Stoaks? Besides the fact your school nickname is stupid?"

"We work with what we got," she said with a shrug. "And I kinda doubt Mr. Berry actually murdered that girl, but there's no way I could prove it."

Reed snapped his head around for that one. "Why do you

think that?"

"Berry's not that type," Isolde said, shaking her head. "Look...I'm not a good girl, right? If he was into the student bodies...he could have had me. And he knew it." Her eyes flashed with malicious, sensuous glee.

"Maybe you're too old for him," Reed said, looking her over with vague disgust. "I mean...you must be eighteen."

"Yeah?" Isolde almost sneered. "So what?"

"So he's into younger girls, clearly," Reed said, "and innocent ones. Which you also aren't."

"Clearly." Isolde's eyes had a look in them like fiery coals on a dying flame. "Berry wasn't that kind of guy. Don't get me wrong, he wasn't Captain America, either, as you can see by his girlfriend, if you ever meet her, but the idea he was going around diddling sweet, innocent fourteen-year-olds? Nah." She shook her head. "Like condoms and cheap earrings...I don't buy it."

I tried to gallop on past that last statement. "So you're swearing this as a character witness?"

Isolde chuckled. "As a character witness with no character whatsoever, sure." She puffed out a long stream of gray smoke. "Do whatever you want with that. Just telling you how I see it."

"So how would you answer another girl coming forward and saying Berry raped her?" Reed asked, and now his eyes had taken on the burning charcoal quality. "Another ninth grader?"

Isolde faltered not a bit, just shrugging. "I'd say...I did a lot worse at her age and she should probably count herself lucky to snag a lay that decent-looking."

I cringed. "Oof."

Reed's eyes just about caught on fire. "Let's get out of here," he said through gritted teeth.

"Nice to meetcha, Sienna Nealon," Isolde said, easing

away from us, her plaid schoolgirl skirt twirling around tanned legs. "If you ever change your mind on the vodka, you should come party with me. I'm at Club Labyrinth in Oakdale on Saturday nights. And every night I can get away."

"Don't count on seeing me in a bar ever again, but thanks," I said, turning the corner after Reed. The cops were gone, so we broke into a run for our car, trying to cover the distance quickly and get the hell out of there before we could land ourselves in still more trouble.

CHAPTER THIRTEEN

"Can you believe that girl?" Reed was seething as we hit Highway 36. We planned to cross the bridge ahead, where it would turn into Wisconsin State Highway 64 and take us all the way into New Richmond, a place I thought I'd been but which defied my attempts to remember it. I wanted to cite Rose as the fault behind this, but I had a vague memory of small-town streets and a Walmart, so I suspected it had more to do with the town being forgettable than the Scottish harpy.

I tried not to let my brother's seething rage get me down as we rode. Green grass filled the berms and banks that straddled the highway, a pleasant change from the concrete and steel and tumbling buildings that surrounded the busier parts of the I-94 corridor through downtown St. Paul and Minneapolis, or the 494/694 Loop with its abrupt changes between urban and suburban landscape depending on which part you were on.

Things were different out here; commercial suburban development gave way to sections of green woods, and ahead I could sense a step change; the St. Croix River waited in its glory just beyond the near horizon, and past that, Wisconsin.

"Can you believe–" Reed started to say again.

"Yes," I said.

He looked at me, blinking in surprise. "What?"

"You asked me if I can believe that a hard-drinking, smoking, slutty eighteen-going-on-thirty-five-year-old like Isolde would be out there acting how she acted. The answer is yes."

Reed's face crumpled in amazement. "She just justified a fourteen-year-old sleeping with a teacher twice her age."

"Yeah," I said calmly, "and I disagree to the death with her view of it, but..." I shrugged. "...She is what she is. What her upbringing and her choices have made her into. Do I believe she slept with an older man at fourteen? Yeah, probably. And also...*ugh* to the maximum, because at fourteen I was mainly contemplating what a dish Leonardo DiCaprio was, and how well he must kiss, and definitely was not thinking quite as adult thoughts as she was. But could I believe that someone else, someone like her, would be that naughty? Yeah. I think she's kind of edgelord, and she was trying to get a reaction from us. Which you totally gave her."

Reed's disgusted look did not fade one whit. "Good. She needed to see that reaction. Because she's probably spreading that toxic idea to her cohort and passing it off as cool rather than repulsive."

I thought about it a second. "Yeah," I agreed. "Probably."

He shook his head, focusing on the road, but his words came out filled with bitter spite. "You could have come out a little harder on her."

I pursed my lips, started to respond with a little fire, but it faded. "Yeah," I finally said. "You're right. I should have."

Reed blinked a couple times looking out the front windshield. "...Say what?"

I leaned over, almost to his ear, and whispered, "I said

'You're right.' You need me to say it again? For your ego and enjoyment?" I leaned back against the far door. "Fine. Maybe if I, as a role model, had properly said, 'Hey, sleeping with older men like that? Is gross, and exploitative, and it cheapens the shit out of you because they're basically using your body and all you're getting out of it is the equivalent of a dog receiving a pat on the head,' she might have listened. Probably not. Still, I could have tried." I shrugged, burning a little inside because while I wasn't sure I had a proper angle on the approach, I did feel the sting of Reed's point, that I'd let this popular girl talk judgment free while edgelording her crazy opinions about teenagers having sex with adults.

Not that it'd do one whit of good either way, but still...maybe I shoulda said it.

Reed sighed, a deep, discontented sound. "Well...that was a Charlie Foxtrot all the way around."

"I know you're trying to sound all military when you say things like 'Charlie Foxtrot,' but you just can't pull it off, bro. Maybe if you had a tactical operator beard, but as a long-haired, clean-cut hippie looking dude...just no."

He smiled, very slightly. "Fine. It was a disaster, though, you agree?"

"I think we can agree we burned a couple bridges just now at Stilloaks," I said, "and we definitely don't want to go back there. Also, it is possible that Stillwater PD is going to be seeking us out for hampering their investigation – when, really, we just opened up a new avenue for them – but on the whole, I think it was a rousing success."

Reed blinked a couple times. "Explain."

"We just turned up another potential victim."

Reed stared dully. "We were there to try and prove him innocent."

"Right," I said, "but still...additional evidence."

"*Against* him," Reed said. "This is the opposite of progress. You said he's innocent...now it looks less like he is."

"Okay, you have a point here," I said, trying to remain buoyant, "but still...progress."

"I think it's technically called 'regress' when you go backwards."

I sighed. "Fine. It didn't go well for our pre-conceived point of view. But I'm choosing to call this a win because if the evidence leads me to the fact that Aaron Berry actually killed Greta Oliver in a drunken stupor, I am fine with hammering the nails into his coffin with our investigation."

"But you said he didn't."

"I said he got blackout drunk and didn't *remember* doing it." I settled back in my seat, arms folded in front of me. "Crucial distinction. If the evidence leads us a different way, then it's entirely possible he did it while retaining no memory of it."

Reed nodded, settled back in his seat, and was quiet for a moment. Then he dropped the boom. "This hitting home for you?"

I shifted uncomfortably in my seat. "Maybe. Can we talk about something else?"

He shrugged. "I guess." Then his face got intense. "I was thinking about an episode of *Lost* earlier. You ever watch that?"

"Great show. Terrible ending."

"Yeah, that one," he said, keeping his hands on the wheel as we rolled down the hill toward the Wisconsin bridge. "Remember in season three when Dominic Monaghan is about to get written out, and they have that last episode before his farewell, where he's thinking about all the great things in his life? Like a top five list of awesome moments?" My brother sighed. "I was thinking about that. But for Minnesota."

I squeezed my hand into a fist, then relaxed it. "Why?" I looked at him, squinting. "Is this because you 'died' last night?"

"Kind of, yeah," Reed said. "But also because we're getting the boot here. And it got me thinking, because you never really appreciate something until it's gone. Y'know?"

"If only you were talking about me."

"Heh," he chuckled. "But seriously...I didn't choose Minnesota, remember? I chose you. You're the reason I'm here, not this frigid hellscape with its psychotic weather and hateful people who masquerade as nice–"

"Some are nice. Some are not. In the same proportion as anywhere else. Roughly."

"I'm just saying 'Minnesota Nice' is surface deep, at best." He settled both hands on the wheel. "But I was thinking...there are a few things I'll miss after having spent all these years here."

"Me too," I said softly.

Reed drummed fingers against the wheel. "And they are...?"

I looked out the window at the sun shining down on these green, rolling hills. The St. Croix River waited ahead, and beyond, the verdant, tree-lined bank that indicated Wisconsin. "Before you joined us at the Directorate, Scott, Kat, and I were doing intensive training with Parks. You remember Parks?"

"Gray-haired, long beard? Turned into a bear when he got mad?" He smiled. "Tough guy to forget."

"He had me over in the woods on the campus one day," I said, staring off into the distance. "It was kinda like it is today, y'know? Sunny, warm...one of those perfect summer days Minnesota comes up with like a down payment on the fact that the winters are just shit. 'Stay here,' Minnesota says. 'For this.' Like...hang on to the memory that it'll be like this again, because winter is long and forever, and drives an ice spike into your frigging veins." I sighed.

"Anyway, we're out in the woods, and he's showing me how to make a fire," I said, and I could see the moment in my head, one of the blessed memories Rose hadn't bothered with. "And Parks is standing there–"

I closed my eyes, and it was like I was there. He stood over a simple cairn circle of rocks, dried pine needles mounted upon a bed of old twigs which lay atop a couple good rocks. Parks was old by now, his beard all gray, showing the twilight of his years and all the experiences he had on that craggy, lined face.

His bright eyes played over the fire pit I'd made in the course of a very few minutes, and he nodded that great, old head, which did make him look like a bear. "That's not half bad for a first try, Nealon," he said in that voice, which sounded like whiskey poured over parchment paper, crackling and filled with character.

And something else, too.

Pride.

"That's what sticks out for you?" Reed asked, jarring me back to the present, to the car and its air conditioner running hard to keep the warm day at bay. "That's in your top five?"

I looked back out the window at the perfect sapphire skies. "Yeah." Then I looked back at him. "Maybe it's hard for you to believe, but...on that day, I went back to my room? And I cried for like...an hour." I bit my lip. "Because that was the day I realized what it would feel like...to have a dad who was proud of you."

Reed's expression melted away; he looked stricken. "Oh," was all he said, though.

I let us sit in silence for a few minutes, the car bumping as we rolled over the length of the long bridge across the St. Croix. About a million sun sparkles twinkled up at me from the blue surface, enticing, almost begging me to come down and look, come down and swim. A few boats dotted the water, from here to the horizon, either bobbing there or trailing a white wake as they ran up and down the river, their masters looking for fish, or for fun.

Only a small sign at the far end of the white concrete suspension bridge informed us that we were entering Wisconsin, and St. Croix County, no less. I broke the silence. A couple large, aluminum grain silos on the left side of the road informed us more effectively, in my opinion. “Didn't mean to bust your balls there,” I said. “Sometimes I get a little envious of the fact you actually knew Dad.”

“Sometimes I forget you didn't,” Reed said, sounding a little choked. “So...top five. That's...number five?”

“Sure,” I said. Not that I'd given it much thought, but I'm sure it would make it somewhere in there, if I was thinking about Minnesota. “What about you? What's your top five?”

He opened his mouth, but didn't say anything. “No,” he finally managed to squeeze out, clearly around the lump in his throat, “let's just leave that one for now.” He smiled at me sadly. “Maybe we can count it down later, but for now...” He focused back on the road, on the gray asphalt line plodding into the distance of rural Wisconsin, “...I don't think I can compete with that.”

CHAPTER FOURTEEN

New Richmond, Wisconsin was small town America to a T. The main street was State Highway 65, which we picked up in the middle of town, where it became main street, complete with faded brick buildings that had clearly seen better days.

"This town is a micropolis," Reed said, gently pushing the brakes because the speed limit had dropped precipitously just inside the town limits. "Biggest one between here and Hudson and Eau Claire; there's not a bigger one north until you get to St. Croix Falls, and south...well, there's Hudson, I guess, and not much other than River Falls beyond that of note for quite a ways. Maybe Red Wing, over the river in Minnesota."

"I haven't been out here in a while," I said, racking my brain for times when I'd gone to Wisconsin. They were few, and almost entirely mission-related, near as I could remember. "You were with us that time on Highway 8, when Omega...?"

"Blew up our car on the way back from Eagle River?"

Reed asked sourly. "Chased us through the woods? Killed Andromeda?"

"I think that was Century, actually," I said. "And her name was Adelaide. Clearly you remember, though."

"There aren't many times in my life I've been in a car and it's been blown up by a rocket launcher, so...yeah, it sticks."

I smiled. "I can't get into these small towns in Wisconsin without thinking of that. Or the Eagle River mission. Or that time I chased my mom – actually, that was the same mission, wasn't it?" I shook my head. "I really don't get over here much."

We passed a small, rundown motel with a brightly painted sign to summon in all the possible traffic they could. I wondered how many options there actually were for motels in town; it couldn't be that many.

"I wish I could live in a small town," Reed said. "Getting kind of tired of the fussy newness of Eden Prairie."

"You could have gone farther out," I said, leaning on my elbow as the town passed. "Young America is like this, I think."

"I'd have to go that far out," Reed said. "Chaska, Chanhassen...they're all like Eden Prairie. All those same-y suburban box houses. I want some space, y'know?"

"Brother, you are talking to the right person," I said, catching a glimpse of slightly more spread out housing down one of the side streets, homes built in the sixties on half-acres, with pretty painted mailboxes and tall trees in the front yards. "I lived in New York and DC this year, and now I'm perched in the basement of a friend's suburban McMansion." I let out a sigh of my own. "I would just about kill for some acreage, some distance from humanity." My brother gave me a suspicious look. "For privacy, not because I want to get lit on my own. Geez."

"Sorry," he said. "Forgive me, given the history."

"It's fair," I said, as Reed's GPS chirped and he turned onto a side street where a two-story apartment complex stood. I could tell by the windows it was old, even though the brick seemed fairly ageless. A couple kids were playing with a ball on the grass in front.

"You get ahold of Paula?" Reed asked as we headed up an exterior stairwell. Weird choice for a complex in the freezing cold of the upper Midwest, but I guess this was why I wasn't an apartment mogul.

"Said she was on her way when I texted," I said, jonesing for a cigarette. And a whiskey, if I was being brutally honest with myself.

"Time frame?"

"Didn't say."

But there was no need for us to worry, because Paula was in front of the door to Berry's apartment, familiar cloud of smoke hanging around her head. I almost bummed one as I was walking up, but she hurriedly dropped hers and ground it out beneath her shoe, a nice, slightly sparkly flat that reminded me of a ballet shoe but looked comfortable. Then she fumbled for keys and unlocked the door.

A ripped piece of yellow police tape was still plastered on the door, warning all who passed that something ominous had happened here. Berry's apartment had a dark aura, though a little sunlight flooded in from somewhere out of sight. I sniffed as I started to enter; it smelled fresh. When I stepped inside, I could see a window at the far end of the place had been cracked open.

"Who leaves the window open on a crime scene?" Reed asked with a frown as he stepped inside, taking immediate note of the obvious.

"Well, they did process it already," I said, stepping deeper into the room. It wasn't a big apartment. Looked like a one bedroom, because I could see it from where I stood next to the TV.

"They told me I could come back," Paula said, trailing behind us, still reeking of fabulous smoke. "I haven't since the day of, you know, 'cuz I still have my own place, but...they said I could." She rattled the keys, putting them back in her purse.

"I'd ask for the tour, but I think I get the gist," I said, glancing around. Every drawer had been gone through, every item out in plain view disturbed by a forensics team looking for clues. When a search warrant was executed on a scumbag's place, cops were not known for being sticklers about cleaning up afterward. Their contempt for Berry was clear here.

"Uncomfortable question: how much time did you spend here?" Reed asked, not looking at Paula as he made his way into the kitchenette. It was an L shaped arrangement of cabinets with a stove and sink stuck right in the middle and a fridge bookending one side.

"Why's that uncomfortable?" Paula asked, leaning against a wall by the entry. "I was here probably every other night. I don't sleep well in a bed with someone else, so I was kinda working my way up to doing that. Figured we'd move in together...I don't know, maybe a few months, maybe a year. I wasn't in a raging hurry."

Reed's eyes met mine, and I could tell he was thinking something snarky. Which he did not say. Something about Paula and commitment, I figured, but I rolled my eyes rather than connect the dots fully.

"So do you think he had someone here on the nights you weren't?" I asked, stepping up to the bedroom door.

Paula bristled behind me. "I thought you saw he was innocent?"

"Let's not mince words: your boyfriend was blackout drunk when the murder occurred." I stared into the bedroom; the mattress was on the box springs, which itself was lying right on the ground, no frame to hold it up. "So while I *think* he didn't do it, I can't be a hundred percent certain. And I know nothing about whether he was diddling his students."

"I don't think he was cheating on me, no," Paula said, voice a little strained. "And I especially don't think he was doing it with the kids he taught. He wasn't a pedo."

"Mmhm," I said, easing into the bedroom and circling that bed.

I caught Reed's look from the door, and this time there was no assembly required for me to suss out his meaning: *Sure*. With all the sarcasm that required.

The mattress was totally askew, clearly had been lifted. No sheets, either. Standard procedure for cops clearing through a potential crime scene, all part of the local PD's turndown service. No mint on the pillow, though. Which was a bummer, because in the absence of alcohol and a cigarette, I was suddenly craving sugar.

I lifted the mattress myself, because something about it cried out to me.

And I was not disappointed.

"Reed," I said, putting the mattress off to the side. My brother swore behind me, easing up on the box springs, which sat lonely on the gray carpet.

A pair of tiny panties and a training bra lay crushed on the box springs, the dark crotch unmistakably crusted. I looked away, drawn off by a strange sense of propriety and discomfort.

My brother moved up, and even without looking at him I could sense him cringing beside me. "These are...small. You think they're the right size for a fourteen-year-old?"

"I couldn't have worn them when I was fourteen," I said, lump in my throat, my face to the wall. "But yes."

"What is it?" Paula asked from the doorway. "What – oh, shit." I heard her thump against the wall. "Oh – oh, shit."

"Would you like to take a bet on whether the DNA on those things is his?" Reed asked. I had managed to pry my eyes open enough to look at him, and while he was still cringing in disgust, it was starting to fade as the realization of exactly what this meant began to settle in.

"No bet," I said. "It's his for sure. They wouldn't be here otherwise."

Paula had made it back to the door, but she had a hand on her chest, and the look on her face was pure pain. "What are you talking about?"

I looked past her, at the open window to the outside. "Someone screwed up."

Reed nodded out of the corner of my eye. "Big time."

Paula followed our gaze to the window. "What do you mean?"

"You call the cops?" I asked, looking over at him. He nodded, and gracefully went past Paula, already looking up the number for the local PD. "Chain of custody on this is going to be a mess. We're going to have to answer questions."

"I know," Reed said wearily. He was already dialing. "Hello? Yes, this is Reed Treston. I'm a private investigator – yes, ma'am." He practically ground his teeth. "Yes, that Reed Treston. And I have Sienna here with me. I'm at Aaron Berry's apartment, investigating on behalf of the fiancée, and we just turned up a piece of potential evidence. Yes, ma'am, I'll hold."

"I don't understand," Paula said, her angled bangs hanging in front of her eyes. "Who screwed up? Why are you smiling?"

I hadn't realized I had been. I wiped it off my face. "Sorry," I said. "It's just...this is the first actual break in the case we've had."

"But you think this," and she waved her hands at the discarded panties, "with the kinda obvious DNA all over the front...you think is...?" Her eyelids fluttered as she tried to connect the dots. "How is this in any way good?"

"Because there's zero chance," I said, patiently, and this time unable to keep the smile off my face, "that even in a burg as small as New Richmond, that a forensic team fails to turn this up the first time they go over an apartment."

"But if...you're saying it wasn't here when they went through the apartment the first time?" Paula asked.

"Exactly," I said, watching Reed pace in front of the door, on hold, "which means that somebody planted these after the fact, hoping to increase the evidence against Aaron." My smile broadened. "And that someone is almost certainly our killer."

CHAPTER FIFTEEN

The New Richmond, Wisconsin police department had questions for us. Oh so many questions. They were presented to us – me and Reed, at least – separately, to him by a hard-nosed, broad-shouldered female detective whose name I didn't catch, and to me by a thin slip of a man with big ears and a tiny face who looked a little like a Dick Tracy villain and went by the name McGee. He had no sense of humor, which made the whole process of describing everything we'd done and seen in the apartment take practically forever. Thankfully, it was only about sundown when he finally let me go, and I was able to join Reed outside. Paula, unfortunately was still speaking to a third detective who was boring in on her with the evil eye, so the two of us just walked out.

"That was unnecessarily long and brutal," Reed said as we walked along the exterior hallway of the apartment building.

"Could have been worse," I said, taking the steps two at a time, wishing Paula had been able to accompany us out so I could have bummed a cigarette. When my brother looked at me questioningly, I added, "The Stillwater police could have caught up to us here."

Reed's shoulders slumped. "They're going to eventually, you know."

"And won't that be a fun interrogation," I said as we headed for the car. "Surprised the New Richmond PD didn't inform them we were here, give them a crack at us."

Reed sighed. "Really? Because I'm just thankful for it, honestly." He looked at the orange-colored state of the sky; it was already after six PM, and while it wouldn't set for a bit yet, sundown was definitely coming. "What now?"

I started to answer him, but a dog barking nearby stopped me. It was close, too close, and the skittering of claws on the pavement caused me to turn in time to see a dog the size of a gym bag charging full out at me. It was puffy, gray and white, and looked like the tiniest Alaskan husky on the planet.

"Cali! No!" An older woman was hobbling after the dog, which was locked on and laser-focused, heading for my ankles like a guided missile, leash trailing behind her and owner at least thirty yards from catching her with a rapidly opening distance.

I thought of Priscilla, queen of the animals, who'd sicced a lion, a tiger, a bear, and a jaguar on me only last night, and said in my sternest voice, "Cali. Sit."

Cali sat, skidding to a stop on her rump and letting out a barking squeal as she did so. She came to a halt mere inches from me, absolutely upright, and I knelt to scratch her on the head. When I put my hand on her, I realized she was about 90% fur, puffy as hell and probably the size of a hamster underneath all the fuzz.

"Pretty dog," Reed said, helping himself to petting Cali, under the evil eye of the woman hustling forward to collect her escaped pup. "What is she?"

"She's a pomsky," I said as Cali barked in answer. "Pomeranian Husky mix. Cali – shush." She shut up.

"How did you know that?" the woman asked suspiciously.

She was gray haired and crabby as all hell. When she stooped and took hold of Cali's leash, she tried to pull on it. Cali didn't move, other than to be dragged about an inch. She was anchored in place by my command.

"Because you've said it in front of her," I said, peering at Cali. I couldn't read her mind, exactly, but there were things contained in Cali's barks that made sense to me in a way that they wouldn't have before I'd partially drained Priscilla.

Reed gave me a sideways look. "So you're talking to animals, now?"

"What do you mean? I've talked to you for years," I said, then fixed the woman with Cali in my gaze. "You live here?"

She seized up, midway through trying to jerk Cali off her rump. "Maybe." Hostile, unfiltered. She was too young to be so cynical, but too old to give an F that I was asking her something she didn't want to answer. I had suspicions, mainly that she knew who I was and why I was here.

"You probably know who I am," I said, "and maybe you've even guessed why I'm here. But you'd be wrong." I leaned in a little. "I'm trying to figure out who framed Aaron Berry."

The woman jerked Cali off her rump so hard the dog squealed. "Nobody framed Aaron Berry," she said with a savage hiss. "He's a kiddie-raping little shitbag."

"Cali, go with her," I said, and Cali's back legs unlocked, thankfully, before her master could rip her head off pulling so hard.

"You don't tell my dog what to do," Pissed Granny said, eyes lighting up in a fiery glare.

"Cali, nip her on the ankle once," I said, and boy, did that little pomsky do it. A great, yelping howl came from her master's throat as her dog got her on that pale, age-spotted ankle. Almost like she'd been waiting for years to strike back.

That did not improve the situation. The woman retreated, pulling Cali with her, and Cali, now returned to my previous command to follow her master, did so docilely, casting the occasional look back at me – but not barking. Her master, for her part, was shooting me devil glares, like I was a witch, and I watched her retreat up the stairs and appear again at the second floor.

"So...she's neighbors with Berry," Reed said, meta-low, hanging at my elbow.

A warm breeze rolled through just then, interrupting our standoff with the old cow. "Yep," I said, "but somehow I doubt we're going to get any more out of her today."

"I think you mean 'ever.'"

That was a fair point, but I didn't feel the need to tell him so. "I do feel bad for Cali, though," I said, trudging back to his car. "I shouldn't have done the ankle biting thing. She's going to get a cuff on the ear for that."

Reed's face soured. "Great job. Well done."

"Sorry," I said, and I genuinely meant it. Cali might have been a nippy little shit, but getting her thumped by her master wasn't a thing I could feel good about. "So...what are you thinking?"

"I'm thinking somebody fairly amateur came up with this frame." He opened the door to his cute little SUV. "Why try and sneak that extra evidence in later?"

"It's a pretty basic bitch frame-job," I agreed. "It does raise a question, though – seriously, how did they get access to his DNA? Because they've used a decent amount of it now, right?"

Reed settled into his seat, face twisted in disgust. "I did not wake up today thinking I'd be talking this much about some other dude's man juice." He paused, then tilted his head in thought. "Actually...I didn't exactly wake up today, did I?"

"No, you did," I said, settling into the seat beside him, knowing exactly what he meant. "You came out of a drug-induced couple hours of sleep in the early morning. Me, on the other hand...I caught about thirty minutes, maybe an hour since yesterday." I rubbed at my weary eyes. "So you've gotten double what I had. Plus I woke up to my brother's brains being blown out on a fifty-foot hologram."

Reed shuddered. "I know the blood was fake that they threw on me, but it was still gross."

"Yeah, they were a bunch of real sweet kids," I said, "at least compared to whoever's putting Berry's balls in a vise. And then milking him, apparently, for evidentiary purposes." I sighed, and it felt like a lot of my strength went out of me in that moment. It had been just the longest damned day. "I think we call it a day and return to the office. Get some sleep, get rested and refreshed, start again tomorrow." I rubbed my eyes.

"We need to talk to the victim's parents, don't we?" Reed asked. "You know...at some point?"

"At some point," I agreed, but I really didn't want to, ever. Hard to tell someone that you were trying to refute that the person they thought murdered and abused their little girl had actually done so, at least not without a different suspect to put forward in his place. "Though I might need a drink before I tackle that one."

Reed made a sound of disapproval deep in his throat.

"Kidding," I said. "I mean, not about wanting it, because I totally want a drink. I'm just...not taking it." I rubbed my eyes again. "But yeah...take us back to the office. At least for now."

"You got it," Reed said. And under that tangerine sky, we drove in silence back to Minnesota.

CHAPTER SIXTEEN

We'd just crossed back into Minnesota at the St. Croix River when my phone lit up. I didn't recognize the number, exactly, but I saw it was a 615 area code.

Nashville, Tennessee, my phone informed me. As if I hadn't already known.

Reed and I had settled into a tired silence, one filled with a strange peace between us. At least, strange in the context of pre-yesterday. After all that had happened in the last twenty-four hours, it actually felt very comfortable.

"Hello?" I answered, suspecting I knew what was coming next.

"Please hold for the mayor of Nashville." A click.

Reed's face showed a non-subtle reaction. A tightening of the brow, narrowing of the lips.

"Well, hey there, darlin'," came the rich voice of Clea Brandt, the mayor of Nashville. "How's your day going?" I could almost picture Brandt on the other end of the line, a playful smile perched on her ebon face, a mischievous light in her eyes.

"Mayor Brandt," I said, and watched Reed's eyes flutter

slightly, his lips a tense line. "This is so out of the blue. Whatever could prompt you to call me today?"

"Why, nothing, nothing at all," Brandt said, still playful. "I just thought I would call and do that occasional follow-up thing that a good politician does. Strictly on my behalf and most definitely not with any ulterior motives or because of a conversation with the governor and Senator Foreman this very morning."

"I do like the way you name drop," I said, settling back in my chair, leaning against the headrest. "It makes me feel almost connected to important people. Like I'm only two degrees from Kevin Bacon."

"I don't see you as the type who actually flaunts that sort of thing, honey, but I always appreciate your wit," Mayor Brandt said. "You just don't get enough credit for it."

"So kind of you to notice." I smiled. "So...job offer?"

"Let's call it...giving you a place to hang your hat," Brandt said. "I know you weren't interested in our previous offers to become Tennessee's very own superhero–"

"But to quote Dylan," I said, "'the times, they are a-changin'?"

"The times are always changing, sweetie," Brandt said, now very seriously. "I know you've probably gotten a million calls today. I just wanted to make sure we were in your thoughts before you decided anything."

"You are in my thoughts," I said, my smile fading. I had gotten calls today. I'd ignored them all; most had been from unfamiliar numbers, but the area codes told the tale: Florida, New York, DC, Illinois, Ohio – the only really glaring one had been California, which, after my little adventure in LA last month, was a surprise. "If you wouldn't mind sending me the terms of your offer again...?"

"I will absolutely do that, if you'll keep us in mind," Brandt said. "I know you've probably got things to do right now, and I don't want to keep you from them. Just let us know if we need to start...making some preparations. Hm?"

"I'll talk to my team. We'll let you know," I said.

"Take care."

"You too, Mayor," I said, and hung up.

Reed didn't say anything, but his neck muscles looked tight enough that they might cause his head to do a full-blown *Exorcist* spin atop his shoulders. "We have an offer?"

"One of many, I'm sure," I said, turning to look out the window. Minnesota 36 was rolling along, and I could see the green signs indicating that we were coming up on the 694 junction that would take us back to the office. I checked my voicemail. There were twenty or so messages.

"I got one from Texas and Florida," he said.

"Pretty sure I've got Florida, too," I said, "and maybe New York and some others." I watched the green grasses roll by on the shoulder of the road. "We're not short on places to run." It was just disappointing we had to run at all.

"You want Tennessee, don't you?" Reed asked, voice tight with dread.

"What do you want?" I asked, looking over at him.

He sighed. "I don't know. To not have to do any of this right now. To have that vacation weekend I was supposed to be on right now." He looked at me with weary eyes. "To not have to tell my fiancée that we're going to be forced out of town and away from her job."

"She's a teledoc, I'm pretty sure she can work from wherever."

"Oh, well then I guess it's just fine we're being run out of the state, then."

"Yeah." I looked at my hands. The smell of Cali was still on them. "We should have left before it got to this."

"That's the problem with being broke-ass poor," Reed said. "It limits your options."

"Preaching to the choir, brother," I said. Because it was very possible one of those calls I thought was an offer was really just a debt collector howling at me about my maxed-out credit card that I had yet to make payment on this month. "You are preaching right to the choir."

CHAPTER SEVENTEEN

"How'd it go?" Olivia asked as we came into the bullpen. The place looked completely different, because we'd left a half-dozen metas in charge of moving and, true to their super-strong selves, they'd...well, moved. Everything was boxed and packed and stacked in the receptionist area except the desks, which appeared to be emptied, their surfaces cleaned and cleared for the first time since I'd been here.

"We have a case," Reed announced, looking around the room. The cubicle walls were still mostly up, though it looked like someone had made a start on disassembling them, at least at the far side of the room. "It's going to be keeping us busy in the next couple days."

"Lucky you," Jamal said, a screwdriver in his hands. He cast a baleful look at the partially disassembled cubicle desk in the corner. "The rest of us will be here lifting heavy things and practicing our fine motor skills, I guess."

"Who knew we were going to end up the beasts of burden up in this place?" Augustus asked, a hammer in his own hand. He twirled deftly in his fingers, the speed of its movement belying the weight of the thing.

"I think we can all agree," I said, running a hand through my rough, destroyed hair, "if anyone's the beast in this place, it's me."

A couple of them chuckled, at least. Olivia let out a way-too-enthusiastic borderline howl. "That's so funny!"

ArcheGrey stared at me from where she sat in the corner, a laptop stretched across her lap, the silver metal a contrast against the blue in her jeans. "It was mediocre, as her cracks go."

"Still here, I see," I said.

Arche shrugged lightly. "I paid for a weekend. I will have my weekend." She cleared her throat. "Though it would appear I'm going to be flying out of a different airport on Monday. Perhaps Madison."

"So...we got a plan for what we're doing yet, boss?" Angel asked, sidling up to Reed. A sheen of sweat lay upon her forehead, her dark hair brushed back behind her ear falling out as she leaned on one of the remaining cubicle walls.

"Same as before," Reed said. "Tomorrow we get a couple U-hauls, load this stuff up, and beat feet to Hudson, Wisconsin. We'll figure out where to go next from there." He fixed me with a look. "Though I think we're going to have to make some decisions on that pretty soon. Like, by end of day tomorrow."

"We don't have to, do we?" Scott asked, frowning, leaning against the door frame in Reed's office. His arms were bulging, and I could see that Reed's desk was now gone from inside, as well as his filing cabinets. I thought I'd seen them in the entryway; all that was left now was his chair, which Scott had sitting in the middle of the room. "I mean, we could play this out for a bit as we think things through. Just camp in Hudson for a month?"

"Charming as it is, western Wisconsin is not going to be a

solid base of operations for us for long," I said. "Without access to MSP airport, we won't be able to take jobs."

"Which we will desperately need to do," Reed said. "Also, there's the little matter of setting up our new company. It needs a physical address, and quickly, if we don't want to lose business to our emerging competitors." He glanced briefly at Angel, who looked a little stricken. "So...we need to make some choices fast, lest our bank accounts dwindle to nothing."

I cleared my throat.

"Or, in some cases, to...is there a less than nothing...?" Reed asked.

"It's called credit card debt, and yes," I said, "there is."

"Can't you just walk away from that while we're burning everything else down here?" Augustus asked.

"Um, no," I said. "Personal bankruptcy is different than business bankruptcy."

"Your debts could just disappear, you know," Arche said, looking at me through those smokey eyes of hers. "It's not hard."

"That's, no – no, no," Jamal said, shaking his head fervently. "That is a felony."

Arche shrugged, a languid smile on her lips. "It was a mere discussion, dearest."

"Speaking of discussion," Augustus said, "your boy Berry is innocent? That's why you were out all day chasing this?"

Reed looked at me, his expression pained. "Seems that way."

"Someone appears to be framing him," I said. "We discovered some – almost certainly – planted evidence. But we also turned up another student accusing him of, uh..."

"Impropriety?" Scott asked.

"Child rape?" Olivia asked, much tauter than usual. When we all looked at her, she shrugged, blushing beneath her blond hair. "What? We fight the most powerful supervillains on the planet and we can't just come out and call the crime what it is? When a teacher sleeps with a fourteen-year-old, it is rape. They cannot consent. Assuming she even wanted to."

I cringed at that one, but mostly because I knew Olivia's history, and it wasn't that different from the victim's in this case. She didn't talk much about it, and I didn't ask, but it was there in her eyes, filled with a kind of fire that I seldom saw in her.

"What was in Berry's head?" Augustus asked.

"Some, uh...blackout drinking, the night of," I said, shying away from looking anyone straight in the eyes on that one. "So...the evidence of his innocence is a bit tenuous. Still, the fact that we uncovered some clumsily planted shit at his apartment weighs in his favor."

"How's that other allegation of child rape figure on the scales?" Olivia sniped.

"I don't know how to take that one," I said, trying to be honest. "Is the girl lying? Is she telling the truth? Is he guilty of that but not the murder?" I shrugged. "I need more information."

"Didn't you...y'know, read the man's mind?" Jamal asked. "Shouldn't you know whether he's diddling kids in his off hours?"

"I focused on the night of the event," I said. "I didn't realize I was going to have to question his entire sexual history." I cringed; when I absorbed those sort of memories, I *felt* them, and I really hadn't wanted to delve into his escapades with Paula...or anyone else, for that matter. The last thing I needed was to be having a conversation with her and then experience a flashback of their sexytimes mid-conversation. "Nor do I particularly want to now, though it appears it might be germane to the investigation."

"Let's table this until tomorrow," Reed said, rubbing his

forehead. "Looks like you all made a good start here. We'll get it all loaded up in the morning, move it out and over to Hudson. Find somewhere to park it for the next day or so. Then we can start focusing on our...y'know...residences. Apartments and whatnot." He pulled his hand back from his eyes. "I don't know about any of you, but I'm tired for some reason. Maybe lack of sleep. Maybe from being so recently 'dead.'" He used finger quotes. "Either way...let's just call it a night, okay?"

"Works for me," Angel said. Her head was now lying sideways on the cubicle wall, her eyes narrowed from sleepiness. "Anyone want to help me move tomorrow?"

"If we make it a team effort, it'll go quicker," Augustus said. "What say we share the U-haul expense?"

"I vote aye on that," Olivia said, raising her hand. "I could use the help."

"Same," Angel said.

"In," Jamal said.

"I'd love to," Reed said, rubbing his face, "but I think it'd be unfair to you if I did." When we all looked at him, he added, "I've got a fiancée who has a doctor's salary and an affinity for heavy furniture. She's not bound to a deadline like us, so she'll probably get movers to pack us."

"I've, uh...got movers, also," Scott said, blushing to his blond roots.

I looked at him. "How pissed was your dad about the cabin?"

Scott blew air out noiselessly between pale lips. "The cabin? I'm not sure he cared. It's the loss of the ability to, y'know, live and work in Minnesota that's up his ass presently. That, he's pissed about."

"At you?" Angel asked.

Scott looked right at me. "Not entirely."

I sighed. Great. Philip Byerly being mad at me was not

the scariest thing that had happened to me in the last twenty-four hours – not even close, really – but it wasn't nothing, either. "I'll worry about him tomorrow. Or the next day." I frowned. "What about Amy?"

"She's already packing and about to catch a plane to Rapid City," Scott said. "My parents have a vacation home in Spearfish, South Dakota, so I think she's going to hunker down there for a little bit while Dad figures out what to do next." He straightened, putting his hands in his pockets up to his bared wrists, his white dress-shirt sleeves rolled up to the elbow.

"And how best to visit his revenge upon me, surely," I mumbled.

"All right, well," Reed said, sighing. "No point in hashing this further. Let's call it a day and meet back here tomorrow morning, say...eight?"

"I won't be in until after nine," I said, checking my phone. Five more missed calls from unknown numbers across the country. When I looked up, everyone was watching me, and I could tell there were questions. "Oh. I locked up some personal possessions in a Minneapolis safe deposit box a few years ago. Y'know, to keep them safe from the inevitable destruction of whichever residence I was in at the time. I need to clean it out before we skip town."

"Ah," Scott said, relaxing slightly.

He didn't say it, but I could sense the eggshells I was walking on. Everyone would be thinking, every time I was late: "Is she drunk? Hung over? Hiding from us?"

"If anyone wants to drive me...?" I asked, trying not to take it personally. "I don't really have a car, or money for a rideshare anyway..."

"Yeah, I can do it," Olivia said. "Need a ride home tonight?"

"Please," I said, smiling tightly. My least favorite option, but she offered, so...there was that. I glanced around. "Unless Lethe is around?"

"She headed back to the hotel a couple hours ago," Scott said, blushing slightly for some reason. "Pleaded tiredness, I guess from flying up here last night?"

"Makes sense." I nodded. "See you all tomorrow."

"I hope we pick Nashville," Augustus said "Then you can get used to saying 'y'all' like a civilized person."

"I'll never be confused for a civilized person," I said as I grabbed my bag from where it lay beneath my cubicle desk. Olivia had hers a moment later, and out we went.

"You could at least try!" Reed called after me. Hard to tell whether he was joking. Either way, everyone fell silent as the door shut behind us. Though I felt sure the moment we were out of earshot, they'd be talking about me again.

CHAPTER EIGHTEEN

The orange was starting to fade in the western sky as Olivia pointed the car east back across 494 on Prairie Center Drive. She held on nervously to her steering wheel, drumming way out of rhythm in the most nervous fashion I could imagine. Frankly, I was surprised she wasn't accidentally triggering her bubble and launching the wheel to the side every couple of seconds. Of course, we'd end up in the ditch, but that might be preferable to this awkwardness. We were metas, after all. We'd survive the crash. Probably.

"You seem like you have something you want to say," I offered, once we were across the freeway and stopped at the traffic light at Valley View.

Olivia tightened slightly, the muscles in the side of her neck visibly bulging. "Ahhh...I don't...uhm..." She sagged, exhaling. "Okay. Yes. I do."

When she didn't say anything for a few seconds, I prodded, "And it is...?"

"I'm sorry," she said, words gushing out, "that I wasn't there for you when you needed the help."

I blinked. "...What?"

She looked at me, right in the eye, her own filled with desperate pleading. "I'm so sorry. I let you go through it alone. I promise I had no idea–"

I blinked. "...Because I hid it from you, Olivia. I hid it from everyone." I looked out the window; the sky before us had darkened to that purple twilight haze that came right after sunset. "How could you know?"

"But I did know," she said, sagging. "I didn't know how much you were struggling, but I knew you were drinking. Hell, we all did. Maybe not to the extent, but we knew–"

"Look, you trusted me to be an adult," I said, "and manage it. I couldn't, which is why I was trying to hide it from everyone. That's on me, not you."

"But I failed you," she said, and boy was she just bleeding the emotion. "Back when we were up against the state, and those mobsters, and the bald guy with the momentum sapping power? I got kidnapped and–"

"You cannot blame yourself for that," I said, shaking my head. "That's like me blaming myself for Rose holding me hostage." Which...I had done, usually with the self-applied 'stupid bint,' and a fair application of self-loathing. But all that hadn't gotten me anything but into the current mess of alcoholism, so it was definitely better if she didn't go that road.

"I just feel like there was more I could have done," Olivia said. Someone honked behind us, and she anxiously gunned the engine, because the light had turned green. "And I feel terrible that you faced it by yourself when–"

"But I chose it, Olivia," I said, focusing hard on her dashboard, which was way better than looking her in the eye. "I pushed you all away because I didn't want any of you to see me for what I was. For what I was doing to myself. That's on me. And I'll dig myself out, and do better, and hopefully never touch the bottle again." Now I looked at her. "It's not your job to save me from my self-destructive tendencies. You can call them out, if you see them, but...this is maybe one of the things that, as a hero...you can't save someone from."

"I wish I'd tried anyway," she whispered.

"I think you would have gotten yelled at," I said softly. "If it had happened before the cabin. I don't think I was ready to listen until after...all that." I rubbed my eyes. They were a little moist. "But I appreciate the concern. It means a lot."

"Just don't leave me out next time," Olivia said. "I don't want you feeling like you're alone in all this. You know? Because that's what I feel like. That I failed you that one time, and you–"

"I picked up a bottle and I drank from it, knowing that I shouldn't," I said firmly. "You didn't take it and shove it in my face and make me drink. I can't control what anyone else does. What you do. What villains do. What the State of Minnesota does. And that...that drives me crazy sometimes, especially when it crosses my life so directly. I had no money, no power, no ability to fight back, really. That was harder than all those years on the run. That was crushing. Depressing. And I handled it badly. Note – *I* did. Not you. Me." I patted her on the arm. "This is on me, okay? And that's good."

She was a little teary, and she blinked it back as she turned onto the side road that led to Ariadne's subdivision. "How is that, in any way, good?"

"Because if I did it, I can stop doing it," I said, with as much firmness as my tired ass could muster. "It's in my hands. I can't control everyone else...but I can control myself." I let out a ragged breath. "And that's going to be the rub, I guess. I have to find a stronger reason not to pick up a glass than I have for wanting to down one. Y'know?"

She nodded, but didn't say anything. "Those BCA cops are behind us again."

I blinked and looked back; sure enough, I could see Tang and O'Rourke a couple cars back. I hadn't noticed them all day, but then, I'd been a little busy. I wondered if they'd followed us into Wisconsin...?

"It'll be okay, Olivia," I said, taking another deep breath and trying to find the assurance in it.

She looked at me through misty eyes, and I got the feeling I was like a parent being asked by their kid for some form of reassurance. Which was a scary thing, because I was an alcoholic who wanted nothing more than to crawl in the damned bottle to get away from my problems, and to not bother waking up tomorrow.

But...she needed this, and I could give it, so I said, "Absolutely. We're going to make it through." I forced a tight smile. "All of us."

And I meant it.

CHAPTER NINETEEN

I went to the front door of Ariadne's house rather than sneaking around back as I had been lately. It felt like the right thing to do, to make a change that could be seen, could be felt. I was done hiding like a thief creeping around in the night.

So I went to unlock the front door...

And my key didn't fit.

"Shit," I whispered, and rang the doorbell, feeling that pit of dread settle in my stomach as I stood there under the porch light. I scanned the street, which was quiet; Olivia was already driving away, and Tang and O'Rourke were parked just out of sight. Not for me, but for their BCA bosses, presumably so they could tell them, clear of conscience, "Nah, she definitely doesn't see us."

A shuffling of footsteps came from behind the door, and the blinds covering the long window beside the door moved slightly. I tried to stand there and look...remorseful, but honestly I probably just looked like I'd been through a wood-chipper.

The deadbolt clicked slowly, then the door lock followed, and Ariadne opened up – a sliver, anyway.

"Hey," I said, trying to put the appropriate amount of humility into my words. There was not ever going to be enough, though, so I did the best I could. "If you want to just...bring up my stuff, I'll wait here on the porch and then...be on my way."

She opened the door a little wider, and looked at the bag on my shoulder. "Do you even have any other stuff here?"

"Uhm...you bought me some nicer clothes, but I can just leave those if you want," I said. "So...probably not, I guess? Other than...bottles or whatever. I don't need those." I shrugged, shifting my weight back and forth between my feet. "Uhm...I do want to say, though, before I go – thank you." I looked up, trying to meet her eyes where they peered out from the crack in the door. "You tried to help me when I needed it and...I really screwed things up for you. I'm genuinely sorry for that. Not all of it was my fault, but enough of it was that I'm sorry for the things I brought down on you. I never wanted any of it to happen, and...I've been shitty. And hiding, maybe from myself almost as much as you. I'm just sorry. I'm so sorr–"

The door popped open then, and Ariadne rushed out onto the porch, her arms finding me, wrapping themselves around my shoulders. She pulled me close to her, and I happily let her because it felt good, it felt right, like absolution from all the shit I'd done was here.

I wept into her shoulder as she pulled me back inside, out of full view of the neighborhood, and I said, "I'm sorry...I'm sorry..."

"Shh," she said, and shut the door on the warm summer evening. "Shhh. It'll be okay."

CHAPTER TWENTY

"Thanks for this," I said to Olivia the next morning as we pulled into the parking lot of a bank just outside downtown Minneapolis. I'd been thinking of the threat once brought to Minneapolis by Aleksandr Gavrikov when I'd chosen it, but also of the more pedestrian worries of a bank robbery.

"No problem," she said, a little more happily than yesterday. She looked me right in the eyes and said, "You seem a lot better today. More...something."

"Sober?"

Her mouth moved a couple times as a contrite expression cropped up on her pale face. "No...no, that's not what I...I just meant your eyes are...clearer. Less hazy. Y'know."

"Are they?" I asked, conjuring – lightly – the memory of Amanda Gustafson, and staring at Olivia.

Her eyes widened. "Did your pupils just turn red?"

I laughed and let the memory of Amanda Gustafson and her eyebeam powers fade. I was not above using powers as a joke, especially when it was called for. "Wait for me here?"

Olivia laughed weakly. "Sure."

There was a little more overcast skies today, gray and hanging a few thousand feet above me as I hurried across the parking lot and into the bank branch. Nobody said anything as I passed a security guard, though I did get a double take. I made my way to the bankers sitting at their desks in the corner of the room, and walked right up to one who was fully occupied in carefully scrutiny of her computer screen, a frown on her broad face as I announced, "Hey, I need to access my safety deposit box."

She did not look up for a moment, continuing to peer at the screen. "Just a sec...Oh my Gaahhhhh–!" She flipped her coffee over into her lap when she finally did look up, a supreme exercise of clumsiness that ended poorly for her. I was laughing inside.

"Sorry about that," I said once I got ahold of myself. She was desperately trying to keep the spilled coffee from running off the side of the table and down onto her crotch. And failing miserably at it.

She forced a smile between gritted teeth. "So sorry, Ms. Nealon. You wanted...what, exactly?"

"I have a safe deposit box here," I said, trying to iron all the amusement out of my voice. "Number 213."

"Okay," she said, and gestured, wildly, for the man at the neighboring desk, who was taking great notice of everything that was happening at hers. "Tom, you mind helping me out here?"

"Seems like you're doing just fine on your own," Tom said, taking a sip of his own coffee rather ostentatiously. His eyes were twinkling, and he winked at me.

I tried not to take that the wrong way. Maybe he was just a fun, middle-aged man enjoying the misery of a co-worker he disliked.

"Ooooookay," the woman said, abandoning any hope of keeping her coffee from draining off her desk. Instead she pushed back so that at least it would stop staining her skirt, and by her sagging shoulders I could tell she'd given up on this situation getting better in the short term. Now she was just gutting her way through it, and the forced customer service smile on her face and that slightly pandering tone she adopted was resigned. "Let me just check the book, Ms. Nealon..."

She did, and found, to what I'm sure was her surprise, that I was in fact the holder of safety deposit box 213. It wasn't much of a surprise to me, though, since I'd taken it out before anyone in this town knew my name.

I was led back through a vault door that I would probably have struggled with breaking down, even if lives were at stake, and through another gate of heavy bars to the safety deposit box vault. She unlocked it for me, then opened the box, removing the container within and placing it on the large table in the middle of the room.

"I'll just leave you to it, then," she said, smiling politely, a little strained but well within the bounds of civilized decency.

"Thanks," I said, and meant it. She retreated quietly, leaving me alone with my most prized possession.

I opened the inner safe deposit box slowly, and found it exactly as I'd left it.

Inside the safe deposit box was a foam cutout, lovingly shaped to fit perfectly within. By me, of course. I'd brought the foam and done the cutting myself when I'd made my deposit. Sandwiched within its depths was a simple, golden watch with roman numerals on the pearlescent face.

I could almost feel myself back in my bedroom at the Directorate on the day I'd walked in and found it waiting for me with a note: *Your father would want you to have this*. I'd worn it for all of a week or so before realizing that given my lifestyle, if I didn't put it somewhere safe, it was going to be destroyed.

Hence, how it came to be here, in this bank. I'd prepaid for years in advance, back in the days when I had money, and here it had remained, through the destruction of the Directorate and several agencies, as well as the annihilation of my house and all my other subsequent misfortunes. Reed had given it to me – left it for me, really – and through that gift, I'd felt a connection with my father that I'd never felt before.

Closing my eyes, I could see him as he'd appeared to me once in a drug-induced fever dream. Tall, strong, brave and loving. Until I'd gotten the watch, and Reed had admitted he was my brother, it had been just Mom and me for all my life.

The watch was like a revelation; a line of sight to a world I'd never been able to fully visualize until I'd held its shiny links in my hand. Sure, I sort of had friends by the time he'd given it to me, but I hadn't had family, really. And I had no idea who my father was.

It was a broadening of my horizons wrapped up in the form of a timepiece. I cradled the cold metal in my hand and sighed. "Tempus fugit," I whispered.

Getting the watch, and feeling that experience of family, of my roots, of connections that I couldn't have imagined before that moment? Of realizing I had a brother...and all the years of frustration and happiness that came out of it?

Yeah. That definitely made the top five.

"I'm finished," I told the banker as I walked out. "And I'm not going to be renewing my box when the term runs out. For obvious reasons."

"Right," she said, lingering outside the vault door, fussing over her ruined skirt. "Well...best of luck." Another tight smile. Boy, I got a lot of those. Or, to be more accurate, I prompted a lot of them.

Off I went, out the swinging glass doors of the bank,

holding my prized possession in my hand. I'd deposit it another place when I got to wherever we ended up, but for now I held it gingerly, the ticking of the second hand audible between my fingers, a reminder that my time here in Minnesota was running short.

CHAPTER TWENTY-ONE

"Mornin'," Scott, shirtless and tanned, greeted me as I came in the office, Olivia trailing a step behind. He was holding a desk upright, waist-high, in one hand, just inside the receptionist area. He waved at the door. "Mind holding that for me?"

I did; I'd seen the U-hauls downstairs in the parking lot. It was definitely moving day, as evidenced by Augustus fussing with Jamal over strapping a desk into the back of one of the moving vans under the summer sun. The day outside was heating up to be a scorcher, and I suspected if I didn't have a case I'd be dragooned into lifting heavy things as well.

"Um, hi," Olivia said, blushing and (sort of) looking away as Scott wrangled the desk past us and toward the stairs. It looked more awkward than heavy, given he was manhandling it with just one hand, and while he was sweating – big droplets were rolling down his forehead and his tanned, muscular back – that looked to be more from the weather than exertion, so I just held the door and let him go, my version of egalitarianism being to let the men do the heavy lifting while I held the door. Olivia's eyes followed his backside as he went, so I nudged her lightly in the ribs to jar her out of her man-ass-induced torpor. "What! Sorry," she said, falling in behind me with one last furtive look.

"It's okay," I said, trying to conceal a smile, but failing. "You can look. You can maybe even touch, if you ask first."

"No!" She reddened to tomato-coloring immediately, and her hands surged up in front of her mouth. "I didn't – I – I –"

I patted her on the arm. "It's okay. Really."

She hung her head, as if there was something to be ashamed of in looking at a very fit man's body. She didn't say anything, though, just sort of moaned.

I had enough hang-ups of my own without wading into Olivia's, though, so instead of engaging her on this I headed down the hall into the bullpen, which was already looking pretty empty. The boys had been hard at work this morning, clearly, and the results were paying off. Angel was in the midst of deadlifting a stack of cubicle walls that had been roped together into a tight bundle, and I averted my eyes because her jeans were surprisingly low rise and her shirt was not.

"Can someone get the door for me?" Angel asked, carrying the bulky wall segments with both hands – again, not because they were heavy for her, but because they were awkward as hell.

"I got it!" Olivia rushed away from me, probably pleased to have an out. As she fled, I noticed Arche in the corner, hand hovering over her laptop, subtle lightning dancing between her fingers like one of those plasma globes had been unleashed from the keyboard.

"WiFi still working?" I asked, thinking maybe I should check my email. Sure, it was rare anyone sent anything to me other than stupid forwards from Mimaw, but it wasn't inconceivable that I could get an email about a case.

"No," Arche said, lightning dancing in her eyes as well in a strangely hypnotic effect. She was clearly jacked into the internet, and she said nothing else about the matter. I guess they'd packed the routers already.

Reed popped his head out of his office at my approach, and I noticed for the first time that his chair was now gone. A quick glance around the bullpen told me that someone had taken it already, which was interesting because I would have packed the chairs last. But that's just me, I guess. "How'd it go?"

I came up with the watch from my pocket. "Got it."

There was a flicker of recognition, and he smiled, ever-so-slightly. "I didn't even know you still had it."

"I mean, if you call locking it in a vault 'still having it,' I do," I said. "I don't have that many nice things, y'know? Things I treasure. So I do try and take care of the few...well, the one...that I have."

His smile was wistful, and he looked down. My brother's hair was bound tightly in a ponytail, and beyond him, in the office, I could see a tablet sitting on the floor. He caught me looking and beckoned me forward. "Come take a look at this."

"Sure." I brushed in after him, and he stooped to pick up the tablet, which was the only thing left in his office other than dust bunnies, which were firmly planted in every corner and on the spot where the couch had been. "What's up?"

"I was reading some Aaron Berry articles," he said, flaring the screen to life and tapping in his passcode so rapidly my eyes could barely keep up. "Trying to get a sense of what threads we should tug on, where we should go next."

"Any ideas?" I asked, leaning in and trying to see what he had on the screen.

He frowned. "A few. I know we talked about trying to get in with the victim's parents. Not sure that's among the great ideas."

"Why's that?"

He pushed the screen toward me. "Seems like they're pretty anti-meta."

I skimmed the article he presented, which was a local news piece on Greta's death. When I got to the appropriate part, I said, "Oof."

...Greta's father, Preston Oliver, told us, "This never should have happened. If our legislature wasn't so damned useless, they'd have passed the law against metahumans, and our daughter would still be alive. I can't understand why people don't see how dangerous they are. Greta died because of their failure to act. Her blood is on their hands."

"Yeah," Reed said, tucking the tablet under his arm. "Not sure we'll get a very warm reception there."

I groaned, then leaned against a bare wall. "Maybe we call them? If we're not in their physical presence, it might be less threatening...? Or we could try and play it off like we're investigating Berry...what?"

Reed was shaking his head, and he brought the tablet to life again, then flipped the screen for me.

Sienna Nealon takes role as lead investigator to prove Aaron Berry's innocence.

It was the front page of the Minneapolis Star-Tribune. There was a subhead, too:

Stillwater police announce discovery of second Berry abuse victim, additional evidence.

"Shit," I muttered. "Guess our chances of getting in with them just went from slim to none."

"Maybe," Reed said. "We probably should have visited them yesterday instead of knocking off early and collapsing." He rubbed his eyes, and I could tell he had not caught up on the missed sleep of the last day any more than I had. He suppressed a yawn – barely. "Speaking of...how'd you do last night?"

"I got back to Ariadne's to find she'd changed the locks," I said. "Which was wise, I think."

His brow furrowed. "You got kicked out? Why didn't you call me? You could have crashed with us."

"You didn't let me finish. I apologized, told her how wrong and messed up I was, and she let me in." I shrugged. "We talked it out. She was just worried she was enabling me. Anyway, I'm only staying there one more night, no point in me disrupting your move."

Reed nodded slowly. "I'm not even thinking about that right now."

"I am literally carrying everything I own with me," I said. "Well...not that literally, I guess, since I left my other clothing bag in Olivia's car, but...nearly literally. I didn't leave anything at Ariadne's in case Minnesota gets aggressive or I need to bail early."

Reed sighed. "You still being followed by BCA?"

"Yeah, I talked to Tang and O'Rourke this morning." I folded my arms in front of me. "They were apologetic and all, but I think they're secretly pleased we're leaving. Because of the 24/7 surveillance thing, you know. It's wearing."

"Can't say I blame them, given they're presently living in a squad car umpteen hours a day." Reed loosed a hefty sigh. "You ever think maybe we should just...quit while we're ahead?"

"What do you mean?" I asked. "Like shut this down and do other things? Or work for the government again? Because I am not doing that."

He looked around for a moment, as if seeking a chair to plop his tired bones into. "Shutting this agency down and calling it quits on this line of work. I mean, we could do a lot of other things. We're not incapable people. We're not stupid."

"Sometimes I do wonder," I said, "given the amount of shit I get into. But who's going to save the world if we quit?"

He sighed again. "There you go again, bringing that legendary reason to bear. You're right. World-ending threats would be a real impediment to us living normal lives, free of this crippling scrutiny. Still and all..." He shook his head as a commotion rose in the entry hall. "...there are times I wish we could go somewhere everyone would just leave us alone."

"You mean like a several-hundred-acre upstate mansion property?" I deadpanned.

A slow smile cracked his grim facade. "I guess we can't really get away very well, can we?"

"All I'm saying is that next time – the Caribbean, maybe?" I turned my attention to the bullpen, where someone was striding out into the (nearly empty) room. She wore a pantsuit and there was a gun prominent at her hip, right next to a badge. She had her hair back in a dark ponytail, and piercing eyes that searched me out across the room before she adjusted her long-legged stride to carry her right on over to me.

"Sienna Nealon?" She poked a long finger at the badge on her belt. "Detective Greene, Stillwater PD." There was a grim seriousness in her eyes, and I could tell she was not messing around. "We need to talk."

CHAPTER TWENTY-TWO

"Come on in, Detective," Reed said, beckoning her into his empty office. Once she was inside, I shut the door behind her. There was a clear aura of tension about her, and I had a question that I was yet unprepared to raise, but which was answered a second later when I saw a man with a badge out in the reception area, eyeing what remained of our crew. Her partner, I presumed. "What can we do for you?"

"I think you know why I'm here," Detective Greene said, taking a look around. "Oh, and I love what you've done with the place."

"Really?" I asked. "I call this decorating scheme 'Minnesota-Not-So-Nice.'"

"Well, I'd give more of a shit about your struggles," Greene said, digging in, "but it seems you went and stuck your nose in my investigation. And I don't take kindly to that."

"We generated a load of fresh leads for you yesterday," Reed said. "A new victim, a new piece of evidence–"

"The chain of custody of which is terminally borked," Greene said, looking straitlaced, reserved sort of daggers at him. She was a cool customer, I'd give her that. "As to the new victim...she wasn't yours to turn up. You got to her under false premises."

"I'm investigating on behalf of Aaron Berry," I said.

"You're not a private investigator," Greene fired back.

"She's operating on my license," Reed said, drawing himself up. "Which is legal. And do you really want – going into this extremely public trial – to give his defense attorneys the ability to say that they weren't able to conduct a full investigation of the facts and evidence because the police blocked them?"

Greene didn't give an inch, but she did slide her eyes off him and onto me. "Your time is running kind of short, don't you think? You've got...what? Two days?"

"More than enough," I said. Little bit of a boast, but I didn't feel it was totally unwarranted.

"Hm." Greene pushed her tongue against her lip, pouching out a little space in her lower cheek. "You don't lack for confidence, that's for sure."

"Why's your partner out there instead of in here?" I asked, finally getting to the question I'd been thinking about since she'd charged in here.

"He's new," she said, putting her hands on her waist, elbows bowed out. She walked up to the window and looked out, nodding across the near-empty bullpen at him. Then she whirled around on us. "So...about this bullshit underwear you found."

"I did find it a bit suspicious," I said.

"Unless the New Richmond PD is utterly incompetent," Reed added, "yeah...fake."

"Helpful news flash: they're not incompetent," Greene said, pacing in front of the window. "I was at the scene when they tossed the place. Because they're cool like that. There was nothing under that mattress when we examined it the first time. So..." She looked right at me, then at Reed. "Did you plant it?"

"We just got the job yesterday," I said. "Where do you think we're going to pick up teen undies and your suspect's semen in the course of a few hours?"

"Oh, I don't know," she said. "I heard you visited him in prison. Maybe it was conjugal."

That stripped all the smirk off my face. "No."

Greene's thin lips broke into a grin. "I know. I already watched your whole interaction with him. Interesting conversation." She paced before the window again. "So...you actually know whether he was guilty or not." She looked right at me. "I could make a case that was you tampering with evidence."

"For examining his memories?" I scoffed. "Good luck making that stick. I only took them because he begged me to, so I could prove his innocence."

"If I may," Reed said, looking at Detective Greene with an aura of suspicion that I thought was well-founded, "you don't seem very confrontational in this...confrontation."

"Because I am not your enemy here," Greene said, that smile disappearing. "You've been on this case twenty-four hours and you're already starting to see that things stink. Try being on it for weeks and watch shit like this pile up. I'm not new to this game, okay? I've got fifteen years in between the beat and this. Never in all of them have I seen this kind of a tsunami of evidence wash up to bury a man." She stopped, putting her hands back on her hips. "If there was a drop of counter-evidence, I'd be screaming that this man is innocent, but he's got nothing. No alibi, all the physical evidence is against him, and we've got a powerful motive for murder." She looked sideways at the bare wall. "Still...there is this nagging feeling something ain't right."

"You try bringing those concerns to your chief?" I asked.

"For a fellow with big ears, he doesn't use them any better

than any other man," she said, glancing at her partner. Maybe he wasn't such a great listener, either? She glanced at Reed. "No offense."

"What?" Reed asked. "Sorry, I didn't catch that."

Greene smiled. "My superiors, driven with the help of the national press...well, they've come to a conclusion. And on the basis of the evidence, it absolutely fits. No one's even questioning whether Aaron Berry is innocent. Too many nails in the coffin. And yet..." She held up a fist. "It's just...too damned perfect."

"You think he's innocent?" I asked.

"I think if he's guilty, he's the dumbest *and* most unlucky sonofabitch there's ever been on the planet," she said. "You've talked to him. Does he strike you as dumb?"

"No," I said. "And I'll do you one better: I've been in his head, and he's definitely not stupid. His alibi? Seems to be true."

"That he was drunk and passed out during the murder?" Greene sighed. "Perfect time to frame a man, though, if you know he's out for the night." She made a noise of frustration. "Look, I'm not working with you on this, and the official position of the Stillwater police is that we've got our suspect." She looked up at me. "But I'm telling you this, investigator to investigator: I think your client is innocent. You try and pin me on that in the press, I'll deny I said it. But there it is. And if you manage to dig something up that proves that, it'll do my conscience a lot of good."

"And if I don't?" I asked, as she started to turn for the door.

"Well, then your super special ass took a crack at it and couldn't disprove the going thesis," she said, hand on the doorknob. "I'll take that as proof, too, that maybe I was wrong, in my gut, and he really was guilty. Either way...hopefully I'll sleep all right at night, knowing I didn't help send an innocent man to jail." She shrugged. "But as a detective, I do have to tell you," and here she opened the door, and raised her voice for dramatic effect, a message to all who witnessed it, "stay the hell off my case and out of my way – or I'll arrest you for obstruction and hold you until Monday. Then you'll be someone else's problem."

Message received. She turned, walked off, just a little more spring in her step than she'd had when she came in.

I waited until I heard the slamming door to turn to Reed. "You believe that?" he asked, beating me to the punch.

"That the lead detective in the case thinks our client is innocent?" I looked into the dark hallway to the receptionist area. "And that she drove all the way over to tell us so? Doesn't really change anything." I folded my own arms over my chest with newfound determination. "But it does mean we're going to have to work fast – and maybe twice as hard – to see this thing done by tomorrow night."

CHAPTER TWENTY-THREE

"So," Reed said, after Detective Greene was definitely gone, "where does this leave us in terms of places to prod?"

I stood there in his musty, dust-ridden office, watching the motes stream across the beams of sunlight creeping across the bullpen. I had to ponder the answer for a few moments. "Well...let's assume he's innocent."

"Easier to assume given we've just been told by the chief detective that the evidence is a little too convenient."

"Right," I said. "But that leaves us with an interesting conclusion: someone had to plant this convenient, excellent-looking evidence."

"Who could it be, though?" Reed asked with a slightly exasperated air. "There are hundreds of students at Stoaks we haven't met, and four we have. We've got the cool burnout lurking outside the office, the way-too-nice-and-helpful headmaster..."

"Paula," I said, and Reed sort of goggled at me. "I'm not saying she's a serious contender, but we should consider all possibilities. Like the trio of besties that threw us another victim yesterday."

Reed's face scrunched up into the most appalled look. "You're going to blame the pre-teens who leveled a rape charge? Are you kidding?"

I shrugged. "Not saying they did it. Just pointing out that everyone's a suspect until we prove otherwise."

He sighed. "I guess. I'm not sure how we're going to narrow things down in the next two days given we're...well, at a dead end."

I gave that a little thought. Something was brewing in my mind, a possibility. "Remember that older lady with the dog outside Berry's apartment?"

"The one with Cali?"

"You remembered her by her dog," I said, "you are such a little bitch for puppies. Yes, the lady with Cali."

"What about her?"

"She seemed a little...off," I said, "and it occurs to me: if someone planted evidence in Berry's apartment, there's every possibility there's a witness around there somewhere. The sort of small-town person who is irritable but suspicious and always watching to see what her neighbors are up to."

"Maybe," Reed said with a deep frown, "but I think the New Richmond police department will be deeply unhappy if we start canvassing the place, given what happened yesterday. And Detective Greene will flip a – well, something."

"It's okay to say 'flip a tit' about a woman, Reed. We have them. We know you notice."

My brother sighed even more deeply. "My point is...our job is possibly a little harder now."

I tried to hide the mischievous grin that was threatening to bubble up on my face. "What if we could do this...without going all the way to New Richmond? And thus keeping ourselves in the good graces of local law enforcement?"

"I think 'good graces' might be pushing it." His lips thinned, pushed together as he watched me through slitted eyes. "What do you have in mind?" Pure suspicion.

I looked through the open blinds to the bullpen, and found ArcheGrey still sitting in the corner, messing about on her laptop. "Well...I did have this one idea about how to get that bitch to talk..."

CHAPTER TWENTY-FOUR

ArcheGrey1819, the world's foremost hacker, looked at me through dark eyes, a little twinkle in them. "You don't do these things in half measures, do you?" She was seated on the floor, legs crossed and her laptop upon them, small trickles of lightning dancing from her fingertips between the keys, flashing against the dull beige paint.

Reed let out a pained grunt; we were all three sitting in his office, the muted sounds of our fellows moving the furniture out of the place through the closed door. "I don't like this. At all."

"Your formal objection is duly noted," I said, holding up a hand to shush him. "In fact, if you want to step outside and supervise the move, it'd give you and your conscience some plausible deniability."

Another pained grunt escaped him. "You really do find all the cracks in the law and work them the hell open, don't you?"

"I'm like rushing water in that regard," I said, keeping my attention on Arche. "What do you think?"

Arche shrugged languidly beneath the brown trench coat she habitually wore. "It's doable. When did you run into her?"

Reed was looking out through his fingers, as though trying to avoid seeing a particularly terrible accident about to unfold. "Late afternoon. In the parking lot of Aaron Berry's apartment."

Arche looked up for a moment – and I mean that, she looked up, eyes flashing white as her pupils rolled up into her head, sparks radiating from her eyeballs and crackling across her cheekbones. She spun the laptop around so we could see the screen, and on it a satellite overhead image popped up of a parking lot.

Reed stooped slightly to get a closer look. "Yeah. There."

A couple dots slipped into view a moment later, in synchronized motion, corresponding with where we'd parked in the lot. Then they glided smoothly across the lot and onto the building. After moving around minimally within the apartment for a few revolutions, joined by another, then many more – presumably representing when we searched the apartment and talked to the cops – they started to retrace the path to the steps and into the parking lot–

"There," I said, pointing at another dot that streaked across the parking lot to our position. It stood off just a little ways, and suddenly the action paused. "That's when she came up to us with Cali."

"Creepy that you can reconstruct our movements this precisely," Reed said. "Which begs the question...how are you doing this?"

"The dots are the ping of cell phones in the area," Arche said as she continued to trance, her eyes still rolled eerily back in her head. "Working off of the local towers."

"Nice," Reed said. "Any chance you can get one of those for the night of the murder?"

"The police would already have done so," Arche said, "but give me a minute. Let's finish this first." She cocked her head slightly. "If the cell phone record is accurate, her name is Mona Daniels."

A picture appeared, and sure enough, we had Cali's owner ID'd positively. "That's her," I said.

"Damn. Also, wow, and scary," Reed said, still frowning. "This is surveillance state shit."

"Don't like it? Turn off your cell phone," Arche said. "Mona Daniels is 54 years old. Works at Farm and Home in New Richmond. Assistant manager. Most frequent online purchases: dog food and toys. Also: puzzles."

"Really digging on the old lady stereotype there," I said. "Where is she now?"

Reed let out a low moan, presumably at my surveillance state-iness.

Arche just smiled smugly. "In her apartment. She lives a couple doors down from Berry." She stiffened. "Ooh. Look at this."

A video clip started playing on the laptop, of Mona Daniels talking to a local reporter. "I never liked him," she said, in that simple, mean way of hers. "He always gave me a feeling that he was up to no good."

"What a stinging character slight against Berry," Reed said dryly. "The cranky old lady of the complex doesn't like him."

I tapped a finger against my lips. "So...about getting whatever she knows out of her..."

Reed stared at me. "You don't know that she was holding something back yesterday."

"Oh, but I do," I said, "and I intend to have it. In a way that won't cause us any other problems."

Reed sighed in exasperation. "Scaring the shit out of her can only cause us further problems." He must have seen something in my grin, because he broke a few seconds later and asked, "Okay, fine. How are you going to do this, then?"

I looked at Arche. I didn't even have to say anything; she knew better than I did what she could do. All she did was smile, and I knew we were golden.

CHAPTER TWENTY-FIVE

Mona

It was not Mona's best day ever; Saturdays seldom were. She worked retail, and weekends weren't weekends to her. Twenty years working at the same store and she still hadn't fully climbed out of weekend shifts. What a shitty job. There were days she just wanted to throw it all away, maybe find somewhere else to work. But then she'd lose her seniority, probably, and instead of working two weekends a month she'd probably be back to four. And there weren't a ton of good jobs unless she wanted to drive over that Minnesota state line – and she didn't.

Cali barked.

"Shut up, stupid dog," Mona said. All she needed was that dumb dog to go barking like crazy at someone out in the hall. She always was. And these idiots in this complex indulged her, which made Mona's life harder.

Well...at least there was one less of those morons now. Mona chuckled at that. Good riddance to bad rubbish.

Her TV program was blaring at her, a stupid commercial on for some denture cream. Useless to her, she didn't have dentures. She thought about hitting the mute button, but just about the time she reached across the couch and got the remote, the commercial would be over and she'd have to turn it up again to hear. Still, Mona grunted. She'd scooted out of the hot seat on the couch to a cooler cushion – she'd been sitting ever since she got home from work – and now her butt was getting warm here, too.

She didn't want to move, though.

"Why don't you do something useful and fetch the remote, you stupid dog," she said, glaring down at Cali, who was barking again. Silly little thing. Of the dogs Mona had owned, this one was the most damned useless. Every once in a while she did consider pulling the tags off her collar and just making that drive to Minnesota. Drop her in the middle of the road in Stillwater at midnight, she'd never find her way home and then she'd be someone else's problem.

"Why don't you get off your lazy ass and do it yourself?" the TV asked.

Mona froze, leaning halfway across the faux leather couch. Her eyebrows knitted close together. Had she just heard...?

No. The program was coming back on now, and Mona shook her head. It was just a...something. Delusion, maybe? She'd definitely heard something. But it wasn't someone talking at her. No. That was crazy talk.

The phone rang, just on the other side of the damned remote, and Mona grunted. She couldn't see the caller ID from here, so she shuffled her ass over a cushion at great effort expense to her, then over one more, snagging the remote and then the phone from the table.

Lifting it up so she could see, she read the caller ID, then squinted at it in disbelief.

MOTHER

"My mother's dead," Mona said to herself, then answered the phone. "Who the hell is this?" She was not putting up with this nonsense. Probably a prank from one of her stupid co-workers. Jane, maybe.

"Your mother," said a sassy voice on the other end of the line.

"Well, my mother's been dead twenty years, so I guess I'm talking to someone beyond the grave," Mona shot back, practically crowing. She'd figured out their game.

"Or maybe you're dead, too, Mona. Did you consider that?"

Mona made a loud, hissing scoff. "Yeah, I'm sitting here dead in my living room, watching my programs from beyond the grave. Sure thing."

"Didn't you know that in hell, *The Real Housewives of New Jersey* is popular entertainment?" the voice came back. It didn't sound...right. There was a hiss in the line, something that made it seem...well, wrong, somehow.

"All right, I'm hanging up now," Mona announced. She'd had about enough of this stupid game.

"You can hang up, Mona," the voice came back, "but you can't get away."

"Sure," Mona said, and hung up. She tossed the phone down next to her, already rolling her eyes. Stupid Jane. She was a little shit who went to the local high school and always butted heads with Mona. Just hard working enough to keep from getting fired (barely) but defiant enough to always be a thorn in the side.

The hum of something in the next room made her cock

her head. Was the microwave running? Mona leapt up. She hustled into the kitchen, rounding the corner to find–

It was the microwave, going empty somehow. She hadn't touched it; somehow she must have left it running.

"Dammit," Mona said, hitting the cancel button. It stopped, and she slapped the top of the thing for good measure. It was an older model, but still, she'd never had it do anything like that.

She was halfway back to the couch when something else went off in the kitchen. She stepped back in, and–

The dishwasher was making a thumping noise, like a cat was trapped inside and trying to get out.

Tentative steps, that was what she took over to the white-finished door, and bent down to get a look. None of the lights were burning to indicate it was running. She reached out, popped it open, and–

Hot water sprayed out at her like it was coming out of hell itself. Mona screamed and leapt back, feeling the damned burn because it had got her right in the eyes. She shrieked, fumbling for the towel she habitually left on the counter. Finding it, she mopped away the water and some of her makeup, too.

"What in the hell is going on around here?" Mona asked, kicking the dishwasher closed. It was still spraying wildly, and only once the white door was shut did it stop, though hot water continued to leak out the sides onto her linoleum floor.

"Hell...is going on," came an ominous voice from behind her.

Mona froze, cold finger tickling the back of her neck. She eased away from the dishwasher, following the sound of the eerie voice into the living room, sliding her head around the corner and peering in, wondering what could possibly have spoken.

"Monaaaaa..." the voice came again, just as frightening as

it had been before, and terrible in its way. Mona stared as Cali barked, loudly, behind her.

"Shut up, you," she whispered, but the edge of terror was creeping into her tone, evident even to her.

There came a loud hum from the fridge, and Mona looked back. Putting her hand against the metal, she jerked it open. The lights flashed within, and from the living room again came a voice, "Monaaaaa..."

"What do you want?" she cried. She was tempted to run out the front door, but she'd have to pass through the living room for that, and part of her didn't want to run. She wanted to find this thing, this voice, and give it a piece of her mind.

"Justice," the voice whispered, and she realized at last, it was piping in through her television.

She relaxed a little. Clearly someone was just playing around with her, interrupting the satellite signal or something. "What the hell," she murmured.

"I'm a ghost, Mona," the voice came again. "Coming to you the only way you can hear me – through your TV." An unnatural screech was added to the voice and Mona bristled. Cali was barking like mad.

"No, you're not," she said, her mouth suddenly dry. "You're just a – you're messing with me somehow."

The lamp to Mona's left exploded in a shower of sparks, and Mona loosed a scream she didn't know she was holding. "What do you want?" she cried, and the first tear of fright escaped her cheek.

Something exploded in the kitchen and Mona didn't dare go back in to look, she just shrieked again: "What do you want from me?" She eyed the front door, but the lights had gone dark around it, and she could just imagine running outside only to get picked off by something. Sunlight was barely leaking through the curtains, and it didn't inspire her with feelings of safety, just knowing the sun was out.

"I want justice," the voice came again, and now it sounded like a little girl. "You saw something, Mona. Something that might bring me justice."

"No – no – I only - I didn't see nothing!" Mona shouted. Maybe a little too quickly, she realized after she'd said it.

"You *know*," the voice came again. The lights flickered again, then went out, leaving her in darkness but for the wash of light coming off the TV and the sudden buzzing of her cell phone. The face plate was lit again, the caller ID pronouncing that MOTHER was calling again.

"I – I only saw – I just –" Mona stuttered to get the words out. "It was nothing!"

Everything settled into silence for a second. Then two. Then three.

Finally, that voice came back, more horrible than ever: "You...saw...*something*."

"Fine!" Mona shouted, wilting, "I saw Aaron Berry's stupid cow of a girlfriend creeping around his apartment smiling like she'd gotten one over on him, okay? After he went to jail. And I knew what it meant, and – no, I didn't say nothing, because there wasn't anything to say or anyone to say it to. All right? That's all!" She shouted it, and she meant it.

The lights flickered once more, and came back on. "You should have helped me, Mona," the voice said, crackling into static, and returning to the program she'd been watching before. "You shouldn't hide...the truth."

When the sound came back on for her TV show, Mona jumped again, one last time. Her heart was racing madly, and she wondered if she'd ever be able to breathe over that thundering in her ears ever again.

CHAPTER TWENTY-SIX

Sienna

"Well, that was interesting," Reed said. Arche's feed was still going on the laptop, even though she'd just shut down the ghost psy-op we'd been running on Mona. A little electrical control over her appliances, the local cell phone tower, plus me whispering to Cali in the background noise had produced just about all the chaos Mona's febrile mind could handle.

Et voila – a ghost of justice, speaking to her from her TV.

"I'm just amazed it worked," I said. "I gotta admit, I only gave it 50/50."

"It's the talking back that does it," Arche said coolly. "If you just talked at her, she'd reason her way to it being a scam. But the minute you show that you're listening to them? Most people can't wrap their brain around it. They don't realize how easy it is to hack a cell phone and make it into a microphone."

"Well, now we know that Paula lied to us," I said, standing up straight and crossing my arms in front of my chest. "Which is an interesting and suspicious factoid."

"Not necessarily a factoid," Reed said. "We're going on Mona's word. The woman's not super stable in my estimation."

"Nor in mine," I said, "but as a data point, you gotta admit it's compelling."

"If true, yes," Reed said. "And it gives us a suspect to look into."

"Speaking of," I said, and looked at Arche. "Can you dig into this Paula? Background, all that?"

Arche's eyes narrowed slightly, and she waited a moment before answering. "Yes, but only because it is something Jamal could do, if you were to pull him from his current task." She waved a hand toward the hallway out of the bullpen, where the sound of grunting was still making its way through Reed's close door. "If this was something else, you could count me out unless there was pay. Understand?"

"You're willing to help very little," I said. "Got it."

"Good," she said, turning her attention back to the computer, the lightning sparking in her eyes. "Your family already owes me enough of a debt."

I frowned. "Hades hasn't paid up yet?"

She kept her eyes sparking. "No. I will collect, though, probably when it's least convenient for him."

"He's sitting around the golf course drinking Mai Tais and schtupping old ladies," I said, "I'm not sure when it wouldn't be convenient for him."

Reed made a face. "Didn't need to know that. Also, sidebar: this? Is why you don't trade in favors."

I shrugged. "So, anyway, Paula. Pretty weak tea, but she might be our planter and framer. How do we prove it?"

"'Pretty weak tea' doesn't begin to cover it. Seems strange

she'd recruit us to help Aaron if she was framing him, doesn't it?" Reed asked, frowning. "He was toast, bound to be convicted before we got involved. Why not just make excuses and run out the clock until we were driven out of town? It's not like it was going to be a particularly long wait."

That was a reasonable point. "Good question," I said. "If I had the answer, I'd have this thing solved. Still, a credible witness putting the girlfriend at a place she told us she hasn't been..."

"Yeah, yeah," Reed said, then, to Arche, "are there security cameras around Berry's apartment?"

"Broken," Arche said without even stopping the eye and fingertip sparking. "First thing I checked."

"Because that would have made checking awfully simple." I sighed. "Well...I guess we could question her."

"Electronically?" Arche gave a sliver of a smile.

Reed's handsome face turned disgusted. "You enjoyed that, didn't you?"

Arche shrugged. "This Mona abuses her dog. She strikes me as a piece of shit, and worthy of some fear in her life." She clapped her hands together, rubbing the palms tightly, a malicious smile lighting her features. "I think I will visit her again later, make sure she doesn't hurt that little dog any further."

"That's using your powers for good," I said. "But I think given the situation, we should probably talk to Paula face to face."

Reed sighed. "So we're going to western Wisconsin again? Long drive."

"You could stay here and move boxes and furniture," I said brightly. "I'm sure one of the others would love a respite, maybe drive me around a little."

A pained flicker in Reed's eyes told me his real motives: he wasn't letting me out of his sight any more than he had to over the next days and maybe weeks and months, until he could be assured my sobriety was rock solid. I chafed a little at that, but I couldn't blame him, and it was a conflict for another time. "No. I'll come with you."

"Let's roll, then," I said, wishing I had a coat or something to grab, but instead I tossed my ever-present bag o' crap to Arche on my way out. "Make sure this gets to my destination?" I asked. "Kinda afraid if I take it with me, it'll get destroyed."

Arche's face got all screwy for a second, then relaxed. "Right. Destruction is bound to follow you."

"Nailed it," I said, clicking a finger gun at her. Sunbeams caught a dust motes floating thickly in their shine. Moving had really turned up the amount of particulate matter in the air given how much we'd disturbed the natural order in this place.

"We needed a cleaning service, I guess," Reed said as we strolled through into the reception area.

"Maybe in our business's next life," I said. "You know, when we're not laboring under the weight of all that crushing debt."

Reed's look slipped back into pained territory. "I never meant for it to get this far out of hand. It's just...Greg Vansen is expensive. Veronika's not cheap. They do great work–"

"You don't have to justify saving me to me," I said softly as we pushed through into the outside hallway. Someone had propped the door with a desk, partially blocking hallway access to the mortgage company down the way. Oh, well. That was their problem, not mine, and if those guys needed to suck in their guts to squeeze through, well, there were worse things that they could experience. Like my foot up their asses. Bunch of tools, always not-so-subtly checking out my ass as they went past in the hallway.

I might miss them a little.

We found the rest of the crew down in the parking lot,

playing Tetris with the rented trucks. "No, the desk needs to go in first," Scott was explaining, shirt off, dripping sweat down his muscled chest.

"How many times have you actually moved furniture in your life?" Augustus was saying, perched in the back of the truck, holding a desk upward at a forty-five-degree angle. The far end just hovered in the air, and if it fell right now, someone would lose a toe. Probably Jamal. That he was standing there in what I would call the mash zone was clearly an indication of his faith in his brother's strength. "Not directed other people. Loaded a truck and done it yourself." He, too, had his shirt off, and sweat glistened on his ebony skin as he balanced the desk perfectly.

Angel and Olivia stood back a few feet, pretending to listen to the argument, arms crossed, almost shoulder-to-shoulder, heads inclined close. As Reed and I approached, I caught snatches of their conversation, meta-low, so low that there was zero chance Augustus or Scott could hear it over their argument.

"...You think so?" Olivia was saying. "I don't know. I have no complaints about either."

"Oh, neither do I," Angel said, in the same incredibly quiet tone, "I just think Augustus has more of that raw masculinity going on, you know? Like, he's lived a little more? And it shows."

"But Scott's rich," Olivia said, like she was really weighing it. "Not that it affects the way they look with their shirts off."

"Mmm, if I'm being brutally honest, I think it does, actually," Angel said, tilting her head slightly. "Maybe just a little, anyway, since I haven't been able to afford a beef short rib in months and fifty percent or more of my diet is composed of Maruchan Ramen at this point."

Reed cleared his throat, loudly, and both Olivia and Angel nearly jumped out of their skin. They both sprang into action in wildly different directions, Angel toward a pile of filing cabinets that had been taped and roped closed, Olivia almost sprinting for a pack of office chairs that was slowly drifting apart due to the curves of the parking lot surface.

"You're just jealous they weren't talking about your manly chest," I said, meta-low, once we were away from them.

"No," Reed said gruffly. Then, a few steps later. "Maybe a little."

I chuckled, then paused. I heard something that made the hairs on the back of my neck tingle. Cocking my head slightly, I turned. There were footsteps coming from the far edge of the parking lot.

"Don't move!" someone shouted, and I turned in time to see a gun barrel pointed at me.

Then another.

And another.

Shit.

CHAPTER TWENTY-SEVEN

The sun was beating down as I watched people with guns crossing the parking lot at a run toward me, weapons up, ready to pump rounds down range–

Into me.

And Reed.

Normally this would have been cause for a fight. Powers out, murder afoot, a thrilling battle and dangerous defense in which we would smack down our attackers, crushing both their will to battle and also their big brass ones for daring to come up against me, Goddess of Death.

Unfortunately...this was not a case where that was going to be possible. Because even Lady Death had her limits.

"What the helllllllll," I moaned, hands in the air, as BCA agents came swarming in around me like mosquitoes on a Minnesota summer night.

Tang and O'Rourke were leading the charge. Tang with his mussed dark hair and red eyes, probably from sleeping in the car, and Britta O'Rourke with her pantsuits, blunt face, and jaded eyes. They were leading with their dart guns, too, and I was only encouraged by the fact that I'd already filled the space under my shirt with ice armor in the critical seconds since they'd begun their charge. And also, that my partner in (apparent) crime today was an Aeolus who could probably blow their darts away before they stuck in us.

"Yo, what's going on over there?" Augustus called from the back of the truck.

"Stay out of this," I called back, mostly because the half-dozen BCA agents that had moved in on us hadn't so much as pointed a gun at my colleagues yet. Clearly, they were here for me, and I needed to keep it that way. I'd put my friends in enough danger for this week. "Tang...O'Rourke...what the eff?"

I didn't recognize the other suit and body armor wearing agents, but Tang and O'Rourke being front and center reassured me slightly that this wasn't going to go straight to hell in a Honda without good reason. Reed, too, had his hands up and a sour look on his face, like he'd supplemented his morning coffee with pure lemon juice.

"Let's let cooler heads prevail, huh, guys?" O'Rourke said. "She's not resisting." She waved her free hand, the one not pointing a dart gun at me, in a bid to get them to lower their weapons. "We heard about your antics over in Stillwater at that school yesterday."

"...And?" I rolled my eyes. "You were following me at the time. Why did you need to 'hear' about it?"

Tang and O'Rourke exchanged a look, neither lowering their own guns. "Okay, we knew you were up to something," Tang said, "but we didn't know you were interfering in an active investigation."

"That's a problem, Nealon," O'Rourke added. "You can't do that."

"I'm still a licensed private investigator in Minnesota," Reed said. "We were engaged by a client to look into the prosecution of Aaron Berry. Where's the wrong in this?"

Tang and O'Rourke exchanged another pained look. "Take a walk, guys," O'Rourke said to the agents backing her up as she holstered her gun. Tang followed suit, then so did the other BCA clowns. "Tang and I have this."

The BCA agents did break off, though it took about thirty seconds or more for them all to file away, and there were a lot of diamond-hard looks at me during that time, as though defying me to start some shit. I wasn't sure exactly what I'd done to piss off the ranks of the BCA, but apparently I'd done so somehow.

O'Rourke waited until they were out of earshot. "We had a conference call with the governor this morning," she said. "All active agents on your investigation." Her eyes flicked to me. "She's pissed about your Stilloaks visit and what it turned up. Makes our boys look incompetent that you had to draw it out."

"She got especially salty once she found out we'd followed you there and done nothing to keep you out of it," Tang said, cringing. Bet that was a fun call.

I snorted. "What were you supposed to do? Dart and arrest me for existing? Because that law doesn't go into effect for..." I checked my phone for the time. "...thirty-six whole hours."

"Basically that's what she wants, yeah," Tang said, almost sheepishly. "Sorry."

"You should do it," Reed said, voice taut. "The countersuit against Minnesota would be very fulfilling – to our wallets."

"Look, we're just trying to do our jobs here, okay?" O'Rourke said warily. "It's not easy to deal with the kind of pressure Shipley is putting on our department. And it's not healthy, either. Tang here's going to have a heart attack if this keeps up."

"What?" Tang snapped to attention. "I am?" He frowned. "My cardiogram was healthy."

"You cannot eat pie with every meal and be considered healthy," O'Rourke snapped back at him. "I don't even know where you put all that." She waved a hand at his frame angrily. "It's so unfair."

I glanced at Tang; he wasn't rail thin, but I had to agree with O'Rourke. If he ate pie at every meal, it was just wrong that he got to stay slim. "Look...we have to do our jobs, you have to do your jobs. How can we stay out of each other's way over the next thirty-six hours?"

"Yeah, you're going to have to drop this case," O'Rourke said, "and probably you should leave town early." She looked at me with great significance. "Seriously. We're only on until about three today, and then another crew is coming on, one much less likely to be kindly of disposition...if you know what I mean."

"I'm picking up what you're laying down," I said, smiling tightly.

If we still had BCA on our tail at three o'clock...

...We were going to be darted, and maybe put in jail.

I say again...shit.

CHAPTER TWENTY-EIGHT

Paula Cunningham worked at a salon in a town called Roberts, Wisconsin, which was about ten miles south of New Richmond and right off I-94 about ten miles past the state line. We passed great woods that hugged either side of the freeway for almost the whole journey once we left Woodbury, Minnesota, and with the exception of the suburban center that was Hudson, Wisconsin, right on the state line, trees and fields were our view the whole way to the Roberts exit. And kindasorta the view once we were in the town of Roberts.

"Busy place," Reed said, watching the midday traffic roll by on US Highway 12. The sun was beating down pretty hard, and I sensed that if we didn't get into an air-conditioned space soon, I'd be sweating through my blouse in minutes. Not a fan of the heat, the idea of being driven out of Minnesota for what was almost certain to be more hot and humid environs held little appeal for me.

On the other hand, the lack of bitter winters might be nice.

The hair salon where Paula worked was in a newly renovated strip mall, a row of chairs in the back for stylists to use and clear-domed hair dryers up front filled with three old ladies that didn't even look up from their gossipy conversation as we entered. The waiting area was fairly minimal, but Reed and I helped ourselves to a chair as soon as Paula took note of us. She was in the midst of a cut and – based on my sadly not-limited experience – a dye job. It'd be a few minutes, but she did nod, then put her shoulder to the wheel and got back to work.

Reed looked about as uncomfortable as I'd ever seen him, glancing about furtively as though he'd gotten caught somewhere he shouldn't be. The three old women were looking at him and talking under their breath about his gorgeous locks, and I knew he could hear every word over the sound of the dryers, because I could.

"At least they're not Olivia and Angel," I said, trying to accentuate the positive. "You know...because you don't have to awkwardly work with them every day after this?"

His sour look was becoming such a regular thing that it made little to no dent in my effervescent cheer.

Tang and O'Rourke drove slowly past the window a few minutes after we entered, leaving us no doubt (probably on purpose; damned decent of them, I thought). We skimmed our phones while we waited.

Paula got her customer checked out and beckoned us to follow her. "I'm taking my break," she announced to another stylist who was deep in the middle of a conversation with someone's grandma about their precious baby darling, and we were led out the back after Paula stopped off in an employee locker room to pick up her cigarettes and lighter.

The area behind the strip mall wasn't exactly a paradise; cracked asphalt pavement and a neglected rear facade conspired with the occasional piece of litter and an open, smelly dumpster to give the place a crappy look. A few cars were parked out here, none fancy, none new.

Paula, with fumbling fingers, dug out two cigs and offered me one. I took it, then lit both with my finger, saving her the trouble of trying to do so with shaking hands. Which was an interesting, if not wholly unexplainable, tic. "Found anything yet?"

"That the State of Minnesota and Stillwater PD really want to hammer your boy," I offered, taking a drag. Reed, his face so twisted in distaste I worried it might freeze that way and reduce the interest of old ladies under dryers, stayed silent, holding his breath. "Not that that's news to you."

She shook her head slowly. "No. That ain't news to me. They been hot on him since this started."

"Not without reason," I said. "There is a good deal of evidence that appears to be...not in his favor."

"You mean like the underwear?" Paula asked, reddening.

"And the DNA on the body," I said, ticking a couple of points off, just for fun. "Etc. We did find something interesting from a witness this morning. A little inconsistency."

Reed's face was pinched; I could tell he was not impressed by my immediacy at getting to this. "Really? Right off the bat?" he asked, meta-low.

"What's that?" Paula asked, taking a lungful of cancer in.

"That you have been to your boyfriend's apartment since the murder," I said, watching her reaction very carefully.

It was subtle. She blew the smoke out in what she probably thought was a casual manner, but that vastly differed from the way she'd done it moments before. "I don't know who told you that, but they're a damned liar."

"Mmmm, I kinda doubt it," I said, taking my own inhalation and savoring it. "Anything you want to tell us? Because we're going to find out anyway. Eventually."

Paula flushed only slightly. "Nothing to tell. They're mistaken."

"Yeah, not so much," I said, making my face into a smirk. "But that's all right." I turned to Reed. "Tell me something. When a material witness lies to you...what does that make you think about their motives?"

"Nothing good," Reed managed to gasp out between subtly held breaths. Subtly to Paula; it was obvious as hell to me.

"Nothing good," I agreed, settling one of my more penetrating gazes on Paula. "After all...why would you lie about a thing like that? To the people you supposedly want to prove your boyfriend's innocence?"

Paula stumbled over her next words, but she turned a brighter shade of red. "I – not lyin'. You're just wrong. That's – it."

I looked at Reed. "That was convincing."

She reddened by a couple more shades. "This is an ambush." Throwing down her cigarette, she stubbed it out with her foot. "I don't have to put up with this."

"No, you don't," I agreed. "Nor does your boyfriend have to put up with your ass much longer. Because you know the thing about the Cube? There are no conjugal visits, even for spouses." I continued my smirk, which was not hard for my arrogant, irritable, want-a-drink-bad ass. "Or maybe that's something you were counting on."

She made a sort of muddled noise, then stormed past us, back to the door. Once she had it in her hand, she wheeled on us. "You're supposed to be investigating his innocence. Not me." She waved a finger at us. "I don't care what you think. I didn't do nothing wrong. I'd never hurt Aaron." She dangled her finger out in front of us, but a bit limply. Then, never taking her eyes off us, she stepped back inside, letting the door slowly close on her weak denial.

CHAPTER TWENTY-NINE

"Why do you think she lied?" I asked, about five hundred feet over the city of Roberts, Wisconsin, in a cloud bank, my brother aloft beside me. We'd left behind his car in the parking lot, because dodging BCA was going to require it. I was flying at a lot less than the speed of sound, and at a theoretical height that wouldn't piss off the FAA, so long as I stayed away from airports. Of course that only worked in places that weren't actively angry at me (Minnesota) and trying to hamper my progress (also Minnesota), so getting caught crossing the border while in flight was a quick path to criminal charges.

Which was a bummer, because flying the friendly skies made my life so much easier.

"Why does anybody lie?" Reed asked as we began our descent. Hudson wasn't exactly a far flight, especially for two people as swift as us. "She's hiding something. Ashamed of something. Actively conspiring against Berry, maybe." He frowned. "Did you get any memories from him of their relationship?"

"No, like I said before, I kept pretty focused on the one night."

"Of course you did," Reed muttered. "Because why make our job easier by having access to a broad range of information about the man and his potential crimes?"

"Because making our job easier would also involve turning him into a vegetable," I said. "Those memories that you wish I'd sapped? They're gone forever. So no, I did not touch his relationship memories, nor did I delve into his student relations, even lightly. Maybe I should have browsed a little. Sorry."

We set down just to the side of the strip mall and walked down the length of it to the rental car office. I paused just before crossing in front of the shop's window and gestured to Reed to go on. "If I go in, it'll just turn into a zoo event. Besides, I don't have any money anyway."

He sighed. "You can't be bothered to brave the obsessive fans in order to keep me company while they go through the ten tons of paperwork, signatures and initials required?"

"No," I said, and waggled my phone. "Besides, I have to make a call."

He shook his head and ducked into the rental car place, probably suspicious that I was going to chug a beer or something the minute he was inside. But he was in luck, because I had no beers (or they'd have already been chugged, honestly). Instead, I dialed up a familiar contact and let it ring.

It was picked up quickly. "Hey," Lethe said. "Been wondering when I'd hear from you."

"Sorry, got busy with the case," I said. "How are you doing?"

"I'm helping your friends lift heavy objects at the moment," Lethe said, and in the background I heard Augustus say something about poor placement of a table. "We're at Olivia's place."

"You mean her old barn of an apartment?" I asked. "At least it shouldn't take too long."

"I heard that!" Olivia called from in the background. "And also...I agree. But still."

"I heard you got a lead," Lethe said. "I trust you're keeping yourself under control."

"Or at least Reed is," I said. "Don't worry. I'm not downing shots when he's not around." I darted a look through the window, and found my brother talking to a squinting, slightly confused clerk. "Though he seems to believe I am."

"It's going to take a while to build back trust again, kiddo," Lethe said. "You want me to come join you?"

"Honestly, I just need to solve this case and get to...wherever I'm going," I said. "After that, maybe we can take some time and hang. It's just that right now..."

"You're busy solving a case while getting kicked out of a state," Lethe said. "One sympathizes. In my day, when I got driven out of a place, they just gathered a mob with torches and spears and came after us."

I pursed my lips. "Is this supposed to make me feel better...?"

"I doubt it," she said. "But at least they were more honest about their intention. It seems to me your state is doing roughly the same thing but in a more subtle and underhanded way."

"True, true."

"Anyhow," Lethe said, "you want me there, I'm there. Otherwise...I guess I'm loading shit to help out over here."

"Such a shame you didn't make it in earlier this morning," I said. "You could have come with us. And been threatened by the Minnesota BCA in the process."

"Well, I wasn't told I needed to be in by a certain time," Lethe said tartly, "or maybe I would have set my alarm. I like to wake naturally. Still...communication. You might want to get better at that."

"I'll work on it after the alcoholism," I said. Reed popped out the door to my right, followed by that befuddled-looking clerk, so I said, "Gotta go. Evading the law and all that."

"Right. Good luck."

I pocketed my phone and followed Reed and the clerk around the corner of the building, silently coming along behind them. "The nice thing about these Ford Fusions," the clerk said, "is that it's got a pretty spacious trunk for a sedan, y'know?"

"That's super important to me," I said, causing the clerk to look over his shoulder and realize I was there. Which was promptly followed by the most spastic, scared-cat body contortion of a jump I'd maybe ever seen.

"Whoa," Reed said, watching him nearly twist himself into a pretzel, "have you considered cutting the caffeine intake?"

When the clerk landed, he slapped his hand to his chest, trying to get his breathing under control. He was a little taller than me, but not much, bald, with thin-framed glasses, and a nametag that read *Gene*. "You scared the shit out of me!"

"Don't feel bad, I do that to a lot of people," I said, nodding ahead at a couple of slightly more weathered Ford Fusions that looked like they had been in the rental fleet for about the maximum time. "The car?"

"I knew you looked familiar," Gene said to Reed, fixing him with a suspicious glare. He got his brain unstuck a second later and said, "Follow me." Gone was his early, chatty politeness. I guess Gene wasn't a fan. "You want the insurance, right?"

"Oh, yeah, we'll definitely need that," I said. Reed's eyeroll arrived as expected.

"Car looks fine," Reed said brusquely, moving from side to side on it. "I'll take it."

For all his disdain for me, Gene did check us out quickly, with the car, and had us driving off the lot minutes later. My theory was that he wanted me out of there, but I didn't really care enough to ask.

"Think this will fool them?" Reed asked, dialing his own phone as he drove, navigating the streets of Hudson as he headed for the nearest on-ramp to I-94.

"Who knows?" I asked. "Hopefully, though. It'd be nice to have BCA off our backs for a little bit. Maybe get some work done."

"Which would entail...?" Reed asked. "Work-wise, I mean?"

"Great question," I said, "and I think the answer is...we have to do the one thing we really, really don't want to do."

"Ugh," grunted Reed, because he knew what we had to do next.

It was time...to meet Greta's parents.

CHAPTER THIRTY

There were, of course, cops posted out front of Greta Oliver's parents' house. Not because they were under guard, I suspected, but because BCA had lost us and were hoping to reacquire us using local PD as their birddogs.

It didn't really work, though, because Reed and I saw them from about six blocks away and turned off, parking a couple streets away and stepping out under blue, majestic skies and into the warmth of the summery sun. There was a smell of somebody barbecuing, the strong odor of cooking meat that sent my stomach into a rumbling tizzy.

"You're just now realizing you haven't eaten lately, aren't you?" Reed asked. I guess my stomach was just that loud.

"You either?" I asked. "Because maybe we could hit McD's after this? Your treat, of course."

He chuckled. "Of course."

The Olivers lived in a suburban neighborhood in Stillwater, a hillside city built like steps into the side of the rising bank of the St. Croix River. It was an old town, the oldest officially in Minnesota, and the trees in this place reflected it. This was the haven which the Olivers called home, and it was fairly magnificent. Much of the Twin Cities suburbs had a post World War II aesthetic; the houses were small, minimalist, a few bedrooms and some living space all packed into an economical box.

Not so, here in Stillwater. These houses had real nineteenth-century grace, with turrets and bay windows and sweeping gables like an Addams' Family house – but in immaculate repair. It kind of took my breath away.

"Like stepping back in time, isn't it?" Reed asked, watching me out of the corner of his eye.

"A little," I agreed. "I like new stuff, too. You know, a McMansion neighborhood? It's not the worst thing. They're tidy. New. But this..." I sighed, looking at a two-story home that looked just...graceful, with sweeping lines and new siding and paint. "...It's a classic look."

"Agreed," Reed said, halting me just next to a thick planter around a thick, tall maple. "Now..."

I sighed again, but for a different reason. "Yeah, yeah. All right. Let's do some sneaking."

We checked the street before disappearing into the planter. Bent low, we crept along the side of the pretty house's yard. According to my GPS, the Oliver house was directly behind this one, and a pretty white fence at the back was the only thing separating us from them.

"How guilty do we look right now?" Reed asked, meta-low, as we huddled in a thicket of bushes that offered us some cover from the nearest house.

"On a scale of one to Sienna Nealon, we're all me, baby," I said, and leapt the fence without hesitation, hoping that bushes on the other side would conceal me from the street where the cops were sitting.

It worked. The entire backyard was a beautiful, wooded and shrubbed paradise of greenery, blooming flowers providing some lovely offset colors against the beige of the house and its stucco'd exterior. A small water feature flowing into a miniature koi pond the size of a large pothole gave this peaceful oasis a placid soundtrack.

Until I heard the scuff of shoes that didn't come from Reed.

I swiveled toward the sound. Beside the pond was a bench, and upon the bench sat a couple. Late forties to early fifties, both of them. He was Midwestern dad that fit the mold: cargo shorts, a little extra weight around the middle, graying hair at the temples and a strong chin. She had long, platinum hair that came off her small head in waves, and her eyes were red from crying, any pretense of makeup that had ever been on her face now long gone.

Greta Oliver's parents stared at us as Reed landed next to me; I could feel him tense upon landing, having now seen the same thing I had.

We were caught.

CHAPTER THIRTY-ONE

"Hi," I said, trying to break the ice before the screaming started. "Sorry to intrude." I slowly stood up, keeping my hands open at my sides, as non-offensive as I could be. "Really. Uhm..."

The backyard garden was silent, other than my babbling and that of the water feature feeding into the koi pond. Mr. and Mrs. Oliver just stared at us, standing at their bench overlooking the placid water at their feet.

"We just need to talk to you," Reed said, mimicking my posture of surrender. "We're not looking for any trouble."

I was watching the faces of the Olivers; her red eyes blinked at his words, but Mr. Oliver's...

Well, his face hardened.

"You're not welcome here," he said, voice in the range of guttural harshness.

"Fair enough," Reed said, and started to turn to leap back over the fence. Smart move.

"Wait," I said, easing slightly closer and trying to sound as non-threatening as possible. "If I were in your shoes, I wouldn't want to talk to me either."

Mr. Oliver cocked his head at me. "Yes. So?"

"But, uhm..." I was grasping at straws here. "...I have a problem, see." I tapped my forefinger against my temple. "When I find out about a crime...I have this obsessive drive to make sure it gets solved correctly."

Mrs. Oliver blinked at me. "And you don't think it is?"

"Let's put it this way," I said, "I have a source in the Stillwater police that tells me things aren't adding up behind the scenes." I took her words as an invitation to get a little closer. "And the things I've seen since I got on this case?" I shook my head. "If you know me, you know I've solved a lot of crimes. Brought a lot of bad people to justice. Now, my jury is still out on Aaron Berry. Maybe he's the guy. But...something is rotten in the state of Minnesota, I'm telling you. Evidence is showing up that's almost certainly planted to fry him. Witnesses are coming forward way after the fact to try and make him look worse. The picture is suspicious. And..." I bit my lip for a second. "...whatever you may think about me, I really want to see your daughter receive some justice for what happened to her."

"You really look at everything they've got on him and think it's...what? A frame-up?" Mr. Oliver laughed. "Did you ever consider the possibility that he's just that guilty?"

"Maybe," I said, trying to sound eminently reasonable, and not like a crazy crank who'd just leapt their fence and intruded on their peaceful sanctuary just to question them. "And if that's the case, I'll gladly pile the kindling and light the fire when it comes time to burn him. But..."

"You don't think he's the one who did this to our daughter?" Mrs. Oliver's voice was a thin, reedy thing, almost on the breaking point.

"I don't know," I said, as gently as I could muster. "But I'd like to ask some questions so maybe I can find out."

Mr. Oliver turned harshly to his wife, his mouth a hard line. "You heard the police. She works for *him*."

"I do," I said, "but if he's guilty, I told him flat out I'd help put him away. To my knowledge, this is the first time I've ever taken a case where I'm looking at someone as possibly innocent rather than trying to catch them and put them away."

Mrs. Oliver was looking at me with a sort of dawning curiosity. Something was getting through to her.

So naturally, Mr. Oliver was trying to put a stop to it. To his wife, he said, "You can't possibly believe this. You know what they say about her." He favored me with a disgusted once-over. "She's dangerous."

"Yeah, I'm a real lightning rod for trouble," I drawled. "I get it. I take on the kind of problems that no one really wants to come their way. In my way of thinking, everyone would be pretty happy if metahumans would just leave them alone so they could go about their lives." I inched closer. "But as you know, now...that just doesn't happen. Unfortunately."

Mr. Oliver bristled, but Mrs. Oliver's face fell. "Preston," she said softly, "would you go fix me a cup of decaf?"

Preston Oliver looked down at her with near-incredulity. "You want to talk to her?"

"For a minute, I do. And I know you don't." She looked up at him, eyes glistening. "Would you do this for me?"

Preston gritted his teeth, looked ready to say something hard and mean and ugly – but he stopped himself just in time, and turned on his heel, and removed himself to the sliding glass door, coming very close to slamming it behind him as he went into the house.

When he was gone, Mrs. Oliver slowly sat back down. Her every motion spoke of the stillness of a woman wounded, as though movement hurt. Even the damage she'd taken to her heart from her daughter's death appeared to manifest physically, in much the same way as I would limp after getting the shit kicked out of me.

I came a little closer, dropping my hands to my side. "Do you have anything you want to tell me?" I asked, as quietly as I could without getting into the range of meta-low.

Mrs. Oliver stared at the bubbling waterfall as it rippled endlessly into the pond. "I do."

I stepped closer, now only a few feet away. "Something about this...it doesn't sit right with you?"

She shook her platinum blond head slowly, the wavy locks moving back and forth like wheat grass in the wind. "I knew my daughter." She took a breath, so quiet it would have barely stirred a tissue poised at her lips. "We talked every day. With her and me, it wasn't like one of those mother/daughter relationships with a constant sprain."

She smiled, a tiny little one, the last light of joy at remembering her lost child. "I talked to the other mothers at Stilloaks. They warned me what was coming. 'She'll turn thirteen and cut you out of her life,' they said. 'She'll never tell you another thing.' And I said, 'Not my Greta.'" Her eyes got teary. "I was right."

Mrs. Oliver bowed her head. "I knew my daughter, Ms. Nealon, all the way up to the end. She was still the sweet, smiling, big-hearted girl I raised." She looked up. "We had her late in life, see. Thought maybe we just couldn't and then...she came along and changed my world for the better. We doted on her. She was my...my best friend." One of the tears slid down her cheek, and I could tell she was holding back, trying to keep her composure in front of us strangers.

She looked me in the eye, clear and bright and green. "So when that Stillwater Police detective told me my daughter was having an affair with Mr. Berry – I told them, 'No.'" She raised a finger, wagging it. "Not my little girl. I knew her, Ms. Nealon. We talked every day." She looked up at me, straight-backed and strong in spite of the glinting tears coursing silently down her cheeks. "My daughter was not having an affair with a teacher. He may have gotten her that night, but she wasn't...she didn't get secretive or furtive, she wasn't sneaky or hiding a secret love. She was just the same as she ever was. Just...my Greta."

Mrs. Oliver lowered her eyes again, chin to her chest, sagging. "She was my innocent girl, all the way to the end."

The sliding glass door opened, and Preston Oliver emerged, a steaming cup of coffee in one hand and a sheaf of papers in the other. He didn't even look like the same man; all the anger that had caused his neck veins to bulge out had gone, allowing them to recede back into the surface of the skin like a shark slipping beneath the waves. He walked slowly over to us, and offered his wife the coffee cup. She gratefully accepted with a mournful smile, but did not sip.

"Maybe you're right," Mr. Oliver said, his voice on the verge of cracking. "I have my doubts, too, about whether Mr. Berry killed my little girl." He sniffed. "When she died, I logged onto the account for our cell phone provider. I'd never checked her phone, her text messages, anything like that."

"We trusted her," Samantha Oliver said, looking into her husband's eyes tearfully.

He nodded, smiling back at her, so mournfully, and extended the papers in his hand to me. "Other than the night of her...her death...I couldn't find a single text message or phone call from Mr. Berry to her." He brought his face down to the sleeve of his bright red polo shirt and wiped them there, leaving dark spots of crimson behind. "If they were carrying on some affair...wouldn't it be there?"

I took the pages from him delicately. "It's possible," I said, trying to play the role of detached investigator. "Sometimes people who are looking to hide something like an affair use chat apps." I decided to go for broke, even though I already knew the answer. "Did you see anything like that on her phone?"

"We don't have it," Mr. Oliver said, shaking his head. Then he pointed to that paper. "But there's a record in there of every single app she ever downloaded from the store. If there's something like that hidden in there, you could find it."

"Thank you," I said softly. Reed, behind me, was barely breathing. I drew up slowly. "Is there anything else you want to tell me about Greta? Or any of this?"

They looked at each other once more, and she shook her head, lowering it onto his shoulder. Mr. Oliver looked at me, and from his eyes I could tell his heart was full. "Would you mind just...leaving us in peace, please?" he asked, and finally his voice broke.

"Yes sir," I said, backing off. "I will find whoever did this to your daughter. That I can promise you. One way or another."

"Thank you, Ms. Nealon," Samantha Oliver said, her head nestled in the wrinkles of her husband's shirt.

I left them there, on that bench, and leapt over the fence as quietly as I could, hoping that not only had I not wasted these people's time, but that I'd be able to fulfill the promise I'd just made to them.

CHAPTER THIRTY-TWO

"What are you seeing in there?" Reed asked, once we were safely away from the Oliver house and back in our rental car, heading for Highway 36 so as to get the hell out of Stillwater ASAP. No point hanging around where we knew they were looking for us, after all.

I was shuffling through the paper printouts that Mr. Oliver had given me, trying to decipher a list of phone numbers without any contact names attached. "Not sure," I said. "This came straight from the phone company, so there's no ID or contact data along with it, like you might have if he'd downloaded it from her phone. Which I assume is in evidence in the Stillwater PD."

"Right," Reed said, nodding along, eyes on the road. The sun was overhead; it was midday. A peal of thunder originating in his stomach reminded us both that we'd been light on breakfasts, lunches, and dinners for the last few days through only a little fault of our own. Still, he kept his eye on the ball. "That's a quandary."

"Not really," I said, and brought out my cell phone, having the number I was looking for pulled up in seconds.

It was answered on the second ring. "Hello?" Jamal asked, the roar of a vehicle engine and the open road passing in the background.

"Hey," I said, "I got evidence I need to send you." I put my phone on speaker, then started snapping photos of the sheets that Mr. Oliver had given me. "It's phone records from Greta Oliver. All her calls, text messages, and supposedly all the apps she'd downloaded. Only I don't know the numbers she's talking to, so...can you provide some clarity?"

"Yeah, maybe in a bit," Jamal said. "I'm driving a big rental truck right now over the bridge into Hudson, remember?"

"Oh, right," I said. "Who all did you get packed?"

"Olivia's and Angel's apartments are all cleaned out," Jamal said. "So that leaves me and Augustus. And Eilish, though I guess she's still in Cali with Kat?"

"Yeah," Reed said. "You have her spare keys, right?"

"Angel does. She's following along behind us. Gonna pick us up, then we're going to get your car in Wisconsin, then back to wherever Augustus and Scotty are loading at that point, I guess?"

"So the office is done?" Reed asked.

"Office is done," Jamal said. "End of an era, huh, bossman?"

"Yeah," Reed said tightly. "Just not a good era. About that app list Sienna is sending you? Can you check it and see if there are any chat apps hidden in there?"

Jamal sighed. "Me? Not for a while. But...m'dear? You mind?"

There was a great, electronically-muffled sigh on the other end of the connection, and then ArcheGrey's accented voice came on. "Sure. Whatever. For you. Taking control of your phone, Sienna. No offense, but this is just too slow."

"Hey, you don't need to 'take control,'" I said, a little irritable. "I'm snapping as fast as I c–"

"Holy shit," Arche blurted. "Maybe I'm not taking control of your phone. What the hell is that thing?"

"A Cassidy Ellis special," I said, admiring the dinged-up craftsmanship of my mobile. "Is it invulnerable to hacking?"

"At a distance, yes," Arche said. "Up close, I could probably crack it. Send me these photos. I was bored anyhow."

"Just sittin' here cuddling with me bores you?" Jamal's voice cut in on the other side. "I see how it is."

"What is it with these nerds we hire finding love among their own hacking kind?" Reed asked. "First J.J. and Abby, now these two...?"

"We should play up the matchmaking perks of our employee benefits program," I said. "Y'know...if we ever end up hiring again." I was on to the text messages photos now, the pages of phone call data already sent along.

"This girl only called a very few people," Arche said. "Like...ever. I have both her parents on here, her house line. Aaron Berry is on it as well, but their only contact was on the night of, and almost at the time of, the murder–"

"Important staging there," Reed said. "If he was framed, that's a neat piece of evidence."

"Yes, he was her last call," Arche said. "I have three girls here on the list as well. Lucille Thompson, Syrena Gaston, and Ashleigh Simone?"

"That was her three amigas," I said. "The headmaster suggested they were all inseparable."

"Plus, Syrena was the new alleged victim we stumbled over yesterday," Reed said. "So it tracks that they're all connected."

"Somewhat connected, yes," Arche said. "It seems like Greta was in regular contact with Syrena and Lucille. Much less so with Ashleigh. I count a total of four calls between them. Ever."

"That's a lot for millennials and below," I said. "Generationally, I mean? We don't call people. We text."

"Well, send me those and I'll sift them, too. Or better yet..." She drew a breath on the other side of the phone. "Okay, I'm in the phone company records," Arche said as casually as if she'd told us she stepped over a concrete parking block. "No need for photos. Hmm. Interesting."

"Want to share with the class?" Reed called out.

"Do you know the time of death?" Arche asked. "For Greta?"

"No," I said, glancing at Reed. "Though that does seem like something we should get. Maybe hit the morgue, get the coroner's report somehow?" I paused, then said, a little slyly, "Unless someone would like to save us a trip...?"

Arche laughed, a short, sharp bark. "Get it yourself."

"Hey," Jamal said from the background, "I haven't had a chance to do any due diligence on this Berry guy yet. You mind looking into his bank account?"

Arche sighed. "The things I do for you." A few seconds passed, and then she made a grunt of intrigue. "Standard stuff for a teacher - low pay, lots of bills. Hm. There is one standout thing. Every pay period, he takes almost a thousand dollars out in cash from the bank."

"Hm," I said. I looked at Reed. "Could be a gambling habit. Turtle Lake Casino isn't that far."

He pursed his lips, thinking over his reply. "Neither is Treasure Island Resort down by Red Wing. Or Mystic Lake."

"There are also some strip clubs in the area," Arche said, "but all these places you mention? Have ATMs, I presume."

That was a good point. Casinos did like to make it easy for people to spend money with them. Why not withdraw there? Was he one of those, rare, disciplined gamblers who walked away from the table when he hit his limit? Who knew when to quit? Unlikely. “Where's he spending this money, then?”

“Another interesting point: the day after he was arrested, someone made a withdrawal from his account,” Arche said. “In person. Authorized.”

“Okay,” I said, listening for the shoe to drop, “who was it?”

“Paula Cunningham,” Arche said, “and I'm looking at the video footage from the bank right now. It was definitely her.”

CHAPTER THIRTY-THREE

"What does this mean?" Reed asked, keeping a steady hand on the wheel as we rolled onto Highway 36 in Stillwater, heading east. It was about half past noon, and we were out of ideas about where to go next. ArcheGrey was enlightening us as to a twist in the tale, though, by informing us that Aaron Berry's girlfriend had made (apparently) the last of a series of regular withdrawals of a thousand dollars from his bank account.

"Could be a bill he pays in cash?" I asked. "Maybe he sends money to charity...?"

"I'll look into it a little deeper," Jamal said. "In a bit, when I get parked."

"Oh, fine, I'll do it," Arche said, sighing. "Keep driving. I'm going to track her cell phone and those of people around her after the withdrawal, see if I can figure out where she left the money or what she used it for."

"That's a thing you can do?" Reed asked.

"Not a thing I can do," Jamal grunted. "At least not quickly."

"I'm going to tie in local security cameras with the cell

phone records," Arche said. "It's a bit more complex than anything my man here has attempted."

"I mean, I've done stuff like it," Jamal said. "You're talking about her passing a lot of cameras, and western Wisconsin? Not exactly covered in security cams compared to say, the Twin Cities. Or New York."

"Leave it with me," Arche said. "I'll figure something out."

"Awesome," I said. "Because that feels like it could be important. Teachers like Berry don't get paid enough to just toss aside a thousand bucks every pay period without noticing it's gone."

"But it kind of explains why he lives in sort of a shithole," Reed said. "And far out of the city."

"She brought up another interesting point earlier," I said. "Do you think as PIs working for the accused, we could get access to the coroner's report for Greta?"

Reed shook his head. "Through Berry's lawyer, probably. It is part of his defense, after all, and has to be handed over during discovery."

I frowned. Paula hadn't mentioned who Berry's lawyer was. Which was funny, since whoever they were, they'd be quarterbacking the defense, and would be a good person to converse with about the case. "I'm starting to realize...there's a lot we don't know about working this side of the investigation."

"Great, you two strategize and I'll just dig into this professional hacking, okay?" Arche said. "It's mind intensive, more so than carrying on a conversation with you, so...bye." A click, and she was gone.

"So what should we do now?" Reed asked.

"Well, it'd be nice to get a peek at that autopsy report," I said. "Think we could just jet out to the coroner's office and ask for one? Not sure I want to try and talk to Paula right now, given how our last conversation went."

"Wouldn't hurt," Reed said with a shrug, "as long as there aren't cops hovering around. You know where the coroner's office is for Stillwater?"

"By not-strange lack-of-coincidence, I do. Stay on 36 and head into St. Paul," I said, and noted the perplexed look form on his face. "I know. Stillwater is Washington County, St. Paul is Ramsey. But I swear, that's where it is."

"Okeydoke," he said, apparently prepared to take at least this small thing from me on faith.

"Do you think if I live long enough, I'll just drop the pretense of manners and do stuff like hang up on people with minimal explanation?" I asked, staring at my phone screen, blank now that my call was over.

An impish smile formed on Reed's lips. "I think you 'lived long enough' by about age twenty."

I thought about smacking his arm, but let it pass. It was true, after all, at least a little.

CHAPTER THIRTY-FOUR

I recognized the coroner's office as we drove into the Regions Hospital complex, only a block or so away from the state capitol. I thought about stopping in there, see what kind of reception I got. But only in the same way as I sometimes pondered what it would feel like to catch a lot of bullets in my internal organs all at once.

The coroner's office was a nondescript, single-story building of sculpted concrete blocks that gave it a slightly more aesthetically pleasing air than regular, bland, dull concrete blocks. These had a randomized pattern to them, like waves atop the beige concrete, or maybe fingerprints dusting the foam atop a latte.

"You've been here before on a case?" Reed asked as we breezed through the glass doors into what looked passingly like the waiting room for a medical practice, if a bit more cold and sterile. Tile replaced carpet and there wasn't much in the way of chairs, but otherwise it was only a few degrees of décor off from a doctor's office.

"Yeah, some murder investigation or another, I think?" I frowned. I'd picked up a lot of cases over the years, including some weird normal-human homicides in which I, as the resident expert, had to rule out metahuman involvement. I'd ended up here on one of those, I thought, but one so forgettable I couldn't even remember the particulars of it. Or they might have been ripped from my memory by Rose. That was always a possibility.

"No one here," Reed said as he sauntered up to the counter, plopping an elbow down as he scanned the waiting area. He was just reaching for the countertop bell to give it a ding when a chubby black dude in scrubs came waltzing out from behind a set of stainless steel double doors, head down as he looked at a clipboard.

He was humming something under his breath, and it took me a minute to realize it was the Nat King Cole classic, "Stardust." He made it across the entire area behind the counter without looking up until I announced, "I love that song."

He jerked slightly, looking up and taking me in with one solid, quick look before reacting. It was fun to watch, actually. "Jeez! Shit! I didn't know anyone was here. Let alone..." He waved a hand at me. "What, uh...what can I do for you?"

"What's your name?" I asked.

"Terrell," he said. Still more jaded. This dude had seen some things in his life. Which made sense, given where he worked.

"My colleague and I are working a case," I said, plopping my own elbow comfortably down on the counter like Reed. "Greta Oliver?"

His hair was short, and he was balding up top. He had jaded eyes, too, and I got a full glimpse at those now. "Look...I know who you are, and you have been around the law for a while. So I know that you know I cannot give an autopsy report for a super sensitive ongoing case to someone who just walks in the front door. No matter how famous she is."

"That's fair," I said, plopping my other elbow on the counter and doing a solid lean. "But I'm working as his PI, see, and I'm going to get a copy of it as part of the discovery process – y'know, from the lawyer – anyway. So, really, what I'm asking for here? It's a favor. From you, a man who knows the greatness of Nat King Cole to me...a person who it is occasionally advantageous to be able to call on."

His jaded eyes got a little more so, and he cocked his head to the side. "That advantage doesn't really accrue for people in Minnesota. At least not for very much longer. Am I right?"

Reed sighed. "Well, you're not wrong. Here's the thing–"

"Let me stop you right there, my dude," our new friend said. "See, I'm just a working guy. Not the boss. Not in charge. Not particularly high up the ladder. And it seems to me, from my low position, that there's very little advantage to me handing over a report as incendiary and controversial as this one...and having it blow back on *moi*. You feel me?"

"I totally understand," I said. "And honestly, I would just wait for it to show up in the paper in a couple weeks, because we both know it will–"

"Yes," he said cheerfully, "once the lawyers get ahold of it, that tends to happen."

"–But like you mentioned, I'm on a timetable here." I gave him my best smile. "So...pretty please?"

He returned the smile, putting his own elbows on the counter. "I'm sorry...but no."

"Well...it never hurts to ask," I said.

Then I hopped the counter and pushed through the stainless steel double doors, in search of my report.

"Wait, what are you doing?" Terrell asked.

"I could be wrong," Reed said, deadpan, "but I think she's going to just go find it and then walk out with it."

"No, no, no!" Terrell pushed through the swinging double

doors after me, skidding on his rubber soles. "You can't be back here! I need this job! I need to not get fired!"

"I appreciate that," I said, finding myself in a white-tiled, scuff-floored beige hall with so many doors to choose from. "Which is why I'm not involving you."

"I am definitely involved!" Terrell called, rushing to keep up. "See, I'm chasing you down a hallway, and I'm having to run, which is how I know I'm involved. Because I hate running, see? And I'm doing it. In order to keep this job. Dammit!"

Pushing into the first door I came to, I found myself in an examination room. There was a body waiting there, under a sheet, and I thought about picking it up to look, but it probably wasn't anyone I knew, so instead I moved on.

"You know all the records are computerized now, right?" Terrell was hot on my heels, as much as he could be for a man who was huffing and puffing. "There's not a hard copy of that thing sitting on a desk, waiting for you to pick it up."

I pushed through into another examination room. This one was decorated with pictures of flowers on the walls. Daisies, to be exact. "That's ironic," I said, pausing for a second to take it in.

"We have our own exam rooms," Terrell said, puffing. "Lisa likes hers a little brighter, that's all. To take her mind off what she's doing, maybe, I never asked."

"You don't see the obvious connection?" I asked. "As in, the people Lisa is working on will, shortly, be pushing up daisies?"

Terrell stopped short. "Oh, shit. I never noticed that." He looked at the swinging doors into Lisa's exam room. "Those are daisies?"

"This would all be easier if you'd just help a girl out, Terrell," I said, moving to enter the next room.

"No, no, no – wait!" Terrell charged ahead of me, apparently catching his second wind, and dodged in front of the next door. He was holding out his hands to either side, and clearly this was his Gandalf moment and I was not going to be passing.

"Okay," I said. "I will wait for you to deliver me the autopsy report."

Terrell sagged. "You know I can't do that. See what we have here? It's conflicting cathexes. You wanna go your way and get what you want, but I am diametrically opposed. So it's an impasse, you see, because I ain't moving and you ain't–"

I leapt over his head and landed on the other side of him, shoving my way into the doors. "It's not an impasse when one person can break it unilaterally, Terrell. But – what in the ever-living *fuck!*"

"What?" Reed almost tripped over Terrell, then me, as he charged into the room behind me. He took it all in with a sweep of ever-widening eyes, and then said, "Is that...?"

"Aww, man," Terrell said, only a little above a moan.

It was suddenly blazingly obvious to all present why this was the room where he'd chosen to make his stand to keep me out. It wasn't for reasons of grace, or because he wanted to maintain the integrity of the workplace or keep his job or any of that other stuff.

No, Terrell had chosen to try to block me from this particular room because every freaking surface in the place was decorated with highly stylized, hand-drawn art...

...Of me.

And it was not tasteful pictures of me subduing criminals in the course of my job or something. No mere photo-realistic splashes of color and pencils taken to an artistic level beyond that conveyed by the constraints of a photograph.

No, these photos were...well...

"I'm...not wearing anything." I pointed at one of the more prominent ones. Because it was seriously me topless, with exaggerated proportions, facing away from the artist and looking back seductively, hair slightly over my face.

"That is some serious sideboob." Reed made a face of mild disgust. "And that look? Really quite disturbing."

"The fact that I'm giving a come-hither look is more disturbing than my nudity?" I wheeled on him. "My ass is right there! Uncovered!" I waved a hand at my artistically rendered, white-as-milk backside. "What color did the artist even use for that?" I turned on Terrell. "Are these yours?"

"NO!" Terrell thundered, waving his hands in front of me like he was trying to sway a T-Rex from attacking in the Jurassic Park movies. "These belong to Kevin. And Kevin..." Terrell sort of rolled his eyes in exasperation. "...Well, Kevin is...something else."

I looked over the Sienna Nealon portrait collection with vague horror. One had me drawn in a Japanese anime style, complete with a schoolgirl uniform, but with my proportions rather than the stick figure ones usually found in that style.

The click of a camera phone made me turn around again to find my brother taking some snaps, close-up, of each work. "What?" he asked, zooming in on another. "Whatever your feelings about your depiction here, I have to tell you, Kevin's skill is impeccable."

And right he was, which did not make it any easier for me to stomach. "This one is..." I cocked my head, looking at another.

In this one, I was naked, straddling another figure in the picture. This one was closer to photo-real, and the seductive look on my face (again) almost made me heave the lunch I hadn't yet had. The man's features were in shadow, and my fingers were clutched tightly around his face, my legs across his hips. It was clear from the slightly occluded look of ecstasy on his features that I was...draining him. Maybe in more ways than one, given that while he appeared to be wearing pants, the brushwork and size of my artistically represented thighs left open for interpretation whether they were zipped or not.

"That's a little creepy," Reed said, snapping a photo of that one up close for good measure.

"So of course you take a picture of it for posterity," I said. "Okay, where's Kevin? Because I need to find him and kill him. Like...right now."

"He's on night shift," Terrell said. "And no killing! Aren't you in enough trouble in Minnesota already?"

Annoyed as I was, I saw the reason in what he said, so I favored him with a sour look. "Fine. No killing." I swept my eyes over the buffet of Sienna Nealon-oriented artwork with great distaste, and said, "Seriously, though...ugh. Why couldn't he have been doing this someplace I'm unlikely to visit, like Rochester? Or Tallinn?" I shuddered.

"That's in Estonia," Terrell said.

"Thanks for the geography lesson, Mr. Art Critic," I shot back.

"Come on," Reed said, putting a hand on my shoulder, and steering me toward the door. "Let's get out of here before you strike a pose worthy of commemorating on the page."

Once we were outside the swinging doors, I fumed, "How can you see all that and not be pissed? He drew me in various states of undress!"

"Because in your life, you have burned your clothes off in public with alarming regularity," Reed said. "And also..." He furtively looked back, but Terrell was still hanging around in Kevin's workspace, separated from us by the doors. Still, he lowered his voice to meta-low. "...This is our way to get the autopsy report."

I made a face. "You want me to play nice with the guy who did *that*? Do you even know who I am?"

Reed's smirk was so self-satisfied it made me want to

punch him. "Y'know, based on the artwork...I don't think he'd be bothered by you not playing nice. It actually might get us further if you didn't."

"Ugh," I said, my stomach churning. I didn't like anything about that plan. But I didn't have to, because as annoying as I found it, I knew my brother was right.

CHAPTER THIRTY-FIVE

"Did you find anything?" Jamal asked, the speakerphone blaring in our car.

"A supply of heebie jeebies," I said. "In fact, enough to last me all the days of my life, no matter how long that may be."

"We found some awesome fanboi art of Sienna by a very talented – and maybe slightly demented – guy who dissects people for a living," Reed said, putting a dimension on it which I hadn't considered in my outrage. Ew...?

"That sounds cool. Did you get any pictures?" Angel asked over the speaker.

"I did!" Reed said, all gleeful. I gave him the killing look I offered to people in whose ass I was about to insert a steel-toed boot. He returned my glare with an outsized grin. At least one of us was having fun.

"Any chance you put together that cell phone data or tracking or whatever on Paula Cunningham?" I asked, since Arche hadn't said a word yet. I took it as a sign she hadn't, but hell if I was going to drive around in circles for hours with Reed with nothing going on as we waited for night shift to begin so we could talk to Kevin, Succubus Worshipper and Resident Morgue Artist.

"You must think this is easy work," Arche piped in. "Let me assure you it is not."

"I noticed you didn't actually answer my question," I said.

Arche sighed audibly, crackling the line. "Yes. I have something, at least. After making the withdrawal, Paula immediately drove south from New Richmond to River Falls, Wisconsin. Not a short jaunt."

I exchanged a look with Reed. No, River Falls and New Richmond weren't a quick trip from each other; it'd be about thirty minutes one way. Not the sort of thing most people would do on a lark, especially after picking up a quick grand at the bank. "That she's picking up the money suggests the gambling addiction is not a viable theory. Unless she was always the one whose addiction was being fed."

"Also, there's no casino in River Falls," Reed said, frowning. "I've been there a few times. It's just a little-ish college town. Cute place, nice ambiance. But I struggle to see where you'd drop a thousand bucks every two weeks there."

"Agreed," I said. I'd been there, too, and Reed was right. "Maybe a car dealership?"

"Maybe," Reed said, "but in cash?"

"Have you considered the possibility it's for a payday loan?" Jamal asked. "Interest on those puppies is lethal, man. A thousand bucks every two weeks sounds about right."

"She went to a residence there," Arche said. "Stayed for only a few minutes, then back on the road to New Richmond."

Boom. "Well, that blew up our theories about paying for a normal product or service," I said. "Got the address?"

"An apartment complex on Wasson Court," Arche said. "Texting it to you now, with directions, in case you struggle with these sorts of things."

"I don't, but Reed could probably use the help. He's averse to asking directions." He shot me a fiery look. "What? You're a man, I assume, but it's a fair assumption."

"Any idea whose place this is that we're heading to?" Reed asked, the irritation clear in his tone. He kept his hands on the wheel, and at ten and two positioning, even as he steered us into a corner.

"Mail being delivered there is to a Faith Holloway," Arche said. "I'll work up a profile based on banking records, education history, all that."

"You can do that?" Jamal asked.

"Never mind, I guess I won't, since apparently he can't," Arche said. "Unless you'd like to make a deal...?"

"NO," Reed thundered. "We'll figure it out ourselves," he added, more at a mutter. "Thanks."

I hung up and looked carefully at my brother. "No deals, huh?"

"I think you've made enough deals for both of us already," Reed said, a little more evenly.

"Maybe," I said. "But she could tell us something interesting. Might be helpful."

"She could also tell us nothing, and then we'd still owe her. No deals."

"Fine, we'll wait until after we talk to this Faith Holloway," I said, and saw my brother's eye twitch.

Didn't matter. He kept us steady, heading for Interstate 35E, which would take us down to 94, and back to Wisconsin. Again.

CHAPTER THIRTY-SIX

"You know, Wisconsin is kind of underrated," Reed said as we crossed the mighty bridge over the St. Croix River and it glittered beneath us all the way to the southern horizon. It was catching the full reflection of that midday sun, and boy was it doing some sparkling beneath the glorious, cerulean skies. These were the kind of days Minnesotans lived for: perfect, amazing weather, a warm memory for us to hold in our hearts when the temps plunged to negative ten for thirty days solid in January.

"Oh?" I asked, leaning against the window, watching a boat go by on the river below. Traffic on Interstate 94 was steady and a little busy, but not terrible considering it was a Saturday. I raised my eyes to the horizon and noted there were a hell of a lot more boats than just the one. Probably thirty, forty, just on this side of the bridge. I let my eyes drift along the natural curve of the water against the high, beautiful, wooded banks.

"You get days like this in Wisconsin," Reed said, a little more chipper than our day would have suggested. He cracked the window, and the wind caught his hair. "It's not so far from the cities–"

"Which we will not be allowed to go to," I said, stirring to lift my head and hand. "So...that's pointless. If you need anything from a major city, you'd have to go to...what? Eau Claire, maybe? Which ain't that big."

"Milwaukee's on the other side of the state." He smoothly switched lines of attack. "It's a solid metropolis. Center of the country, in terms of flights–"

"It's at the extreme north middle," I said, "like Minnesota. Not exactly optimal, if one was selecting for that."

His lips twisted sourly. "So that means Texas at the extreme south, you're not so keen on, either?"

"No," I said, shaking my head. "I don't have a grudge against Texas. But I don't have any motivation to go there, either, Lethe's desires aside."

"They made us an offer," Reed said. "Some tax incentives and whatnot. Plus, Miranda's down there. Might be nice to have our lawyer close."

"She's only close if we're in Houston. If we're anywhere else in the state, it's like...hours away." Texas was massive. Bigger than many countries.

"So it's a no on Wisconsin and on Texas?" Reed asked, and he sounded...grudging, maybe?

"You're in charge, Reed," I said, weary of the whole thing. "I'm an employee who's on the ragged edge. You'd be well within your rights to just can my ass and go wherever you want."

He was quiet for just a moment, long enough for us to rocket past the wooden *Wisconsin Welcomes You* sign. "I don't want to do this without you."

"Well, I'm not keen on doing this in a place where I know the state government is wobbly or unfamiliar or actively hates me," I said. "I don't know about Wisconsin. Don't think I've had any contact with their government one way or another. Have you?"

"Not really," Reed said. "Some state-level agencies, I have, but not their governor. What about New York? They seem to like you there."

I shrugged. "New York, in the minds of basically everyone, unfortunately means Manhattan or NYC, to the chagrin of the entirety of upstate. And I can't do NYC again. Too crowded. Plus it has its own heroes already."

Reed smiled, almost ghostly. "Yeah, Captain Frost has got it covered up there. Evil is always on the run."

"More like he's evil, and he's got the runs," I said, smiling right back. "And you know I meant Gravity."

"I do. But...in fairness to the rest of beleaguered, forgotten New York...what about upstate? It's nice there."

"It is," I said. "But I feel like we should be centered on a major metro area. Somewhere close to an airport, since we're currently broke and will have to fly commercial to our gigs for the foreseeable future. Which rules out upstate. And most of New England, unless you're real close to Boston."

Reed grimaced. "If we're doing brutally cold weather, I'd rather stay in Wisconsin. A little more nature, a little less...people-y."

"Yeah, pretty as it is, I'm not keen on New England, either," I said with a sigh. "And it may sound funny for a person who can literally generate fire from her skin, but I'm not big on the heat. So if it were up to me, I'd rule out anything south of Atlanta. And maybe Atlanta, too, because...whew. Warm."

"North Carolina is nice," he said. "They have mountains. Several decent-but-not-huge metros. Good amount of flights."

"But not exactly central," I said. "Which, by the way,

would be my argument against Portland or Seattle, where I think we're also generally liked."

Reed nodded. "Got an offer from Washington this morning, in fact. Not as good as Texas's." He fixed his eyes on the road, preparing as the exit for River Falls loomed ahead, the green highway sign hanging overhead as he shifted lanes. "So...north of Georgia, but west of Carolina and east of...Nevada? But south of Wisconsin." He got a shifty look. "...Illinois?"

"Chicago? Horrendous traffic and they've never forgiven me for Soldier Field. Hard pass."

"Oh, right," Reed said. "So...probably south of Illinois. Arkansas? Indiana? Ohio? Iowa–"

"Don't joke. You know Iowa is a no. Why would you even bring that up?"

"Fine, fine. But the others?"

"Maybe."

Reed nodded slowly. "Okay. Ohio. Indiana. Colorado?"

"Possibly. Did we get an offer?"

"Yeah," he said, almost grimacing. "Third tier at best, I'd say. We go there, we're on our own, but we're welcome. Utah had a nice one. How do you feel about Utah?"

"I was once tossed in a dumpster there."

He stared at me, as though trying to decide what that meant.

"It's okay," I deciphered it for him. "Not among my favorite places, but it's fine."

He nodded, then frowned. "Who tossed you in a dumpster in Utah...?"

"Some bitch jealous of me riding around with her ex," I said. "Don't worry. I got her back."

His face froze, and you could see he was doing the mental leaps to try and figure out how all that had played out. "But...she's alive, right...?"

"Alive, yes. Probably still smells like she bathed in a porta potty – which she did – but she's very much alive."

"Right," Reed said. "Should I rule out Nebraska, Kansas–"

"Please do."

"Ouch," Reed said. "No on the flatlands. Which is a shame, because Kansas made us at least a high second-tier offer."

"What about the Dakotas?"

"North Dakota...so so, at best. South Dakota, a little better, but not exactly one that has me chomping to get my ass out there right away." He looked sidelong at me. "If we're being honest...New York and Texas offered the best terms. Tied with..." And he waved his hand at me in a leisurely way.

"Tennessee?" I asked. He nodded, and I smiled. "Nice to be wanted somewhere."

"I suppose," Reed said, and we settled into a few minutes of quiet as we cruised down Wisconsin State Highway 35, the open fields on either side and the occasional copse of trees, the odd occasional hill providing some variation in the landscape. "It is pretty out here, though," he finally said, as we reached the city limits of River Falls, a quaint town that started off with the same sprawl of commerce as every other suburban community I'd been to. But maybe ten percent nicer.

"You know what would kill me about being here in Wisconsin?" I asked, watching the small businesses in strip malls slip by. "Minnesota is right across the river. I mean, not only would we have to drive to Madison to catch a flight, since we can't go to MSP, but – it's right there." I gestured to the west, and the St. Croix. "A strip of water and there's home. Where I was born, where I mostly grew up, and it'd be...right there." I looked out the window; the river was far from here, in spite of the town name. It referred to the little

Kinnickinnic River, not the sprawling St. Croix, which was a tributary of the Mississippi.

"That's fair, I guess," Reed said softly, taking the turn onto a cross street marked Division Street.

We slid through quiet, small-town streets, past older homes, a church, tall oaks, and then an empty soccer field/retention pond, it seemed. Taking a turn onto Wasson Court, we drove down a road that could have been pulled out of any neighborhood in America. It was peaceful, trees stirring in the wind, and green lawns that were a perfect reflection of summer.

At the end of the road was an apartment complex, which stuck out in the midst of all this regular housing. We pulled into the lot and Reed peered at the spots, looking for one that said "Visitor" instead of bearing an apartment number. He found one after some searching and pulled in, and we stepped into the warm day.

"What do you think we're going to find here?" he asked, as we made our way over to the apartment Arche had sent us. "Other than Faith Holloway?"

"Maybe not even her," I said, checking my phone. It was almost two in the afternoon. "She could be at work."

"On a Saturday?" Reed asked. "I suppose. Maybe she works retail."

"Would have been useful to know something about her," I groused. "Maybe Arche could do us a favor and teach Jamal some of her tricks?"

"Doubt those are the tricks he's interested in learning from her," Reed said, with almost a straight face. Not quite, though. My brother was still a guy.

I knocked on the door and waited, my breath almost held, listening for any sound beyond the threshold. I heard movement back there, and someone called, "Just a minute!" in a high-ish female voice.

She opened the door a moment later, and we were greeted by a thin girl who was probably not old enough to buy alcohol, in a tank top that hid what little she offered and boy shorts that revealed pale but well-shaven legs, which was more than I could boast at the moment. Her reaction to us upon opening the door was for her eyes to widen in shock, and to jerk backward a step.

"Faith Holloway?" I asked, catching the door before it had a chance to bounce back and smack her unawares. "I'm...well, you know who I am. Mind if we come in and talk?"

CHAPTER THIRTY-SEVEN

She probably minded, but she invited us in wordlessly anyway, with a hand gesture, as she staggered back from the door on those wobbly, pale, stick-like legs. It might not have been enough of an invitation for a vampire to enter, but Reed and I came in just fine, following her over to a living room area just to the left of the entry, where she collapsed, wordlessly, onto a sectional sofa and looked at us with big eyes.

"Mind if we sit?" I asked, looking past the living area. A small kitchen occupied the back of the apartment, light streaming in from windows there and illuminating the faded linoleum. Back at the entry, a staircase curled in a reverse L up to the second floor, where presumably the bedrooms were.

She gestured to the edge of the sectional. "Sure. How...how did you find me?"

"We have methods available to us that the normal police don't," Reed said, very smoothly.

Faith sagged a little (more). "Oh."

"Can we ask you some questions?" I tried to smile gently

at her. It was always hard to tell how well it worked when I smiled at someone in what I thought was a gentle manner.

She cringed, so I guess I failed. "Okay."

"How did you know Aaron Berry?" I asked, leaping right past bothering to ask *if* she did. I caught Reed's frown out of the corner of my eye, but I was light years ahead. Let her deny it rather than giving her the advantage of asking if she did.

"I mean..." she stared past us, at the window, "...He was my history teacher at Stoaks."

Reed's neck muscles bulged as that one landed, but he and I kept our eyes front. "So you're from Stillwater?"

Faith settled her hands on her skinny knees, which looked red, like she'd been crawling around on them recently. There were carpet imprints on both. "Yeah. I just moved out here last year. You know, to go to college part time. While I'm working."

"Where do you work?" I asked.

"Walmart," she said, near lifelessly. "In Hudson."

A couple small thumps from upstairs drew my attention. Could have been a dog. Could have been a man. Or woman. I listened, but the breathing I heard was too faint to quantify. "Who's that?" I asked.

Faith tensed, balling her hands up, squeezing her kneecaps. "Can we just...not do this today? It's my day off."

"Hm," Reed said, drawing his own conclusion about the noise upstairs. "Let me ask you something – how well did you know Mr. Berry?"

Faith flushed. "He was my teacher, like I said. He was a nice guy."

"He's really nice," I agreed, "but not so nice as to just randomly pay you a thousand bucks every two weeks out of the kindness of his heart, I think."

Another thump from upstairs, louder this time, focused

my thinking. It proceeded in a steady series, thumping down the stairs until a little blond head became visible, peering through the black, wrought-iron balusters at me, at Reed.

"Momma?" the kid called. It was a boy, two years old, max. "Momma? Who that?"

I looked at Faith Holloway, and she looked wrecked, all the color washed out of her already pale face, and I knew the secret she'd been so determined to keep hidden.

Because the kid on the stairs was – obvious as hell, really, just by one look at him – Aaron Berry's son.

With a former student.

CHAPTER THIRTY-EIGHT

"I was eighteen when it happened," Faith blurted out, like a solitary gunshot in the silence that followed the dropped bomb of a revelation that our client – so very innocent, it seemed – had knocked up an entirely different student. "I was out of school. Had been for months. I ran into Mr. Berry in a store – and we talked. And...then..." She waved a hand futilely as the little boy came down the stairs and scrambled across the gulf between us like he was crossing a minefield. He vaulted into the safety of his mother's lap and then peered at Reed, then me, as suspiciously as any reasonable person should.

"Okay," I said, trying to fill the silence while I gathered my thoughts, which had been blown all to hell with this revelation. "So...then this happened," I pointed at the little boy, "and you decided to...what? Keep it off the books?"

"I liked Mr. Berry - Aaron," Faith said, "but we weren't in love. And I knew what it would do to his career if the parents found out he had a child with a former student."

"Especially one only a few months former," Reed said. "I can see why you decided to keep quiet. Very altruistic.

Although the more cynical part of me wonders if maybe that tax-free $26,000 a year he pays you has anything to do with it...?"

Faith flushed a bright scarlet. "He wanted to take care of his son. To be involved in his life. But he knew what it would look like if anyone found out." Her lips curled like she smelled something sour. Maybe her kid's feet, because I could smell 'em from here, and they were a little rank. "Imagine what this news would do for his defense."

"Yeah, his defense is pretty well toast at this point," Reed said. "The only way you could destroy it any further would be to launch a nuke from orbit."

"He's a good man," Faith said, blushing bright red all the way down her neck. "What happened between us was a mistake. But he didn't do anything to that other girl. He's not interested in students. He never showed a hint of interest in me until after I graduated."

"Were you, like, out and proud about your relationship?" I asked. "Going on dates in the cities and hanging out at clubs and such? Meeting the parents?"

"No," Faith said, like what I'd said was completely absurd. "We were both aware of the danger if our...relationship became public. Besides, we started as friends, meeting for coffee and talking. It went a different direction for a while, that's all. I was an adult when it happened." She bent her neck slightly to kiss the wild-eyed, staring, smelly little boy on her lap. "I have no regrets."

"I suspect Aaron might have a few if word about this gets out," I said, clapping my own knees for exclamation as I stood. "Nice try hiding it, though. The only reason you probably got away with it is that the police were already so gorged on evidence they didn't feel a need to dig deeper."

"If they look closer, though," Reed said, joining me in

standing, "they'll find you. So you should be ready to answer some questions if they do."

Faith looked away, but she nodded. "Are you going to be able to prove him innocent?"

I exchanged a look with Reed. "You can't prove innocence, you know," I said. "Or at least you're not supposed to have to. The court has to prove guilt, and right now...boy, do they have a lot to work with. But..." I lowered my voice a little. "...that doesn't mean it's over. Just means...wow, does it look bad. Thanks for your time." And I turned to head for the door.

"Please," she said, picking up her kid off her lap so she could stand. "He didn't do this. He wouldn't. He's not that kind of man."

"What kind of man is he?" Reed asked, trailing after me on my path to escape. "I mean...other than the kind who knocks up former students?"

"He's kind," Faith said, following him. "And gentle. He wouldn't hurt anyone. Certainly not someone like a kid."

I glanced back, the open door in my hand, and looked at the little boy on the couch. "I sure hope he wouldn't," I said, and met Faith Holloway's eyes. I think she got what was I alluding to, because she looked away. "Have a good day off, Miss Holloway." Out I went, and when Reed slammed the door behind us, I could have sworn I heard the death knell of our case in the boom that followed.

CHAPTER THIRTY-NINE

"Well, that's the end of that," Reed said as we hooked our turn back onto Main Street in River Falls. The ubiquitous trees that girded the heart of this town gave it such a lush look. One of the prettier small towns I'd been through, really. "I guess we should meet up with the team and help finish up the move?"

I stared out the windshield. Clouds were floating by overhead, and one was blocking the sun. Just a little; the skies around it were still blue, and the beams of light were making the puffy white mass almost glow. "I don't think so," I said, rubbing my chin.

Reed turned to look at me. "...Why not?"

I pursed my lips, deep in thought. "Something's...not right."

Reed made an exasperated grunt. "You already admitted you didn't look into Berry's sexual proclivities. Clearly, he does have a thing for students. He was blackout drunk the night he did it; it's perfectly reasonable for him not to have a memory of something that awful if he was that messed up." He shook his head. "Come on, Sienna. This thing is over."

"Think about the underwear, though," I said, my phone buzzing in my pocket. "Yes, this is bad. But two things can be possible at once: Berry has slept with a former student in the past. Bad judgment? Yep. Two, he's not a murderer, and the evidence against him is circumstantial because someone is framing him. Hang on." I answered the call and put it on speaker. "Hello, Paula. Can't pretend I'm not surprised to hear from you."

"Why'd you have to go looking for her?" Paula's voice was wrung out. "Why couldn't you have just left that alone and proven him innocent, like I asked?"

"Because we don't control where the evidence leads," Reed snapped back, "and when you tried to hide it, you made it impossible to ignore."

"He's right, Paula," I said. "You block us, we go around. You cooperate, we're left with much less suspicion."

"Okay, fine," she sobbed after a pause. "Can you meet with me? I want to clear the air about this."

I looked at Reed, he shrugged in reply. "Sure," I said, because we literally had nothing else going on. "Where?"

"Hudson?" she asked. "It's between me and River Falls. I could be there in about thirty minutes."

"Okay," I said. "Target parking lot?" I'd seen the Target right off the I-94 freeway, and it seemed a noticeable landmark. "2:45?"

"I'll be there," she said, and hung up abruptly.

Reed looked tense, hunched over the wheel. "What do you think is going to happen when we talk to her? Contrition? Confession?" He raised an eyebrow. "Assassination?"

"If she wants to try and kill us, I'd almost welcome it at this point," I said, staring at the flat fields as River Falls gave way to the empty farm lands between these towns. "But I kinda doubt that's what's coming. At least...not just yet."

CHAPTER FORTY

Paula was about five minutes late, pulling up at the far, empty edge of the Target parking lot in Hudson as promised, her eyes red and swollen from her tears, and her hands empty of any possible weapons. Her Chevy Aveo glided in next to us and she threw open the door, sniffling and wiping her nose as she got out.

"You had to know we'd find out," I said, figuring I'd hit her with the immediate broadside first. I was running out of patience and out of time, and not feeling all that much pity.

She rubbed her nose on her shirt, then dabbed her eyes with the same part of her sleeve. I could feel Reed cringe even though his back was turned to me. "I didn't think it mattered," she finished lamely. "She told me what she said to you. So now you know. But you also know that it wasn't like...well, this."

"I don't know that it's going to matter if this goes in front of a jury," Reed said. "It gets admitted into evidence or, hell, just gets reported on the news, the only thing people are going to hear is that he slept with a student before. Why wouldn't he again?"

"As far as behaviors go," I said, "this one's not going to add any jurors to his side. Except maybe the pedos in the audience."

"But he didn't do it," Paula sniffed.

I folded my arms and leaned on the car roof. "Doesn't matter. How do you think a prosecutor is going to present it at trial?" Which they were conducting these days in the Cube, oddly enough. A huge departure from the days when I ran the place and justice was dispensed at the point of my knuckles. Or, in one memorable case, from the barrel of my shotgun.

"It's going to look terrible," Paula said, hanging her head. "But he still didn't do it."

"Is that what you were hiding from us earlier?" Reed asked. "What you did at his apartment?"

She sniffed, wiping her nose. "Yeah. When they arrested him, they had...I don't know, probable cause or whatever, but they didn't have a search warrant for the place. So I went in and gathered up all the stuff that might point them to Faith before they got back and did the full search. I was just trying to..." She sniffed again, head still bowed.

"Well, you could have saved us most of a morning that we spent hunting this down working on proving him innocent instead," I said. "So...anything else you want to tell us? Because time's starting to run short."

"Nothing I can think of," Paula said sadly. "You're...you're not going to make it, are you?"

I looked at Reed. "Well, just to be clear: we have basically no leads, and in...what? Less than thirty-six hours now, we're going to have to leave the state, probably forever, so..." I shrugged, doing the math in my head. "...It doesn't look promising."

"I'm sorry," Paula sniffled. She didn't look like a girl who cried much, if ever. "I should have just said."

"You can go ahead and squirrel that guilt away for later," Reed said. "Right now we should get moving." He flashed his phone screen at me. "We have an appointment in St. Paul at...what? Seven? Eight tonight?"

"Quick question," I said, looking back to Paula. "Did Aaron have any enemies? Anyone who disliked him?" I screwed up my face in concentration. "Faith's parents, maybe?"

"Um, I don't think they know who the father is," Paula said, thinking about it for a second. "And the other...I mean, he doesn't always get along great with some of his older co-workers? Otherwise, no. And I wouldn't call any of them an enemy."

"Got a name we could look into?" Reed asked. "Anybody?"

"Um," Paula thought about it, eyes glazing over and looking into the distance. "Kellen Henderson, I guess? He's the math teacher for the older kids. He and Aaron argued sometimes."

"About what?" I asked.

"Just teaching styles," Paula said. "Aaron was more new age, I guess? Mr. Henderson, he's old, a fixture at the place."

"The very definition of old school, being that he's old, and in the school," I said.

"I guess." Paula wiped her nose on her sleeve again. "But I can't imagine any of their arguments over teaching style making him want to frame Aaron for rape and murder. And using a student to do it?" She shuddered.

"Let me inform you of something, since it appears you haven't met with Aaron's defense attorney yet," I said, leaning hard on the car. "Presumption of innocence is a fun legal term, but when you've got an overwhelming surfeit of evidence against you, that presumption vanishes, especially in heinous crimes. Aaron's in a hole, and in order to just get back to ground level of 'presumed innocent,' he's going to need to not only explain away the mountain of evidence he's buried under, he's going to have to provide a compelling theory as to why he's not guilty."

"I know," she said. "I know. I just have no idea who would do this to him."

"Yeah, I'm struggling to see anyone else who would do it, either," Reed said, too cute by half. I got it; Paula didn't. Reed was starting to believe that Aaron had done it.

"We'll go kick some anthills," I said. "See what scurries out." I thumped the roof of the car and slid back inside. "Call us if you think of anything else."

"I will," Paula said, leaning down to look at me through Reed's open door. "And I'm sorry. Really."

I didn't say anything to that. I didn't need to. She was already tasting the consequences of wasting our precious investigatory time. We drove off without saying another word, not one of affirmation, nor absolution, leaving Paula standing there in the empty parking lot, wondering if she'd just cost her boyfriend his freedom.

CHAPTER FORTY-ONE

"I don't see how he's not guilty," Reed said as we slid back across the bridge into Minnesota for umpteenth time in the last two days. "I know there's not always truth to that old, 'Where there's smoke, there's fire,' adage, but in this case..." He tilted his head, staring out the window in the slowly setting sun. "...Where there's a guy who'd diddle a former student..."

"Maybe there's a guy who's willing to diddle a fourteen-year-old and then kill her so stupendously that they bring in superheroes to investigate?" I shook my head. "Which begs a question that I'm hoping we get answered by the autopsy: What's the *us* of this whole equation?"

"You mean why do they think a meta killed her?" Reed asked. "Don't know. I imagine they're saving that for the trial."

"Hm," I said, shaking my head. "Nope. I'm not sold on that explanation. There has to be a reason. Something atypical. Something beyond damage to the body by someone strong. Something else got done to her. Something distinctly metahuman. And that's why I don't think Berry was the guy."

Reed chuckled. "I get that there's a disconnect between getting sexually entangled with an eighteen-year-old former student and getting in with one who's fourteen and current – but it's not nearly as thick of a line as you're making it out to be. It feels like for most people, one's beyond the pale and the other is–"

"Fifteen thousand light-years beyond it," I said. "Let's be absolutely clear about this: I can frown on Aaron Berry fathering a child with an eighteen-year-old former student. I think it's shitty, and exhibits bad judgment, because he's probably playing on at least the trace remains of the power dynamic between them when he was her teacher and she was his student. But still, it's legal. If he did anything with Greta Oliver? It's fucking not. Period. No equivocation. She cannot consent, he has power over her as her teacher, and it's really frigging gross."

Reed nodded slowly. "Point."

"But you know why I really don't think that it's him?" I leaned against my palm, feeling the strain of the tendons in my wrist from the weight of my head. I was tired, hungry, irritable, and something that had been nagging me since the beginning of the day was blossoming, full-flower into my mind. "No one's tried to kill me yet."

Reed blinked. "Someone doesn't try and kill you on every case."

"No," I said, "but on the major ones, they do. And you cannot tell me this is not a major case. We've already agreed, this waterfall of evidence? Is not natural. Berry's odious character aside for this Faith Holloway thing, there is someone doing him wrong for some reason – and they killed and abused a fourteen-year-old to make it happen."

"Maybe," Reed said, frowning. "But when you asked Paula that question, there wasn't a lot of direction for us to go.

Investigation-wise, I mean. What would we even poke at? That Henderson guy?"

"I don't know," I said, "all I know is that when I'm scaring people who have a murder secret, they try and kill me. Just like when you're over the target, you catch the most flak. We're getting zero flak."

"Because so far all we've done is turn up stuff that improves the state's case," Reed said. "Is that your contention?"

"Yes," I said. "If we were knocking over pieces of evidence as plants and sniffing up the right track? I guarantee we'd be spooking the person behind this, and they'd be trying to kill us. Because murderers in our world are never content to try and quit while they're ahead. So this person, whoever they are? They're not afraid right now. At all. And small wonder, given how much we've buried Aaron in the last couple days with our findings."

"You're making some sense here," Reed said grudgingly. "But that still leaves us with the question: where do we look next? Because it seems like we've got ourselves a proper dead end, and our only lead is a very tepid recommendation from the girlfriend saying that he had a rival at school."

"I don't feel like we got a complete picture of Greta's situation," I said. "I feel as if we got like a blurry snapshot, at best. If you're asking me where I think we go with the investigation, I say we fill in the gaps on her school life. You heard Arche; school people and her parents were all she talked to."

"But you don't think it was the parents?" Reed asked.

"The father was a little suspicious," I said, "but not a lot. So I'm not putting them first on my list. They're more of a double back and check later, the next time we run into a dead end."

"So who do you want to check with now?" Reed asked. "That Kellen Henderson?"

I shook my head slowly. "No." Then I told him who I wanted to talk to.

He was not pleased. And I couldn't really blame him.

CHAPTER FORTY-TWO

Headmaster Prestegaard was spending the afternoon in a coffee shop in Oakdale, according to a cell phone trace reluctantly performed by ArcheGrey, at the nagging of Jamal, who was busy driving Reed's car back to load the next apartment.

"We already talked to this guy once," Reed said, slamming his door as we got out of the rental car. "What do you think a second round is going to turn up? Other than him immediately calling the cops because of how you lied to him last time?"

"I prefer to think optimistically," I said, walking across the parking lot. Some dude strolling along under the awning of the mini mall the coffee shop was located in had his phone out and was clearly filming me. I heard him mutter under his breath something about it being awesome that he'd just seen Sienna Nealon. "Hey, how's it going?" I called to him.

"He's probably livestreaming this, you know," Reed said, meta-low. "We need to hurry."

"Slay Queen!" the guy called. I nodded back, smiling tightly, as Reed held open the door to the coffee shop for me.

When we walked in, Headmaster Prestegaard was sitting in an overstuffed chair next to a dormant fireplace, a book in his hand, his glasses low on his nose.

"Excuse me?" I asked, shuffling up to him so as not to surprise him. He looked different today; his hair was not as carefully combed, and he was in cargo shorts and a T-shirt with NEW YORK JETS on it. "Headmaster Prestegaard?"

He glanced up at me through the thick-rimmed but thin-lensed glasses, and I caught a moment of calculation; a hint of anger, but it settled quickly, and disappeared with a sigh. "Call me Dan."

I slipped into the chair across from him. It was comfortable, and the scent of strong coffee and a little chocolate lingered in the air. "I appreciate the magnanimity," I said.

He sighed again, a hint of irritation slipping out. "I wish you'd just told me why you were there. I like to think I'm a decent guy. I believe in due process, and that Aaron deserves a chance to mount a defense. I would have talked to you just the same." He hesitated. "Though I probably wouldn't have allowed the girls to. That was a mistake on my part...anyway. How did you find me?"

"We have means available to us that are beyond those of the police, let's say," Reed answered for me.

He settled back in the chair, putting the book down and folding his hands over it on his chest. "So you violated my privacy." He looked sidelong out the window. "I guess I shouldn't be surprised, given what you did at the school." He looked back at us, and I had this feeling that this was what it was like when a father was disappointed in you. "What do you want?"

"We have plumbed the depths of all the leads we had," I said. "And obviously it got a little...crazy after we talked with you. We left a little earlier than we might have wanted to. I was hoping we could ask you a few more questions?"

Another long sigh. "I suppose. If it helps Aaron. I owe him that much."

"Uhm," I said, figuring it would be best if I just laid it all out, "I read his mind – at his request. He has no memory of killing Greta, or of leaving his place on the night in question."

Dan's brows furrowed. "Really? That's good, then. It means it was someone else, right?"

"Maybe," I said. "Just because he doesn't have a memory of doing it – well, it doesn't mean he didn't. But let's just say I'm inclined to believe him, because things keep popping up in the investigation that suggest someone's trying to frame him."

"What kind of things?" Dan asked. "I mean, the police came out again yesterday, after your visit, and the girls..." He sighed, putting his head down. "Sorry. It's just...what a nightmare. For the students, you know?"

"It's probably going to hurt you some, too, isn't it?" Reed asked.

"Oh, I should say so," Dan said, surprisingly levelly. "Two girls were abused by a teacher under my nose? Yeah, the buck stops with me. So I'll probably be out of a job. And I'm too young to retire, too old to outrun this blemish on my reputation. Which was spotless before this happened." He offered us a tight smile. "Come to think of it, maybe I have an ulterior motive for wanting Aaron to be innocent. And I do. I want him to be innocent. It's a lot easier for me to think that the guy I knew all these years was decent, and he loved the kids – and not for the reason of wanting to prey on them."

"Totally understandable," I said. "Can you tell us a little about the rivalry between Aaron and Kellen Henderson?"

A flicker of surprise echoed in his cool eyes. "You heard about that? Look, any faculty is going to have chemical sort of differences in personalities. You ever meet someone and just not like them from the jump?"

"All the time," I said. Reed gave me a withering glare. "What? I'm trying not to lie to him. Again."

Dan chuckled. "That was Kellen and Aaron. Kellen's an older gentleman, been with the school since before I started, and when I came on as headmaster, he and I butted heads. He didn't respect me, a stranger, coming in and making all these changes. It took a few years for us to build up to that level of mutual respect. He's...prickly."

"I like him already," I said.

"You'd change your mind if you met him," Dan said with amusement. "He's an acquired taste. Not a bad guy, just...the kids like him well enough. Knows his stuff. Our kids that pass Trig and Chemistry and Algebra with him? They get rave reviews from their college professors. They know within the first week of class if this was a Stilloaks kid. That's down to Kellen."

"But he and Aaron had beef between them?" Reed asked.

"They had disagreements," Dan crossed his legs, laying the book down on his lap. "Again, down to that chemistry thing. Kellen has his way: it's very by-the-book, established, 'this is what works,' whereas Aaron is more on the bleeding edge. Again, both methods have their merits, and at Stilloaks we've always been willing to try new things. They taught completely different subjects, so there wasn't much reason for them to argue; it's not like they had immense influence over each other."

"But Henderson was more senior?" I asked. "He had some kind of sway over Aaron's job?"

"No," Dan said. "Absolutely not."

"Interesting," I said. "So you don't think that whatever was between them would rise to the level of motive for...any of this?" Trying to be delicate.

"I should think not," Dan said. "Unless Kellen is secretly a sociopath, and I really doubt that. He's strongly passionate about people, about doing the things the right way, about the kids."

"Okay, well," Reed said, "if you don't mind, we'd like to talk to him."

"I don't mind, I'll give you his info," Dan said, messing with his phone. "But it's up to him whether he wants to talk to you."

"Another question," I said. "Is there anyone else you know of that was having any difficulty with Aaron?"

Dan settled back in the chair, looking up at the ceiling. "I don't think so. He got along pretty well with everybody. I don't think I ever heard him even raise his voice with anyone but Kellen."

"What about students?" I asked. "Were there any students – prior to this, I mean – that had an axe to grind with Mr. Berry?"

Dan sat up a little straighter in his seat. "Look...faculty lounge gossip is one thing. But I can't give you information about students when you're not directly involved in the investigation."

"Oh, I don't need specifics," I said, "I'm just asking in general: is there anyone in the student body who you know would have a grudge against Berry?"

He chuckled weakly. "Anyone he's ever given a bad grade to, I suppose, though I doubt it would rise to the level of malice needed for...murder and...all this." I could see he felt as much need to dance around the ugly edges of this one as I did.

"Did he give a lot of bad grades?" Reed asked.

Dan paused, sucking his lip. "You know...I don't think he did. That was probably one of the key areas where he disagreed with Kellen. Kellen's a rough grader. Very into the idea of the bell curve, you know? I had to put a stop to his policy of pushing passing grades down into the fail range in order to fit his ideas about averages. But Aaron?" He shook his head. "He's failed very few students, to my knowledge. And given that a failing grade is something I would see...yeah, he doesn't hand out many. Maybe a couple a year, tops, and always well-deserved."

Out the window, I saw my "friend" with the phone camera bob into view, pointing his weapon of choice through the glass and peering in, holding his hand over his face to cut through the glare, presumably. He saw me and waved.

I waved back, still wearing that tight, plastic smile. "Did any of the students he graded poorly take it...badly?"

A jaded look rolled over Headmaster Prestegaard's face. "Look...I don't know what you think my student body is, but..." He looked around, as if afraid to be overheard, and lowered his voice. "...They're mostly rich kids, okay? Some of their parents don't often tell them no, which means when I have to, it can result in...unpleasantness. It's a tight balance we walk at Stilloaks, trying to keep the parents happy but also enforcing high academic standards."

"Bet it makes you long for the days of the boarding schools where the parents just handed the kids over and expected them to take a good flogging for misbehavior," I joked. Probably joked.

"You're not wrong," he said with a wry smile. "Anyhow...yeah, a few kids have reacted poorly to receiving bad grades. From any teacher, not just Aaron. As to who...I can't tell you. That violates student privacy."

"Hm," I said. "Greta kept a very tight circle, it seems. You don't know of any enemies she had in school?"

"Greta was one of our best students," Dan said. "I never saw her in my office for a disciplinary matter – except once, and she was the accomplice with some other girls who'd gotten into mischief. Definitely not the ringleader, and embarrassed to be there, I would say."

"Would that be the girls we met yesterday?" Reed asked.

"I can't say." Dan looked pained, like he wanted to, but was caught. "Look...nothing that happened with her in that case would rise to a level beyond what I would consider basic, ordinary mischief associated with the age group. If you're looking for some sign that any of my kids were working their way up to murder, I can tell you – there's nothing that would suggest it. I've met some real bad kids in my education career. You know the kind, I'm guessing; the sort where you look in their eyes, and the void stares back at you."

"I've met a few like that, yes," I said. "But you haven't seen any in your crop?"

"No," Dan said, "not in years. Some bad seeds every now and again, but this has been a good crew. All my troubles are minor." He sighed. "Or were, until now. I guess I'm making up for lost time with this one."

"Thank you for your help," I said, rising to my feet. "For what it's worth, I am sorry that I lied to you to try and get you to cooperate. And I appreciate you giving Aaron the help. He's going to need it."

"I would never have guessed this from him," Dan said, looking wistful. "But then, if this came from someone else Greta knew, at school...I would never have guessed it from any of them, either. So maybe my estimations aren't worth much. Either way, I hope you find the truth." He smiled up at me, mirroring my tight one, because he'd just done something that was probably unpleasant for him, talking all this over. "Good luck."

"Thank you," I said, and headed for the door, Reed trailing a step behind me through the tightly packed tables in the coffee house. Luckily it was nearly abandoned on this Saturday afternoon, otherwise we'd have been fighting through people all the way.

"You know what I'll miss about Minnesota?" Reed asked

as I held the door for him this time. "Caribou Coffee." He glanced at the coffee shop. "Though I guess there are locations in other parts of the country."

"Life's chock full of sacrifices," I said, nodding at the guy still filming me. He tittered wildly at my acknowledgment, bellowed something else about SLAY QUEEN and about missing me, and I tried to acknowledge it without engaging, just a wave of the hand or something.

"Well, what the hell are we supposed to do now?" Reed asked as we stepped off the curb and he came up alongside me. "Question Kellen Henderson?"

"Do you see any other leads leaping out at us?" I asked, heading for the car. There was a low rumble nearby, some dull undertone in the background noise I was trying to put a finger on. I looked up, looked around–

Just in time to see a semi-truck jump the curb and lumber into the parking lot at over fifty miles an hour.

Headed straight for us.

CHAPTER FORTY-THREE

"Um..." Reed said, pointing at the truck. "...um...um..."

The engine on the big truck roared as it accelerated toward us. It smashed aside a Tesla, then a Honda minivan, then ripped right through our rental car, crushing the three vehicles under its carriage like they were nothing. The trailer hooked to the back of the vehicle bounced hard over the curbs separating the road from the parking lot, causing the trailer to bobble.

I saw the big truck's grill getting closer and closer by the millisecond, and I snaked an arm out and wrapped it around my brother's waist like the love interest in a movie. "Don't kiss me for luck," I said–

Then I leapt into the air as the tractor trailer ran through the space beneath us, the top of the trailer not-so-gently clipping the sole of Reed's shoe. He grunted in pain, and the truck went on beneath us, smashing into the tutoring business two doors down from the coffee shop and coming to an abrupt stop.

"You okay?" I asked, scanning the area around us from thirty feet up. I couldn't see anyone watching us other than the guy with the camera, who was still filming the whole thing.

"Other than a turned ankle, I'm fine," Reed said through gritted teeth. "Put us back on the ground?"

"Sure," I said, "though even Minnesota cops would have a hard time getting mad at me for hovering at this height. That's way below the airspace requirements."

I brought us down near where the tractor trailer had smashed into the building, on the driver's side. It was popped open, and the driver was grunting, trying to crawl out but favoring his side.

"Hey," he said, nodding when he saw us, "you okay?"

"No thanks to you," Reed said. I sensed the tension of his body where I still had him around the waist. He wanted to throttle the guy. "What the hell was that?"

"My truck," he said, grunting as he took the last step down. He cringed hard, and I could tell he'd done a little damage to himself coming to such an abrupt stop. "It was like it got possessed or something. I couldn't turn the wheel, couldn't get the brakes to go, couldn't make the pedal stop accelerating. Nothing worked."

Some of the tension bled out of Reed as that hit home. "So it just...malfunctioned?"

"I guess," the driver said, still cradling himself. Sirens were blaring in the background; cops and paramedics were on their way. I shot a look over my shoulder. Our rental car was utterly destroyed, the engine pressed flatter than Paris Hilton. "Never had anything like that happen before." He reached up and doffed his hat, revealing some seriously mussed, over-long and alopecia-ridden scalp. "Ever. And I been doing this a long while."

"Come on," I said, tugging at Reed. "We gotta go."

He wheeled on me. "Are you kidding? Leaving the scene of an accident?"

"We weren't involved," I said. "Thus we're not obligated to stay. And I'm not pressing charges on this guy. Are you?" I gave him a look of great significance.

"Right," he said, settling down a notch. He turned on the driver. "Help's on the way. Try and stay out from behind the wheel...maybe ever, in the future, because..." He looked over the damage; the storefront was obliterated, the trailer buried in almost halfway through the front windows. Glass was everywhere, and the smell of engine exhaust, pointed and oily, hung thick around us. "...Yikes."

"Are you kidding?" he looked mournfully at his truck. "Like a ghost took control of the damned rig. How am I even going to explain this to insurance?"

"Call it an accident," I said. "Because if you call it anything else, they're not paying up." I grabbed Reed by the arm and started to drag him away.

He complied, letting me pull him off the side of the parking lot, down a short, grassy hill as we headed around the back of the strip mall. The sirens were getting close, and I didn't want to get seen at the scene. It'd be a prime way for Minnesota BCA to reacquire us, or worse still, dart and arrest us, holding us for the next thirty-two hours until we were in violation of the new state law and they could just send us right to the Cube. "What the hell was that?" Reed asked once we were around the building and heading into a leafy copse of trees.

"That...was flak," I said with a small, satisfied smile. "Which means I think...for maybe the first time in this case...we're getting close to the target."

CHAPTER FORTY-FOUR

"So that was an assassination attempt?" Reed asked, as we loped through a softly wooded area of Oakdale, Minnesota. We were sticking to the trees as much as possible, and the sirens summoned to the crime scene behind us were receding in the distance as we covered ground at a meta-jog. Which was like a sprint for normal people.

"Yep," I said. "A clumsy one, posing as a random accident, but I think we can safely say that was an attempted kill."

"Well, you asked for it," Reed deadpanned, "so I guess you get what you wish for."

I chuckled. "Maybe."

He paused for a second, catching me by the elbow. "You do thrive on danger, don't you?"

I sighed, looking back at him. "I mean...probably? Yeah. I'd say so. Why? That a problem?"

"For the people who love you?" he asked, breaking back into a jog. "Yes. But only because we want you around, and violence directed at you would tend to decrease the likelihood of that happening. One way or another."

It took me a second to reason through what he meant

there; he was talking about how if I got killed, I'd be gone. But also about how if I went too far in stopping someone coming at me...I might also be gone, thanks to the current heavy and ever-increasing restrictions on my use of force, at least in Minnesota. "We all gotta go sometime," I said, trying to blow off his concern.

He stopped again, catching my elbow. "This is not a joke."

"Come on," I said, "some Magneto-type just clumsily threw a tractor-trailer at us. At us! People who can fly. That's at least a little funny. Or sad, maybe, depending on how serious they thought they were being."

"None of this is funny," Reed seethed, surging ahead of me as he broke back into a run. "Not the crime. Not the fact that if Berry actually is innocent, he's being framed. Everywhere hope pops up for this guy, it gets slammed down."

"But clearly we just hit a nerve for someone," I said. "I think interviewing Prestegaard suggests that whoever is behind this? They don't want us looking at the school."

"Unless," Reed said, puffing slightly as we took a hard turn to avoid the end of the treeline, "this is Paula or someone else in his personal life trying to convince us with that clumsy hit attempt that we're on the right track."

"Maybe," I said, following the bend in the treeline. I could still hear the sirens, though they were quite distant at this point. Less clear was what to do next, other than run. "Though that's convoluted."

"Well, it's not as stupid as trying to whack someone when they're on the supposed 'right track,'" Reed said, and now he came to a stop again, putting his knuckles on his belt, leaving his elbows out. "Where are we even going now? We have no car."

"I did notice that, being as it was ground beneath the wheels of the semi trailer."

"What's your plan, then?" he asked, breathing a little heavier. "Other than running from the cops?"

"Yeah," I said. "Who knows what they'll do, so let's just stay out of their grasp."

"I agree with that," he said, "Because I don't want to get darted and held in the Cube until the time to run is out and they hand us over for violating the state law. What I'm saying is...what do we do? Where do we go?"

"Well," I said, doing a little heavier breathing myself, "being as my theory of this thing is now bending toward Stilloaks Prep being key to the murder and the frame job, I say our next move is to find that teacher, Kellen Henderson, and ask him some questions. Then...I don't know." I paused, putting my own hands on my hips. "Hey, you remember that gal outside the office yesterday?"

"The 'cool' chick with the old world name?" Reed asked. "Isolde?"

"Yeah, her," I said. "You remember where she said she hung out on weekends? Some club around here?"

"Club Labyrinth, I think," Reed said, frowning. "Whatever that is."

I pulled out my phone and looked it up. "Hm. Looks like it is in fact a club, for teens and the youth here in Oakdale." I looked up. "I say we hit it tonight, see if we can find her. Push her for an intro to some of the other movers and shakers at Stilloaks. Take what we now know about some of the dynamics of the place and, uh...ask around among the cool kids."

"Okay," Reed said. "We also need to visit Kevin at the coroner's office when he gets on shift. Say...seven? Eight, maybe?"

"Since we're making a list of things we want," I said, "I'd also like a full night's sleep, at Ariadne's, for the last time. I want to be able to say goodbye to her, especially since she's put up with my drunken bullshit. I owe her a decent farewell."

"That's totally fair," Reed said. "Here's a question, though: how do we get to our next destination? Should we warn the others about the scrutiny on us falling on them? Because if Shipley is pissed enough at you and me to turn loose BCA with dart guns a blazin'–"

"It's not a stretch to imagine she'd do so on our friends, that's what you're saying?" I chewed my lip. "Good point. They might need to dodge the cops, too."

"Yeah," Reed said, phone already up to his ear, dialing. "Hey, Scotty. How's it going?" He flicked the speakerphone button.

"We just finished up at Augustus's place," Scott said, sounding a little wheezy. "Moving on to Jamal's. You sure you don't want us to get yours, too? We're making good progress here."

"No, Isabella has got it," Reed said. "Listen, Scott, BCA is still dogging us right now, and we're a little concerned they're going to expand their operations to include you all, too. How much more do you have to do?"

"Jamal's place, then Eilish's," Scott said. "I'm leaving mine to movers my dad's paying for. Another few hours, we could beat feet to Hudson. Maybe be out of the state by tonight, if you need us to."

"It's a good idea, Scott," I said. "My handlers said that they're ready to dart first, ask questions later, and it seems to us that the logical play is to keep us in custody for the day and a little more until the law takes effect. Then they've got us on a felony, and we're in the Cube for a bit."

"That's some dirty pool," Scott said. "But I could see Shipley doing that. She does hate you. All right, we'll hustle up here and get done ASAP. What about you guys? Where are you heading next?"

I looked at Reed; he looked at me. "Depends," I said. "Is Jamal there?"

"Yeah," Scott said. "Just a sec."

There was movement in the background, and a few seconds later, Jamal came on. "Hey. Y'all in some trouble?"

"You know it," I said. "Lost our rental car in a tragic metahuman-induced accident."

Jamal let out a low whistle. "I was monitoring east side police traffic online and heard the truck thing in Oakdale. That what you're talking about?"

"It is," I said. "Do they know we're involved yet?"

"No," Jamal said, "but they got a low-key BOLO out on you already. Not to detain you, but rather to let any local that runs across you report your position to BCA immediately so they can show up in force."

"You guys need to wrap this moving up quick," Reed said. "You definitely need to get out of the state tonight, this bull-shit about waiting until tomorrow at midnight is turning into exactly that. They're going to put us in jail before we can even get out."

"Sounds about right," Jamal said. "We'll hustle. You need anything else?"

"No." I traded a look with Reed. "Just...stay safe."

Jamal just laughed. "You might want to take that advice yourself, you know?" He hung up.

He wasn't wrong.

CHAPTER FORTY-FIVE

Jamal found us the least advanced rideshare that he possibly could, a guy named Marty, who seemed very much in the mold of my favorite driver, Tom, from over on the west side. He grunted when we entered his Hyundai, and said nothing as he pressed the accelerator, our destination address already visible on the GPS built into the dashboard.

When we arrived at an immaculately kept, if small, house in White Bear Lake a few minutes later, Marty didn't say anything. Reed gave him a solid tip and five stars, and asked, "We're only going to be a few minutes. Want to wait for us?"

Marty grunted noncommittally, but he didn't drive off the moment we got out of the car. Instead, he reached over onto the seat next to him and pulled out a well-worn paperback copy of *Marine Sniper*. I nodded in respect to his choice and headed for the house.

Kellen Henderson's residence was a split-level that probably dated back to the sixties, built about six or so blocks off of the actual White Bear Lake, playground of Minneapolis-St Paul's east side elites. On the lake itself, the houses were amazing, inspiring, and probably worth millions. A little further out like this and you found normal, middle-class neighborhoods of the sort Henderson lived in. His home was covered in wood siding, painted in a light brown and blue color scheme. Which was a little dated, but it worked.

We climbed the small concrete stairs off the driveway up to the split-level entry, between the basement floor and the upper one, and Reed stabbed the doorbell with surprising viciousness. My brother's whole frame indicated tension, though whether that was because he had just nearly been run over and participated in a not-fun run, or because he'd just had enough of this day, it was impossible for me to say. I stood a couple steps back, though, trying to smooth down my hair, wild from all the action, and make sure my RBF was not on full display when the door swung open.

Which it did moments later, and standing there was a short, white-haired, wrinkled and balding man with thick glasses. "Whaddya want?" he asked, all pretense of Minnesota nice just straight out the window.

"Mr. Henderson?" Reed led. "I'm Reed Treston. This is my associate, Sienna. We're here to ask some questions about–"

"What, do you think I'm stupid?" Henderson asked. "I know who you are. And I know why you're here. You're poking around about that simp Berry, aren't you?" His accent did not seem Minnesotan. It felt transplanted from Jersey.

"No, we're here about the peonies out front," I said. "They're really quite lovely. Do you have some gardening tips?"

Henderson stared at me with the same attitude for a couple seconds, then he chuckled. "I like you. You've got spunk." Then he stepped back from the door. "Well, come in if you're coming in. Don't leave the door open, I'm not paying to air condition this godforsaken sauna of a day." And he retreated slowly up the stairs to the next level of the house, leaving us to come in.

Reed followed him, and I came after, shutting the door quietly. We walked up to the upper level of Henderson's house and found a nice wood-floored design, with an open doorway ahead leading to a kitchen. Henderson retreated within, and I could smell something cooking on the stove, something that involved garlic and onions...no...shallots.

I took the lead since he seemed to like me more than Reed, and entered the kitchen to find a place sparingly decorated. A small table sat in the corner to my left with a microwave on it. Here the wood floors gave way to a gray tile, and stainless steel appliances that looked new. It was a real contrast to the decor of the living room we'd just passed, which seemed to belong to the original house. He'd even had an old, square box TV blaring in the corner, loud enough we could hear the Saturday matinee playing some western.

"So you're the one looking into whether or not Berry was schtupping that girl?" Henderson was focused on whatever he was cooking. Then he walked past the stove top and around a corner, where I heard him rustling in a pantry. He emerged with a giant can of tomatoes and a big plastic container of what looked like granulated sugar. He paused in front of the spice rack next to the stove, then set it all down beside the piping cookware.

"Do you think he was?" Reed asked, leaping right in like an idiot a second later.

Henderson turned to favor him with a look that indicated he felt sure Reed was stupid. "Why don't you let the grownups talk, little boy? You know, before you say something even dumber than that."

Reed's eyebrows rose, and he folded his arms across his chest, then sauntered past me with a wary look as he made his way back toward the living room.

"We heard you and Berry crossed swords about teaching practices," I said, waiting until Reed was out of the room. "But you don't think he did it?"

"I thought he was a jumped-up little shit who was too easy with A's and too friendly with the kids," Henderson said, opening the tomatoes with a manual crank can opener. The garlic and shallots were wildly fragrant, and I found myself covering my nose with my sleeve because of how strong they were. Henderson finished opening the can and dumped the entire contents of whole, peeled tomatoes into the skillet, muting the smell somewhat. "But no...if you'd asked me before this happened if I thought he was messing around with little Greta Oliver? Not a chance in Hades."

I perked up at the mention of my great-grandfather, but then I realized that he was just using it as a turn of phrase. He seemed very intent on stirring and breaking up his tomatoes. A decent amount of basil followed the tomatoes into the pan, and then he stirred with his tomato-spattered wooden spoon. "But now...?" I asked.

"Well, they found the boy's juice in her, and I'm old enough to know that doesn't happen by accident," Henderson said. "So maybe he did. Maybe I misjudged him. Maybe he wasn't being lenient on the kids because he's a soft sister, maybe he was doing it to curry favor to get in their junior-sized panties. I don't know." He shrugged. "A dirty business, that, though. Real dirty. I wouldn't have seen it in him."

"So your arguments with him were just about teaching philosophy?" I asked.

"No," Henderson said, taking a giant spoonful of sugar and dumping it into the tomato mixture. "I didn't like him personally, either. But there's a difference in my world between not liking someone and thinking they're a murdering, perverted skeeze. I thought he was weak on the kids, because he was. I thought his methods of teaching were bound to produce soft, pitiful children unprepared for the world ahead." He shrugged. "But now we're in a soft, weak world, and so maybe I was the one who was wrong, in hindsight. But I recognized that my differences with him were there, on that battleground. Not with his character. I wish I could have predicted that he was this kind of rat, if he is. I have my doubts, in spite of the evidence." He shook his head. "Looked him in the eye a thousand times. Never saw this. But," he said, and looked at me with great significance, "drink has been known to do funny things to a man. Or woman."

I ignored the not-so-subtle jab present there and declined to contemplate how much shit the press must be talking about my own leap from the wagon of late in favor of pursuing the current line of inquiry. "You knew he was an alcoholic?"

Henderson guffawed. "You could smell the whiskey coming out of his pores in the morning. Surprised he didn't just give up the pretense and take his coffee straight Irish." He put another spoonful of sugar in his tomato sauce.

"Do you know why he was drinking?" I asked.

"Because he liked to drink, I imagine," Henderson said, giving his sauce a stir. "Does he need a reason beyond that?"

"Not necessarily," I said. "Anything else you can tell us about him that could help?"

Henderson set down his wooden spoon and looked at me with piercing eyes. "Help who? Him? Or help his victim find justice?"

A tightness in my chest suggested my exasperation was tunneling its way into my physical being. "Anything, really. Mutters and rumors of students. Whispers in the fricking wind. Whatever might suggest there was something else going on here behind the established narrative of a teacher messing around with his student and it going fatally badly."

Henderson paused, thinking deeply. "You know..." He

shook his head. "No. It's probably not even worth mentioning."

"Well, now you have to mention it," I said.

"It's stupid," Henderson said, "and maybe the ramblings of an old man who needs to retire. But...all right." He gave the sauce a gentle stir, clockwise, and the aura of tomatoes and shallots and garlic and sugar and basil all strangely combined in my nose, making me hungry for pasta. "There's something different about the kids this year. Don't ask me for specifics, I couldn't tell you, exactly. It's a thousand little things, mostly in their attitude." He held up a hand. "I know, believe me. Old man bitching about the next generation. But there's something in the air in Stilloaks this year. Kids are always getting sassier. But this year...there was a step change. Especially among the older ones. They're flat-out defiant, in a way I've never seen. But this whole Greta Oliver thing...it also has 'em whispering in the halls, behind the scenes. These are the popular kids I'm talking about, mostly. There's some secret. Maybe it's related, maybe it ain't. I don't know what it is either way. Don't care to." He stirred again, lifting the spoon with a smooth red sauce upon it, then dipped his finger down to catch a dribbling. "Needs more sugar." Then he offered me the spoon.

I caught a dribbling of the sauce on my palm and tried it. He was right; too acidic. "Yeah. So you're saying this feeling of yours...it's about the popular kids? Not the...not unpopular ones? Like Greta?"

"Exactly," Henderson said, dropping another tablespoon of sugar into the mix and beginning to stir. "And I'm not the kind of teacher the cool kids confide in. The only one I can imagine they would is..." He smiled.

"Berry," I said, my mind swirling around the possibilities there. "This begs a natural question. Who's the coolest of the cool kids in Stoaks?"

Henderson blanched, possibly at my question, or my bastardization of the school name. "That's easy. Isolde."

I frozen. "The oversexed girl with the braids?"

"That's her," Henderson said, going back to his stirring. The sugar dissolved into the red like it had never even been dropped in, the sauce turning fully red again. "You've met? Because she's quite the wild card, that one. But bright."

"In passing," I said. At least I knew where she'd be tonight. Or probably, anyway. "Thanks for the info, Mr. Henderson."

Henderson waved us away. "Leave me to my cooking, will you? And get to your truth." He pursed his lips. "If Berry did it, I hope you help put him in jail a long time. If not..." He smiled, almost wistfully. "...well...I wouldn't mind arguing with the sonofabitch again. See yourselves out. I'm busy." And he turned his full attention back to his tomato sauce, apparently nothing else to say to me.

Once Reed and I were out the door, he said, "That was vaguely interesting. Not much of a lead, though."

"Same as all our leads, then," I said "We've been dragging from shit possibility to shittier possibility this whole investigation. We weren't even properly focused on the school, the actual center of her life, until we met with Prestegaard. Talk about chasing our tails at a time when every second is crucial."

Reed hoisted up his phone. "Well, we've got all of thirty-one hours left. What do you want to do next?"

"Three things," I said, in order: "First, check out the actual murder scene. That ought to keep us busy for an hour or so, until Kevin gets on at the coroner's office. Then we, uh...get him to give us the report–"

"Oh?" Reed was smiling at me impishly. "And how are *we* going to go about that? Out of curiosity."

"However we have to," I said, only a little shamefaced. "Within the bounds of the law. Then–"

"Let me guess – go to the club and meet up with Isolde."

I snapped my fingers at him. "Nailed it."

He surveyed the street slowly as we made our way over to Marty's car. He was still waiting. Sunset was a ways off, and the air was warm, almost moist. "All right. Next up – the murder scene. What are you hoping to find there?"

"At this point? Anything I can," I said. "Because so far, it feels like we're just grasping at straws."

CHAPTER FORTY-SIX

The streets of downtown Stillwater were packed, the summertime traffic in the town nearly unbelievable. Coming down off the hill we could see the parking lots filled to the brim all the way up to the edge of the St. Croix River, and suddenly I felt very fortunate to have a driver. He took us down through the mixed streets of the old town with the aged brick, and down to the main road, the St. Croix Trail, pushing us through the traffic until we reached the north end of town and a turnoff just where the buildings ended and the cliffs began their climb again.

"You going to Marina?" Marty asked as he pulled off the road. To our right lay a very definite marina, then one last building with a sign that said The Zephyr, a theater of some sort. Then trees, endless trees, separating road from river.

"No," Reed said.

"Theater?"

"No." Reed pointed to the left-hand turn, which led into a small parking lot shrouded by trees. "There."

"You need another ride?" Marty asked in his strong accent, dropping us in the parking lot.

"Probably a good idea," Reed said, and waggled his phone. "I'm adding an extra large tip for you to wait."

The driver nodded, and we hiked away from the car, Reed checking his phone's GPS. "I think it's just down here," he said as we reached a yellow perimeter of crime scene tape.

"What was your first clue, detective?" I asked, dipping under the tape and finding myself on a steep slope down to the river without a lot of mercy. One false step and I was going to end up in the drink. I studied it for a moment, rolled my eyes and said, "Whatever," and just drifted down in hover mode.

"That's cheating," Reed said, apparently unwilling to disturb the sensitivity of the scene with the high winds it'd take to loft his ass down. "I'll wait here, I guess."

"Be my eye in the sky," I said, taking the short, steady drop down to the shore. There wasn't much to stand on down here, mostly a marshy promontory that was more swamp than actual riverbank. In the distance, I could see a white riverboat starting a slow cruise down the St. Croix, paddlewheel slapping against the river and jovial passengers clinking glasses and laughing. The glorious sun was trending lower in the sky, but it wouldn't set until much later.

This was Minnesota in the summer.

This was the part I'd miss.

I hovered a foot above the water, on the near impassable bank, and called up to Reed, "I don't know how he got down here."

"Probably just dumped the body from here," my brother called back. He was only a few feet above me, maybe five or so, but it was enough. "Killed her up here, maybe?"

"We need that coroner's report," I muttered, flying low over the rocky bank. "Look at this. No white chalk outlines–"

"They only use those when they're moving a person who's still alive."

"–no shell casings, no flags left behind to mark pieces of physical evidence. All we've got is a riverbank without a single sign that anything bad happened here." I swept up the shore about thirty feet where a small, sandy beach about six feet in length sat under the eaves of a pine. Settling my feet upon it, I stared up, then down the river, watching a red speed boat motor past. "What the hell are we supposed to get from this? We're so late to this investigation there's nothing left."

"Like being invited to the party after the buffet table's been picked over," Reed called down to me. The burbling of the river as it passed didn't stop me from hearing him. "I'm not sure, given the constraints, this one's going to produce any leads."

It'd hardly be the first case I'd failed, given how many I'd touched over my years. But to fail this one as I was just coming back to the profession from a long interval with my other addiction–

I shook my head. "No. There has to be a way."

Reed sighed. "Sure. Get the coroner's report, hope there's something in there."

"No," I said, looking across the river to Wisconsin, my temporary promised land and deliverance. "We need more."

"Fine," Reed said, "we talk to Isolde, see what we can unravel from the student body."

"That's not enough." This much I knew.

"Well, what else do you propose?" Reed asked with a sudden, surprising burst of exasperation. "Because if you're seeing other options, I'd like to know. Psychic visions? Pretty sure Harry took those with him. Telepathy to get to the heart of the problem? I wish you could control it, but speaking as someone who felt the effects of you trying it just the other night, please no. So..." He shrugged. "What else? You want to try and travel through time to witness the murder? Cuz that could be useful. How about we just–"

I looked up from my feet so quickly I thought my neck might break. "What'd you say?"

His eyes narrowed. "I think I was about to propose finding a bloodhound sort of meta to–"

"No, before, the time travel thing," I said, "but never mind. I don't need to hear it again."

"What?" Reed peered down at me. "Sienna, you can't be serious."

"Shhhhh," I said, plopping down on the beach. It was a little wet, not going to lie. My ass felt the dampness and I did not like it. But neither did I leap back up. Instead, I sat there, and I concentrated...very hard...

On the night of the murder.

I held it in my mind, this flimsy idea and flimsier hope. I'd tried this once before to no result, but if there was one thing I'd learned in my use of meta powers, it was that having a proper emotional incentive as fuel seemed to help make their use even easier.

Years ago, I'd shaken the hand of Shin'ichi Akiyama, a man who could control time itself. He'd held my grip long enough for my powers to work, just a little, on him, taking a little piece of him with me. From that, I'd gained the ability to withstand the shakes, rattles, and heaves of time trying to set itself right when things had gone a bit wild, temporally, a few years later.

That incident, not so very long ago, had ended with me absorbing some very painful memories straight from Akiyama himself. No mere touch, I had a feeling I'd picked up something a little stronger than passive resistance to time's eddies, but the only time I'd really tried it out I'd been in a rush, and without much emotional motivation to really give it a go.

Now...now I had some emotional motivation.

I pictured in my head the night of the murder. Tried to imagine the river bank, and the sky all black above, stars peeking through like holes punched in a blanket. I closed my eyes, squinting...

"What are you doing?" Reed asked.

I didn't answer; I was busy focusing.

On Greta Oliver.

On her fate, which she met, here on the bank of this river, weeks ago.

Something changed around me. The warmth of the sun faded from my skin. The sound of the river's run became garbled and distorted, like electronic interference.

I opened my eyes.

The world was dark around me, the only illumination bleeding in from down the river, where Stillwater stood, glowing on its banks from every shop and building that left the lights on at night.

My ass was no longer cold and wet, or at least I couldn't feel it. I got to my feet, taking in the scene. There was a shadowy, distorted effect around me, like the world had taken on a haze. I raised my hand and air rippled at my very touch.

Something was different.

Something was...wrong.

Yet I stood on the bank of the river at night, and heard the crunch of branches. And...

Something else.

There was a whimper and a whine that came over the sound of the river, which was...right...again, somehow. I looked down the shore to where Reed had been, but he was gone, no sign of him in the dark of night. The moon was high overhead, and somehow I knew I'd done it.

I was here at the night of the murder.

CHAPTER FORTY-SEVEN

The moon hung overhead in the starry, sky, and my skin was clammy, my stomach upset, like both knew that I was somewhere I wasn't supposed to be. My boots seemed to make little impact on the shore of the St. Croix River, burbling past in its mad rush south.

One sympathized. I wanted to be rushing south right now, too, but instead I had to witness a horrific crime.

Which I knew was coming by the sound.

It was obvious as hell, even as strangely distorted as it was. A voice, crying out in the night, from within the woods where Reed had been standing in the present. He wasn't here in the past, in this moment, and instead I saw the shadows moving between the trees, the whimper and whine of someone being moved against their will through the rustle of grass and branches and dead leaves.

"I'm here now," I muttered. My mind was under a bizarre sort of strain. I was holding this moment in my mind, intent on seeing, on knowing for myself what happened. It was a little like hanging onto a chain over an endless drop. I could sense the chasm below; death wasn't waiting, but the future was, and if I took my mind off this moment, off living it...

Well, I'd end up right back where I started.

My head was already aching, threatening to split, and I felt weakness slipping into the tips of my fingers, like I would struggle to so much as ball up my fist at the moment. I stood, on wobbly legs, there on the bank of the river, and watched, listening as the figures moved through the darkness toward the short cliff's edge where I'd left Reed.

The muffled cries remained muffled, even as they drew closer. The crashing of footsteps through the brush meant I knew where my foe – and the victim – were. Still, I peered into the darkness, listening as they drew feet from the place where – I assumed – it was all going to happen.

Greta Oliver's cries sounded pitiful. She was already terrified, plainly, but they were muffled as though she had duct tape over her mouth. I stared into the shadowy haze that hung over this vision. It wasn't a real fog, I somehow knew; it was an artifact of my amateur attempt to travel time to reach this moment. A visual reminder that I wasn't supposed to be here, that I wasn't a natural swimmer in the currents of time like Akiyama but rather an amateur and an invader.

My eyes blurred, my headache gradually increasing like a vise had been placed over my temples and another run along the sides and back of my head. The pressure ramped up, pushing ever harder upon my skull.

I ignored it. I needed answers.

I needed to see this for myself.

With a muffled cry, Greta Oliver burst from between the trees on the shallow cliffside, her feet dangling just off the ground as though she were being carried by the back of her neck. She was resisting her kidnapper, but to little effect, and in the shadowy dark I could see another figure behind her, wearing a hoodie.

It was hard to tell much about them other than that they were man-sized. Taller than most women, and certainly towering over Greta Oliver. But that description probably fit a majority of people on the planet, because though it was hard to be certain that this distance, Greta did not look terribly large.

I tried to tap into my flight power, and the world wobbled around me as though the earth had shook. A sound, louder than rushing water overwhelmed me, and I realized that it was blood rushing through my ears.

Sinking to one knee, my head swelled with pain. Trying to summon forth the memory of Gavrikov, the world rocked around me again, and no additional light came from my hand or my body.

While here, I realized I was powerless, my whole attention focused on keeping myself present in this moment in time. To try and interfere would mean loosing myself, like kicking the lever on a catapult to release the tension that kept it down. Such was my place in time; I didn't belong here, and I could feel time itself trying to propel me back to where I did belong. My concentration was the only thing holding me here, and to try and summon forth another power would mean slippage followed by a prompt – and possibly explosive – return to my own time.

"Mmmmmm," Greta Oliver moaned. I couldn't see in the darkness whether he'd grasped her by the neck or was holding her up in some other way, but regardless of how he was doing it, he was strong. Not necessarily meta-strong, but it certainly seemed that way. From the angle of his body, he had no more than one hand on her, and appeared to be keeping her aloft effortlessly.

No words were spoken; Greta was muffled. Her moans were plaintive, and cut through the fog of pain squeezing my head like the fingers of a giant looking to rupture my skull.

"Shhhhhhh," came a voice from somewhere in the darkness. The hood was keeping me from seeing the face of the killer, the shining lights of Stillwater just behind him, pushing through the trees, giving me little but a silhouette of a body and the outline of a hood. The woods were thick and tangled behind him. I couldn't see anything over his shoulder.

The pain was near-crippling, squeezing my head so tight I could barely concentrate, yet I tried to climb the short cliff nearest me, to draw closer to the scene. What I could hear, what I could see, was all marred by the steady series of pain spikes driven into strategic points around my skull. Was this the price of using a power I hadn't fully claimed? Or did it feel like this for Akiyama when he did it, too?

I dug my fingers into the cliff, and with a little leap, made it up to a higher level. Trees grew tightly up to the edge of the cliff, and I staggered, landing a hand on rough bark, leaning against it as my equilibrium threatened to invert, sending me right back over the edge. I steadied myself, listening to the muffled cries of Greta Oliver, then thudded with heavy footsteps toward the scene of the crime unfolding before me.

"Shhh, shhh," the voice came again, and by now my eyes were blurring so strongly, either from the effect of the time distortion or the pain in my head, that I couldn't see more than a few feet in front of me. I pitched over, crunching leaves and causing the action in front of me to pause.

I lay still, pressure of the world threatening to crash in on me like water rushing into a diver's helmet at the bottom of the damned ocean. I listened as best I could, and heard a steady breathing over Greta's whimpering. It was deep, and regular, and sounded strangely...sedate?

With a hard shove, I was back upright and on my feet, staggering the last few paces through the woods to the scene of the murder. I needed to see, needed to witness, and there was no chance of that if I couldn't get my head together.

The dark-hooded figure swayed in silhouette, a shadow against the lights of Stillwater shining through the skeletal tree trunks. His feet seemed to be off the ground, I realized, drifting an inch or two above the earth. I peered through squinted, painful eyes at him and stumbled ever closer.

With a last stagger, I lurched forth and grabbed him, almost falling over myself in the process. I grasped at his lapels, securing myself from tipping over, and looked him right in the eyes–

And I *saw*.

Then, like a sudden snap, I was ripped away from the hood, from the face, from the figure, from the squealing, muffled cries of Greta Oliver as she came to her death. Flung back through time by the force of a vengeful, angry god of time – I could feel Akiyama shoving back hard against what I'd done here – I came back in a bright flash of light into the late day by the riverbank, feet thumping onto the rock cliff next to my brother, who did a double take at my sudden appearance.

"What the...?" he muttered, looking me over.

I had no time to reply, though, because after only a single look at him, my eyes rolled back in my splitting head, and I keeled over into unconsciousness.

CHAPTER FORTY-EIGHT

"Hey."

Soft fingers touched my shoulder, leaves crackled in my hair. I woke to the sun poking my eyes through branches swaying above, and everything in my head hurt like I'd gotten sledgehammered squarely in the skull. Probably my brains had come out of my ears in the process, though it was hard to be sure.

"Are you okay?" Reed asked, fingers brushing my shoulder as I peered at him through that blinding light from above. I closed my eyes because I did not want to look at him, nor the sky, nor the branches, nor anything. The mere shape of those things, the fact that they existed in my universe was an affront to my eyes and the pain god nesting in my skull. "You've been out for like an hour." He sagged. "I was about ready to give up and call an ambulance. What happened?"

"I discovered another power that I have which should not be used unless I'm suicidal," I said, not bothering to even slit my eye to look at him. Hell, right now I was wishing I could turn off my hearing, too, because the sensory overload of the river running beneath me? Like a cheese grater on my damned eardrums. "Again, I mean. Unless I'm suicidal again."

"Wait," Reed said, "what did you do?" His voice dropped a timbre. "Did you actually travel time?"

"Yes," I said, my voice a rasp. "Now stop talking."

He did, but only for a second. "What did you see?"

"My brain exploding in the future," I said. "The very near future. Possibly like one of those *Mission: Impossible* tapes, in the next five seconds." I brushed my head with my own fingers, miming an explosion. "Boom. See?"

"Sienna," Reed said sternly. Didn't matter. I couldn't see him, I wasn't reacting. My head hurt too much. "What happened?"

"Akiyama got pissed at me for screwing with time, I think. And shoved me back to the present in the least gentle way." That was all supposition. But it was decent supposition, I thought, given what I knew of the man and his distaste for others messing with the flow of time. Weissman had mentioned Akiyama's predilection for pushing back against longer-term affronts against time. Well, I'd just made a hell of one, and something had sure shoved me forward back to now, and in spite of my splitting headache, I was fairly sure it wasn't just my meager, fledgling time-control powers failing me.

I was pushed back. And now I was here, lying on a river-bank in a fair amount of pain, wishing like hell I'd never even considered doing the nutty thing I'd just done.

"But what did you see?" Reed asked. "Did you get to the night of the murder? What happened?"

"I...sort of," I said, the ringing in my skull like someone was playing a conga beat on the top of my head with knives for drumsticks.

"Well?" Reed's fingers dug into my shoulder. I doubted he even knew he was doing it, his excitement was so high.

"What happened? Who did it?" His voice was a rising tempo of excitement. To him, this was the end, perhaps, the answer to all we'd come here for, to everything we'd done in the last day to solve this thing.

But my answer...was not going to satisfy.

"I saw...a man," I said, hedging as I opened my eyes to bright sun streaming in overhead, painfully glaring from the heavens above. "In a hoodie. And he had Greta...he had her...there. Right where you were standing before."

"And?" Reed's finger's tightened on my shoulder. "Did you see his face?"

I nodded slowly. "It'd be hard to miss at that distance." I couldn't control the shudder that ran through me, as though the knowledge I now contained didn't want to be held in. But I couldn't find voice to speak it aloud, into the world, because I feared it.

Because it was the end of everything.

My last dance with Minnesota.

"Who was it?" Reed's voice was soft, gentle, but prodding.

I closed my eyes again, embracing the dark, such as it was. Light flooded through my eyelids, and my skull screamed from its time-traveling abuse. Still, that face hung in front of my eyes, the face of the hooded man, glimpsed in the moonlight, the rush of the river and the whimpers of Greta Oliver the soundtrack to his shadowy, remorseless mien.

"Sienna?" Reed shook me gently.

"It was Aaron Berry," I said, the words leaving me in a frantic rush, the last gasp of breath before death. Because now I had no more need to stay in Minnesota; this case was over, I'd seen its truth with my own eyes, and it was answered to my legal satisfaction.

But not in any other way.

"It was Berry," I whispered, as though that could quiet the

thundercrack of truth I'd just released into the world, destroying it, at least for me.

The case was over.

It was time to leave home.

Forever.

CHAPTER FORTY-NINE

"Well..." Reed said, when we were back in the car, Marty at the wheel, taking us south through the hamlet that was Stillwater, "...at least now we know."

I sat slumped in the backseat, leaning low against the cloth covered headrest. I felt hot, achy, like I had a fever. Sweat stuck my shirt to the small of my back, and my pants were all bunched up and clinging from my climbing at the river. One leg had gone capri, creeping up to mid-calf and causing a back-up along the rest of my leg. I felt too weak and pained to even bother adjusting it, like inching it back down to my ankle was the least of my problems right now.

"We can head out now," Reed said softly, and I didn't know if he was talking to me or Marty. "No more worries about Minnesota catching up with us while we're chasing things down. We can head for the hills and it'll all be good."

I cocked my head at him. "Why do you sound like you're trying to convince yourself as much as you're trying to convince me?"

Reed's handsome, open face was slightly twisted. He pursed his lips, clearly holding something back.

But only for a moment. He leaned in close to me and said, meta-low, "Okay. So...who tried to kill us at the coffee shop?"

"I don't know," I said wearily, turning my face back to the window and closing my eyes. "Maybe it was an accident. Massive brake failure. They do occasionally happen from time to time. The fact that we were there? It could just be coincidence."

"But what about the planted evidence?" He pressed on. "You can't tell me that Greta Oliver's underwear, covered in Aaron Berry's semen, is a naturally occurring phenomenon." He hesitated, and I could almost sense him making a face. "How does that even happen, anyway?"

I turned my face slowly to him. "...You really need me to explain it to you? Because I feel like at this stage in your life, the birds and the bees talk is really more Isabella's job than mine."

"I mean how did the evidence get in his apartment?" Reed asked. "What is the genesis of it?"

"He took a trophy and...used it on himself at some point after the murder," I said tiredly. "Or before, maybe. I don't know and I'm tired of contemplating it. It's possible that the New Richmond PD missed it in their search. Sometimes it happens."

"That's two major coincidences," Reed said, leaning in closer to me. "The truck nearly obliterating us and the evidence 'planting.' I don't know about you, but I don't believe in coincidence. Not like that. Not at this level." He sat back in his seat. "I think this bears at least a little closer look."

I stirred, turning my head to look at him. "Closer look at what, Reed? I just watched the lead-up to the murder, live."

"But you didn't see the murder itself," Reed said, his eyes alight and dancing. "I feel like..." He clenched a fist in front of him. "...Something else is going on here. We have a bizarre picture of this whole thing. True, Berry does not seem wholly innocent–"

"What was your first clue? That he hid the bastard offspring he sired with his ex-student?"

"–But absent your placing him at the scene, everything else about this stinks," Reed went on. "You heard that Stillwater PD detective, Greene. Even she thought it reeked of a setup. The outrage spurred by the case was just too much for her to swim upstream against."

"Because the evidence is overwhelming," I said tiredly, "and I just added another irrefutable piece: Aaron Berry was present at the scene on the night of the murder, walking Greta Oliver to the slaughter moments before she died." I was still leaned against the back seat at an odd angle, and finding no comfort for my pain. "He was just a drunk and a lech, Reed. A failure as a human being, a burnout as a teacher–"

"And that brings up another question," Reed said, really building up a head of steam. "What made him an alcoholic? Why was this young guy, in the early years of his career, already a blackout drunk? Huh? What was driving that?"

I just stared at him. "Sometimes people are just worthless drunks, Reed. Sometimes they just can't deal, even with the little things, and they curl up in a bottle every chance they get. Not because they're driven by some big mood or past trauma they can't outrun. It's just their way of giving up on all the little cuts and pains that attach themselves to you in the course of everyday life." I settled my head against the window, staring out into the fading sunlight as we slipped along the cliffside road out of Stillwater.

"Are we still talking about Aaron Berry?" Reed asked, after a small pause.

"Maybe not. I don't know," I said, feeling just so damned bone-weary. I wanted the conversation to be over, the day to be over, this case to be over, and maybe my life to be over. It was a hard, dragging moment, one that cried out for a drink to suppress the writhing feelings of angst and weariness. If I'd had a whiskey in my hand, I'd have downed it and the bottle beside to calm these jangling nerves.

"Hey." Reed's hand was on my shoulder again, but this time truly gentle. "You're making it, okay?" I turned to find him looking at me, his eyes brown and warm in the midst of that feverish sense causing my skin to go clammy. "You're getting through. One day at a time."

"Why couldn't it have been a day when I had nothing going on?" I asked. I felt a spike of nausea; part of me wished it was true, alcoholic withdrawal, just so I could have something to hang my hat on as I went through this, but I didn't experience the physical symptoms of withdrawal the way a human would. This was the sickness from my time-travel excursion and subsequent temporal bitchslapping, and it left me wondering if I could heal out of it.

I conjured forth Wolfe, and the sick sensation vanished, but left the jangling nerves behind.

"If it came in manageable chunks, it wouldn't be a case," Reed said with his usual wry, understated humor. "You know that's not how these things work. It's feast or famine, calm or overload, no in-between."

"And you wonder why I became an alcoholic," I grumbled, sitting upright, giving my weary spinal column a break from the discomfort of my slumped position. "Okay, genius brother, riddle me this: we now have Aaron Berry at the scene, just prior to the murder. Who did it, if not him?"

"I don't know," Reed said. I must have looked at him strangely, because he shrugged. "I'll be the first to admit, I do not have a plausible alternative explanation. All I know is we've got is a puzzle whose pieces are not fitting together. Let me turn this around on you – okay, Berry's at the scene. Let's stipulate to that. How could that happen and him not be the murderer?"

I blinked, trying to thread that verbal contortion through my fuzzy brain. "Wait...what?"

"Give me alternative explanations for how Berry could have been there you like you saw, but not guilty," Reed said. "Like...he was sleepwalking. Or under the influence of someone who was sleepwalking him."

"Drunkwalking, more like," I said, frowning. "It feels like you're violating the hell out of Occam's Razor here."

"Yes," Reed said, "and I'm all for the simplest explanation – when it actually explains everything. But with the truck attack, and the evidence being so neat and overwhelming...I just don't buy it. It's still a frame, Sienna." He leaned closer. "How would you say they did it? Meta-power wise?"

I sighed, deeply. "I mean...they would have to get him out there somehow." My frown deepened. "He did seem to be moving a little strangely."

"Right," Reed said, pointing a finger at me. "Maybe he had a metal coat on. To let a Magneto-type walk him around like a doll. Which would also explain the truck."

"A not-so-little doll," I murmured, closing my eyes for a second. "I don't know about the Magneto thing. Maybe. Another alternative, though, is an invisible meta."

Reed stiffened. "Wait...they have those?"

"Yeah, didn't Angel tell you? We fought one in LA."

Reed stared at me blankly. "No, Angel did not tell me. And neither did you."

"Yes, there are invisible metas," I said. "So it could conceivably be that. Also, it would make it easy to plant evidence if you're invisible."

He frowned. "What about a speedster? They can appear almost invisible, right?"

I shook my head. "A speedster wouldn't be invisible while

walking Aaron Berry to the scene of the crime, and they're not so impossible to spot that you or I would miss one zipping away from the truck that almost splattered us. I don't think it's a speedster. If we're dealing with someone other than Berry at all."

"But you're starting to see the possibilities." Reed's eyes were alight with them, and he was wearing a very small smile. "Come on. What else?"

I closed my eyes. "Can't think of anything else right now. Maybe I'll just let it brew for a bit." I let out a small exhalation. "What now, though?"

Reed leaned forward and tapped our driver on the shoulder. "Change of destination. Take us to Regions Hospital complex." His eyes flashed as he looked at me. "Get us to the coroner's office."

My heart sank slightly, and I said, meta-low, "Kevin."

He nodded. "We need to know how she died, what they found on the body. If nothing else, maybe it'll fill in another of these insufferable blanks we're tripping over."

I matched his nod with one of my own and settled back against the seat. "Thank you," I said softly.

He looked over. "For what?"

"For not giving up on me."

His smile was warm, and there was a gleam in his eye of real affection. "Never have. Never will." He clasped his hand on my wrist, fingers against the cloth of my sleeve, and I matched his move as best I could. It was holding hands for a succubus, or the nearest we could get at present, and I felt his warmth through the sleeve of my shirt as we rode on, toward the orange-colored sunset.

CHAPTER FIFTY

"We should be careful here," I said as our driver got close to the coroner's office. "Terrell might have called the cops after our last visit."

Reed nodded and leaned forward to talk to our driver. "Can you let us out around back? And cruise real slow into the parking lot?"

If Marty the driver thought our request was odd, he didn't say anything. He also kept his mouth shut when we both slumped down in our seats below window level, though I did catch his questioning eyes peering at us in the rearview.

There were no obvious cop cars in the parking lot of the coroner's office, which I took as a good sign. Marty dropped us around back once we were sure we were clear, and Reed kept his head on a swivel as we walked around the building.

I elbowed him in the arm. "Try not to look so obvious," I said, keeping my eyes front and scanning with my peripheral vision. I also glanced around behind me, but I tried to make it more natural. "You want to look at least a little casual."

"If there are cops watching, it doesn't matter whether I look casual or panicked, they know who we are," Reed said, maybe altering the wide-swinging arc of his head by about 20% in either direction.

"So look cool while you're getting arrested, instead of like a spaz."

"'Spaz?'" Reed craned his neck at me. "Did we just stumble out of a John Hughes movie?"

"Yeah, it should have been 'Sienna Nealon's Day Off,'" I said, "but I don't see a parade and frankly my singing voice doesn't lend itself well to...anything, at this point, actually."

"I've heard it, before and after the glass-breaking thing," Reed said, cramming his hands deep in his pockets. "The only difference is the broken glass, because our eardrums bled either way."

I elbowed him again, and he chuckled, a little, "Oof!" from the fervency of my blow not stealing his cheer one bit. He held the door for me and in I went, this time finding the front desk of the coroner's office manned. Ish.

Kevin was obvious on sight, sitting on a little stool behind the desk with a spiral-bound art pad spread out in front of him, in the middle of a sketch. Why they had a coroner manning the front desk, I couldn't imagine; budget cuts? No business tonight? Whatever the case, there he was, a selection of pencils with varying tips laid out next to the pad and his full attention on his work. A wispy beard extended almost to the rumpled collar of his shirt. His dark hair and glasses didn't improve his image; dude was a dork through and through, and not one of the new, geek-chic types. He was an old school nerd, the kind who'd probably kept pocket protector companies in business all these years.

"What the hell...?" Reed muttered, meta-low, as we approached the desk.

Kevin was in the middle of putting some vaguely impressive nipple detail into a curvy, slightly shadowy female figure that seemed both familiar and not. Familiar in the sense that it was supposed to be me; unfamiliar in the sense that I saw myself naked more frequently than anyone these days, and I thought he was being a little generous in every area that counted.

Was I flattered? Hardly. But neither was I as all-fired annoyed as I'd been earlier. My emotions felt muted, possibly from the brain-splattering-agony that had followed from my time travel experience, and maybe a little from the crushing disappointment of the revelation about Aaron Berry before Reed had pulled me back into the case. Either way, I was considerably less murderous and ambivalent than I had hours before, which was lucky for Kevin.

He took no notice of our approach. So when I got right up to the counter, I reached down and planted a finger on the desktop bell, and it rang out under my meta strength, dinging like a fire alarm.

Kevin jerked his skinny neck back in order to give his four eyes a chance to take me in. The non-stylized, full-clothed, dreary, weary, make-up smudged and tired AF me that bore little resemblance to his sketch. His mouth dropped open, he banged his knee on the counter getting up, and promptly folded in half as he grabbed for his knee. "Owwwwww," Kevin moaned, hopping on one leg.

I considered waiting for him to settle down, but a quick check of my phone revealed that it was already close to six thirty. "Kevin," I said, trying to be diplomatic to the troglodyte whose hobby was picturing me naked, "You know who I am, and I know who you are and what you get up to in your free time. So let's dispense with the bullshit, hmm? Because I've had a trying day, and I would really like to not start my night off by murdering the shit out of you."

He stopped, standing on one foot, his wounded leg curled around the other like he was a tropical bird. "What?"

"What my sister is trying to say," Reed intervened,

smoothly, "is that we're here for some information. Also, we're deeply creeped out by what you're doing here." He gestured toward the topless art of 36DD me without looking at it.

"Yeah, so let's make a deal," I said, the edge creeping into my voice. "You give us the autopsy report for Greta Oliver, and I'll leave your skeleton right where it is, in your skin, and in its current, mostly-cohesive state."

Kevin slowly set his wounded leg back down, straightening it experimentally. "You...you're why Terrell said I should man the front desk tonight." He leaned his head back, a wolfish, oddly-relieved smile parting his lips to reveal coffee-stained teeth. "He knew you were coming."

"And now I'm here," I agreed. "So get me a copy of Greta Oliver's autopsy report and I'll be gone, forgetting I saw any of this."

"As well as the art gallery in the back room," Reed added, not so helpfully. Because I was trying to forget that rather than indulge my natural instincts and burn the whole thing down, probably along with the building.

"You saw that?" A weird glow bloomed in Kevin's eyes. "What did you think?"

"That you're creepy and I'd like to put you through the countertop, face first," I said without missing a beat. "You're drawing nude pics of me. How did you think I'd react?"

"Well, I didn't think I'd ever see you in here," he said, completely unabashed, looking me right in the eye, "but now that you're here..." His smile got wider. "...I'm glad you know. I think you're...you're just great." His eyes roamed over me in ways that made me wish I was wearing a sackcloth and ashes, and I suppressed the urge to heave right there.

"Okay, creep-o," Reed said, stepping squarely between us so he couldn't molest me with his eyeballs any longer, "let's talk turkey. Autopsy report. Now. Or you're going to be on the menu for some cat's Thanksgiving."

Kevin peered around my brother. "Is that literal?"

"Yes," Reed said, "I will literally throw you in a spin cycle with the sharpest things I can find, and you will end up in chunks so small that only the birds and worms and other carrion will find you. Thus, you shall become cat food."

"But...birds aren't cats," Kevin said, leaning to the other side to get another glimpse of me. I didn't shrug away, but I did give him a look that reflected my true distaste for him.

Reed put a hand on his shoulder, clamping down in a very unfriendly way. "You know what I think? This is not the face of a man who wants to be cooperative in any way." He shot me a look. "I think it's time to start breaking parts of him. You know, that aren't already broken." He pulled back a fist, and I got a sense he was about to pummel Kevin for realsies.

"I can't give you the autopsy report," Kevin said, craning his neck to look around Reed.

"That's going to be a real problem for your bone structure," Reed said, and his voice revealed the strain. Was he really that bent out of shape about Kevin's invasive artwork? It seemed so, but I didn't stop him. Mostly because I was feeling somewhere in the vicinity of that level of anger myself, though I was so tapped out it was not finding outlet in my usual violent tendencies.

"No, I mean I can't give it to you because I don't have it," Kevin said. "Terrell locked me out of the computer before he left." He pointed at the device next to him. "That's why I'm manning the counter tonight. I can't actually do any real work, because I can't record the results in the system."

Reed sounded a little strangled when he spoke. "Call Terrell. Get him over here right now. Or we'll pay him a visit."

"Can't," Kevin said, shaking his head. "Said he was leaving town. Going north for the weekend. Sounded spontaneous."

He managed to look around Reed's long hair and found my eyes, whereupon he smiled. "I guess I know why now."

"Sonofa," Reed said, and let loose of Kevin, who stumbled back a few steps. He wheeled on me. "You believe this?"

I didn't have a lot of emotional range; mostly I just felt cold and tired. "Yeah," I said. "I believe it. He wanted to get us out the door, so he fed us this guy, who he clearly doesn't like very much. Then he locks Kev here out of the system and beats feet out of town, leaving this dumbass to face the consequences."

Kevin was wearing a goofy grin. "Call me a dumbass again."

Reed turned around on him, his face split with absolute disgust. "Is this part of your kink, freak?"

"Reed," I said gently, catching his arm before he could raise it to pummel Kevin. I was shaking my head slightly when he came around. "You've kinda got me in a bind here, Kev."

"I would really prefer *you* bind *me*," Kevin said, foisting a brand new entrant into my all-time list of "Things I Wish I'd Never Heard."

Reed raised his fist again, and I caught it just in time to keep him from splattering Kevin's skull. He seethed quietly under my grip, and I could feel him radiating heat. Or possibly hate. Instead he grabbed Kevin by the throat with his free hand. "Give. Us. The. Report. I don't care how."

"I can't...I don't have it," Kevin rasped. "Also...could you have her do this? If you're going to hurt me?" He made eyes at me, even with Reed's hand now around his throat.

Reed cast him away, but not hard enough to actually hurt. He fanned his hand wildly, as if appalled to have touched his very flesh, even at the neck. "I can't do this," Reed said, making a heebie jeebie face. "I wanted to help you, to spare you, 'cuz I know you've had a rough few days, but...I just can't beat the shit out of a defenseless cretin, no matter how creepy."

"It's okay," I said, patting him on the arm. Then, with a sigh of pure exasperation, "Kev...we have a problem here. I'm trying to solve a case. I'm tired. I need info. I don't really want to threaten you. I've already nearly been run over and gotten slapped through time today. Can you just..." I put my head down. "...just tell me about the report."

"I have a suggestion," Kevin said, and boy did his eyes light up. "I'm okay with you hurting me for it. But...in the right way." He touched his fingers to the side of his head. "Then...you get what you want, too. Because I've seen the report! It's all in here, even if I can't recall all the details off hand, you can...you know, drain them out. Right?"

I made a grunting, pained noise from deep within my diaphragm. "Can't you just tell me? I really don't want to go in there," and I waved my hand at his depraved skull.

"Not really," he said, looking slightly abashed. "I do like...five, ten of these a week. And it wasn't one of mine. I will say this – the girl died in a way that made it clear a meta did it." He grimaced. "There was...power exerted on her in a way I've never seen before. Pure force. But no handprints. No ligature marks. Something killed her that was not human or machine...just strange." He tapped his temple. "It's all in here. Photos. Full exam of the body, because I was in the room at the time. You go in...you get it all. See for yourself."

I took a couple sideways steps and planted my head on the counter. Not too hard, just enough to ring my bell. I loosed an unintelligible burst of pure frustration.

"What...what did she say?" Kevin asked.

"She said she doesn't want to go in your effed-up brain, Kevin," Reed said.

I sighed, lifting my head and looking at my brother. "Are we sure this is worth it? Are we sure there's a conspiracy to frame Berry going on here? That we're not just grasping at straws to keep the case going a little longer?"

"Wait, Berry's not guilty?" Kevin appeared to give this some consideration. "That kinda makes sense, actually. Did you guys hear about the convenient underwear from his apartment?"

I ignored that and turned on Kevin. "All right. Let's find a place that you can lay down while I do this thing."

He jerked a thumb up. "There are morgue slabs in back. And it'd be real handy in case you got a little carried away, and y'know..." He waved his hands in an overly enthusiastic manner in front of him in a way I interpreted as to represent me vacuuming his whole soul out of him. He was smiling the entire time. "...Hm?"

"Yeah, that's not going to happen," I said, leaping the counter and grabbing him by the hand, letting my powers warm up as I dragged him through the doors and down the hall. "Keep your soul – and everything else – in your pants."

CHAPTER FIFTY-ONE

I put Kevin unceremoniously upon the morgue slab in the nearest room (and not the one with my nude art, fortunately). He was giggling with uncertainty and delight, and part of me felt like a mother taking her toddler to the doctor for an exam.

Reed trailed into the room behind us and cringed at the rattle as I put Kevin on the metal surface with a not-so-gentle thump. He closed the swinging door behind us, looking nervously out the windows into the hall. "You sure you want to do this?"

"I am one hundred percent sure I do not," I said, rolling up my sleeves for some reason. Probably because I viewed this as work, and of approximately the same sort as a sanitation worker about to dive into a shit-filled cesspool to unclog a drain. Maybe even less clean, come to think of it. "Yet here we are, on day one million of Sienna doing things she vehemently does not want to do. *C'est la vie.*"

"This is so awesome," Kevin said giddily. "When you get done, can you let out a little gasp, like, 'Oooooh?'" He shivered all down the length of him, and I barely kept from dry heaving.

"When I get done, you'll be lucky if I don't upchuck on you," I said, and plunged my hand down on his forehead as I looked away and closed my eyes. "You should have worn a poncho."

"Wait, this is a beautiful moment for me," he said. "Don't go and ruin it by – gyaahhhhh!"

The cumulative working of my powers across the moments in which I'd dragged him into the room meant we reached full-throttle succubus drain before he could finish his perverted thought. His eyes were wide now, verging on panic, because this was not feeling how he thought it would.

Getting his soul ripped from his body was not turning out to be the lusty, raw sexual fantasy he'd built it up to be. I knew from experience that it burned, that it churned your stomach, that it made you feel woozy and sick when it was over. Kevin was realizing this, but a little too late.

For me...well, I was having a good ole time. As a succubus tended to, when exposed to the chance to rip out a soul.

I plunged into the dark depths of Kevin's mind, trying to focus in on the one thing I needed with my usual single-minded discipline. It was difficult not to breathe hard, not to enjoy this thrumming intensity playing down my every nerve, like tingles of joy running across my skin. This was the shit that caused my Aunt Charlie to lose herself, the feeling that Rose Steward had willingly jumped into and never looked back.

In moments like these, I always tried to think of them, the people I hated most. They were my dark doppelgangers, the blackest elements of myself, the faces in the mirror that I never wanted to see.

Because of them, I leapt into the Kevin's head the same way I had with Aaron Berry's – with one intention and one only, after which I needed to GTFO before I could enjoy myself a little too much.

I broke away seconds later, the autopsy memories and report tingling in my brain, a pleasant replacement for the mule kick that Akiyama had levied on me earlier. I staggered into a nearby cart, knocking off a set of sterile tools under a cloth. They clattered to the ground and rang out with excessive sound and intensity as I closed my eyes, savoring the last taste of Kevin's strangely pure soul.

Reed was at my side before I opened my eyes. "You all right?" He was holding me up, the dear.

"I just engaged in a compulsive behavior that's way more addictive than alcohol," I said, opening my eyes. The world was somehow brighter, and my very skin called out for me to step right up and let myself back into Kevin's soul, to take more, because by God I deserved it after the day I'd had. Maybe just a little more. At least to start–

I shook my head, trying to push away that cloying thought. "Sorry," I said. "The pull to finish the soul drain...it's..."

Reed nodded, though he wouldn't look right at me. "You got it under control?"

"I got it," I said, taking a deep breath. "Under control, the report...I got it all."

Kevin sat up on the table like a zombie coming back to life in a horror movie. "Whoa." His face was ghostly pale, his glasses askew on his nose. He sat there blinking for a second–

Then he turned to the side and heaved his guts up right there on the floor.

"Welp," I said, looking away so as to avoid adding my own contribution to his vomitive mess, "I think it's time we moseyed on out of here." I grabbed Reed by the arm and pulled him toward the door.

"Wait," Kevin said weakly, leaning over the table's edge. "Did you...did you take anything else?"

"Nope," I said, not even missing a step as I pulled Reed through the swinging double doors. They squeaked as I made contact and shoved them open.

"Well...call me?" Kevin shouted after me.

"Sorry, Kev," I said, "but I'm leaving the state tomorrow night. And also – I'm not really sorry. Get a new hobby."

"You should have taken his desire to draw you naked," Reed said, surly, pulling his arm loose from my grip.

"Now, now," I said, my boots ringing out a steady rhythm as I headed down the hall, "I can't go nuking all my fans." I looked over at my brother, who was frowning. "Otherwise, who'd be left to love me besides you?"

CHAPTER FIFTY-TWO

"What did you learn?" Reed asked once we were out the door of the coroner's office. Our driver was around back, waiting, I presumed, and the sun was moving lower in the sky by the minute. Sundown was coming, and a bright shade of orange where blue had been not too terribly long ago was my sign of its approach. Feeling the sticky cling of my shirt to the small of my back where I'd been sweating all day, personally I welcomed the night. Maybe I'd get some sleep, and get to hang out with Ariadne one last time.

"I learned that our victim got bent out of shape," I said, and when Reed cocked his head quizzically, I added, "Literally. Someone about broke her in half. Snapped her spine at the small of her back, ruptured her internal organs at the waist. She bled to death internally and was paralyzed from the hips down."

"Well, that sounds meta," Reed said. "Especially if it was done, impromptu, on the shore."

"Seems it was," I said, beckoning him to follow me. I blazed a trail to the back of the building, wanting to get out of sight of the highway, in case any cops went by. Better to not make it easy on them. "But as the perv said, there's no handprints on her. No ligature marks from rope. No physical sign that she was manhandled by someone strong, or that she was...I dunno, fed into a machine that broke her in half. That means someone folded her in half without leaving a mark." I reached the back corner of the building and sure enough, our driver was still parked where we'd left him.

Reed slipped behind the corner with me, and we stood next to a really smelly dumpster, neither of us ready to head back to the car and discuss this in front of the driver yet, even meta-low. "How does that fit with what we've already postulated?"

"Honestly, I don't know," I said, feeling at my brow for sweat. There was only a little; absorbing a fellow human being (or Kevin, in this case) was not a stressful thing. Pulling off before I ripped his entire soul out? That probably jumped my heart rate a few beats per minute. "If we're talking an invisible meta, this doesn't fit. If we're dealing with a magnetic one..." I shrugged. "...You'd think they'd put, like, metal rings on the victim in order to do this sort of thing. But that'd leave a mark."

Reed nodded, deep in a frown. "What about the, uh...genetic evidence?"

"Right," I said sourly. "It was there. In the, uh...in her..." I was waving a hand in front of me, frantically. The only relief here was that my brother was apparently as skeeved out by discussing the technical details of the rape as I was.

"In the place you'd mostly expect it to be...?" Reed asked, cringing.

"God, we're a pair, aren't we?" I broke away from looking at him, because it was just easier. "Mom forced a course of anatomy and physiology plus sex ed on me when I was ten, and she answered everything in clinical terms when I asked questions. Probably the function of her radiology background. I still couldn't escape the feeling that since I was the only one in the, uhm, class, that she was judging me when I'd ask anything. What's your excuse?"

"That I'm talking about a sex crime with my sister," Reed said. "I like my villains more murder-y, less sleazy, personally."

"Right," I said. "Anyway...yeah. It was in the...front hole." That actually made him snicker. "They matched it with a sample compelled from Berry by court order. I guess the poor guy had to...y'know...in jail."

"I'd say there's a lot of that in jail," Reed said. "That and back hole action." He kicked at the ground, knocking a pebble into the next parking lot as he tried to look casual before spitting out his next brainwave. "Did she, uh...when there's an assault, there's usually signs in the uhm...the tissue around..." His finger was spinning at about waist level, and he would not look at me for anything. "...Y'know...of trauma...bruising...hints of, uh..."

"There was no sign of forced penetration," I said, closing my eyes and visualizing that segment of the report. Kevin's memory was clearer to me in my head than it had been in his. I could recall specific moments of absorbed memories, even down to pages in a book someone had been reading. That sort of memory wasn't evident in my own head, where everything seemed to be hazy these days, unless I'd recently had coffee. "But then, if you're a meta who can apply pressure to flesh and bone without actually leaving a mark on the skin..."

Reed nodded. "But let's be clear here. Absent some strange, flesh-manipulating power – which I don't rule out – I think what we're talking about here is someone who can spread the pressure they applied to Greta Oliver's body along the entire surface."

"Thus keeping her from bruising where they would have grabbed her," I said. "So...you're talking about–"

"Something new," Reed said pensively. "Or at least something we haven't run across before."

"And something really dangerous," I said, looking up at the deep orange sky, and the hints of color lighting up the western horizon. "What's the term for someone who can move objects with their mind?"

"Telekinetic," Reed said tightly, "and if that's what we're dealing with..." He shook his head. "Someone who can reach out and crush us without us laying a finger on them...how are we even going to stop them?"

CHAPTER FIFTY-THREE

"It does fit," Reed said, once we were back in the car, the driver taking us east, back toward Wisconsin, the river, and our actual destination, Club Labyrinth. When I looked up at him quizzically, he added, meta-low, "the telekinetic thing."

"Of course it fits," I said, looking out the window. "It's a thesis, and it logically works. But it might not be *the* thesis. We have to prove or disprove it. Also, I don't even know if telekinesis is an actual thing, meta powers-wise."

"If only there were some resource we could consult," Reed said dryly. "Some person whose knowledge of metahuman abilities stretched back over an appropriate period to have seen...y'know...a lot. But sadly, with the fleeting human life span and lack of expertise, this person would have to have lived thousands of years–"

"Yes, I get it, thank you," I said, fishing my phone out of my pocket and summoning up Lethe's contact info. I hesitated before hitting the button to dial.

"Okay," Reed said, catching my wrist in a non-harsh manner. "What's the deal?"

"No deal," I said, still not pressing the button to call her. "Just..." I looked back out the window. "...I'm not exactly at my best right now, Reed. And it's not easy for me to lean on people even when I am. Life or death situation, back against the wall? Yeah, I'd call her." I looked back at him. "But this isn't that. So it's a little harder for me to...face her right now."

"She's here to help," Reed said softly. "I mean, she lifted boxes for hours yesterday. And she's...well, she's *lived.* I get the feeling she's been in your boots before, since she's done probably everything under the sun by now."

"Yeah," I said. Still didn't press the call button.

"...But?" Reed asked.

"I feel weak," I said, whispering even beyond meta-low. I looked at him, and I could feel the stricken sensation on my features. "Because of..." I waved a hand in front of me, indicating me. "...I'm...I'm an alcoholic, Reed. And I just tanked down to rock bottom. I'm feeling a little exposed here. Also, ashamed." My cheeks burned with scarlet fire, and I didn't dare look in a mirror right now. "The shame is...deep. Bad enough that I had to go through the intervention with all of you. I just had my every vulnerability exposed by Madison's consortium. I mean, you've seen it all from me before. But Lethe..."

"She watched you fight a war with her dad and then annihilate the Network," Reed said, scoffing. "You think this is you at your worst? Lemme tell you something, sis, and not for nothing – this ain't your worst. Scotland was worse."

I nodded slowly. "Scotland was worse."

"I've never seen you so drunk and emaciated," Reed said. "I know you don't like your body type, but seeing you like that?" He shuddered. "You were like a hundred and thirty pounds of muscle and bone and gristle." Now he shivered more. "But we made it through. The period after, though?

Almost as bad. When you were lounging around that condo in Florida? Way worse than this."

I nodded slowly. "Still...she hasn't seen me like that at all. When I look at her, she doesn't look much like Mom. But then she'll turn a certain way, and I see...Mom. Her bearing is different, her attitude is different. Miles different, really. But I'm just afraid...like, if she really sees me, when I'm rock bottom..." I couldn't even look him in the eye.

"Maybe don't get to rock bottom again, then?" Reed said, and when I looked up he was smiling. "Or if you do, lean on your brother? Before you get there? We could cushion the landing next time. Make sure I don't end up coated in fake blood and you don't go all Dark Phoenix on a bunch of randos who are trying to make you feel some empathy for their losses."

"Yeah," I said, and drew a deep breath. "That'd probably be easier."

"You know what I think you need to do?" Reed patted my wrist above my sleeve. "You need to call her...and invite her to come with us. Or at least pick us up after we go all wild at the club." He made some sort of mimed dancing, moving only his hands and upper body. It was very much of the white boy rhythm style.

"Sure thing, old man," I said, still holding my own phone. "Anything else I should ask my grandmother for, besides a ride?"

"She's not going to hate you, Sienna," he said. "She loves you. She'd do anything for you. I got that from her when I reached out. She'd walk through fire for you. She's not going to turn her back because you dove into a bottle for a while." He hesitated. "Though...a thought I had, too..."

"What?"

"Maybe we don't just consult with Lethe on this?" His eyes were glimmering. "Don't just ask her questions.

Maybe...we take her with us for the rest of the case? She knows things, after all. She's seen things."

"Yeah, like what entrails look like from the inside," I said, then sighed. "But you have a point." I hit the call button and waited until it was picked up on the second ring. "Hey, it's me. You know how you've been wanting to spend some quality time? Well...we could use a ride."

CHAPTER FIFTY-FOUR

Club Labyrinth was a dance club/bar that apparently catered to the teenage and young adult set. It was sandwiched in the corner of a strip mall in Oakdale, Minnesota, maybe ten minutes away from Stilloaks Prep by car. The building it was in was faded, with blue lettering spelling out Club Labyrinth in neon large enough to see it from some distance.

"Need me to wait this time?" Marty asked as he pulled into the parking lot. "Because I have fares downtown I could be getting to, so it will cost you now."

"Nah, you head out," Reed said, tapping away at his phone. I watched him sign a rather sizable tip to the guy, then end the ride. "Thanks for your time today."

The driver grunted and drove off almost the second he let us off. Reed and I both looked up at the awning above the club's entrance; two thick bouncers were watching from the door, one in a blue blazer and the other in a muscle shirt cut off a little above the bicep. It looked like it might have been a couple sizes too small, but it displayed his bulk quite effectively, like a message to idiots: Don't get in a fight here or I'll be forced to eject you, possibly from the planet.

A show of strength. I could respect that.

There were a couple of late teen/young adults hanging by the door, looking like they were thinking about going in. I shrugged at Reed; he did the same to me, and up we went to the bouncers, who also controlled the door.

"No trouble in here," the guy in the muscle shirt said warily as I approached. "You understand?"

"I solemnly swear I will start no trouble in here," I said, holding up my right hand. This much was probably a pledge I could keep. Probably.

He caught my verbal trick, but it seemed he couldn't find fault with it, so he just scowled. Then touched his ear. An earpiece was buried within, and a black cord snaked down his neck, a bulky segment indicating where the microphone was, and then the cord trailed all the way to a unit on his belt. Blue Blazer had one, too. They were both wired for sound. "Let's see some ID," Muscle Shirt said, like it was a demand.

"It's a teenage club, right?" Reed asked.

"Yeah, but she's not a teenager," Muscle Shirt said.

"Sure she is," he said, flashing his own driver's license at him. "And you should treat her accordingly."

"What the hell does that mean?" I asked. Then I got my answer.

The guy in the blazer grabbed my hand – fairly swiftly – and marked a big, black X on it with a magic marker. I probably could have pulled it away before he laid the felt tip on me, but honestly...why? Then he beckoned for my other hand, and I gave it to him. Another big black X went on the back of my hand.

"Okay, you can go in," Muscle Shirt said. "Cover charge is $20."

Reed peeled off two twenties from his wallet, then walked

through after Muscle Shirt opened the door for us. We entered into a darkened space with multi-colored spotlights flashing in the dimness, the music turned way the hell up.

I showed the now-marked backs of my hands to Reed. "What the hell is this?"

My brother slightly smirked. "It's a club for teens and adults. The X's show who can drink and who can't."

"Ohhhh," I said, feeling the mark of the underage beast upon me. "So basically, for tonight, I'm back to being sub-twenty-one."

"I thought it was best," Reed said, his smile dimming. "Mainly cuz, uh..." He jerked a thumb over his shoulder. "I'll find you in a minute. Call of nature." And he disappeared behind a smoky glass divider that encircled the dance floor. I caught sight of him a moment later cutting a path toward a glowing red Exit sign in the distance. Another sign beneath told me the bathrooms were over there, too.

"Really feeling the trust here," I said to the empty space around me. I took in the layout of the place with a quick sweep of my eyes.

There wasn't just one bar in Club Labyrinth; there were two, and they were long. In addition to the typical beer taps and infinite liquors that were present at any bar – and so beloved of me – there were also visible soda machines and Icee makers lurking behind the longer bar, nearer to me. The one in the distance, and shorter by far, seemed to be exclusively oriented toward alcoholic beverages.

Naturally, I turned my back on it ASAP, so as not to be led into temptation.

The music was all beat and little melody, a constant, thudding bass that reverberated through my ears and my skull, twanging at the distant, near-forgotten pains of hours past. I'll say this for it; it was loud, and there was plenty of it.

Apparently the club hadn't gotten busy for the night yet,

either. A field of circular tables crowded the space to my right; the dance floor lay to my left. Every color on every surface I could see looked like a shade of black except the tables and the bars. A girl passed in a white T-shirt that was tied up to show her midriff, and her T-shirt glowed under the black lights shining down from above. A sparkle of glitter also refracted from her midriff, like someone had done a shot of Gold Schlager out of her belly button.

Which...hey, maybe they had. Though, like many of the patrons I could see, she was probably a little young for it.

"Hey," came the voice of a dude from behind me, over the thrum of the bass notes in the currently playing "song." I turned to find a not-bad-looking guy leering at me. "Buy you a drink?"

I knew from his face that I already didn't like him. I wouldn't have let him buy me a drink even if I were already three sheets to the wind. So I held up my hand and said, "Sorry. Can't. I'm just not old enough."

He snorted a laugh. "No, but seriously. You want something?" He gestured with his thumb over his shoulder. "I'll get you anything you want."

Anything I wanted?

What I wanted was to walk behind the bar, grab the nearest bottle of whiskey, and upend the damned thing. I already knew what would happen if I did; the music in here would suddenly sound good, instead of like a rock drill loosed against my eardrum. The guy standing in front of me, a six or seven at worst, but lacking any personality to take him from being a horrendously, vanilla preppy jerkoff trolling a teen club, would suddenly become much more handsome, maybe even an eight or nine, someone I'd want to rub against while the beat resonated through my bones.

My eyes would dilate and the ridiculous spotlights flashing across the floor would seem cool instead of bright and intolerable when they turned my way, and the bitter taste of my fast food dinner and the bile that had threatened to come up after my Akiyama mule-kicking-through-time would give way to sweet, sweet liquor and maybe whatever mint was wafting off this guy's breath after I stuck my tongue down his throat for a while.

Steady, Sienna, Brianna said in my head.

I cocked my head at him quizzically. "Are you trying to contribute to the delinquency of a minor?"

His smirk vanished. "N – naw. That sounds like a crime. I wouldn't do that. Uh...see ya." He turned and walked away at double speed.

"You can always tell the repeat offenders," I said sadly. "Thanks, B."

I'm here if you need me, Brianna whispered. *Glad you're back.*

"Am I back?" I wondered aloud.

"Did you ever leave?" Reed asked, arriving just in time at my elbow. Didn't hear him coming, either. The music was way too loud in this place.

"I neither leaved, nor relieved – unlike some people I know," I said. "What now?"

Reed made a show of scanning the places. We were catching a few eyes, but not a lot of attention. The crowd here, sparse as it was, was far too self-centered to worry about the old people – by which I mean us, false evidence of the back of my hands notwithstanding – in their midst. They were here in tight knit little cloisters, maybe divided by school or friend groups. "I don't see anyone we know. Do you?"

"No, but look at how empty the dance floor is." It was; the whole space had to be big enough to handle a few hundred people and there were maybe ten out there right now. "I don't think it's rush hour for this place yet," I said.

"Maybe we should settle down at a table over there. Keep an eye on things." I smacked my lips. "Get a water."

My brother caught the unsubtle movement of my lips. "If it's water you're drinking, I'm buying. Grab a table," he said, heading for the bar, "and we'll settle in and wait."

CHAPTER FIFTY-FIVE

"Were we ever this dumb?" I asked, after about an hour – or maybe a year – of watching teens and slightly post-teens (and the occasional waaaaaaaaay post-teen, ewwww) interacting in Club Labyrinth. "And carefree? And–"

"I get the point," Reed said, cradling a sweating water bottle. The population of this joint had increased dramatically in the last hour. Now there were a couple hundred people, at least, on the dance floor. Bright, multicolored spotlights were sweeping over them at a frenzied pace in time with the music, providing a bizarrely entrancing spectacle for my tired eyes. "And yes, I assume we were. Maybe just at an earlier age, since we were busy saving the world and whatnot before we could drink." He looked sideways at me. "Legally, anyway."

"Pffft. You weren't saving the world until you met me, bro, and you were like twenty-three when we met, so I call bullshit."

"Subtle jab at my age," he said. "Nice one...little sis."

"Well, shorter sis, at least. And younger. And pr–"

"Don't say prettier. It goes without saying that you're prettier."

"I dunno, I've heard Olivia and Angel talk about you. Fairly sure the word 'pretty' was used."

"Thanks." Reed chuckled, eyes scanning the dance floor. "We're kinda hanging our hopes on this Isolde chick, aren't we?"

"It's a thin reed to hang onto, yes," I said. "Unlike–"

He closed his eyes. "Ouch. It's the long hours and the stress. And dad bod preparation. That's all."

"You look like you're putting on the weight nicely if you're planning to get pregnant," I said. "Really nesting."

He knew I was kidding, and his sly grin reflected it. Thankfully my brother was secure enough in the fact that he had nowhere near a dad bod. "No pregnancy. Yet." He shifted in his chair. "And maybe ever. After all, Isabella is...older than me by a bit."

"That'd be a real shame," I said, taking a sip of my water straight out of the bottle. "You'd be a good dad."

He smiled almost sadly, then perked up. "Hey...isn't that...?" And he nodded his head over my shoulder.

I turned; there were two girls at the bar who looked both young and incredibly familiar. Mostly because I'd met them yesterday, at Stilloaks, when they'd been sitting on either side of a student who'd quietly accused Aaron Berry of sexual assault. "It is," I said. "Lucille, I think? And..." I frowned, trying to pluck the name out of my memory. "Ashlynn?"

"Ashleigh," Reed said. "Should we talk to them?"

"Tempting," I said. "Since we're just waiting for Isolde anyway, and we're looking for her so she can shed light on the Stilloaks situation. Stillwater PD isn't going to get all up in our junk about it if we chat with material witnesses without them around, y'think?"

"I can't see how they'd be upset with us for that," Reed

said, standing up. "Or at least, not in a legally actionable way. They're people, after all, not objects under the control of the police."

"But they are minors," I said, "so we've got to be at least a little cautious. Keep a light touch."

Reed cocked his head at me, favoring me with a dry look. "Because I'm the one who comes in hot on these things."

Fair point. I drank down the rest of my water bottle and we crossed the sea of tables between us and the long bar. I wondered if there was a natural limit for how young you could be and still come here; I would have thought eighteen, or maybe sixteen. But here we had two fourteen-year-olds hanging out, albeit bellying up to the kiddie bar, with the Icees and the fountain drinks rather than the one where you could pick up a shot of Jack Daniels. Still...

"Hey," I said, because Reed let me take the lead. Made sense; an old man like him approaching teenagers in a place like this was a bad look, the kind Aaron Berry was currently grappling with. Lucille and Ashleigh turned to find us standing behind them, the music pulsing so loudly that I was surprised they heard me. But then, I would have been surprised if they'd heard a herd of angry buffalo approach in this din. "How's it going?"

As opening salutations went, I thought that one was muted. Right down the middle of the road.

These girls erupted like I'd just told them they'd won free tickets to...well, to whatever sort of concert girls of that age would be into. Jojo Siwa? I really don't know.

"Ohmigosh!" Ashleigh said, her eyes lighting up as she saw me. Her hands flew up to her face. "I can't believe you're here!"

Lucille giggled, reminding me of that annoying habit of hers. She fanned the minimal cleavage presented by her low-cut top, and said, "This is so amazing."

I did not look back at Reed for support, but I thought about it. "Huh?"

"I did not get a chance to tell you yesterday," Lucille said, "because of the y'know, creepy talk and whatnot," and here she locked arms with me, making me suddenly thankful I was wearing long sleeves, "but we are just...such fans of yours." Her eyes were alight with excitement, moving and lively. "And very disappointed that Minnesota is giving you, like, the rawest deal. It's the sushi of deals."

Well, I couldn't argue with that. "Yeah, it sucks," I said. "Um, uncomfortable question real quick – how are you here?"

Lucille giggled, of course. "What do you mean?" Her voice was a lot higher pitched, and I knew an obvious lie when I saw one.

Ashleigh knew the score. "Well...we kinda have fake driver's licenses, see."

Ah, so the club did have a lower limit, and they were both safely under it. "Nice," I said.

Lucille looked suddenly very uncertain. "You're not going to bust us for that, are you? Because my parents will literally kill me."

"Relax, I'm not from the liquor board," I said, "nor am I your principal. But this does beg a question – how did you get here?"

"Rideshare app." Lucille flashed her phone at me, giggling – God, that was annoying. "Like...duh." She blushed and straightened. "Uh...no offense."

"No, that's fair, I should have guessed that," I said. "Just wanted to make sure you didn't, y'know, ride your bikes over or something." In the dresses they were wearing, that would have been quite a sight. They were definitely experienced clubbers based on their attire. Short skirts, lots of sparkly fabric to catch the lights in this place, and tops low enough to have clued the dumbasses at the door in on the fact that these girls had some puberty yet to go through.

That wiped the guilty smile off of Asheigh's face, but it quickly regenerated, like one of my limbs after a severing. "So...what are you doing here, slumming with the kiddos? There are cooler clubs, y'know. Like Myth."

"We're still on the clock," I said. "Just trying to figure a few things out." I looked around. "I take it Syrena is home, recuperating from her ordeal?"

"Oh, yeah," Ashleigh said. "She talked to the police for like...hours yesterday. And I don't think her parents are ever going to let her out again."

"Yeah, they totally withdrew her from Stoaks already, even," Lucille said. No giggle. Guess that was sad news.

"Mmhmm," I said, taking that news in. "When did she first talk to you about her relationship with Mr. Berry?"

"Um...recently?" Ashleigh said, looking at Lucille as if really questioning it, looking for confirmation. Lucille was – not quite stone faced, but sort of staring blankly ahead. "Yeah. Pretty recently. Like in the last couple weeks."

That was interesting. A teenage girl keeping a secret like that? From her best friends? Not impossible by any means, especially given the strong possibility of an element of shame involved. Still, I felt like I had equations floating around my head like Zach Galifianakis in the gambling scene of *The Hangover* trying to deal with the factors in play. A person's natural desire to connect with their peers would have to be overcome by a strong other factor – like the shame or guilt that came from being abused, maybe?

Yeah. That could probably possess Syrena to keep her mouth shut. Especially if, like so many victims, she thought it was somehow her fault. Self-blame was a deadly thing.

"Did she, uhm...change at all?" I asked. "In the last few months? Personality-wise? Behavior-wise?"

"She did some, like, self-cutting," Ashleigh said, looking me right in the eye. Then she glanced at Lucille, who nodded solemnly, but let out a soft giggle that she quickly suppressed beneath a hand.

"That's...awfully obvious, isn't it?" Reed piped up from behind me. "Didn't anyone else notice?"

"Uhm, we only noticed in the locker room," Ashleigh said, looking past me at him. "Changing for PhyEd, y'know? She kept it where no one could see it."

I frowned in concentration, mulling that over. Yep, that'd be a classic outlet for a sexual assault survivor. Almost textbook, in fact. "Yikes. Any other signs?"

Ashleigh half-shrugged, raising a tanned shoulder. "I dunno. She was always quiet before that, so she never really changed in any other way? Y'know?"

That made sense, too. Predators picked off the weak. If a teacher was going to prey on a student, it made total sense he'd pick one that was socially isolated – then her response might be to make herself even more isolated. Ugly stuff.

"Thanks," I said. "This is helpful."

"So are you really investigating this for Mr. Berry?" Ashleigh asked. "Like, to prove him innocent?"

"I think everyone deserves a chance to defend themselves with the facts available," I said, giving the rote-est answer possible. "Regardless of the crime."

"But, like...the facts are bad for Mr. Berry," Ashleigh said, giggling almost like Lucille, who joined in nervously. "I mean...come on. They found his DNA in Greta. How does that translate to innocence?"

It was my turn to half-shrug. "Maybe he's guilty of rape but not murder. Maybe someone planted the evidence."

Ashleigh twisted her face up almost comically. "That's not a thing."

"Absurd as it might sound," Reed interjected, "you just never know until you investigate every possibility."

"But, like, he slept with our friends. And killed Greta." Ashleigh folded her bare arms in front of her. "How do you get 'innocent' out of that? I mean, if he hadn't been caught, he might have done the same thing to Syrena. Or Lucille and me. I mean, he totally made, like, a move on me once."

"Did he?" I asked, leaning closer.

"Yeah," Ashleigh said, sticking out her chin almost defiantly. "I mean, why wouldn't he have? But I was like, *no*. Because ew. He was so old." Her shoulders were tense.

"Why didn't you tell any of this to the police?" I asked, trying to keep my voice very neutral. I didn't want to come off like I was disbelieving her; it was entirely possible she was telling the truth. It was also possible she was jealous that Mr. Berry might have had sexual interest in two of her friends and never displayed any in her. Sure, that was dumb, but teenagers were not world-renowned for their exceptional judgment.

"It's not a big deal," Ashleigh said. "It's not like he was the first."

That time I did look at Reed, who'd stepped up to stand beside me. "There were...other teachers who'd hit on you?" he asked.

"Sure," Ashleigh said, unfolding her arms so she could put her arms out to indicate herself. Like, of course there were grown men falling over themselves to be interested in her.

Reed was looking at her with narrowed eyes. "You should tell that to the cops. I'm pretty sure they'd be very interested."

"Maybe I will," Ashleigh said, taking a step back. I got the sense our conversation was almost over, because she was looking around at the dance floor like she wanted to fly. "Are you guys going to just be a drag all night?" Now she was looking at me. "Or are you here to do some actual partying?"

"Strictly business," I said with a thin smile. "You go have fun for us."

"Fine," Ashleigh said with a hint of impatience and a smirk. "Later." And she waved a mocking toodle-oo, dragging Lucille, who was not smiling, along with her toward the dance floor. Without their drinks, which were sitting on the bar.

"That was odd, right?" Reed asked, eyeing the drinks like I was. "I mean, I don't know teenage girls, but..."

"It wasn't completely out of the realm of normal," I said, watching them disappear into the dark crowd at the dance floor. "But it was unusual. And I think that Ashleigh's at least a bit of a self-involved narcissist."

"I was getting the, 'In A Relationship With My Own Instaphoto Account,' vibe from her," Reed said, leaning an elbow on the bar. "You feel anything sinister?"

I frowned. "No. It's not unusual for her age bracket to be somewhat self-obsessed and sure the world centers on them. Even before social media. What we saw here is not ridiculously out of line for an alpha mean girl. I think." I shrugged. "I didn't go to high school, after all, so most of what I know from the social interactions of this cohort is from my required psychology texts and a steady diet of John Hughes VHS tapes."

Reed frowned. "Your mom didn't even spring for the DVDs?"

"Why would you want clear picture, flawless sound, chapters and instant, digital rewind when you could have the soft whir and clack of mechanical gears turning in your VCR?" I asked with a half-smirk. "Also, we had one of those old, square TVs until like 2010, so a DVD player, while nice, wouldn't have been as useful as after the HD revolution."

Reed surveyed the area around us. "Well. Technological

woes of your deprived childhood aside, I'm not sure whether that conversation was enlightening or a horrifying glimpse into the mind of teenage girls."

"It can be both."

"She was just so damned callous," Reed said. "And do you believe that Berry actually ever made a pass at her?"

I screwed up my face thinking about it. "For the moment, I neither think that he did nor that he didn't."

Reed's eyes narrowed as he tried to untangle it. "Huh?"

"I'm not a cop anymore," I said. "I don't have to put together a case on it either way. He might have. He might not have. He may have signaled something to her sexually that she picked up on and refused; he may have just been nice to her and she misread it. To me, this story is like one of those really dark pieces of a puzzle that goes somewhere in the middle but doesn't really change the picture much. Either Berry is the kind of scum that she's describing, and he totally did it, in which case him hitting on her is kinda the least of his sins. Or she's wrong, and he's innocent, and she's either wittingly or unwittingly trying to put another nail in his coffin."

"Unwittingly?" Reed stared at me. "How do you figure that?"

"Like I said, maybe she's jealous of her friends getting that attention and trying to socially justify that she never got it."

"Here's a dark thought," Reed said. "What about these two? Doing the deed and somehow framing Berry."

I thought hard about my reply before speaking. "It's not impossible. But it's complex, getting all that, uh...proof...for the frame. And it's real dirty, so I would need more evidence that they're anything other than slightly mean girls. After all, it's a pretty big leap from being shitty to people in school to cold-blooded murder and frame-ups. To me, the possibility that Berry is just a child predator is more likely. Whether he's guilty of the murder or not."

Reed's lips turned in disgust. "But if Berry was really guilty of being a pedo without being a murderer, would she need to craft this kind of story to get attention? Or to justify to herself that he never went after her?"

"If Berry is, in fact, a pedophile sleeping with his students," I said, calmly and clearly, over the thudding beat in the dark club, "going after Ashleigh would have been, in my estimation, the single dumbest thing he could have done."

Reed's face got completely screwed up now. "...Huh?" He looked back over his shoulder; there was no sign of Ashleigh or Lucille. "Maybe you're seeing this differently, because you're a girl. Let me explain – of the four, Ashleigh is the prettiest of these friends." His face flashed almost white for a second. "I mean that in as non-creepy a way as I possibly can."

"There's no objective, non-creepy way for you to gauge their looks, old man," I said with a smirk. "But your point is taken. Now catch mine – Berry's not moving solely on looks, if he's doing this pedo thing. He's making his decisions based on other criteria – like attainability, risk mitigation–"

"Right," Reed said, putting a hand on his forehead. He looked disgusted to even be having this conversation. "Like you said: predator and prey."

"If he's been doing this, he's a clever one, not some burning-hot-under-the-belt fiend seeking immediate release. He's cold, calculating. He's been angling to not get caught," I said. "So yeah, he's going after the weakest and most isolated, not the prettiest, boldest, and most connected." I looked over the dance floor, where teenage and near-teen bodies were packed in close, tight. "He was culling the weak from the herd. Not the strong."

"Like a wolf," Reed said. "Which sort of answers my question for how you learned to think like this."

I smiled, but only faintly. The smells of this place, of the crowd, and the way my brain interpreted them, left me in no doubt that he was right. Forever, I'd been changed by my association with a real predator, one who knew the exact hunt that someone like Berry – if he'd done what he was accused of – was partaking in. The sly, dirty logic, the evil games. I'd seen them firsthand, in memories from the worst and best teacher of the sort I could have had. "Let's go back to our table and wait," I said, nodding him back to the empty table from which we could survey the crowd.

He nodded, but I could see the uneasiness weigh on him at my insights. And I couldn't blame him, really. The ghost of Wolfe was, after all, still with me. Always.

CHAPTER FIFTY-SIX

The club was filled with a thumping, driving beat and there seemed to be nearly no difference between the songs, at least not to my aching, aging ears, just a steady stream of bass with some lyrics thrown in every now and again for variance. I couldn't tell if the DJ, over at the far end of the dance floor, was just synthesizing the song as he went, or if this was a track from some artist whose name I couldn't have told you if held at gunpoint.

Reed, too, appeared pained, a steadily deepening cringe on his face. "Really works on you over the long term, doesn't it?" I asked, tossing back a little water and still wishing it was cut with whiskey. There was an itch under my skin and an ache in my eardrums that wasn't going away until I got out of this acidic sound bath. Maybe not even then.

"Do you even hear what they're saying at this point?" Reed asked. "It feels like someone's jabbed a hot icepick in my ear over and over again. I keep waiting for blood to seep out."

"If you want, I could sing for you and get that started," I said. "Maybe burst the eardrum entirely."

"Might take you up on that if we're here much longer," he said, then turned, reacting to me waving to some teenager who was waving furiously at me. She didn't approach, but her grin and excitement was palpable, her eyes glued to me as she went past. "Friend of yours?"

"If I've met her before, I couldn't tell you," I said. "It's a normal reaction in crowd situations. You get used to it."

He rolled his eyes. "I'll never get used to it, and it happens to me, too. Just less than to you."

"I could do without the fame," I said, looking around. Others had noticed us, too, but few enough. Lots of the kids here were buried, nose-down, in their cell-phones. There was little to no chatter of conversation, I realized at last. Just the damned death beat of the music, and the noise from the dance floor. There was no conversation otherwise. "Have you noticed...?"

"That other than the enforced murder music and dance floor, it's kinda like a wake in here? Except with cell phones?" My brother's grimace lightened. "Yeah, I noticed. Kids nowadays aren't much for actual socialization, I guess."

Whatever my brother was going to say to that, I missed it, because I caught a flash of motion coming in hot behind him and stood to address it. My movement caused him to come to his feet quickly, sensing the danger before it swooped in–

–To give me a hug.

"You came!" Isolde shouted, catching me right under the arms, which I threw up just in time to keep her from pinning them to me in a bear hug, and indefensible. Girl was strong, too. I probably could have broken her grip, but it would have hurt her, and based on the tenor of her voice, I realized a moment after she had me–

–She was drunk.

Like...really, really drunk.

I looked down; there were no X's on her hands. Unlike mine.

Isolde set me down quickly, her head lolling slightly in that way drunken people get. "I can't believe you came out tonight. This is so amazing."

"Yes, amazing," I agreed, grabbing her a chair from the next table and guiding her into it before she could fall down. "Uhm...fake ID?" I cut right to the chase.

She looked around mischievously, then held a finger to her lips. "Shhhhh. I'm totally twenty-one plus."

"How many times have you failed twelfth grade, exactly?" Reed asked dryly.

Isolde turned around on him, grinning, and planted that finger right on his lips. "You're cute. I've always thought you were cute." She turned back to me. "Isn't he cute?"

"I'm no Cersei Lannister, but he's a handsome enough fellow," I said, trying to get her to focus. Her being drunk could end up being a bonanza for us in the interrogation department. Or a patience-trying disaster. She was likely to be more cooperative, but I could already see her attention was going to be tougher to corral in her current state. "Isolde, I've got a couple questions for you. About school."

"Ugh, school," she said, sticking her tongue out. "I am just so over that place. It's...like a constant funeral these days. I mean, I enjoyed it for the longest time. Good energy, y'know. A real youthful vibe to the place. I'm starting to think I might need to move on, though."

Reed blinked a couple times. "I...I think that's called graduating."

She turned back at him, smiling sweetly. "Yes. Yes, that's right. That's what most people do. Graduate." She patted him on the cheek, then turned back to me. "But seriously, seriously...I have to tell you..." Her face went blank. "What was I going to tell you?"

"Something related to the murder?" I asked, hoping, just hoping, that it was germane, and not some drunken tangent she was going to drag me on. I mean, if she did I probably deserved it, because she was the spitting image of how I'd looked the last few months while drinking, but still...

"Ugh, the murder," Isolde said, pitching her head back slightly. "Seriously. Seriously. A drag. Total drag. Stoaks has been just terrible since it happened. It was such a cool place to be before this. Now you might as well stream black crepe paper down the halls and put a coffin in every corner. People aren't partying like they used to. It used to be all...YOLO up in there. Now it's like people have no lives to live. They're staying home on Saturday nights, their parents all afraid the ghost of Mr. Berry is going to get out and rip their precious babies' virginities away." She snickered. "Which is hilarious, because...it's just hilarious."

I traded a look with Reed. "Why?" I asked.

"Because...a lot of those party girls aren't virgins," Isolde said, collapsing into giggles. "And if they haven't slept with someone older than Berry by now, I'd be shocked." She smacked her lips together. "I need a drink. Do you need a drink?" She pointed at me, then Reed. "You?"

"I'll get you something," Reed said, standing up quickly and looking at me with great significance. "You two keep talking."

"Mm, okay, I'll take a Moscow Mule," Isolde said. "Heavy on the vodka, light on the ginger beer and lime juice? Okay?"

Reed opened his mouth to argue, but apparently thought the better of it. "Be right back," He said, and off he went.

"He didn't even ask you what you wanted," Isolde huffed once he was away.

"He knows what I want," I said, thinking happily – but not really – of a water bottle. "So, uhm...we've had some conversations in the last day..."

"Yeah, I saw that thing on the internet with you and the headmaster," Isolde said. "Learn anything good?"

"From Prestegaard?" I shrugged. "He's a nice guy. Not sure he's got the pulse of the school, though, from where he sits. At least not the student body portion, y'know?"

"Yeah, it's kinda tough for the old farts to get down with us *yutes*." Isolde laughed. "Same old story, right? We want to live fast and die young, and they can't identify."

"Oh, yes, you're horrendously misunderstood, with your grandiose ideas and non-fully-formed prefrontal cortexes," I said. "So anyway...uhm...we're struggling a little, to be candid, with motive for why someone would want to kill Greta Oliver."

Isolde shrugged. "Well...just look at it from the point of view of a potential killer."

I tried not to smirk. Failed. "That's kind of my job. The problem is that we don't know these people, we don't know the dynamic at the school. And it seems likely it came from the school. Greta Oliver didn't really know anyone else, go anywhere else that we can find. Which means–"

"That I know the murderer?" Isolde sounded so jaded by this that I wondered if she'd just gotten used to the thought of it by now with Mr. Berry being accused. "Yeah. Probably."

"But you don't think it's Berry?" I asked.

"I don't know, but I don't think so," Isolde said with a shrug. "Tough to know a person, really, like what they'd do in all circumstances, but...nah. I don't see him being like that."

"We heard the same from his rival, Mr. Henderson," I said.

"Which is interesting, because I would have definitely pointed the finger at Mr. Henderson way before Berry," Isolde said, slouching back in her chair like we were having the most natural conversation in the world. And about nothing to do with murder and all else. "Hell, I'd have pointed the finger at Prestegaard before Berry."

That was interesting. "Why them?"

Reed came sliding up beside her and delivered a drink to her which she quickly snatched up. She held it just in front of her lips, pausing to answer. "Well, why not? They both work in close proximity to teenage girls, right? Just like Berry."

"But there are lines," I said. "It sounds like Berry was chummier with the teenage girl set than either of those other guys."

"Yeah," Isolde scoffed. "Which would be something you wouldn't want to be seen doing if you were going to, y'know, shag and murder one. So either Berry's a complete moron, making it obvious by being the teacher that everybody loves, and being close with the kids while screwing one or more of them, or he's as smart as I always thought and wasn't. And looked close to the kids because he actually cared, not for nefarious reasons."

"That's an interesting alternate theory," Reed said.

"Yeah, well, I'm interesting," Isolde said, and toasted to him before taking a slug of her drink. She promptly spit it out in a cloud of moisture that reflected all the shades of the rotating LED spotlights in the club. "What the shit is this?"

"Moscow Mule," Reed said with a thin smile.

"I think you mean 'Virgin Moscow Mule,'" Isolde spat, wiping her lips like she'd just had a drink of toilet water. "Ugh. I'm not into anything virgin, okay?"

"I could have guessed that about you," Reed said, "But I'm not contributing to the delinquency of a minor. They'll arrest me."

"Ughhhh," Isolde said. "You could have just said that's what you were going to do. I would have gotten my own drink." She started to get up, but three large bouncers converged on our table just as she did so. She stood there, staring at them, drink in hand. "What do you want?"

The largest of the three was in the lead. He had the same belt-radio setup as the guys outside, with a thin cord snaking up his back to a terminus in his earpiece. "Gonna need to see your ID, ma'am."

"For a virgin Moscow Mule?" Isolde sighed, then put down her drink and fumbled through a tiny clasp purse I hadn't even noticed she was carrying. She came out with an ID and presented it to him for inspection. "Here."

He looked at it for a moment, then back at her; she definitely did not look twenty-one. But then, most days, neither did I. "Thank you," he said, then clicked the button on his radio. "She's good."

"No, she's not," Isolde said, putting her ID back in her purse, "but after a trip to the bar maybe she will be." She shot an ugly look at Reed. "Thanks for nothing."

Reed started to reply, but couldn't; the earpieces of all three bouncers were hit with a massive squeal of radio feedback, and my brother cringed terribly as it bled through the distance between us and them. Reed's head jerked back in sudden shock, as did my own–

And so did Isolde's.

The guys wearing the earpieces? Cringed. But that was all.

Because none of them were meta.

But Isolde, apparently...was.

I came to my feet, as did my brother, a little behind my own reaction. Isolde, though, was still cradling her head. She'd been closer to them than we had, but she hadn't failed to notice...that we'd taken notice. She was watching us both with a sort of uncomfortable look frozen on her face, and she put her little purse down on the table. "So..." she said, sighing as she dropped back into the seat, "...I guess we should talk about that, huh?"

CHAPTER FIFTY-SEVEN

"Are you over twenty-one?" I asked, easing myself back down into my chair. I wanted to keep a close watch on Isolde from here, the memory of Eve Kappler front of mind in case I needed a non-lethal option for dispensing with any trouble she might be ready to dispense.

"Yeah," Isolde said, sighing deeply.

"How over?" Reed asked.

"I'm a lot older than you, prettyboy," she said, clearly losing her patience. "Let's leave it at that."

"What the hell is up with the teeny bopper routine?" I asked, almost laughing. "I mean...my teenage years were like the least fun of my life, and I didn't even go to school. Why would you want to perpetually be locked in the state of classes, peer pressure...clearly you've skipped the 'no alcohol and sex' suggested portion of teenager-ing, but still...why?"

"Oh, I don't know," Isolde said. "Why would I want to anchor myself in a stage of life where responsibility is small and the fun is always? Instead of in the part of life where you wonder how you're going to pay your rent and worry about recognizing the signs of a heart attack?" She shook her head.

"It's a real mystery. Are you crazy? The teenage years are the best if you don't have any angst or confidence issues. And I don't. Which is why I'm the coolest kid in school."

"Oh," I said. That made some small amount of sense, actually.

"Okay, so you're a fully developed person living in amongst the natives," Reed said, sweeping a hand around the crowds of teens and early twentysomethings inhabiting the club. "You're basically undercover here."

"For my own enjoyment, yes," Isolde said. "Don't make me sound like I'm going all *21 Jump Street*. I'm not; I like the drugs and the teen keggers and the endless possibilities, okay? I'm not ratting anyone out. I'm just enjoying myself."

A terrible thought occurred to me. "Do you...date boys from Stoaks?"

She sighed. "Occasionally. But mostly I go a little older, okay? Better for my reputation."

"Wow," I said, with so many questions and so few I wanted to know the answers to. "How many times have you pulled this routine?" I pointed at her. "Because...you can't have been at Stoaks since kindergarten and just keep repeating."

"I drop in a school – usually a restrictive prep school where the kids have enough money to be really fun – around tenth, eleventh grade," she said. "Graduate, find a new school, do it all over again somewhere else in the country."

"You're like a vampire," Reed said, pointing at her. "You're like one of those vampires that–"

Isolde grunted and slid down in her seat. "I am so misunderstood."

"Now you do sound like a teenager," I said. "All right, well, whatever. You're not the murderer, right?"

"You should have a drink, because if that's how you ask your questions, you are way off your game while sober." She looked up at me, greatly annoyed. "If I were the murderer, I'd hardly admit it, would I? But no, I am not. And I don't know who it is, either, before you try and push me on that. I would have told you if I did."

"This is an interesting thing you can shed some light on, though," I said. "Because the murderer...they were a meta."

She looked tense; I could tell I'd hit a vein. "Yeah. So I'd heard."

"So the question becomes," Reed picked up for me, "if you're a meta at Stilloaks...one of the fractional portion of the population who is..." He just let that hang.

"Don't try and good cop/bad cop me," Isolde said. "It's been done before, but by much more experienced ones than you two. Like I said, don't know who the murderer is."

"That's not what my brother's asking," I said, watching her tighten up, "and I think you're wise enough to know it. What he's asking–"

"I know what he's asking," Isolde said, sagging. "He's not going to like the answer. And neither are you."

My jaw tightened as I asked the question. "How many metas do you know that are at Stilloaks?"

It should have been an easy answer. It should have been one. Two, maybe.

"I don't know," Isolde said, instead of giving us that. And her face fell, telling us...so much more. "A lot. You have to understand...that meta serum...it's a designer drug now. The hottest ticket. And it made its way around last year on the party circuit. Like...to *every* party. So eventually...everyone took it."

Reed's eyes were wide. Real wide. "So what you're saying is...you don't know because..."

"Because there's too damned many to count," Isolde said, looking from my brother to me. "For all I know...every student at that school over grade ten is a meta by now."

CHAPTER FIFTY-EIGHT

Oh, man.

There were moments in my job where facts came to a clarifying point. Where the information I uncovered cast prior events in a new light, shattering my previous perceptions like a good, solid hammer blow upside the head.

This was one of those moments.

"Oh...for..." Reed swore under his breath, putting his head down. "So, Berry wasn't a meta, but the whole student body was? That's just great."

"I don't know whether Berry was a meta or not," Isolde said. "I do kinda know...he wasn't...well, he didn't ever make a move on me or anyone I know."

"That proves nothing," Reed said darkly. "Except that his tastes ran younger than the people you hung around with."

"Any of the administrators metas?" I asked. "Since you were throwing shade at Prestegaard and Mr. Henderson?"

"Uhm, not that I know of," Isolde said. "And I'd probably know, because this thing that happened just now that blew my cover? Happens all the time at school."

I thought back to when we'd gone through the front

doors of Stilloaks Prep, how the security guards had been wearing radios with earpieces. Static squeal was not a bizarre occurrence for cheaper radio sets, so what she said made sense. "That's not definite, though. You'd have to have been in the presence of one of the teachers or administrators when one of those sonic squeals went off."

Isolde shrugged. "True, I guess. Just never noticed it any of the times I've had to cringe from it." She made a face. "And it happens all. The. Time. Or at least enough to annoy me."

Reed was poking at his ear. "Doesn't take it happening many times to achieve that result."

I nodded, already shooting off down my own train of thought. *What's on your mind?* Brianna asked as I fell into silence, and Reed and Isolde got into a conversation about other everyday noises that annoyed metas.

This whole thing is a dark blanket over my head, I said. *By the way...I appreciate your quiet as I'm working through...everything.*

Just trying to be supportive. You know, now that you're doing the right thing.

Yeah, well, I said in my own head, *let's hope it lasts.*

Amen, sister, she said. *Amen.*

"But first," I said, breaking out of my head, "I really need to solve this crime. And there's a lot I'm not seeing."

Reed and Isolde both looked at me quizzically. "Did we just...miss part of the conversation?" my brother asked.

"Yeah," I said. "And it is thus: we have no clearer idea of what's going on in this case than we did yesterday, other than having snagged character details about our client and the autopsy report."

"You witnessed the lead-up to the murder," Reed said. "Don't discount that."

"Whuuuuuuuuut?" Isolde turned slowly to look at me, her eyes about as narrow as they could get.

"It was a time travel thing," I said, dismissing her with a

wave. "It didn't give me anything except more questions. And a ringing headache."

"I have questions," Isolde said, "specifically related to this 'time travel.' Also – you actually *saw* the murder through time travel? Uhm – seriously, whuuuuuuut? I cannot be the only person who is going to ask this. Just – whuuuuuuuut?"

Uncomfortable stares were coming our way from Isolde's loud reaction. The tables around us were crowded with kids on their phones, and all had looked up to look our way after she'd spoken aloud, which I did not take as the greatest sign.

"Keep your voice down," Reed said, bending in closer to the table. "We don't need everyone knowing this."

"Yes," I deadpanned, speaking meta-low, "we don't need everyone knowing that we know nothing. Let them think we know everything. That will be great for..."

I paused, because a noise caught my attention. It was not a normal sound in the club, at least not normal in the sense that it occurred at the volume and amount that we heard it in this moment.

Because *it*...was the sound of breaking glass.

And it...was not just a single glass or bottle breaking.

It was every glass and bottle along the entirety of the bar. Cascades of alcohol flooded down the shelves beneath the screams of the teens standing nearest to it. The mirrors that ran behind the length of the booze bottles exploded, too, showering the bartenders and filling the air with more screaming and panic.

The spotlights caught the glitter of clouds of glass hovering in the air like great swarms of crystalline insects, sparkling like diamond stars in the night sky. There was a veritable constellation of them, hanging in the air, the lights dancing over the cloud as large as a car. They gathered there for only a moment before moving – of course – in the only direction that they would, naturally–

Directly at us.

CHAPTER FIFTY-NINE

"Get down!" I shouted, throwing our table over, grabbing it by its base and whipping it in front of us as a shield.

Then the table was ripped, without warning, out of my hand, and flew across the room, leaving us defenseless.

"Shit," Reed mouthed, throwing his hands out.

A hard wind blew from behind us as the glass swarms rocketed toward us like tiny crystalline missiles of death. It was clear what was going to happen here; a swarm of glass that size and depth, run through us at that velocity, would be like tossing a human body in the path of a debris field in space. We'd be shredded into strands of meat like I'd once seen Reed do to an army in Revelen. The biggest remaining chunks of us would not look out of place in a stew pot.

"You defray, I shield!" I shouted, counting on my brother to do what I suspected he was doing anyway.

He did.

Blowing the wind as hard as he could, he slowed the progress of those whipping, murderous shards coming our way. The spotlight helpfully turned in our direction as they made it about ten feet in front of us, and suddenly the wall behind them was alive with a disco ball effect of light shining through the glass. Reed was desperately fighting their forward momentum, sweating as he mustered all the air movement he could within this enclosed nightclub, trying to keep them from turning the three of us into a casserole.

While he was doing that, I was working slightly above and below him so as not to interfere with his movement of the winds. Isolde shuddered, stepping back. The shiver was not from fear. Or at least, not entirely.

I built up two full walls of ice above and below us, holding them tightly in place as I filled them in. They went from inches deep to two feet thick in seconds as I threw everything I had into them. Reed's winds began to flag–

And I dropped the ceiling wall down and shouted, "Duck!"

My brother, Isolde, and I, all conditioned by long life experience, dove into the relative security of the shadow of the ice wall as Reed's wind faltered.

Clouds of broken glass flew over our heads, no longer impeded by Reed's wind resistance. They shot past us, paused in the darkness, sparkling like there was some malice being reflected in the thousand glassy eyes, then–

"Jump!" Reed shouted, and the three of us leapt and rolled over the wall as the glass cloud sprayed into my impromptu ice barrier.

Being tuned to the ice, I could feel the places where glass ripped into it. It felt like a shotgun effect peppering my shield, digging into it. Once buried inside, though, the glass didn't stop.

It kept ripping through the ice.

"Run!" I shouted, and grabbed my brother by the collar and Isolde by the back of her top. They were both on their feet and running a second later, all of us hauling ass for the exit.

Another sparkling swarm of glass shot past us overhead, dangling and angry, and I had to wonder why it hadn't just ripped right through us. A glance to my side revealed the answer, as a gust stirred my hair.

Reed had blown it off course. Just enough that it had arced over us.

"What do we do?" Reed shouted, sweating feverishly. The screams of the teens around us were panicked, frenzied. All thoughts of their Instaphoto accounts and Socialite streams were out the damned window. There were a lot of glittering halter tops breaking for the exits, and a lot of high-heeled shoes abandoned in the melee of all these kids trying to exit.

Which presented a certain problem I now recognized, and one which, thankfully, our opponent hadn't.

Yet.

"Lotta hostages in here," I said, meta-low.

Reed glanced at me. "For the moment," he said, getting it.

Then he put his hands up, readying himself for the next round. Because it was coming.

And because he knew.

We were going to have to fight this directionless, disembodied swarm of telekinetically thrown glass right here while these kids escaped.

Because otherwise...

Innocent teenagers were going to get torn to pieces.

CHAPTER SIXTY

"Isolde, if you see an opening, you might want to bail," I said, lighting my arm from shoulder to knuckles and setting my clothing on fire in the process. Out of that, I extended the flames in a circular motion, a Spartan shield of pure, superhot flame I could crouch and duck behind.

On the other side, I was building a shield of ice that would run the length of my body, an ovoid slab of hardened frost. It was part of a strategy, really, to see how effectively I could combat the swarms of glass. Fire or ice? Which would work better?

I had a feeling I was about to find out.

"Go!" Reed shouted, shoving Isolde to the side as a blast of glass came our way. He threw out his hands and a roar of contained wind blew past.

It parted the glass above, below, and to either side of him, sending it rocketing off in all directions.

"I have an idea," I said, "but I'm not sure whether it's a good one."

Reed cast a look of pure desperation at me. His forehead

was drenched in sweat. "At this point, I'm willing to try anything."

"Well," I said, "you might want to cover your ears, cuz I'm about to burst into song."

"Okay. Maybe not that?" Reed paled, then blasted Isolde toward him with a gust of wind. He grabbed her and shoved her hands over her ears, then ducked down, looking at the glittering minefield of death that was, even now, reversing course in anticipation of coming back and cutting us to shreds.

I pictured Brance Venable in my mind, narrowing my eyes as I stared at the cloud of twinkling glass.

Then I let loose with a burst of unadulterated, absolutely terrible, autotune-worthy song.

The sparkling shards burst, going from a constellation of stars into a sparkling field of stardust. It writhed, then dropped, and I looked around as it coated the floor, dropping out of my song–

Our attacker was in earshot, and had been stopped by my bloodcurdling singing.

"Reed!" I called out, and he nodded, still crouched with Isolde. He'd seen it, too.

The crowd was filtering out of the club, and there wasn't much left to exit. That meant our enemy was one of the malingerers here, hiding either in the shadows or not even bothering to hide. I cast a look around the mammoth club, which I realized, wasn't a labyrinth at all, given I could see almost all of it from where I stood – seeking a hint, something, anything, that would tell me where they were, who they were. The shadow behind this whole thing was clearly watching, and had acted the moment they heard Isolde say we had witnessed the murder.

We needed to get unpinned here, to destroy this threat against us and get down to the important business of catching our quarry. This was the first time they'd exposed themselves, and now we not only had their power locked down, we knew the range at which they were using it. Somewhere in the room.

The glittering dust cloud of glass rose up and surged at me. I lifted my ice shield, throwing my body behind it–

Glass dust shaved its way through my ice shield at the top and around the sides, skimming along my cheek and drawing blood. A warm trickle ran down my face, and I whirled as the glass dust surged around me like it was caught in a wind current.

This told me a little something about the meta's control of the glass. It was finicky and imprecise. Was that a feature of the power? Or a quirk of someone who didn't know how to use it?

Of course...I had a bad feeling about who this attacker might be, too, but I didn't quite want to leap to it. Yet. Not when they were right here in the building and I could still chase them down and confirm it.

Yeah.

Them.

Whirling to put my fire shield in place, I had to hope that the heat of my flame would be enough to digest shards of glass.

It was. Mostly.

Specks of surviving glass passed through my flame shield and dotted me, bouncing off my face and hair, threatening to start me on fire. I went and flamed my hair out just to hold that at bay.

"Sienna!" Reed called. He watched as the last of the glass spent itself against my shield. "Watch ou–"

A little too late; I got clobbered from behind by a discarded chair, and it rocked my world. Another followed, shattering against my ankle (and also shattering the ankle).

They were coming hot and heavy now, minus the hot, and my hair had caught one of the seats on fire.

"Holy shit!" Isolde shouted, and I heard her shoes slapping against the floor as she retreated some distance, then vaulted over the bar. The splash of liquid against her shoes told me where she'd sought cover.

"You all right?" Reed asked, lifting his hand and sending another chair shattering against the wall.

"No," I said, snuffing the fire on the chair next to my head with a thought as I healed. Reed had set up a wind break, and these larger objects being hurled at us now – chairs, tables, part of the lighting rig – were flying off course harmlessly, burying themselves in the wall behind us. "But give me a minute..."

I shot to warp speed right there, almost cracking the sound barrier inside the club. I came to an abrupt halt at the far end of the room, almost sure I knew what I was going to run into.

Those damned girls, Lucille and Ashleigh. They had to be here somewhere.

I skimmed the dance floor and shot into the women's room just beyond. There were windows at the far end, and girls climbing out of them furiously.

None of them were Lucille or Ashleigh.

I blasted around the corner, ignoring the half dozen scattered, unfamiliar people still lurking around – idiotically, gawking – on the dance floor. None were making offensive movements.

Into the men's room I went, where I didn't really find any men. Mostly squealing little boys, also trying to get out the window.

"Huh," I said, returning to the dance floor. I hovered a couple feet above the ground, looking over the entirety of the place.

"Sienna!" Reed called, beckoning me toward him. The furniture had stopped flying, and I caught his meaning.

Mostly because I could hear the sirens in the background.

"Yeah," I said, and shot over to him. "Wanna fly?"

He shook his head. "We're already fleeing a scene. We really don't need that additional trouble from Minnesota right now."

Couldn't argue with that. "Fine," I said. "We'll try it the traditional way. But you'd better hope Lethe made it here by now."

"Gotta check the bar for Isolde," Reed said, making his way over to where I presumed she'd disappeared. "We can't leave her behind–"

I made it a second after he did.

Isolde was gone. A trail of debris that looked like crawl marks hinted at her path through the spilled liquor and out an emergency exit to the side of the bar.

Reed followed my gaze, then met my eyes. "Wanna go out that way?"

"Well, I sure as shit don't want to go out the front," I said, and off we went, coming out behind the mini mall and into a dark, barely lit alley.

Teens and young adults were running around, having escaped out at least one other emergency exit back here, but Isolde was nowhere in sight.

"Where'd she go?" Reed asked, looking around. He stared into the darkness of flickering lights at either end of the strip mall's back parking lot.

"She ran," I said, feeling the drag off all the power usage I'd just pulled, like a tiredness worming its way into my mind. I'd already been feeling the ass-kicking Akiyama had laid on me for violating the rules of time. I usually didn't feel the effects of using my powers, even after using them hard like I just had, keeping that fire shield burning.

"That seem suspicious to you?" Reed asked.

"Yeah," I said. "Almost as suspicious as us getting attacked when Lucille and Ashleigh were in the crowd tonight."

Reed's face dissolved into shock. "Wait...now you think it is the girls? Because I was just coming around to the idea that Isolde's been stringing us along the whole time and just tried to bushwhack us."

"No time to talk about it now," I said, listening to sirens railing in the distance, drawing ever closer. Bright car headlights slid around the corner to our left, highlighting the two of us and a half dozen other straggling teens, who all immediately fled down the embankment in front of us.

The car came squealing to a stop beside us, and Reed and I waited for it to do so, mostly because I had a feeling I knew who was driving it. Lethe stuck her head out the window and bellowed, "What are you waiting for? Your boober app or whatever to beep and tell you I'm here? Because it's not happening. Get in."

"You heard your grandma," Reed said, sliding over the hood like one of the Duke boys, then cramming himself in the back door. "Let's motor."

I slid into the passenger seat. "Thanks for coming," I said. "How'd you know we'd be out back?"

Lethe gave me a sideways look. "The police are coming. Only an idiot would go out the front."

That made sense. She gunned the engine and off we went, dodging teens as we sped off into the Minnesota night.

The last one I'd ever spend here.

CHAPTER SIXTY-ONE

"So, seems like you were having a normal night back there," Lethe said, keeping her hands steadily on the wheel as she raced for the nearest interstate. Her strategy was familiar to me; get as far clear of the incident as possible in the allotted time. Best strategy for that? A road where you could travel seventy miles an hour the hell away from it. "How'd it go?"

"We finally made contact with the enemy," I said. Then, catching a frown from Reed, I added, "Maybe."

"Keep in mind the enemy tried to run us over this afternoon outside that coffee shop," Reed said.

"Okay, that's true," I said. "But now, I finally feel like I have a line of sight to the enemy. It's–"

"Isolde," Reed said.

"–Lucille, Ashleigh, and maybe Syrena," I said.

"No jinx," Lethe said, taking a corner at about forty miles an hour and nearly rolling the car in the process. I pushed against the door and used my flight powers to keep the tires on the ground, otherwise we'd have been enjoying the washing machine effect as we tumbled up and down in freefall. "So...competing theories of the case? Let me hear them."

"I think you should concentrate on keeping the car from going airborne," I said.

"I have you and your flight powers for that," Lethe said, oh-so-sweetly. I guess she noticed.

"It's Isolde," Reed said. "It has to be. She was there with us for the whole attack, never once made a move to help, just watched the attack happen. She was masterminding it the whole time; steering the glass toward us while she was pretending to have nothing to do with it. It started the moment she found out you'd seen the murder–"

"Which was announced, loudly, to the entire club," I said, "and at which both Lucille and Ashleigh were in attendance, and would have heard."

"You couldn't hear it through the *whole* club," Reed insisted. "You'd have to have been paying attention. Besides, Isolde admitted to us that she was an old meta. Old enough to have the power to do what happened in there. No newb is going to control their powers like that."

"What kind of power are we talking about here?" Lethe asked.

"Telekinesis," I said, beating my brother to the punch. "But I'm telling you – Isolde doesn't fit."

"Look, I don't like the mean girl vibe from Ashleigh any more than you do," Reed said. "But like you said before – it's a big leap from being a mean girl to being a murderer. Especially when you're taking out one of your friends."

"Clearly you've never had friends as a teenage girl," I said. "It's always a thin line between loving them one day and hating them the next."

"You didn't have friends at that age, either," Reed shot back. "Unless you felt that way about your teddy bear."

"Mom didn't let me have a teddy bear. And that's beside the point."

"Hold," Lethe said. "What kind of powers did you say? Tele-what?"

"Glass," I said, "chairs. We're dealing with full-on telekinesis here. Moving objects with the mind, you know?"

"Oh." Lethe's brow furrowed. "That is a rare one."

"You've dealt with it before?" Reed leaned forward, planting a hand on each of our seats and peeking his head between. We were in a four-door sedan of some kind, one of those small variety kind nowadays rather than the roomier, pure Detroit cruisers of days past, probably a Ford Fusion or a Toyota Camry. I hadn't been able to tell in the dark as it rolled up.

"I've dealt with just about everything in my day, sonny," Lethe said with a trace of a smile. "The problem with – what was it? Oh. Telekinetics. It's a very draining power to use. And they have to be proximal."

"See, the telekinetic could have floated the incriminating underwear into Berry's window," I said. "And floated him out in a drunken stupor."

"Right to the murder scene," Reed said, nodding. "And maybe even, uh...extracted the evidence that way." The look on his face was priceless. "Y'know...without having to touch him, or despoil the, uh..."

"Yeah," I said. "The, uh...DNA evidence."

"Semen," Lethe said, and Reed and I both cringed. "It's called semen." Her face switched to puzzlement. "You're saying...someone used telekinetic powers to extract that? Like..." She made a motion with her hand that had me cringing.

"I guess?" I shrugged, feeling deeply uncomfortable having this conversation with my grandmother. "I mean, they could have plucked it out of a condom he used with his girlfriend? Or a, uhm...solo emission? But it seems like this would be another way to extract the evidence to frame him without leaving a mark, right?"

Lethe guffawed. "So whichever of these suspects you're talking about, they milked him like a cow with an invisible air hand?"

I looked at Reed, who looked equally pained to contemplate this. "Well," he said, "Isolde is not a teenager."

"Right," I said. "Odds are good she's, uhm...milked...a few in her time–"

"Haven't we all," Lethe said. "Still, I feel like you're soft-pedaling this a bit. Why do this to your teacher?"

"That's the fuzzy part," I said. "And by the way? I still maintain Ashleigh or Lucille could have done this, especially now. If you don't have to touch the person you're manhandling in this way, it's got to be easier to...uhm....do...that."

"Extract semen?" Lethe asked. "Just say 'semen.' There's no point pussyfooting around it anymore."

"I'm not saying it," I said irritably.

"Why?" she asked. "It's not like you haven't seen it, haven't–"

"Okay, either the hectoring stops immediately or this car does," I said, using my flight powers to drag the suspension down. The bottom scraped the road for a second, sparks flying out on either side of us. "I'll talk about anatomical functions however I want to, all right? The point gets across either way, and the point is this: we actually have a unifying theory of *how* Berry was framed now, okay? And that's important."

"Yeah," Reed said, "now we're just lacking consensus on the who and the why."

I frowned, wrinkling my nose at that. I saw a road sign pass, and realized we were heading south on 694 and Lethe was about to take the Hudson exit onto 94 toward Wisconsin. "Hold up," I said, gesturing for her to skip and keep heading south. "I'm staying in Eden Prairie tonight."

Lethe looked at me sideways. "The cops are looking for you in Minnesota. They'll be waiting outside Ariadne's. You must know this."

"I know," I said. "I'll have you drop me a couple blocks away and I'll go in the back door."

She sighed, rather theatrically. She really did seem like Sigourney Weaver in that moment. "You don't think they'll have that covered?"

"They can't watch everywhere," I said. "And they won't be expecting me. They've got to believe by now I'm staying with the rest of you, over in Wisconsin."

Lethe looked at Reed. "What about you? Are you staying with your fiancée tonight?"

Reed tilted his head, getting the most uncomfortable look on his face. "Hell, no. She told me to go to Wisconsin so I don't bring the law down on our place." He must have realized how he'd just dinged me, because he hastily added, "But she's coming to live with me wherever we end up, so...that's a little different, I guess."

"Exactly," I said. "Ariadne's been with me through thick and thin, and she's not coming with. I've really done her wrong these last few months, and I feel like I owe her one last goodbye that's not tainted by alcohol or me being a burned-out husk of a human being. All right?" I looked at each of them in turn.

"This makes no sense," Lethe muttered.

"Logically, no," I said. "But we're human beings, grandmother. We don't always make our choices on logic. Emotion is the stuff of life. I'll watch my back, okay? If Minnesota comes for me, I'll fly off out a window at rocket speed. But I kinda doubt they will, because Miranda is currently burying them in lawsuits using the last of our cash, so I bet they'll think twice about kicking down Ariadne's door without probable cause, which I will sneakily avoid giving them. Okay?" I smiled.

There was low-level grumbling from both of them. Lethe got over it first. "So what are we supposed to do tomorrow? Pick you up out front?"

I flashed my phone at her. "We'll set a rendezvous a few miles down the road. Or I can just fly to Hudson and meet you, if the cloud cover is heavy enough and I start early enough." I yawned. "Last day in Minnesota, after all. I bet it's going to be packed."

"There's still a lot to uncover here, Sienna," Reed said nervously. "We need some kind of break to get this case to open up. Right now, we've got nothing but a theory, and they don't let people out of the Cube for theories."

"Believe me, I know this," I said, looking at the window as we rolled through Woodbury, now heading south on 494. We'd be in Eden Prairie in about thirty minutes if traffic stayed light. I checked my phone again, this time making a note of the...well, the time. It was almost ten.

A little over a day until deadline.

"We'll make it happen," I said, feeling the dragging sense of tiredness that this day had inflicted on me. It felt long. Too long. Too filled with red herrings and too empty of productive leads.

But the mask had started to come off our seemingly invisible enemy, and I took some solace in that as I started to nod off on the journey back to Ariadne's to spend my last night in Minnesota with the woman who'd become a surrogate mother to me.

CHAPTER SIXTY-TWO

"I was beginning to worry," Ariadne said as I crept in the back door, listening for any sound of sirens or police radios anywhere in the distance. The neighborhood was quiet, and the basement widescreen TV was turned down low as I came in. Ariadne was laid out in the recliner, a strange vision given she never sat down here and watched TV. Her place for TV viewing was upstairs, either in the living room or her bedroom. She was wearing a flannel nightgown and the touch of sleepiness was upon her eyes, like I'd woken her coming in.

"You waited up for me?" I smiled as I closed the door as quietly as I could.

"Just catching the local news," she said sadly. She thrust the remote toward the TV screen, on which there was a report playing from a certain local teen nightclub in Oakdale that had a whole fleet of police cars out front for some reason. The chyron read, "Metahuman Incident at Teen Club," and below that, in smaller typeface, "Sienna Nealon may have been involved."

"Exciting stuff," I said, making my way over and sitting on the opposite end of the couch. "And honestly, probably the most thrilling part of my day."

Her face fell. "That bad?"

"It was almost action-free until the end," I said. "I was having a twisty but relatively quiet case for once. Someone ran at me with a tractor-trailer, but other than that it's been all dramatic conversations and revelations and treachery and such. No fisticuffs." I flexed my hand. "Actually, there still haven't been any fisticuffs, which is very disappointing to me since I like to punch faces. But, I did get to sing, and it sounded better than anything the club played. Though their glassware might disagree."

"What...happened to their glassware?"

"I turned it into glass sand. With my killer vocals."

"Oh," Ariadne said, still laid out and leaning back in the recliner. She put the remote in her lap and lowered her eyes. "I was hoping you'd make it back a little earlier."

I slowly lowered myself into the seat down from her. This couch had recliners built in at either end, a helpful boon for when I'd felt like leaning back but Harry had wanted to remain ramrod upright. Personally, I felt like puddling, so I kicked mine back to match her lying-down position. "I know," I said. "I know I've sucked since I relapsed. I've lived here and we haven't really spent any time together because I've been busy...well, dodging you so I could get drunk."

She nodded slowly. "When we lived together before, we'd watch stuff every night."

"Wait," I said, frowning. "You remember that now?"

"A little," she said, smiling faintly. "Thanks to Dr. Zollers's help. And while I didn't think it'd be exactly like when we used to work together...I didn't anticipate how little I'd actually see you."

"I know," I said, lowering my head. "I've let a lot of people down. And I wish I had more time to make amends." I hesitated. "...But I don't. I've got tonight, and that's it, so..." I forced a tight smile. "...You want to watch a movie or something?"

Ariadne smiled. "I would. I really, really would."

CHAPTER SIXTY-THREE

Road to Perdition ended up being the film Ariadne chose. Soon enough I was engrossed in the gangster period piece about fathers and sons, blood and adopted, and the ties that bind us all. There was some real subtext there. I was pretty sure I'd seen it before; fairly certain it was an Ariadne favorite, and somewhere after the magnetic scene in the rain between Paul Newman and Tom Hanks, I managed to tear my eyes from the screen and over to my watching companion.

She was sleeping, slumped in the recliner, eyes closed, her breath coming slowly, evenly, her chest falling with a steady rhythm. The gray roots were starting to show in her red hair; her striped cotton nightgown looked like it had been around since before I was born. The sight of her sleeping stirred a memory in the far back of my mind, one that I felt surprised to still have, mostly from sheer shock that Rose hadn't taken it.

It was from before I left the house for the first time. I was sitting on the couch and I was eight years old. There was nothing but darkness, no light from beyond the blackout curtains that covered every window. The smell of burned

Ramen hung in the air. Stomach acid burbled in my stomach from sheer excitement.

The clock read 10:01, and little me vibrated with excitement and just a little fear.

My mother slept on the couch next to me, her face lit by the glow of Christmas lights. She'd gone out somewhere in the second act of the movie, leaving me to watch on, with a little fear and a little wonder, as I continued well beyond my limit of one hour per day of television time.

Jimmy Stewart was running through the streets of Bedford Falls wishing everyone a Merry Christmas when I heard her stir. I looked over with apprehension, that dull, sick feeling in my stomach like I'd done something very wrong by letting my mother sleep.

She looked at me through half-lidded eyes, her hair all mussed up from the couch cushion, then at the clock. "As soon as it's over...go to bed, okay?" Then she put her head back down without another word.

My heart threatened to explode in my chest. I was staying up past my bedtime AND getting extra TV time.

Mother stirred again, looking at the red clock above the TV. It read 10:17. "Merry Christmas," she muttered, and then went back to sleep.

I remembered that night so well. Another Minnesota memory that easily made the top five. Best one I could recall, period, at my old house.

Best I could, recall, period, involving my mom during my childhood.

"Ariadne," I said, shaking her awake after the movie came to its quiet conclusion on the beach of Perdition and the final destination that followed. The credits were rolling, my eyes were misty for more than one reason, and it was closing time here.

She stirred, putting a hand on mine and giving it a couple

pats. "I'll miss you," she said, looking at me sleepily. "Not the you of the last couple months, obviously, but...you." She slid her hand up to my sleeve. "You need to take care of yourself, okay?" Her eyes locked on mine. "No more drinking."

"I know."

She seized my arm. "No. I mean it. Ordinary people can have a weakness. They get behind the wheel while drunk, a few people die. You do it..." She shook her head. "...It could be thousands."

There was a lump in my throat. "Believe me...I learned about the consequences of my failure to take responsibility firsthand a couple days ago." Even if that hadn't been the lesson Madison had been trying to teach me, it had been one I'd taken to heart. "I won't make that mistake again."

She patted my cheek. "I know it's unfair. To be asked to carry all this...but it's what you were born to do."

"I don't know about that," I said, gently removing her hand before the burning started. "But I did choose it." She cocked her head at me, disbelieving. "I made my mom lock me up so that I could become who I am now." I shrugged. "I didn't choose everything that came from it, but I decided to accept the responsibility for the world when I made that choice. I just need to...get tough again. To pull myself out of the spiral of shame and get back to it, you know?"

She nodded. "I know you will."

"I already am – in a small way, I suppose." I picked myself up from the couch. "Every case is an extension of that ethos, large or small. Me trying to make things better, even an inch at a time, or for one person."

"One is the smallest minority there is," Ariadne said, sitting up. "It's a lot easier to crush a small person, a lone person, than even a group."

I nodded. "I've thought about that sometimes, when it felt like everybody was gunning for me."

"I imagine that's very difficult," Ariadne said. "But to me...that sounds like a feature, not a bug. Like you're the pilot of a plane and yeah, gravity's unfair, always pulling you down, but–"

"But it's my job to compensate for it," I said with a wry smile. "Yeah. I'm starting to get that. I think I just let myself get too down. Too helpless." I stuck out my tongue like I had a terrible taste on it. "I hate that I let it get to that. But I guess I'm fortunate in that I have a chance to correct it."

"You do," she agreed. "And please do." She stood, and drew me into a hug. "Please. Please do."

"Yes, ma'am," I whispered. We'd been around each other so long nothing more really needed to be said.

Which was fortunate, because at that exact moment...

...the window on the back door shattered, and something flew in.

A bottle.

On fire.

It crashed against the carpet and exploded, flames spreading in every direction. Whatever fuel had been used – and I suspected gasoline by the smell – was lit now, and burning, fire filling the basement and blocking the exits.

"Oh my God," Ariadne whispered over the flames, barely audible over the crackling and the sound of the fire alarms blaring all over the house. "We're trapped."

CHAPTER SIXTY-FOUR

I rolled my eyes.

I lifted my hand.

I dragged every single square inch of the fire into me with barely an effort, sending frost out and leaving a thick powder of ice over the black spots on the carpet where the gasoline had been burning only a moment before.

That done, I spun on the broken window and frosted the pane, creating a new shield of ice out of nothingness, a solid block that covered over the hole where the bottle had been thrown through. It thickened and blacked out the view of the backyard in a few seconds.

I grabbed Ariadne by the arm. "We gotta hustle," I said, and pulled her up to my side, then leapt to the stairs.

"What are you doing?" she cried. But she grabbed me around the neck, the better to stabilize herself. "Aren't you going to fight them?"

"It'll be lopsided if I do," I said, leaping up and out the stairwell door into the front hallway. The fire alarms were still blaring, but were starting to settle down now that there was no more fire or smoke. I checked the windows;

they were all still covered, the blinds closed. "And not in my favor. This meta? They can only attack what they can see."

"So?" Ariadne asked as I vaulted us up to the landing, heading to the second floor.

"So with all the blinds down," I said as the last fire klaxon died, "they have no line of sight on us. I need to get you somewhere safe before they decided to bust in. Somewhere like–"

"My closet?" she asked helpfully.

"Exactly," I said, making the final leap up into the house's loft, then racing through the master bedroom and into her closet.

Ariadne's closet was spacious. Ever the fashionable, professional lady, she was currently in the midst of her summer wardrobe, with a few brightly colored outfits sprinkled in among the tamer, more sedate suits. With the change of the seasons, she'd pull her new wardrobe out of one of the three spare bedroom closets. There would've been room for another wardrobe in her closet, but after the cops came for her shotgun, Ariadne had bought a little something extra to guarantee her safety. She wasn't a fool; she knew living with me carried risks.

That was why she had a nice, seven-gun safe sitting in perfectly good hanging rack real estate. To be clear, she didn't have seven guns in there; it was just the smallest safe she could find to accommodate the three she did have.

"Bullets are going to be iffy against this meta," I said, setting her down just inside the closet door. "If you need to shoot, try and blindside them. They've got telekinetic powers. That means–"

"Move things with the mind, I got it," she said, already working the digital access on the safe. It beeped and she popped it open as I ducked back out into the master bedroom, listening for the inevitable sounds of trouble coming.

They didn't take long.

The kitchen/dinette area below opened onto a small, fourteen-by-fourteen-foot wooden deck that had a staircase leading down to the basement level ground below. I heard heavy, thudding footsteps on the deck stairs, and then the scrape of someone grabbing up one of the metal chairs that sheltered around the table on the deck.

A second later, that metal chair was sheltering on the kitchen table, a pile of glass scattering its way across the wood floors, the kitchen slider blind crashing to the floor as it all came in with the heaved chair.

I waited in the loft overhead, figuring I'd ambush my would-be attacker the moment they tried to charge the stairs. For now, though, I was just listening, and suddenly quite glad that Ariadne hadn't activated the alarm for the night. All this shattering glass would have set it off, and instead of hearing muffled grunting from below, my ears would be ringing and I'd be effectively deaf to my approaching enemies.

Shoes crinkled across broken glass, which I thought was interesting. Why wouldn't a person able to lift objects with their mind just float over the glass? Maybe it was because, like my grandmother said, all that heavy lifting wore a body out. I didn't hear the glass tinkling in the air, either, and that made me wonder – was our telekinetic here? If not – why not? And if not...who was visiting me tonight?

Ariadne padded up behind me softly and I waved her off, back to the closet. She had a semi-automatic shotgun in her hands, a big one, the Mossberg 930 Jerry Miculek Pro. Ten rounds, no waiting, no pumping. I'd helped her customize the load out in case she ever had to take on a meta, and I'd gone with double ought buck alternated with less-recoil rifled slugs. Double ought buck was a cloud of murderous pellets that could turn limbs into instant sausage without the casing to hold it together; slugs were just a big lump of metal that'd put a big damned hole in a body. I felt good about our chances if the telekinetic wasn't here.

Though that did raise another question: What the hell was going on here? Or rather: who? And maybe: why?

A thump of feet against the floor below made me lift off the ground, floating, looking down at the staircase below. I was just outside Ariadne's bedroom, and here I could look down into the stairwell and see the hall below. A shadow was moving slowly across the floor, inevitably toward the bottom-most stair...

I readied myself, conjuring to mind the thought of Aleksandr Gavrikov as well as Eve Kappler and Brianna.

Then I looked back at Ariadne and said, "Sorry about this."

And I leapt over the railing and plunged into the stairwell, smashing into my opponent at the bottom of the stairs, driving them through the floor. Beams and plywood buckled under the force of my impact, and together we tumbled into the basement and crashed through the base of the stairs down there.

My opponent grunted; they were big, way too big to be natural. Then their freakishly large hand grabbed me, muscles bulging at the sleeves, the arm, and even the chest and legs.

It was a Hercules, a muscle-swollen freak with super strength.

And they had me firmly in their grasp.

Uh oh.

CHAPTER SIXTY-FIVE

When you find yourself in the grip of someone stronger than you, it's not really the time for recriminations about the bad choices that led you to this moment. When you're in the hands of someone who can break bones with a simple squeeze, who can throw you a dozen yards with the greatest ease, it's not a time for quiet reflection and consideration.

It's time to hit hard, hit fast, and get the hell out of reach.

I slammed my fist into my opponent's solar plexus with everything I had, but encountered a muscular abdominal wall that was totally flexed. I'm not saying it was like punching steel, because I've punched steel, and there's a big difference between the kiss of steel on my knuckles and this, which sounded like a ripe pumpkin getting tapped. My opponent did nothing but grunt.

Ah, shit.

I'd fought Hercules types before. Hell, I was related to one. My grandfather, Simon Nealon, was one, as was my uncle, Friday–

Who I'd once absorbed a memory out of.

Hmmmmmm.

Picturing Friday in my mind, I tapped another shadow power I hadn't even realized I had. My skin began to contort around every muscle group, straining at the bounds of my clothing. It was nothing like a real, true-blue Hercules, who could shred their clothing from Hulking out. But I did feel a boost to my strength as I increased the density and power of my muscle, and as a succubus, I was already pretty damned strong without even being all that ripped.

When I grabbed the Hercules's arm, she – and the noise convinced me it was a she – sucked in a pained breath. I twisted it, trying to knock her out of the fight fast, and she screamed, elbowing me with the strained, mangled joint and letting out another cry as she struck me.

I took the hit in the sternum, and I felt the extra gusto put into it by her Hercules powers. It sent me flying into the bathroom wall behind me and into the tub. When I hit the wall of the shower I stopped, mostly because beneath the tile I'd just crushed was a concrete wall, and an offhand blow from a Hercules wasn't quite enough to send me through that.

It was, however, enough to knock me silly.

There were seconds in which I tried to get myself together. Blood was seeping down my forehead; my skull had been smashed into the concrete, which was just not good for my health, mental or otherwise. Brushing my hand against my scalp caused it to come away smeared red. I held up my hand in the dark and watched it glisten, the light flooding in from the other room where I'd left them on when Ariadne and I had retreated.

I summoned Wolfe to front of mind and felt the clarity and sharpness of thought return as the concussion and brain damage faded. I blinked my eyes a couple times, then floated back to my feet and followed the holes in the wall back to where the Hercules was standing in the light, elbow dangling limply.

Now I had a better look at her. She was dressed in a track suit with a ski mask, like a low-grade sort of tactical chic. The bodybuilder muscles disguised her form, so I couldn't tell if this was someone I'd met earlier or not. No hair was dangling out of the back of the ski mask, and she was disguising her voice under the grunts.

Or...she really, really had a husky voice. Like, "gargled with broken glass and smoked a pack a day" husky.

"Let's try this again," I said, listening for sirens in the distance. Someone had to have heard all this madness, either from the Molotov cocktail or else this beast's entry into the kitchen. I lifted one hand and lit it on fire, then the other and set it aglow with fairy light. "Hi. Who are you? And what do you think you're doing here? Other than experiencing pain."

She shuffled sideways, turning her body to keep her injured arm in back. I respected the move, but I questioned the wisdom of it. Now I just had to deal with one more arm and I'd more or less have her at my mercy. At which point we could get some questions answered.

Deciding to just skip right to that, I blasted her with fairy light, anchoring her good hand to her body and causing her to look at what I'd done with great surprise. Like, "Wow! I can't believe she just did that."

Then I shot at her at (relatively) high speed, figuring I'd knock her over and it'd all be done.

But, as per usual, my best laid plans went badly awry.

Blame it on me being tired; it was after midnight, and I'd had a long day. Somehow, I hadn't connected the fact that while I'd disabled her arms, they were not the only part of her capable of causing me damage.

When she leapt off the ground with both feet at incredible speed and slammed into me with a dropkick so fast I didn't even see it coming, I did remember. In that fleeting second before her foot broke my jaw, oh, yes, I remembered.

I went through the wall – again. Different hole this time. A new one, actually. This time I ended up in the bedroom, smashing through the closet and into cardboard boxes of something or another. Sounded like glass from the noises they made. Or maybe that was my spine.

Don't call it a blackout, but I did kind of lose consciousness for a few seconds there. I opened my eyes again to find a shadowy form over me, way too big to be a normal person, and with a beefy hand extended over me. She draped it over my throat like a necklace...

...And started to choke the life out of me.

CHAPTER SIXTY-SIX

When you're having the life choked out of you, you'd think it might clarify the mind. Focus you on the things that are really important, like the fact you're alive, and how great being alive is compared to the alternative.

Nope. That does happen eventually, but only if you survive.

In the moment, all your brain can do is revert to the same lizard programming that it does when you're drowning, where the only thing you can think about is air, and getting air, and why can't I breathe air, and maybe I should flap my arms like a big, stupid bird, and flail my legs wildly until I get them on solid ground. Anything to stay afloat.

Sure, you can overcome this mental programming with hard training. Get the logical segment of your brain to fire during these times of stress. Navy SEALs train this way, for example.

Me? I'd never actually trained to overcome it, but I'd been choked and drowned a time or two. Not quite enough to have come to the point of zen where I could logic my way through asphyxiation.

Fortunately...I still had a friend for that.

Ariadne's shotgun boomed, and the giant specimen of a woman who was throttling the life out of me absorbed a round of double ought buck right in the back. She let out a scream of pain and her grip loosened.

Another blast, this time of slug, and the spray of blood across my face was immediate as the big hunk of metal burst through my enemy's rib cage just to the side of the heart.

Man, I missed having a gun. If I'd had one just now, I might have been able to pull it, stick it up against my foe's chin, and paint the ceiling with her brains, giving Ariadne another renovation project to charge to my broke ass.

As it was, I had to rely on her to come save me, which was mildly annoying for a woman who preferred to do everything – including her killing – for herself.

The Hercules collapsed to one knee, and her fingers slackened around my throat. I spun, delivering a kick to her solar plexus and listened to her wheeze as she fell over. Probably less from me and more from the fact she had a gaping hole in her left lung, and deposits of lead balls all over in her chest cavity. That was bound to exert a drag on one's enthusiasm.

"You all right?" Ariadne asked as I stepped back from the Hercules, who was now on all fours, bleeding profusely on Ariadne's carpeting. Once beige, it was terminally red now, and let me tell you something learned from long experience: blood does not come easily out of high-pile carpeting. If at all.

Man, these renovation projects were really adding up.

"I'll live," I said, massaging my throat. "Bitch tried to David Carradine me."

"He was alone," Ariadne said, shotgun still to her shoulder, eye perfectly positioned over the sight, a look of confusion breaking out across her slightly wrinkled face. "That's why they call it '*auto*erotic asphyxiation.'"

"Fine, she tried to duo-non-erotic asphyxiate me." I stepped back, flaring my hand to flame. Sirens were going, but way in the distance. My guess? MN BCA was coming, but in force rather than chancing sending in a single officer against lil' ol' me. "Thanks for the assist."

"Don't mention it," Ariadne said, keeping that shotgun on target. If Hercu-Lea tried anything, she was going to get another round of double ought buck, this time to the face. It didn't take a great marksman at this range and with that gun, but Ariadne was more than adequate to the task.

The Hercu-Lea was gurgling, a terrible noise that told me there was fluid in her lungs. Definite pneumonia risk – if she survived the bleed. I felt time slipping away and tried to decide what needed to happen next. The answer seemed obvious.

"I need to get that mask off her before the police show up," I said, lifting a hand. I blasted both of hers to the ground with light webs, hoping they'd hold against her bull strength. Then I did the same to her feet.

"I'll circle over here," Ariadne said, shifting subtly sideways, her nightgown rustling as she did. "Cover you."

I nodded. She'd need to focus on some part of her body that wasn't close to me. "Take a leg off me if you need to. I can grow mine back. She can't."

Ariadne nodded, keeping her gun steady. The sirens were getting closer, and I approached slowly, shuffling across the carpet. I planned to lull Hercu-Lea with my slow movement, then dart in at the last second and snatch the mask.

I didn't get the chance, because something else...surprised me first.

The entire wall of the basement opened up, ripping the door, the supports, everything – completely out.

A cloud of drywall dust and plaster followed that awful,

world-ending sound. The whole house groaned under the strain, part of the facade collapsing as a shadowed, female form appeared in the cloud, floating through it like me, hovering a few inches above the ground.

The murderer was here.

CHAPTER SIXTY-SEVEN

I didn't hesitate. There was no time to, not with a meta this dangerous.

She was there, in the cloud of dust and plaster, clad in black with a ski mask to hide her identity. Long hair was bundled up beneath it, and she was obviously female by the shape of her body. Other than that, in the cloud of dust from her demolition of the wall of the house (new doors, new windows, fresh stucco and siding – that was going to be a whole lot more renovation, lemme tell ya) there was little I could tell about her.

I needed to knock her out of this fight swiftly. The easiest way to do that was get inside her defenses and pummel her so she couldn't use her powers.

Hence, the Gavrikov maneuver.

I launched into top feasible speed from my standing position next to Hercu-Lea, and rocketed toward her, keeping Brianna in mind as I did so. I formed ice along my shoulder, my back, letting my sweat freeze and moisture be drawn out of the air as I flew toward my target–

And suddenly...I stopped.

The black clad telekinetic (or TK, for short) held her hand out, and considered me, her head cocked slightly. I could see the corners of her mouth in the tiny slit in the mask, and they were curled up in amusement.

I was trapped in her grip; so much for getting inside her defenses. All I'd managed to do was get myself caught in her powers.

She motioned with her hand and I flew sideways across the basement, crashing into the built-in wood cabinetry at the far end (but missing the widescreen TV, fortunately, because I really didn't need to cost Ariadne any more money right now). I slammed into that and wood splintered, cracked, and generally made noises like I'd broken bones.

Fortunately, I hadn't. In the uncomfortable period between her gripping hold of me and loosing me into the far wall and cabinets, I'd built up ice armor beneath my clothes. It absorbed most of the damage, though not all. I was still going to be sore for a bit.

Wolfe...I thought.

There. That was a bit.

I decided to play possum, though, let her approach.

Then I remembered, as an invisible force wrapped around my throat, that my foe didn't need to approach to crush me into Spaghetti-O's.

"Oh, come on," I grunted, straining against this invisible enemy. It didn't even feel like a person had me. There were no fingers on my body, no warmth of a hand or press of skin against mine. I was lifted out of the wreckage and it felt like there was uncomfortable, cold contact with almost every surface of my body.

Then I got thrown through the far wall into the storage room, and my ice armor took another beating. My head, fortunately, did not, because it was the only part of me at this point not covered by an inch of frost. Silver lining: because

Madam TK wasn't actually laying her hands on me, she couldn't tell that my clothing was below thirty-two degrees Fahrenheit.

I landed on a pile of suitcases that collapsed when my full weight hit them, and my tailbone cracked against ice, which cracked against the bare concrete floor in the unfinished storeroom. Looking up I could see the bones of the house, two-by-fours and larger beams stretching overhead, shadowed by the light flooding in from out in the basement living area. Ariadne, wisely, had made herself scarce for this. She had a pretty good grasp of when she was outgunned, and seeing me tossed about without any recourse was probably enough encouragement to tell her not to stick her nose in this one. At least not until she could get the drop on the enemy. If such a thing was possible with a TK.

I kept Wolfe front of mind and stayed down, because until I had a strategy, there was no point in sticking my head up to be hammered. I let her come to me, running through my entire repertory of powers for ideas of what I could do that didn't involve things she could throw back at me.

I had a few ideas.

Bringing Friday to mind, I increased my strength to its maximum, letting the ice armor adjust and flow around my bulging muscles. I tried not to look at my thighs, either, because they were already big enough without going swole.

The door to the basement storage squeaked open, and Madam TK came floating in. I guess she'd had enough of the theatrical and decided not to rip open the wall so she could float through.

Or...as my grandmother had told me, this power consumed a lot of strength, and our practitioner was weak. Maybe she was saving her strength to deal with me.

Well, she was going to need it. As soon as I felt her invisible grip take hold of me again, I opened my mouth, brought to mind Brance Venable, and belted out a few notes of the seminal AC/DC classic "Highway to Hell."

Something glass broke behind me on a storage shelf, and Madam TK's grip on me vanished instantly. She came off her high horse – well, invisible horse, maybe – and dropped to one knee, covering her ears.

Too late.

I charged over the distance between us with Gavrikov flight power and slammed a Friday-embiggened fist against her jaw.

It was Madam TK's turn to launch, and launch she did, like a rocket leaving Cape Canaveral on a clear, crisp day.

She smashed through studs and drywall, back out into the basement living area. She clipped the couch as she tumbled head over feet, and caught herself just before she smashed into the far corner of the basement wall. With a flick of her hand, she floated off it.

I opened my mouth to shout a few more notes of "Highway to Hell," but something caught in my throat.

Or rather...some *thing* did.

It felt like a whole fist was being shoved in my mouth, choking me. Another surge of force ran across my body, this time catching me in the gut, across the chest, and it rammed up, up into the floorboards above and through them–

I crashed through hard subfloor and up into the entryway hall to Ariadne's garage. A shelf for stacking shoes collapsed on me, and I hit the glass light fixture on the ceiling like I was the dinger on one of those test your strength contraptions at the State Fair. I'd been good and rung, and I dropped, flightless, into a pile next to the door.

My body hurt in a lot of places, but my Wolfe healing was hurrying to make those things right. I'd definitely taken some cracks to the ice armor, and I hurriedly knitted those back together while trying to shake off the pain that had been inflicted across the whole of me.

The black figure of Madam TK drifted up through the hole, headfirst, and I let out a bellowing scream of Brance voice. She reeled like I'd punched her, bouncing off a shattered two-by-four board and thumping down into the basement below.

I dragged myself to my feet in time to see Ariadne come sliding down the wall of the kitchenette, tilting her shotgun around the corner. I shook my head; she'd climbed the stairs while I was tangling with Madam TK, but her shotgun wasn't going to do shit in this fight. I gestured toward the shattered sliding glass door just across the kitchen table and the wreckage of glass. She needed to get out of here, now, and that was the fastest exit.

Ariadne pointed to her bare feet. Well, shit.

I grabbed her and shot out through the gaping hole in the glass door, hoping to avoid any more entanglements with Madam TK and her bulked up follower, but of course it did not go as planned. Just as I reached the door I felt a tug on my foot, and barely had time to drop Ariadne on the deck before another tug from a different direction radically altered my momentum.

Madam TK mentally hurled me through the frame of the sliding glass door. My back went smashing through the remainder of the glass, the aluminum casing, the solid wood that made up the door frame, and then I crunched through about five or so two-by-fours, a mess of drywall, and several feet of vinyl exterior siding until I hit the frame of the living room window and stopped, the sound of shattering glass tinkling as the window broke from the momentum of my hit.

I wasn't hurt too bad, but I had to admit there were much less painful ways I could have spent my last evening in Minnesota.

However, this was quite on brand for me, getting pushed through a damned wall sideways, so I guess it did have a rough sort of symmetry to it.

Madam TK drifted up behind me, tightening her grip and slowly applying more force. I burst through the frame, dragging arms and legs behind me and let out a cry of surprise to play the part. I traversed through the empty window, saw the sill pass a couple feet beneath my face, sparkles of glass twinkling in the white from the light in the house.

I slammed into the frame of the second window, and still Madam TK kept trying to force me through wall sideways, like a giant using a knife to cut through the place. No knife, though, just me and a hell of a lot of pain. I had enough presence of mind, in between keeping my ice armor together and running Wolfe healing like a background program on a computer, to realize that what she was really doing here was hoping to cut me in half. I imagine she thought that it'd take some of the starch out of my shorts.

Guess she didn't realize I was all starch, all the time. Mostly due to potato chips being a cornerstone of my diet.

I let out a hard grunt as she rammed me, ribs-first, into the frame. If she kept it up, eventually it would break through my ice armor, and then it'd be a contest of Ariadne's home's building materials versus my very flesh and bone. I might win in the short term, but over the distance I was going to get ripped apart. The scraping of wood and aluminum against my ice armor should have been a big clue to Madam TK that not all was as it seemed, but the sirens were now so loud (as was my breathing) that she probably wasn't hearing it.

She floated onto the back deck just as Ariadne was hitting the ground floor from descending the stairs. Ariadne did not mess around; she was really moving like her life depended on it. She wheeled at the bottom of the stairs, and I saw her raise the shotgun and look up at me between the deck supports.

I shook my head. No point getting involved in this mess.

Madam TK said nothing, just gave me another hearty shove and bam, in I went through another series of supports and out another window's frame and sill. My insides felt like they were getting squeezed into jelly, and my ribs felt like someone had been working them over with a baseball bat. No pleasant feelings there, but I'd been hurt worse.

I was wedged once more against a window frame, the pressure incredible, probably enough to kill a normal human, or maybe even me if she'd put my head against it instead of my (protected) right side. The shearing forces were reaching intolerable levels, even through the cracking ice. Which I was having a hell of a time holding together, even with Brianna's full assistance.

Hang on, she said, *just hang on a little longer...*

The sirens were close now, and the reflection of red and blue lights was reflecting wildly against the house next door. No good was going to come of the cops arriving, not even if they were BCA and ready for a full-on meta rumble.

"What's the matter?" I asked, trying to stay in the range of huffing and wounded, but unwilling to let Madam TK take a free shot at me without at least verbally abusing her in my own particular idiom. "You having a little trouble finishing the job?"

She made a deep scoffing noise in the back of her throat, and I hit a Brance note as she started to shove again. That dropped me from her grip, and I started to slide forward out of the window, taking up my own weight with Gavrikov powers. I kept the sonic assault on point and pointed at her, then jetted for her, figuring I'd land a blow of my own to knock her ass out and beat feet before the cops showed up–

Nope. She gripped her ears, got her concentration, and slammed a bone-breaking telekinetic attack on me before I could make contact with her face by shattering it. I felt a hard rush of gravity and force and I flew through the air not under my own power, tumbling. I passed the third story of Ariadne's house, got a solid look at the roof, and then came back to earth, bereft of breath. She'd shattered my chest armor and knocked the wind out of me, stunning me momentarily.

She snagged me just before I smashed into the stones that filled Ariadne's back planters. I hung there, suspended, and again something heavy shoved its way into my mouth, working over my vocal chords and blocking my ability to breathe. I choked silently, no air coming into or out of my body.

"Freeze!" someone shouted from behind me, as my body spasmed under the panicked feeling of losing my breath again. I could feel the presence of someone – maybe more than one someone – just feet behind me, and somehow I knew they were cops. Not BCA, but beat cops, because BCA was holding back like chickens, waiting for more backup.

Madam TK just looked at them like they were nothing, and made a hand gesture spinning me about so I could see, with my own eyes, what she was about to do to them.

CHAPTER SIXTY-EIGHT

The cops were no fools, but neither were they ready for what was coming here. I could see the red and blue flashing of their lights reflecting off their skin, lighting up their scared faces. One of them was aiming at me (of course); the other was taking aim at Madam TK.

I was clawing at my throat, my body jerking and spasming at the lack of oxygen. The warm night air and all the stress of the moment was causing sweat to stream down my forehead, down my back.

Gunfire split the night like summer thunder, and I struggled to get my presence of mind back in spite of the drowning sensation that was sapping my will to think, to fight, to do anything other than twitch and scream internally.

In the light spilling out from the house, tiny specks were visible hanging suspended in the air between me and the police.

Bullets.

Madam TK had stopped the bullets. Just stopped them in midair.

I couldn't see her, but I did hear a faint, silvery laugh, slightly muffled and utterly malicious.

The bullets moved slowly, lining up like a spray of shotgun pellets in front of me. It didn't take a genius to realize what TK was doing.

She was about to plant a dozen rounds into me at full force from about two feet away. They were lining up in front of my face, making it absolutely clear where they'd hit. From this distance I could see the hollow points, waiting to hit my skull and expand until they blew out the back of my head at about three times the size. It was an elegant solution, really; she'd kill me with the police bullets, then crush them or otherwise make it look like they'd been killed by me. Then she'd disappear, leaving BCA to conclude that Sienna Nealon had left Minnesota in the most appropriate way: by killing the police and then having the grace to finally die here, on the home soil. No escape. An ending Governor Shipley could be happy with.

I writhed beneath the grip of her powers, but also under the assault on my mouth and throat. I'd regained some presence of mind, albeit not much. Just enough to call up one more backup program (soul) to run in the part of my brain that wasn't panicking over oxygen deprivation.

But it was a dead useful soul, the one I picked.

Madam TK flung the bullets at me, and I could feel them coming through the air. They weren't whipped lightly; there'd be no gentle impact upon my skull followed by a ricochet, or even a simple OW! as one penetrated my eyeball and stuck there. She was winging them at me with killing force, enough to leave me dead.

But like I said, I could feel them coming. And not in the sense of how a distant whiff of something moving fast by you triggers your skin to goosebump, either.

I could feel them. In the air, before they even started cutting toward me.

Because I'd recently – as in two nights ago – partially drained the soul of one Chad Goodwin, a Magneto-type, and used his powers while I was in contact with him to rip open the door of a metal vault.

I hadn't absorbed his full soul; if I'd been trying to stop bullets over a long distance, I might have really struggled. Similarly, if Madam TK had been an actual Magneto instead of a telekinetic, she could have slapped my paltry hold on the bullets away like momma slapping down a pre-schooler.

But we were competing meta types haggling over the object in question, and she didn't even realize that I was altering their course until they were past my head and embedding themselves in the deck, the house–

Oh, and her leg, in the case of one. She must have lost track of that one in her surprise at feeling someone shoving back hard against her control. She let out a scream as it ripped its way through her calf. All her control over me, over the rest of them, vanished in that moment.

I dropped to the ground, keeping my mental grip on that one bullet. I pumped my fist as I caught myself, sucking in a deep, fulfilling breath, and jerked hard, imaging what I wanted that bullet to do.

It obeyed, ripping up through her leg, skipping along the back of her knee, slipping under the skin along the back of her thigh, and tumbling out of her right buttock. That's right; she had bullets coming out of her ass.

Her scream doubled, tripled in volume, and she took a knee like she was bowing to her queen. Which...really, she sorta was.

Unfortunately, I lost track of the bullet after it exited her, and I was pretty messed up, gasping, feeling some serious phantom pain from bruising along my throat and ringing my chest. I tried to get up on my feet, but fatigue was definitely settling in. I'd used a lot of powers in the last few minutes, and it had already been a long day. I was running on pure adrenaline and spite and that was it.

"Sienna!" Ariadne shouted, and then BOOM! she filled the air with a cloud of buckshot.

She really shouldn't have shouted, though, and I think she knew it a second later, when Madam TK caught the lead pellets out of the air. They hovered in front of her, even as she held on that knee, steadying herself. She turned her head slowly, firing a wicked smile at me, then looked back at Ariadne, her intent clear.

"No!" I shouted, and summoned Gavrikov right to mind.

A burst of flame the size of a coffee cup leapt from my hand and puffed against Madam TK's black mask. It exploded almost soundlessly save for a tiny *whump!*

Madam TK stiffened, lifting a hand to touch the top of her ski mask. Her fingers flitted through the flames crowning her skull like some ski-masked version of Ghost Rider, and after two passes, she screamed as the heat burned her fingers.

I didn't wait for her to recompose herself; I dragged the buckshot out of the air in front of her and slammed it into her chest. It hit with a lot less force than an actual shotgun blast, but it dug into the meat of her shoulder good. It also elicited another scream that tore through the night, and she dove back into the house, howling to beat the band.

"Freeze!" one of the cops behind me shouted, and I looked back to find him drawing a bead on me with his pistol. Should have gone for the dart gun.

"Sorry!" I said, dragging the barrel of his and his partner's guns down as they opened fire. They planted a couple bullets in the yard, missing wide as I shot over to Ariadne and draped an arm around her waist. "Hang on," I said, and blasted off.

I didn't want to leave the cops with Madam TK, or Hercu-Lea, but they were bound and determined to bring me down. That wasn't in my plans, and certainly not with my ability to fight compromised by stunning levels of fatigue. I'd barely dragged those cops' guns down in time; I'd felt the wind of the bullets pass my ankles as I reached tapout levels of weariness from exerting powers I'd never really used before at levels I probably wasn't supposed to use them. Pushing my luck and trying to fight back against the guns of those cops? Was a losing proposition.

Staying in the fight against Madam TK seemed another one, at least from where I was sitting. The side of Ariadne's house exploded a few seconds later in a shower of wood, siding and plaster, and the whole structure started to crumble. A blur of movement suggested to me that Madam TK was on the move, but a host of additional cars was pulling up out front, lights flashing, and I knew I wasn't going to be able to remain in the area.

"I'm sorry, Ariadne," I said, kicking my speed into overdrive and turning east. "I've got to get us out of the state."

Ariadne smiled tightly at me as the sound of her house collapsing echoed down the street just before I throttled us up to over a hundred miles an hour, cutting through the dark summer night. "I'm just glad you're okay," she said, hanging tight to her shotgun with one hand and clenching the other in her pocket. She was trusting me to hold her aloft.

I didn't dare let her down.

CHAPTER SIXTY-NINE

Crossing the St. Croix River into Hudson, Wisconsin for what felt like the thousandth time in the last couple days was an unsurprisingly easy affair. The dark gulf between the last lights of Minnesota and those of that city was clear, the far bank rising up above the black, calm waters.

Finding the hotel where my friends were staying? Also surprisingly easy, even without calling them. I knew, in general, where they'd be, and when I found Reed's car parked next to my grandmother's rental, I knew I was all set. It was a two-story cheap motel with exterior doors overlooking the parking lot and then, after a frontage road, Interstate 94. I brought us down gently in the asphalt lot as I dialed Reed on my phone.

"Hey, it's me," I said after he answered sleepily. "Just got attacked by our bad guy."

"What?" Reed mumbled, then more clearly, "What?"

"I'm in the parking lot of your motel," I said. "With Ariadne. What room are you in?"

"203," he said.

I hung up, and beckoned to Ariadne to follow. "Come on."

"I've got something for you," Ariadne said as I turned away.

"Oh, right," I said, and spun back, reaching for the shotgun.

She quartered her body away to protect it. "Not that." She clutched it tight to her. "I need that. What if they come back?"

Fair point, but I had to admit I was coveting it. Only slightly abashed, my cheeks red, I asked, "Well, what did you have for me, then?"

She lifted her left hand, and I realized for the first time she had something crumpled in it. "I got this off the big one I shot." She hesitated. "Well, it fell off of her, anyway, after I shot her." With a gentle flourish, she opened her hand and I stared in the moonlight and parking lot lamps at the thing crumpled in her grip.

It was a driver's license. From Wisconsin.

"What the hell?" I muttered, taking it out of her hand. It was slightly bent from being snugged in Ariadne's hand the entire flight, but it wasn't unreadable in spite of the rough journey. It did, however, take my brain a moment of working in the low light to reckon with what I was seeing.

There was a familiar face on the ID. Entirely too familiar, given I'd just had a conversation with her today.

The plastic smile of a pale, freckled blond stared out at me from the photo. It looked a little forced, a little wan, and maybe a little chubbier than when I'd seen her. Probably because, in the photo, it looked like she'd been pregnant at the time it was taken. "Sonofa..." I muttered.

It was Faith Holloway, the mother of Aaron Berry's child.

CHAPTER SEVENTY

"What does this even mean?" Reed asked, staring at me through the open door. Everyone was waking up now, and by everyone, I mean Lethe, Augustus, Jamal, Arche-Grey – and now they were working to awaken everyone else. Everyone else being Scott, Olivia and Angel, I suppose. We were gathered just outside Reed's room, and I was leaning against the metal railing overlooking the darkened parking lot. The faint smell of engine oil and the blood that had seeped out of a couple cuts I'd suffered during the fight were my olfactory soundtrack for Hudson, Wisconsin. Seemed apropos.

"It means that Faith was the one who attacked us tonight at the bar, I think," I said, brandishing the ID. "Or it certainly points to her."

"'Points to' is not definitive evidence," Jamal said, his eyes moving slowly about as he shuffled over to the rail and looked out past the parking lot to Interstate 94, which rolled past over a chainlink fence. A big semi-truck went by, engine giving it absolute hell to make it up the hill from down at the river bridge. "By the by, I'm trying to see into her apartment right now? And I'm not getting anything." He brandished his phone, then looked sideways at Arche.

Arche blinked at him innocently, twice. "What? Are you insinuating I have some expertise you do not, my dear?"

"I hate sharing a room with these two," Augustus muttered. But not really, because we could all hear him.

"I hung a sock on the door," Jamal said. "Not my fault you don't know what that meant. I thought you went to college."

"Can we just focus for a sec?" I looked right at Reed. "I say we fly to River Falls right now, check for ourselves. It's no time at all, and we can rule it out if she's home, because there's zero chance a telekinetic could make it from Eden Prairie back to there in that little time." I looked to Lethe. "Right?"

She shook her head slowly. "When lifting themselves, especially over long distances, they're very slow."

"Yo, I want to go along on this," Augustus said.

"Follow behind in the car, then, maybe?" I lifted off the ground.

Ariadne looked up at me, then raised her shotgun in offering. "You want it?"

"Nah, I'd just commit a felony with it and then you'd be out another shotgun," I said. Then I looked at Reed. "You coming?"

My brother sighed deeply, then leapt over the balcony. The wind caught him a few feet from the bottom, and up he went, blowing a little air our way as he went by.

"You want us to follow in the car?" Jamal called after me as I turned to jet off, too.

"Wouldn't hurt," I said, "but priority one is to protect Ariadne. Okay?"

And off I went, following the disturbed wind trail of my brother, hurrying to catch him before he made it to River Falls.

CHAPTER SEVENTY-ONE

Reed and I set down in the parking lot of Holloway's apartment, nothing but a waning moon and a few streetlights in the parking lot for us to see by. They covered the older model cars in the parking lot with a dull, reflected light.

"We kicking down the door here?" Reed asked, meta-low, as we touched down on the pavement.

"I'd think it'd be better if we knocked. One of us on the front door, one hidden around back. That way she can't run."

He nodded. "I'm taking the back." And he turned, ready to make a wind-assisted leap over the long apartment building.

I frowned and reached out, catching his shoulder. Wind rustled my sleeve. "Why do you get to go around back?"

He turned his head enough to give me a smirk in the moonlight. "Because if I knock on a single mother's door after midnight, she's less likely to answer than if a woman does. Right?"

"Depends on the single mother. Some might prefer a visit from you at midnight, if you know what I mean."

Reed rolled his eyes, then leapt over the apartment complex in a gust of wind. I gave him a minute or two to get into position, then strode up to the door and gave it a good, hard hammering so she could hear me upstairs. "Faith!" I called. "It's Sienna Nealon. Open up."

I shuddered slightly in the cool night air, listening as the echo of the thumping I'd laid upon the door faded away. A dog barked in the distance, another dissatisfied customer of my midnight escapades. Waiting about a minute for any sign that she'd heard me, I unleashed another wave of pounding on the door, calling out her name.

No dice.

About a minute after my second round of knocking, a light snapped on inside, and I could hear footsteps. I braced myself, waiting, and put a flaming hand behind my back in case I needed it–

The door opened abruptly, and my brother was there, a grave look on his face. "Back door was unlocked when I tried it," he said, opening the front so I could look inside.

Holloway's apartment looked fine. I headed upstairs, already knowing – or suspecting – what I'd find.

No kid.

No her.

"Shit," I said, looking over the place. It didn't look like there'd been any signs of a struggle. The two of them were just...

...Gone.

"Guess that answers one question," Reed said tightly, and I nodded.

Now we knew who had attacked me at Ariadne's house.

But another persisted:

Why?

CHAPTER SEVENTY-TWO

The flight back to Hudson was mercifully short, and we managed to call back the team before they made it much more than halfway to River Falls. They slid back into the motel parking lot in two cars a few minutes later, by which time Reed and I were hanging silently off the porch rail, staring into the night.

It was nearing two in the morning, and I was dog-tired. Other than a brief period of unconsciousness when Akiyama had booted my ass back to my own time, I hadn't slept since yesterday. And I loved my sleep probably more than I'd ever loved any man. Especially when I was running high on using powers and low on alcohol, the tiredness really started to get to me. Adrenaline could keep me up for a while, as could coffee, but I hadn't had coffee since yesterday morning and the adrenaline burst from searching Faith Holloway's empty apartment had been fleeting and was already gone. As a consequence, I was almost hanging over the second-story rail of the motel, my cheek pressed against the cool metal, when my friends made it back upstairs.

"So they've fled?" Augustus asked. He was speaking meta-low, presumably either as a courtesy to the other guests of the motel, or else as a simple privacy precaution. I could respect either one.

"Mother and child," Reed said. "No signs of a struggle."

My brain was running slowly, like a failing machine. "I think we have a suspect. And she already possesses one of the key skills here that I thought might be lacking in one of our other suspects." Reed looked at me curiously. "After all, it wouldn't be the first time she's milked Aaron Berry for his seed."

Reed's face contorted in disgust. "Right. She could have just slept with him. Boom. Evidence sorted."

I made a finger gun and pointed it at my brother. "Nailed it. Which is also what she would have done."

Jamal slipped up beside us. "What's the motive?"

"Resentment? Anger?" I threw those out, but I was so tired I wasn't feeling much of anything in terms of an emotional resonance for those theories. Usually when I hit on a reason for a crime, or a solid breakthrough, I felt exultant.

Now, I just felt the cool rail pressed against my temple. And what I really wanted to feel was a pillow against it, because the rail was hard.

"I think we should call it a night," Reed said. He looked like he was on the verge of dragging, too, though he was definitely wearing the fatigue better than me. "Get a fresh start tomorrow."

"Tomorrow is the very last day," I said, my eyes sliding over my friends. Angel and Olivia were not in evidence, presumably because they were guarding Ariadne in one of the rooms, but Arche, Jamal, and Augustus were all here. As was Lethe, standing over Jamal's shoulder and watching me with concern in her eyes. "In Minnesota, I mean. This is the last shot. To solve this."

"You'll solve it," Lethe said quietly. "But you'll need a decent night's sleep if you're going to do so."

"Hey," Reed said, "what about Paula?" He looked around, like he was searching for some sort of answer not in evidence. "She and Faith were chummy. She brought her Berry's money, after all."

I stared blankly at him. "...And?"

"And you said there were two attackers," Reed said.

I closed my eyes. "Oh." I dragged myself off the rail, and steeled myself to get ready to fly to New Richmond. "Yeah. We can go check on her. If she's not there–"

"It's a bad sign," Augustus agreed. "But you know what else is a bad sign? You draped over a rail like clean clothes on exercise equipment." He snapped his gaze around to Jamal. "You going to let her fly when you can just handle it here?"

Jamal's eyes widened; he looked slightly stricken. "I mean...I could try, but it'll take me at least as long to set that up as it'd probably take them to get there and back." He drifted his own gaze over to Arche, who was leaning against the railing.

Arche's eyes were cool, and they rolled up when she realized what he was suggesting. Then her nostrils flared visibly, and she said, "Fine. But only because I'm tired and I want to get back to bed." She thumbed up her phone and flared the screen to life, turning it to face us.

I didn't recognize the place she showed us at first, but the photos in the background were all of Paula, with a few tossed in of Aaron. "Is she there?" I asked; I felt like I was getting a decent view of the place, but it was fuzzy, a low light view of the apartment. The main thing in view was a bed, and we were looking from the foot toward the headboard. A curtain blew in the breeze, and I squinted; "Is she in there?"

"Not sure," Arche said, doing a little squinting of her own, "but I don't think so. Watch."

A sound blared, loud and clear and striking over the speakers of her phone, and I knew it was playing in the apartment right now. After a moment without any sound but the klaxon, light flooded the room. "That's me," Arche said, eyes flaring with lightning, "I'm turning all the connected appliances on. Computer, TV. Give us a little more light." The flash wasn't exactly blinding, but it did blot out the screen for a moment, turning it white as the pixels adjusted.

There was no one there.

"Hang on a second," Arche said, eyes flaring, little sparks shooting out of them. "Her cell phone. I'm tracking it and..."

Something buzzed and moved on the nightstand. Now the phone was visible, the screen lighting up as Arche pinged it.

"Left her phone behind," Reed said, easing up beside me to frown at the scene. "She must have known we would track it."

"Or that the police could." I glanced at Arche. "Can you keep an eye out for them? In case either of them come back?"

Arche sighed heavily. "Yeah. I'll set a motion alert in case someone moves." Then she frowned, her look souring. "Ugh. That curtain is going to mess me up. Whatever, I'll map out an algorithm to account for it using wind direction. Just let me get back to sleep, will you?" And off she wandered, toward the room door, which she opened with a spark of electricity against the keypad lock.

"What happens if they don't come back?" Lethe asked, easing a little closer to our little circle.

I looked at Reed; he looked back, imposing, almost implacable. "Then it's them we're after," Reed said, matter-of-factly. "And tomorrow we'll have to track them down."

"Before," I added, "it's too late."

CHAPTER SEVENTY-THREE

Morning came without word from Arche, and it dawned before I woke, my alarm clanging loudly at about seven o'clock, informing me I'd had all the sleep I could afford for today.

"Will you turn that infernal thing off?" Lethe murmured from the other bed. "Some of us don't have to wake up yet."

"I thought you old people were early risers," I said, sliding my legs over the side of the bed and staring at the light flooding in from around the curtains.

"I'm not old, I'm ancient," Lethe said, tucking a pillow over her head. "And in case you missed it, someone had me up way past my bedtime last night."

Well, she wasn't wrong. I let her sleep while I showered and got ready. A text message was waiting from Reed when I got done, as I'd anticipated. *Denny's for breakfast?* it asked.

Damned right. I hadn't had Moons Over My Hammy in way too long.

The gang was all there by the time I yoinked Lethe's keys and tooled my way over to the Denny's in her rental car. A five-minute drive led me to a real retro version of the classic restaurant, with entirely silver outer covering. It reminded me of an airstream trailer, but in building form.

I found Reed, Augustus, Jamal, Arche, Scott, Olivia, Angel, and even Ariadne (wearing new clothes that looked fresh from Walmart) waiting around a booth-table as I threaded my way through the breakfast crowd. I pulled a few looks as I did so; should have worn a disguise, I guess.

"Hey," my brother said, looking a little rough around the eyes. He nodded to a steaming cup of coffee next to him. "You want?"

"Does the Pope shit in the woods?" I asked, sucking the heat out of the coffee with my powers so it wouldn't scald the roof of my mouth when I took my first sip. It was weird; my body could literally take flame against the skin, but burning liquid still hurt me if I didn't make an effort to sap the heat first. Talk about a strange and narrow exemption to my powers. The coffee was already mixed exactly the way I liked it, with just enough cream and sugar to cover the fact that it was mass manufactured and probably overly roasted.

Still tasted great and life-affirming when I sipped it. Mmmm.

Augustus, after watching me take my first sip and react, asked, "Do you need a few minutes alone with that?"

"Shhhhhh," I said, closing my eyes. "For your own protection, I'm going to need you to keep it down while I finish this."

"Rude," Augustus pronounced, making a face. But he did quiet down, and I enjoyed a moment of silence, alone with my thoughts and my coffee.

Then I saw a guy reading a newspaper at the next table, caught the headline, and sprayed a mouthful of my precious coffee all over the table. Scott managed to jerk to life and catch it all with his powers before it drenched anyone.

"What the hell, Sienna?" Jamal asked, the blob of coffee floating in front of his face.

I said nothing, just pointed behind him at the open copy of a local paper that the guy was holding up, and the headline that had caused me to do a spit take right there at the table.

Aaron Berry's love child revealed, it read, and below that, pictures of the kid, with the cleverly snotty subhead, *Not his first time*.

CHAPTER SEVENTY-FOUR

I walked outside and just about overturned the nearest newspaper rack as I did so, cursing a blue streak such that a woman walking into the Denny's with her little boy covered his ears, her eyes widening as she hustled him inside and away from the wicked, swearing, meta bitch.

"Feel better?" Reed asked as he stepped out into the warming day after holding the inner door open for her.

"No," I said, kicking at the sidewalk that ringed the front of the Denny's. The noise of the distant freeway could be heard in the background, a soothing, quiet roar. The taste of the coffee lingered on my tongue, a sweet promise unfulfilled thanks to my stupid spit take. "I probably just drummed up another vote to get me banned in Wisconsin just now." I chucked a thumb after me to indicate the retreating mother, who was standing in front of the servers' station just inside the door, looking back at me worriedly, hands at the ready to clamp over her little pumpkin's ears in case I decided to go blue again, loudly.

"You have never been your own best friend, that's for sure," Reed said with a chuckle, "but you're not your own worst enemy, either. So there's that. Which is more than I can say for Aaron Berry."

"I'm trying to wrap my head around this news," I said, "and make it fit with the attacks last night. Were the two women in his life resentful of him? Did they plan this out and use newfound meta powers to sacrifice one of his students to make him suffer?" I shook my head. "I don't get it."

"That's what it looks like to me," Reed said. "Though I'm a little unclear on why they decided to attack us, both at the club and at Ariadne's house."

"I guess..." I said, "...the same theory holds for them as when we suspected Isolde, or the girls from the school. They would have heard Isolde say that bit about me witnessing the murder. Or at least, whichever one of them has TK powers did."

"That makes sense," Reed said, nodding. "So then they make two attempts to wipe you out, as the sole surviving, awake, non-patsy witness to their wrongdoing?"

"If only I'd actually seen it." I kicked at the pavement again, futilely. When I looked up, I saw two heads in silhouette in one of the cars in the back row of the parking lot. I waved.

Reed looked over at the car. "Is that...?"

"Tang and O'Rourke," I said, watching Tang wave back. "Must have reacquired the team yesterday and followed them to the motel."

"And caught us there," Reed agreed. "Guess they don't have an arrest warrant from Minnesota."

"Guess not, since there's not a SWAT team all over us yet." I looked out across the parking lot. "I don't know what we do now, Reed. With less than twenty-four hours to go, we have no line of sight to the villains, and no damned evidence to convict them. They played this perfectly. They were brilliantly positioned to collect all the evidence to frame him, and they damned well did it. Now how do we disprove any of it?"

"I agree it looks like a perfect frame," Reed said, "and coming from the people he probably trusted most in his life, with what is clearly the darkest secret he had, and one he was paying a hefty price to keep quiet. But that doesn't mean there's no evidence left." He shuffled over to me, and put both hands on my shoulders. "If there wasn't, they wouldn't be freaking out and trying to kill us right now."

"That's the point, though," I said. "They're reacting to faulty evidence – as in the *none* we actually have. Other than the driver's license from Ariadne's house, we just don't have anything. The cops are against us, and the villains have flown the coop. We have seventeen hours before we have to leave the state of Minnesota for good, and honestly, we're screwed if we actually try and go back in right now. You know Tang and O'Rourke have orders to arrest us if we cross the state line."

"Oh, I'm sure you won't let a little thing like that stop you," Reed breezed.

"At some point, it will stop me, yes," I said. "Because at some point, they're going to stop being forgiving of my transgressions, and I'm going to find myself back in the bad old days of two years ago, in the crosshairs of a nationwide manhunt. To put it another way, Minnesota has allowed us to play this border game because they're the ones pushing against the law, but as of tonight, we're the ones breaking it. Hard. And they're not going to just let that stand. It'll get bumped up, we'll get a federal BOLO, Wisconsin authorities will have cause to pick us up–"

"I know how it works, thanks."

Three more cars pulled into the parking lot in a convoy, all SUVs, and they had that familiar police escort look to them; I caught a glimpse of lights on the dashboard of the front vehicle, and I bristled. "You know how this works?"

Reed did a double take; the vehicles all had Minnesota plates. "Minnesota authorities are going to arrest us in Hudson? That's ballsy."

"I'm sure they got permission," I said, steeling myself to leap into the air and straight to warp speed to get the hell out of here. Then I cursed, probably sending that poor woman inside scrambling to cover her baby's ears. "The team's in there." I turned an agonized look on Reed. "We can't run without them."

"Not sure it's wise to run even with them," Reed said somberly. "Where would we go?"

"Any state that's offered asylum," I said. "Duh." Governors had the occasional tendency to allow that sort of thing, and refuse extradition between states on criminal matters. And I was pretty sure I knew one that would do just that. "Nashville."

Reed tensed. "You're still set on Tennessee?" His jaw tightened as the doors to the Minnesota SUVs opened and disgorged–

Not a SWAT team.

Cops, for sure. But not cops with guns drawn, to my surprise. Nor cops on an aggressive footing. They kept their eyes on us, no doubt, and their hands hovered around their weapons, but didn't touch them.

They fanned out around us, and the building, scanning for threats that apparently did not include us. They weren't clad in the familiar tactical gear of any strike force looking for a fight with metas, either. They were plainclothes guys, in suits, with ties, all done up to look nice. Not even wearing tactical armor.

One of them circled behind me, slowly, and entered the restaurant through the front door, then just stood there like a wall, as if to bar exit from anyone wanting to step outside. The others formed a perimeter, and at last, I started to get an idea of what was happening here.

"All clear," one of them, just around the side of the building, said. Another, by the middle SUV, opened the back door.

And out stepped a woman with wire-framed glasses and a blond bob hairdo.

The Governor of Minnesota, Bridget Shipley.

CHAPTER SEVENTY-FIVE

"I've gotta enjoy this weather while I can," Governor Shipley announced, looking at us as she clopped her way across the parking lot in a pair of humdrum tan heels. It was almost eight o'clock in the morning and already in the eighties. Beneath her glasses, her eyes seemed alight. She smoothed out the wrinkles in her skirt as she walked, and her panty hose revealed much nicer legs than mine. As always.

"Well, I'll be damned," Reed muttered under his breath.

"Probably, yes," I agreed, "but not right this second." To the governor, who was approaching us at a slow, non-threatening pace, I asked, "What brings you out to Wisconsin this fine morning?"

"Oh, I think you know," Shipley said, stepping up the curb from the parking lot to stand with us. "You and I haven't had a proper conversation since...well, since last time. And I wanted to clear the air. Make our position crystal, since I don't think it is yet."

I exchanged a look with Reed, who seemed as perplexed as I was. "You want us banned from the state. Forever," I said. "How is that not clear?"

"It's not just that," Shipley said. "I mean, I thought that would be the warning you would take. You haven't, though, given the course of recent events." She smiled, and it was somehow matronly, yet cold and patronizing at the same time. I had a sudden flashback to how I'd heard people describe their mothers-in-law, and I thought...that was her. A mother-in-law who loathed you, but didn't want to say so aloud. "Three incidents in the last twenty-four hours, after all? The coffee shop. That nightclub. And then your friend's house." She clucked her tongue at me.

"I'm trying to leave," I said, "but I'm also trying to solve one last case on my way out. I never started any of the shit that happened." I hesitated. "Not that you'll believe me."

"Oh, I do believe you," she said, faux sweetly. "But this is the problem with you people. You're like monsters in the streets of Tokyo, aren'tcha?" She cocked her head at me. "Do you even notice the damage you do? There are lives ruined behind the destruction you wreak."

"Well, first off, I'm not the one wreaking the destruction," I said. "I'm trying to catch the...wreakers."

She shook her head, almost sadly. "It's never you, even when we catch you at the center of a crater of wreckage. Don't you see? It's always you, even when it's not. Because you're the bringer of destruction. I'll grant you that you don't often do it yourself. But you cause the problem. You escalate the fights–"

"I defy you to explain how us almost getting run over by a rogue semi-trailer was any sort of a fight, escalated or not," Reed said. His eyes were blazing with barely-restrained fire.

"Because they were trying to kill you," Shipley said, just as calmly. "Just like they always are." Then she looked at me. "Just like they always will be. That's why this has to end. It's why you have to leave."

"Fine, I will," I said. "End of day."

Shipley shook her head, still clucking like a damned chicken. "Oh, no. That won't do." She smiled at me, almost sadly. "See, we don't want you here. Minnesota is a nice place, for nice people. We welcome all sorts, but sadly, anyone who's going to bring trouble and destruction? They just need to get the message and move on."

"You hear that?" Reed asked. "'We don't want y'all kind around here, law dog.'"

"I don't know what that means, but it sounds about right," Shipley agreed.

"It's from *Tombstone*, you uncultured swine," Reed said, and I felt like he was almost as pissed that she missed his reference as that she was kicking us out of the state.

She gave Reed a prim and snooty look, pursing her lips. "I don't think we're going to miss you, either, Mr. Treston."

"You'll miss us when it's a smoking crater," Reed fired back. "You realize you're completely eliminating any defense against metahumans by getting rid of us?"

Shipley's eyes remained alight, amused, as if by her own personal joke that no one but her knew. It twisted her lips in a smirk. "By removing you, Minnesota won't have to worry about these things anymore. You're the one who brings the trouble. Without you...we'll be fine."

"You don't have any idea how many metahumans are brewing under the surface in Minnesota," Reed said, way more fiery about this whole thing, which I thought odd. Usually I was the one who was right in the face of authority, but strangely, I didn't feel like yelling at Governor Shipley.

I actually felt...bad for her. Because Reed was right.

"Well, as of today it's a few less," she said brightly. "Bye now." And she waved with one hand. "I don't imagine we'll be needing to see either of you ever again." And she walked on, leaving her back turned to us.

"You know how I know you realize we're not an actual danger to you?" I called after her.

She barely turned, pausing her walk only for a moment. "I don't know where you come up with that idea."

"Because if you thought we were the deadly menace you sell us as in the press," I said, looking her right in the eye, "there's not a chance in hell you'd have come out here with your cops not even having their guns drawn. And you damned sure wouldn't have insulted us, then turned your back as you walked away. Either you are one ginormous idiot...or you're the most cynical, lying politician I've ever met. And I've met a few."

Shipley's eyes flashed dangerously, but she said nothing except a little, sort of choked, "Bye bye, now." And with a glint of triumph in her eye, she turned her back on us again and walked away.

CHAPTER SEVENTY-SIX

"Ordered your Moons Over My Hammy," Augustus said, tucking into a Grand Slam with French toast and a pile of eggs big enough to qualify as a mountain in some jurisdictions. Like Kansas.

I slumped back into my seat, making room for Reed to slide into the booth side of our table first. He huffed as he did so, cheeks mottled with rage. Shipley's entourage had blown out of the Denny's parking lot with their lights flashing, probably in violation of Wisconsin law. They did it anyway. Showing off, I guessed.

"So...did that go well?" Scott asked, pausing a spoonful of fresh fruit right in front of his mouth.

"She just came to twist the knife," Reed fumed. "You were right, Sienna. That was cynical political gamesmanship all the way, her sop to terrified soccer moms that we were going to murder them all."

"Yeah, probably," I said quietly. I didn't feel like arguing the merits of Shipley's case, which, in spite of her cynical maneuvering, wasn't completely empty of reason. "Bet it works."

"Until some meta goes off in downtown Minneapolis," Augustus said through a mouthful of eggs.

"So does this mean we're done here?" Olivia asked from the far end of the table. She'd been mouse quiet since I'd gotten here, which was about par for the course for her.

"Guess so," Reed said, a little huffily. "She told us to get out, and we're going to have a hell of a time flying around Minnesota in broad daylight without getting caught, so..." He looked right at me. "...We done?"

I started to say yes, but something caught me, wouldn't let me do it. The words were there, written on my heart: *Yes, let's make a clean break of this and move on.*

But I couldn't get them out.

"You don't have to fight every battle, all the time, Sienna," Augustus said. Probably trying to be reassuring.

I blinked, staring down at my food, untouched and probably growing colder by the second. Something about his words struck me. "I haven't been," I said softly.

Reed looked over at me. "Uhm...you haven't been? Are you sure?"

I looked up at him. "Yes. That's been the problem ever since I went off the wagon." I looked around the table, at all my friends, in their various stages of eating, and finished forming my thought. "Thank you, by the way."

Scott managed to get the words about him first. "...For what?"

"For standing by me," I said. "For trying to intervene when you saw me going hard down the wrong path." I sighed, taking a deep breath. "You all didn't give up on me, even when everything looked really dark. When I was dedicated to making all the worst choices. When I'd forfeited any right to expect anything of you, when I'd burned my credibility with lie after lie after lie...you're all still here. And I hope you'll stay with me, or let me stay with you, wherever we go from here. But..."

"Hoo boy," Augustus said, "here comes the big 'but.'"

"I started drinking again because I let myself stop fighting," I said. "I let Minnesota get to me. To make me feel helpless in the face of what they were going to bring to bear." I looked at the faces around me, and, with the exception of Arche, who could not have been less interested, they were all watching me. "I gave up and dove into the bottle because I couldn't bear the thought of the rest of you going through what I went through in those two years being hunted by the law. So I let myself wallow in the liquor. In the feelings of complete powerlessness."

"It isn't right," Ariadne said at the end of the table. "What they're doing to you."

"Doesn't matter," I said. "They're going to do what they're going to do. That's fine. I owe it to myself to see this case through before I roll out of Minnesota for the last time." I looked over at Reed. "The way I see it, they're going to mess with me for the next sixteen hours if I'm in the state. After midnight, when the law is in effect, that's when they're going to get serious about dropping the consequences on me." I looked at each of them. "On us, though I wouldn't blame a single one of you if you decided to stay on this side of the line today. Especially since you can't fly."

"Sienna," Reed said, "are you sure about this? This 'sixteen hours' thing...it's a gamble. Minnesota might not be taking it uber seriously yet, but if they catch us, they will almost certainly dart us and ship us to the Cube. For good, probably."

"And they could decide to charge you with some stuff you do today," Jamal said. "Just because the big law ain't in effect yet doesn't mean they won't hit you with every little law at their disposal."

"That's exactly what they're going to do," said a familiar voice. Minnesota BCA Agent Britta O'Rourke was walking up to our table, Agent Tang trailing in her wake.

"'Sup, Nealon?" Tang said, raising his hand.

"Tang, O'Rourke," I said. "You have news for me?"

"Nah," O'Rourke said, slipping into the booth beside us as she took off her jacket to reveal the badge and gun on her belt. "We're just talking to the air, here. Right, Tang?"

"Yeah, you never saw us," Tang said, slipping into the chair opposite her. "And we definitely never talked about the bureau's rules of engagement vis-a-vis *you*."

O'Rourke threw up a hand, flagging down a nearby waitress. "Two coffees? To go, please." When the waitress moved off to accommodate her she looked back at me. "Gotta get back to surveilling our 'dangerous' subject, y'know."

"Right," I said. "I'm so dangerous you feel free to come in and have a cup of coffee next to me."

"I like danger with my breakfast," Tang said sunnily. "A little extra jolt with the caffeine." Then he leaned in closer to us. "You nailed it on the RoE. Minnesota's going to play small ball with you today. Harass, drive, dart, and detain."

"They made a Powerpoint presentation," O'Rourke said. "HDDD, they called it."

"That's a terrible acrostic," Augustus muttered. "Awful branding. Government employees are just the worst at this shit."

"Hey," Tang said, sounding vaguely offended.

"Now," O'Rourke said, "the other part of what you said? Also true. You get caught over the line tomorrow, it's big time. Full SWAT, BOLOs across the state, they'll scramble police choppers and Minnesota Air National Guard if you're in the sky. Today your charges are going to be things like criminal trespass and disorderly conduct. Misdemeanors."

"Tomorrow you go instant felony under the new law,"

Tang said. "Use your powers...sentence is a mandatory minimum five-to-ten without parole."

"So, theoretically..." I said, "...if I were to cross the state line today, solve this case by midnight, show up to the Cube to present the evidence I found–"

"Cube's federal property," Tang said as the waitress dropped a styrofoam cup of coffee in front of him along with a receipt. "No jurisdiction for us staties there."

"Everywhere else in the state you're getting a push," O'Rourke said. "BCA will show up. You might get more leniency from local agencies. Our marching orders come from Shipley, and I doubt she piped that down to every sheriff and PD in the state. Not the kind of thing she'd want known far and wide, that she's doing this before her law goes into effect."

"Because it gives us a case to sue the shit out of the state for harassment," Reed added tightly.

"Yeah, just leave us out of that one," Tang said. "If you could."

"Sounds like you have a window, Sienna," Scott said quietly. He had his cup of coffee in front of him now, the steam rising up in front of his ruddy face. "A small one, but still."

"I have to do this, you guys," I said, the words rushing out. "If I'm going to recover from this...lapse. This...nosedive off the wagon...I can't let the feelings of helplessness just sit on my chest like a damned elephant."

"You could just learn some coping mechanisms. Like the rest of us," Angel muttered, but loud enough to be heard.

"And I will," I said. "I'm going to enter a program, go to meetings, all that jazz, once we get where we're going. But for now...I have to solve this. Or else I'll feel like I gave up again." I felt a new resolve bubble up within me. "I'm done giving up on doing the hard things." I looked around the table at each of them. "I'm doing this. If anyone wants to stay behind–"

"Oh, shut the fuck up," Olivia said, a little louder than I'd maybe ever heard her speak before, her cheeks red as the ketchup bottle on the table in front of her. "Of course we're in. Right?" Head nods and mumbled assents followed. "Great. So...what do we do now?"

"Well, we can't all cross to Minnesota," I said, glancing at O'Rourke and Tang. "Right?"

O'Rourke shook her head. "I'd suggest a distraction. Something that could plausibly keep us busy while you're going over the St. Croix."

I looked at Scott. "A distraction. In the St. Croix River."

Scott smiled. "I think I can handle that."

"Someone should watch Ariadne," Reed said, giving Ariadne an apologetic look. "No offense. I just don't want to see you get taken hostage or taken out while we're trying to wrap this up."

"I long ago made my peace with the fact I was powerless and working with powerful people," Ariadne said. "If you want to give me a guard, that's fine." She sighed. "It'd help if I could go to Target and get a computer so I could get some work done today. Or maybe a book."

"I'm not sure how much help a reflex-type is going to be against someone who can fling anything I throw or shoot at them right back," Angel said. "So...I can stay on guard duty and deal with the Hercules if you want–"

"Hercu-Lea," I said. "That's what we're calling her."

"Ooookay," Angel said. "I can deal with her. But if your TK shows up? Not sure how I'd deal with that."

"I'll stay," Arche said coolly. "I don't want to be in on this anyway, and I doubt her TK powers affect electricity."

"I can double back to the motel when I get done 'distracting' our crack BCA team here," Scott said. "That'll be three of us on guard duty. We should be able to handle a TK and Hercu...Lea..." he stumbled over that one, "...between all of us."

Augustus nodded. "Now we got some power coming off the bench. We ain't breaking up like the Beatles. Go team."

"Sounds good," I said. "Reed, Augustus, Jamal, Olivia – you're with me." I cringed. "Oh. And Lethe, if I can wake her up."

"But now the $64,000 question," Reed said. "Once we're over the river...where are we going? I mean...we have no idea where Paula and Faith even are. They could be here in Wisconsin."

"No, we don't," I said, "but that doesn't mean we're just going to stand fast and let things develop. I'm going to pursue every single end, every single lead, in order to find out *why* this was done to Berry. From that, maybe we can figure out where they are – if they're even the ones we're after." I let my eyes narrow. "Because there's an element of this story that's been bugging me, and I need to pull the band-aid off it and really dig into my discomfort in order to get to the bottom of this." I stood, dramatically. "Come on. We're going to Stilloaks Academy. I need Jamal to dig up some student addresses for us."

He looked pleadingly at Arche. "Or...someone could save us a trip."

She shook her head silently, a highly amused smile playing out on her lips. "I already checked on the other women for you this morning to make sure they were still gone. Also, I'm playing guard. You owe me enough for one day."

Jamal sighed. "Back to school it is."

"Yo, you're going to eat that Moons Over My Hammy first before we go, though, right?" Augustus asked.

I paused, about to dramatically climb my way out of the booth, and looked down. I'd forgotten my sandwich. That wouldn't do. "Hell, no, I'm not waiting – we have to get moving," I said, noting that the rest of the team was just about done eating. Augustus started to reach for my food, and I slapped his hand away. Gently. Ish. "But the nice thing about a sandwich is that it's portable." I waved down the waitress. "Can I get a to-go box? And some napkins? Thanks." I set my chin, boldly. "All right. As soon as she gets back...let's go solve this thing."

CHAPTER SEVENTY-SEVEN

Stilloaks was a pretty quiet place on a Sunday morning, only a single car in the parking lot up front as we drove up the tree-lined drive, Lethe at the wheel of her rental car and still grumbling under her breath about being awakened for this.

"You could have stayed behind," I said, watching the green boughs catch sunbeams from above and dappling the car with little leaf shadows. "Gotten your beauty sleep."

"Let me tell you a little secret I hope you learn for yourself someday," Lethe said. "When you've got a granddaughter like you, always leaping into the chippershredder, it's best not to leave what's happening to your imagination." She glanced over at me reproachfully. "To put it another way...once you told me what you were doing today, there wasn't a chance in hell I was getting back to sleep. I'd be sitting there with one eye open, wondering what was happening to you with every moment that passed. If you were getting into a scrape, if everything was all right. Better I'm here. Maybe I'll worry less."

"Never would have pegged your grandma for a worrier,"

Augustus said. "She's way cool." He nodded at Lethe. "Respect."

"Who says 'respect' anymore?" Jamal asked.

"I do," Augustus said, turning on him. He was in the second row of seats, next to Olivia. Reed and Jamal were in the far back. "And I'm cool enough to be able to bring it back if it was dead, you hear? Actually, here's another one: I'm bringing back 'y'dig?' Because Isaac Hayes was badass."

"Are we there yet?" Reed asked with muted enthusiasm.

"Let me do something real quick," I said, as everyone was piling out of the four-door SUV. I leapt into the air, shooting up about two hundred feet to get a quick look at the campus. There was a neighborhood far off to the north, but otherwise Stilloaks Prep was surrounded by fields and a thick lining of trees on all sides. At the back of the building I saw a parking lot, then a couple outbuildings, one of which looked like it might be a machine shed. Two cars were parked behind it in the grass, hidden from view of the main building.

"Hm," I said, dipping a little closer to the earth to confirm they weren't cop cars. I wanted to remain strictly out of sight of any observers from outside the campus, and thankfully the heavy tree growth ringing it made that possible. I slipped a little closer to the outbuilding and sure enough, the cars were empty, and looked a lot nicer than any that a cop would drive. One was a BMW 500 series, and the other was a luxury foreign sedan of some kind, I couldn't tell which at this distance.

I swept back over to my friends and settled down. "No cops in sight watching the campus. A couple of luxe cars out back, hidden from view, which is a little suspicious, but I suspect they're just student vehicles parked for the weekend."

"What about this one?" Augustus asked, nodding to the only other car in the lot.

I traded a look with Reed; the vehicle was a mid-size SUV.

"Pretty sure that's the headmaster," he said. "It was parked out front of the coffee shop when we were there yesterday."

"I would not have noticed that," I said, shrugging. "You boys and your car fetishes."

"What? I thought about getting one." Reed shrugged. "They look nice."

We made our way to the front door of Stilloaks and found it unlocked. Slipping into the office, I wasn't quite sure what we'd find, other than hopefully Headmaster Prestegaard hanging out and reading a book here, since his favorite coffee shop had nearly been demo'd yesterday. Something that sounded like a radio broadcast was playing, and I frowned, listening. The speaker was a quick-talker, and it was tough to tell at this distance what was being said.

"I need about five minutes," Jamal said, meta-low, nodding at a computer sitting out on the secretary's desk. "What am I looking up?"

"Addresses for four students," I said. "Names are Syrena Gaston, Ashleigh Simone, Lucille Thompson, and Isolde...uh, Isolde. They're spelled–"

"I'll just hack the login info so I can access student records at any time," Jamal said, already focusing on the computer. "It'll be quicker." He paused, then rustled around in the desk for a minute until he came up with a filecard with LOGIN and PASSWORD written along with...the login info and password for this computer. "Actually, I might be longer waiting for this old-ass system to boot up than I will to break in."

"Okay, then." I nodded to Reed. "Let's go have a quick chat."

He nodded and fell in beside me, and I shuffled into the secretary's office, wondering how to stall Prestegaard for five minutes. "Hey," Reed announced, when we were just outside the door. He knocked haltingly. "Headmaster Prestegaard?"

Silence greeted this pronouncement. Except for whatever the hell was playing in the office.

Reed and I met eyes; I frowned. "Maybe he's in the bathroom? Or moving about the school?"

"Could be," Reed said. He looked around. "If so, we should probably..." He nodded toward the office, then dropped his voice to meta-low. Maybe he was afraid Prestegaard was hiding under his desk, or in the closet. "...Make sure he doesn't stumble on our people."

"Yeah," I agreed, and back out we went, into the main office, where Jamal sat at the desk while Olivia, and Scott lingered about looking about as suspicious as one possibly could without a lighted sign saying, "CRIMINAL ACTIVITY UNDERWAY" over their heads in flashing lights. Not Lethe, though. She looked like she'd done this kind of thing before, and worse, and was leaning against a tall filing cabinet, eyes closed like she was asleep.

"How long, Jamal?" I asked.

"I don't know," he said, focusing on the computer. "This thing takes forever to even open a window. We're talking cutting edge 1996 tech. Not sure where this fancy prep school is putting its money, but it ain't in admin hardware and software. Still...a few more minutes and we can skedaddle."

"You guys keep a lookout here. Headmaster isn't in his office, so we're going to scout the school and see if he's about."

"What are you going to do if you find him?" Lethe asked, a mischievous smile turning up the corners of her mouth.

I froze. "Uhm...distract him?"

"How?"

"I don't know," I said, sighing. "But if he's wandering around the school, isn't it better if we try and intercept him before he gets into the office rather than having to explain...all this," I waved a hand at them, "once he's here?"

"Just making sure you're thinking right," she said, and slipped into the hallway next to the office, the one that led to the exit where we'd met Isolde. "I'll keep watch on this entrance." She nodded to Olivia, pointing her to another exit at the far end of the office. "You post up there. Augustus, watch the front door."

"Being bossed by a legend," Augustus said with some satisfaction. "That's some confidence, right there."

"I've got confidence in my plans," I said, frowning.

"And in sunshine?" Augustus said, smirking as he made his way past me.

I sighed again, slipping out the door into the interior of the school. Everything seemed quiet here; there were no footsteps ringing through the hall today, no voices muted in the distance.

"Something about this seem weird to you?" I asked Reed, who was lurking beside me.

"Place is empty," Reed said with a shrug. "It's Sunday."

"Yeah," I said. "But Prestegaard left his phone there on the desk, playing the radio–"

"It was a podcast," Reed said absently, looking around.

"Whatever. Point is, he left it going. Does he not care what he's missing?"

"You can rewind a podcast."

"Okay, fine, so maybe that's nothing," I said. "Still...this has a weird vibe to it. Like he got interrupted."

Reed shook his head. "Didn't see any sign of that. Did you?"

"Yeah," I said. "His book was sitting right there, just to the side of his phone." I pictured the desk in my mind; no paperwork had been laid out, just the phone and the book. "I think he was doing exactly what you were suggesting, using this place as a quiet alternative to his coffee shop."

"Then what?" Reed asked, walking a slow circle around the school seal in the middle of the entry hall.

"I don't know," I said, and then bellowed, "Headmaster Prestegaard!" at the top of my lungs.

My voice echoed down the halls for a few seconds, to the far corners of the school, then stopped.

No one answered back.

Reed frowned. "What do you think is going on here?"

"I have a suspicion," I said, and then, opening the office door, "We might head out back for a minute. Keep an eye out here for trouble."

"What kind of trouble we talking?" Augustus asked, popping his head out through the open door.

"Not sure," I said, and broke into a jog toward the back of the building, Reed trailing a step or two behind. "But we're going to check out the building behind the school, see if those parked cars are anything."

"And after that?"

"We go find Syrena and ask her some hard questions about Berry," I said. "Because I'm getting to the bottom of this – whatever uncomfortable places it might lead."

CHAPTER SEVENTY-EIGHT

The school's back exit was unlocked, and no alarms went off as we burst out into the sunlit day. There was a paved parking lot here, presumably for the students, rather larger than the faculty lot or smaller student lot on the side of the building we'd seen a couple days ago. The tall green trees rustled in the wind a hundred yards or so from us, forming the protective visual brake around the entire campus.

"How should we do this?" Reed asked as we approached the primary outbuilding. Wood shop? Gardening shed? I couldn't tell from here, only that there was a tall garage door, white with windows at about head height on the far end of the blocky brick building.

"Carefully," I said, finding a steel door on the side of the building. It was slightly ajar and the handle was askew, a look I was familiar with since I had a tendency to break through locks in exactly that way...oh, all the time. "See that?"

"Signs of forced entry," Reed said, meta-low, as we drew closer. "What do you think is happening here?"

"Don't know," I said, sparking up a fire ball in my right hand, and conjuring up a light web with my left. "Want to see if there's a door on the other side of the building, try a pincer attack? Distract and assault?"

"You pry the garage door up with your super strength?" Reed asked, nodding to the white garage door with the windows.

I hesitated. "Pretty sure that's trespassing and property damage."

He looked at me almost pityingly. "Like we haven't done that already today."

"When a place is open, you can go inside until someone asks you to leave," I said. "We're on the right side of the law until someone like Prestegaard shows up and tells us to GTFO."

"I forgot I was riding shotgun with a veritable expert at riding the edge of the law," Reed said as he whipped out his phone. "Augustus? Need you and Olivia out here for backup. We might have something." He hung up, smiling. "Bases covered."

I nodded, then tilted my head toward the garage door. "Okay. I'll force entry. You just do the light trespassing."

"Thanks," he whispered, still operating meta-low, and let the wind sweep him off the ground. We were still about thirty feet away from the building when we took flight in hopes of trying to avoid our footsteps giving us away. Reed went left, and I went hard right, my belly about six inches off the asphalt, figuring the lower I was, the less likely someone was going to look out those garage windows and see me. They seemed to be the only windows in the building, at least on this side.

Reed was bound to wait for my move, since I was the one who had to rip open a door. I took my time, giving Olivia and Augustus a chance to catch up with us. Settling my fingers down in the little crack between the garage door and the pad of concrete foundation it rested upon, I took a breath. Then another. Wriggled my fingers in under the door's black plastic seal as much as I could.

My feet were planted firmly, my eyes closed. My ears were pricked up, listening, but all I could hear was the background wind that Reed was whipping up around the corner to keep himself aloft. The drifting smell of greenery permeated my nose, along with a trace of oil greasing the garage door tracks inside. If this sucker was locked, I was bound to encounter some resistance when I did this. I resolved in advance not to let little things like that sidetrack me. I'd launch it toward the heavens; there was no such thing as small amounts of property damage and criminal trespass, after all. At least, not for me.

On the count of three, I ripped it upward.

Light flooded in to a compact, garage-like space, illuminating a most...horrifying scene.

Four people were bound to metal chairs by duct tape in varying states of undress. I recognized them instantly, in order:

Paula.

Faith.

Isolde.

And Headmaster Prestegaard.

They were all at least somewhat worse for the wear, their bodies bearing bloody wounds of some stripe. A variety of objects floated in the air around them – well, chiefly around Isolde, who had turned her head at the shocking sight of me ripping open the door.

Behind them, three more figures waited, unbound, two in the bedraggled, black-clad states that I'd seen them last night when they had stormed Ariadne's house. While everyone seemed surprised, the last figure was much more terrified by far than any of the others, her face a sudden mask of horror at my appearance.

For my part, I just smiled, most especially at her, and when I spoke, it was so sweet and cloying it only added to her absolutely horrified reaction to my appearance: "Why girl," I said, then looked at Lucille and Ashleigh in turn, "...girls...I was just looking for you."

CHAPTER SEVENTY-NINE

Nobody moved when I burst into the garage. Taking the space in with a quick survey of my eyes, but hesitant to take my focus away from Syrena, Lucille, and Ashleigh, who were clearly behind this reign of terror, I wanted to know where I stood on the impending battlefield.

The answer was...not in a good place. Not in a good place at all.

This was the school's gardening shed, and it had all the appropriate implements for cutting and trimming and doing minor repairs. There were box cutters, pruning shears, lawnmower blades...a variety of objects that could be used to rip me to pieces. In fact, judging by the floating pliers and hammer (and a few other tools), that was what had been happening, on a small, slowly torturous scale, before I'd interrupted it by ripping open the door and inserting myself into the situation.

"I...this isn't what it looks like!" Syrena immediately burst into tears.

Not Lucille and Ashleigh, though. Lucille looked choked, for sure, like she'd swallowed a frog.

But Ashleigh...

Her face didn't change a wit. It was still coldly calculating, watching me with chilling eyes.

"So," I said to her, "you're the one."

"Don't know what you mean," Ashleigh said. If I wasn't staring at her with my own eyes, on the set of an industrial torture porn video, I would have been absolutely convinced by her effective, cold-blooded lying. She didn't exhibit one single sign of dishonesty when she spoke. Not one.

I looked to my side and saw a set of keys hanging on a peg. Without missing a beat, I snatched them and threw them at Ashleigh as hard as I could.

She moved a hand in front of her and caught them out of the air without touching them. They just stopped and hung there.

And she still didn't react.

Shit.

"Okay, now I'm clear on the *what* and the *who*," I said, putting my attention for a (very) brief second on Lucille and Syrena in turn. "So...why'd you want to frame Mr. Berry for Greta's murder?"

"It was an accident!" Syrena blurted.

I snorted. "You lifted Mr. Berry out of his apartment with your powers," I said, keeping my attention fully on Ashleigh, "you collected...evidence...from him in the most invasive way possible...and you brought both him and Greta out to the shore of the St. Croix in that isolated spot. And she was still alive at the time! Not sure how that's an accident."

"That's a lie," Ashleigh said, still steely calm, even as Syrena turned her head to look at her, then Lucille, in shock.

"No," I said, smiling smugly. "I was there, Ashleigh." At least now I knew what I was facing. Ashleigh was a stone-cold sociopath, and a damned good one, too. "I saw."

"How?" Lucille blurted.

"Oh, I have time-travel powers now," I said, and tapped into Chase's abilities for a second, letting that red beam slide down my wrist and extend three feet out from my hand. "Among others." I kept the fire of Gavrikov and the fairy lights in mind, too, because I was actually going to use those. This was just a bluff; maybe if they thought I was powerful enough, I wouldn't have to get into a fatal altercation with these three.

Especially Ashleigh, whose powers...yikes.

"You told me it was an accident," Syrena said, burbling with tears already coursing down her face. Of the three, she was clearly the only one grasping the danger they were in here.

"Shut up," Ashleigh said, the absolute chill in her voice sending tingles down my spine. "She's lying."

"Really not," I said. "Dressing Mr. Berry up in that hoodie...was that how you found him, passed out on the couch? Or did you dress him for cloak and dagger?"

"He was like that when we found him!" Lucille shouted, desperation oozing out of her every pore. She caught a slap to the arm from Ashleigh, and a warning look, though Ashleigh barely dared to take her eyes off me. Which was smart.

I could see the wheels turning for Ashleigh, and when she finally realized there was no talking her way out of this, she smiled in a way that chilled me right down to the damned bones. "How'd you figure us out? Was it the attack at the club?"

"Reed suspected you before that," I said, "but I try to keep an open mind, especially since Paula was doing such an amazing job of trying to hide Faith." I looked through the group of hostages, and realized someone was missing. "Where's the kid?"

"He's fine, he's just sleeping back there," Syrena said urgently, and pointed to a door to the back room. It was drawn to, and I saw a flash of movement through the open crack. Reed's hand, if I wasn't mistaken, letting me know he was in position. "We wouldn't hurt a kid."

"Why not?" I asked, staring down Ashleigh. "You killed Greta. She was fourteen. That's a kid."

"By that logic, so are we," Ashleigh said, with a sweet lethality to her tone. "You wouldn't hurt a kid, is that what I'm hearing you say?"

"Not unless you make me," I fired right back. "Why don't you let these people go, and we'll sort this out?" I figured my first priority was freeing the hostages. Then I could deal with defusing the human bomb that was Ashleigh.

"Sure," Syrena said, and started to move, clearly intent on letting someone loose.

Ashleigh stuck out a hand and it was like Syrena ran into an invisible barrier. "Hold up," Ashleigh said, eyes nailed to me. "Don't do anything she says."

"Ashleigh," Syrena said, wide-eyed, "that's Sienna Nealon. You know what she does, right?"

"Yeah, I know what she does," Ashleigh said, smiling. "Or at least...what she did. Nowadays she just drinks herself to sleep and doesn't hurt a soul."

"Oof," I said, feigning a blow to the heart. "That's harsh. Also, false."

Ashleigh shook her head slowly. "You used to have the biggest damned body count. I admired you. For that."

I cocked my head slightly, a pained look coming over my face. "That's not something a normal person admires."

"You didn't take shit from anyone," Ashleigh said, "didn't let anyone get in your way. They challenged you...you bulldozed them over. To death."

"That's not...quite how it would happen," I said, a little defensively.

"Nowadays," she went on, "you go after a lawbreaker

and...what? Tickle them with a feather until they give up? Give them a massage?" She laughed. "You two don't need to be afraid of her. She doesn't have claws anymore. She's housebroken."

"Mmmm," I said, a little pained. "I believe you are laboring under a big, painful misapprehension here. What I've gotten better at is beating people to within an inch of their lives and then tossing them in jail. See, I used to just go that last inch in the beating. I had to learn to dial that back so that the cops weren't chasing me all the time. It still hurts when I bring someone in. Some might describe it as the worst pain they've ever felt. Why, a couple months ago in Los Angeles, I cost a girl her arm...for good." I waved at Lucille. "How do you feel about that arm, Lucille? I almost took it from you during our wrestling match last night. You ready to give it up for good?"

Lucille cradled her arm close to her. Good, she still felt the pain. Maybe when – or if – this fight broke loose into a melee, I'd be able to peel off Ashleigh's support so I'd only have to fight her. With Reed, Augustus, and Olivia helping, maybe we could keep this manageable.

"You don't scare us," Ashleigh said, still wearing that smile.

"No, I don't scare you, because you're a sociopath who feigns emotions in order to get others to follow you," I said. "Lucille and Syrena are terrified right now, because they think I'm going to rip out their spines and play drums with them. A not inaccurate assumption, if you push me." I looked at each of them in turn. "Give up. You can't win this."

"There's a time I might have believed you," Ashleigh said, smirking. "But it was before you got neutered, and then became the town drunk. Oh. And before I could do this–"

Ashleigh swung her hand, and I jumped toward the ceiling. A riding lawn mower flew through the space where I'd been standing a moment before, smashing through the garage door track, and the wall behind it. The air filled with a dramatic amount of concrete dust and powder, but I was already racing ahead of that to strike the blow I knew would end this.

I flew at Ashleigh over the heads of the hostages. One hand burned bright with fire, the other glowed with the fairy light ready to shoot. I plunged toward her at over a hundred miles an hour, intent on slamming her through the wall behind, hoping that Reed had done what I knew he would have done and evacuated the kid.

Unfortunately, Ashleigh did what I hoped she wouldn't do, and got her hand up when I was just feet away from colliding with her.

I halted in midair, unable to go forward, unable to go back, just stuck in space.

She clenched her fist, and I felt the grip of her powers holding my body in place, pressure running all along my flanks like I'd been seized in the fist of a giant.

"Now," she said, possessed of a dark satisfaction, "I think it's time I showed you who the new queen of meta bodycount is." And she started to squeeze.

CHAPTER EIGHTY

Suddenly I was a tube of toothpaste, my innards were the contents, and I was about to explode. Or that was how it felt as the pressure built on my body. My entire surface, front and back, was getting pressed on, arms to legs to guts to my skull. It was all lateral, though, nothing on the top of my head or bottom of my feet. It'd be a hell of a lot easier to just put all that pressure on my guts and watch me pop like a zit, but she wasn't doing that. Her inexperience with the powers was showing, but her strength was unquestionable.

I started to throw flame, but stopped when I heard the roar of a wind gust coming in from behind me. It whipped over me, locked in place by Ashleigh's powers, past the hostages, and slammed into the three girls in front of me.

Syrena and Lucille both hit the wall, rattling the building. Ashleigh leaned in against the surge of wind, keeping her hand on me and another pointed at the ground as the air dispersed, her long hair blowing all around her. "Nice try," she said through gritted teeth, her cheeks flapping under the gust. "But no one's stopping me. Not you, not your brother."

"Don't be so sure about that," I said, and launched another round of flame at her head.

This time, she was not so powerless to stop it. She whipped a hand in front of her, and the flames rolled to the side, dispersing against the far wall like they'd never even been there.

Ashleigh smiled. "There's nothing you can do to me that I can't stop. See, you learned how to use your powers, but you never really learned your limits." She dragged me closer to her, and the pressure increased on my innards. "And now...you never will." We were almost face to face, and her grin was absolutely demonic.

"Oh...I don't know about that," I said, and summoned to mind the mental image of Amanda Gustafson, she of the eyebeam powers. A blast of scarlet energy shot out of my eyes and straight into Ashleigh's baby blues.

"Augh!" she screamed, stumbling back into the wall, thudding against it and clawing at her face. She looked right at me, one of her eyes hideously blood red, the other with a vicious looking welt just beneath it. It looked like I'd done some solid damage, about as much as a good punch would have produced.

"You call that a scream?" I snorted. "Try this."

I let go with Brance voice and really hit a high note. I only maintained it for a second, because I was keenly aware there were hostages in the room and I barely had any control over this power. A multitude of screams came from behind me, and I knew I needed to stop before I burst eardrums.

Ashleigh staggered back again, and this time I felt the squeezing hold she had on me cease. That vicious grip about my midsection was gone, and I put the pedal to the metal, power-wise.

With an elbow to lead, I slammed into Ashleigh at thirty, forty miles an hour, as hard a hit as I could muster. She was clutching at her ears, covering them, and I caught her just above the sternum. A sickening crack was my guide, and I watched her slam into the wall, but catch herself before she hit the floor.

She raised a hand and whipped me to the side; I slammed into the wall of the shed and went squarely through it, just like the lawnmower before me. The concrete blocks shattered as I passed through. Felt other things shatter, too. My collarbone, my shoulder blade, my arm.

Once through the wall, I slammed into a car and spun it around like I'd T-boned it with a truck going fifty. But it wasn't; it was just little ol' me going as fast as Ashleigh could throw me.

I bounced, slamming back against the wall, Ashleigh's grip on me gone, and eventually, I hit the ground and rolled. Blood seeped over my face, and darkness squeezed around the edges of my vision like Ashleigh squeezing my innards.

Somewhere in the midst of all that pain, happily, I passed out.

CHAPTER EIGHTY-ONE

Reed

As Sienna went through the wall, I came in through the door, because I knew for a fact that with her out of commission, Ashleigh was bound to start doing some more damage to the hostages. I whipped a hand out, trying to generate enough wind to shove them out the open garage door. The oily smell permeating the school's gardening shed mingled with the scent of blood and fresh air as I thrust out my hand, mostly for emphasis, since my powers were in my mind.

I failed.

All four hostages froze in place only inches from where my wind caught them; I recognized Prestegaard, Isolde, Paula, and Faith all bound to the chairs with duct tape. I'd caught an inference from Sienna that they were here, and constrained, but I hadn't dared to open the door while she was confronting the girls for fear that I'd blow the element of surprise. Instead, I'd hurriedly evacuated Berry's kid, leaving him on the lawn outside as Olivia and Augustus came bounding our way, hopefully safely out of action while we did this. He hadn't even stirred.

Turning another blast loose in the direction of the three girls, I tried to whip a hard enough wind at them to distract Ashleigh in hopes that it would give me time to get the hostages out of her line of sight and thus, out of danger.

I failed again.

Ashleigh smirked at me, hands out in front of her, wind blowing around an invisible windbreak in the shape of a U that covered her and her friends. "You're not exactly blowing my skirt up here."

"Upskirt vids aren't really my style," I said, redirecting the wind into the gap she'd left at the back of her shield. Apparently she'd failed to realize that I could send them in any direction.

She figured it out when they caught Lucille and launched her into Ashleigh. She, in turn, crashed into Syrena at a rather bone-crunching velocity, and the three of them piled up on the floor as I bowled them over.

"I'm not much for hitting girls," I said. I tried again to sweep the hostages away out the door, but Ashleigh held onto them in spite of my blindsiding her. "But so help me, if you don't let these people go, I'm going to bitchslap you into the next state."

Ashleigh didn't respond to that with words. She did, however, lift her head and jerk her chin at me.

I flew backward, an invisible force grabbing tight hold of my body and ramming me toward the wall behind. It was then that I remembered that old adage about objects in motion tending to stay in motion unless acted on by another force.

So I added some force. A hard wind caught me before I

impacted against the concrete block wall, and boy did I feel the squeeze.

For a moment.

Then...Ashleigh had other things to worry about.

The back wall of the shed exploded, concrete bursting like a wall of water, flowing out and surrounding Ashleigh and her friends. Movement out of the corner of my eye drew my attention to Augustus, who was standing framed as a silhouette in the open garage door.

He blew out three, four more concrete blocks, letting the earth elements within spill over Ashleigh and her friends. She opened her mouth to shout, and he shoved dirt and concrete residue into her open mouth. She made a choking noise and lifted her head as Lucille wormed her way out of the soup of dust that was consuming Ashleigh. So did Syrena, squirming away on the other side, leaving Ashleigh in the middle of it all.

"Augustus, knock her out!" I shouted, trying to get my wits back about me after being crushed by an invisible cobra. My breath had left me, and I was sucking in great lungfuls of the air I'd barely had time to miss. I brought the winds back around me, trying to decide where I might do the most good.

Lucille moved faster than I would have thought possible. She grew as she leapt, like a puma, at Augustus, who was fully engaged with trying to keep Ashleigh choking on dirt. I threw a hand out to blow her off course, but only succeeded in knocking her aside. She caught the ground, swollen to Guy Friday-like size, and ducked around behind Augustus, planting an arm around his throat and lifting him off the ground in a choke hold.

Shit. I leapt into motion; Augustus's attempt to keep Ashleigh down was already flagging; dirt and dust was spilling out of her mouth as she hacked up the garbage he'd tried to choke her with. She made a sputtering noise and gestured to Syrena furiously, pointing at the hostages.

Shit times deux.

Syrena hesitated, locking eyes with me, and I watched determination harden in her eyes. She opened her mouth, as if to speak, but instead of words coming out, she belched out something green and slimy, the very smell of which made my eyes burn.

Acid.

A huge spattering of it sprayed from her lips, clouding and splashing—

Right at the hostages.

CHAPTER EIGHTY-TWO

I didn't have any time to react, hardly, and so the only thing I came up with was pure rote reaction. Acid spray was blistering through the air between Syrena and the hostages: Headmaster Prestegaard, Paula, Faith, and Isolde. There was no time to waste.

So I didn't. I threw up a hand reflexively, and channeled the wind.

The acidic spray, which was making my eyes water even from this distance, reversed course and came right back at Syrena, who stopped belching that crap in time to scream and then leap away.

Ashleigh...was not so fortunate.

It didn't catch her full; the spray pattern was wide and dispersed by the wind. It blew in a ten-foot spatter against the wall, a wooden workbench, a trash can, and...Ashleigh, catching her from top of the head to about mid-chest.

I'd never seen acidic spray powers at work before. I might have read about them, but I couldn't recall ever seeing a villain just open their mouth and belch acid so strong it burned my eyes even ten feet away.

What it did to Ashleigh, though...was a hell of a lot worse.

The effect on the wall was immediate, a hissing, steaming sound rolling up from the surface anywhere a spatter had made contact. The work bench, similarly, began to waft smoke off the surface, and the trash can started to actually dissolve(!), crumpling in on itself like it was made of Play-Doh and someone was squeezing it across the middle.

But Ashleigh...

I've seen some effed-up things since I joined up with Sienna in fighting metahumans. I'd even seen some bad things before that, but teaming with Sienna brought things to a whole new level.

But I'd never seen what happens when you apply incredibly corrosive acid to a human being's face and upper body.

Ashleigh's screams were heartbreaking, even though I now knew she was a crazed sociopath. A clump of her hair and scalp just dissolved, leaving part of her skull exposed, blood rushing down it. Her left cheek, the side that had caught the spray, started to slide down her chin, which was drifting off her maxilla, exposing bloodied bone. Her eye sizzled as it slid out of the socket, her eyelid already eaten by the corrosive spray.

She screamed and screamed, agonizingly, for about five seconds, before I started to feel a tension in the room, wild and dangerous.

"Uh, Reed?" Augustus's voice was choked, guttural. I spun to look at him, and he was fighting for his breath and his life against the superior strength of Lucille, who was giggling as she choked him out like a UFC fighter. "...Lil'...help here...?"

I started to go for him, but Lucille spun, holding him between us like the hostage he was. "Come any closer...I break his neck," she said, in a husky voice that belied how silly and frivolous she'd been before. Her eyes showed her panic; she was taking in the spectacle of her friend being eaten to death by acid, and it was not instilling her with calm.

"Hi," said a friendly voice from just behind Lucille, who turned to look, because the speaker was just beside her. I already kind of knew what was going to happen before it did, but I cringed anyway to watch it.

Olivia Brackett had slipped right next to Lucille, and as soon as she turned to try and position Augustus as a hostage between them, Olivia moved to insert herself between them. She grabbed Augustus, and flared her power.

Lucille went flying. And not a short distance, either. She blasted off like Team Rocket, or Wile E. Coyote in one of those old cartoons. I could have sworn I saw a glimmer of light in the distance as Lucille entered low earth orbit.

"Damn, thanks for the last-second save," Augustus said, reaching for his throat. He turned, eyes got big, and he pointed. "Um."

I turned to look for myself. Syrena was standing over Ashleigh, who was still doing her best impersonation of the wicked witch of the west, half her face sloughing down, along with her shoulder and chest muscles from her neck to just south of her collarbone. Which was showing, unfortunately, along with a dissolving mass of muscle.

The currents of wind in the room were bizarre; something was building, pulsing, and it took me a moment to realize what it was.

Ashleigh was in agony, and she was channeling that pain into her power. Telekinetic currents were thrashing about, grasping at objects and snugging onto them like a pregnant woman in labor seeking a hand to squeeze.

Except Ashleigh was a powerful telekinetic, and all that pain going into this was like gasoline being poured on a fire.

The room was about to explode.

"Get everybody out!" I shouted, grabbing two of the

hostages by their chairs nearly at random and running for it, because I didn't even have time to summon the wind. I sprinted out the open garage door, pinballing off of Olivia, who looked a little surprised but went with it, bouncing up and out the door as Augustus swept down behind me and grabbed the other two.

I was barely five feet out the shed door when the Ashleigh bomb went off. It knocked me over and sent me rolling along the ground along with the rescued hostages. I was battered by earth and chair legs and flailing limbs and when I came to rest, I was almost a hundred feet from where the concrete block shed had stood.

Yeah. Stood.

Because now...

It was gone.

Along with Ashleigh, Syrena...

And, it seemed to me, by the fact that the cars parked on the side of the building were now absent...

Sienna.

CHAPTER EIGHTY-THREE

"Has anyone seen Sienna?" I called, ripping the duct tape from Paula's hands as I struggled to free her from her captivity on the chair. It wasn't particularly strong stuff, but it was sticky and tangled and once I got her hands ripped clear, I left her to stagger closer to ground zero of the psychic explosion.

My ears were ringing and I took a knee because my equilibrium was all effed up. The world was swinging back and forth like someone had hung an anvil around my neck and given it a hearty shove; now it was dragging me side to side like some weighty pendulum.

Augustus lifted his head from where he'd ended up. He was dusted with plaster dust, his dark skin a washed-out gray. "Anyone get the number of the rocket ship that just landed on my head?"

A whistling noise heralded the return of Olivia, who bounced once, then again, just to my left, then cut her momentum and stepped lightly to the ground. "Oh, wow," she said, her hair frizzed. "That was...something."

Both their voices sounded whispered, as if from a

distance, and over a bell that was ringing loudly in the foreground of my mind. "Where. Is. Sienna?" I called, wondering if they could hear me.

Olivia straightened, then pointed.

I followed the direction of her finger. And followed it.

And followed it.

Almost two hundred feet from where the shed had been, both the cars that had been parked behind it now rested, shredded like they'd gone through a crusher at a junkyard.

I blasted into the air and came down beside the wreckage, wondering if I'd find my sister alive or dead. I searched the surrounding area in all directions for fifteen, twenty yards, into the treeline, and then back, covering the ground at meta speed and ignoring the dramatic sway of my run as my inner ear played merry hob with my sense of balance.

Olivia plopped down by the car wreckage, beckoning me over with a waved hand. "C'mere."

I hustled over. She grabbed the bumper of one twisted wreck, and with a heave, we threw it aside to reveal...

An indentation in the earth, and destroyed grass where it had come to rest.

But no Sienna.

We hurried to the other. Each taking an end, we grabbed hold and lifted; I felt her power send the car ripping out of my grasp. She launched it into the trees, where it crashed against a pine and came crunching down to the earth. Distracted by that, I turned my gaze back to the ground beneath it and found–

"Oh, God," Olivia whispered.

CHAPTER EIGHTY-FOUR

Sienna

"You assholes look like you've seen a ghost," I said.

It seemed appropriate, since I was crushed from about the neck down.

Hey. Like they say in *Monty Python* – I got better.

The dimness clouding my vision started to fade as I pushed Wolfe to front of mind. Olivia turned away, gasping and nearly retching.

Reed watched, but the deeply uneasy look on his face twisted into disgust before resolving into relief. "Thought you were dead."

"Another few minutes, I might have been," I said. "Kinda hard to rejuvenate yourself when you've got a car on your body." I sat up, my clothing creased and dusty beyond belief. "Thanks for the assist."

Lethe came running up, and she had good form for someone who'd learned to run back in the days before they had mirrors or video cameras. She wasn't even out of breath as she skidded to a stop just feet from me. "Are you..." she looked me over doubtingly, "...okay?"

I lifted my right hand; the bones in it knitted back together before our eyes. "Getting there," I said, rocking myself upright and feeling a pain in my abdominal region as I did so. Probably some internal organs settling right. "You?"

"I wasn't just in an explosion," she said, unable to take her eyes off of me. I did have a fair amount of blood on my clothing. "I'm fine."

Turning my head toward Augustus, who was helping the rest of the hostages free of their restraints, I saw Jamal run up and give his brother a worried hug. No wonder; Augustus had enough dust on his face to have been in a building collapse. Which...technically I guess he was.

"Was that Ashleigh unleashed?" I asked, pointing to the blast crater that had once been a gardening shed. It wasn't deep, but everything had been flattened out for thirty feet or so around where the foundation had stood. Not so much as a blade of grass remained upright in that zone. The ground looked like it had been sowed with concrete powder.

"Yeah," Reed said haltingly. "She kind of got...covered in acid. And her face sort of...fell off."

"It was the second grossest thing I've seen today," Olivia said, looking rather pointedly at me.

I lifted my shirt and gave it a good wringing out. Blood sluiced onto the ground in rivulets. "Sorry about that." I was pretty sure my internal organs had been visible when they lifted the car. Because when I'd woken up, jagged metal had been buried in me, and it hurt. A lot.

You really do bring the pain on yourself, Brianna added. So helpfully.

"So...where is Ashleigh?" I asked, looking around. "And Syrena? And Lucille?"

"Um..." Olivia looked to the side, then bounced off like she'd been catapulted. She vanished into the treeline in the distance for about two seconds, then came flying back, a large body in her bubble. She landed, saving the lump of flesh that was Lucille from flattening upon impact by cutting her momentum before she cratered in the earth. Olivia dropped her gently at my feet. "Here. For this one." She shrugged. "No idea on the other two."

"Syrena was standing next to Ashleigh when she went off," Reed said, almost cringing. "I don't think there's much, if anything, left of them."

I frowned. There was something wrong with the idea that they'd just gone poof in the explosion, and I said so.

"The boom blew you a hundred, two hundred feet and dropped a car on you," Reed said, "and you think it's improbable they died in it?"

"She's right," Lethe said. "A telekinetic doing what you describe would have blown objects away from her. She wouldn't have blown herself up."

"Um, hey y'all?" Augustus came trotting up. "There's a piece of a jawbone over there. In case you're wondering where those girls went."

I shook my head. "That's Syrena. Not Ashleigh."

Reed just blinked. "...What?"

"Think about it," I said. "She doesn't use her powers inside her own skin. She's not a suicide bomber. When she went off, she pushed things out, away from her skin. Then she left."

"You didn't see," Reed said. "She was burning in acid. Her face was falling off like one of the Nazis at the end of *Raiders of the Lost Ark*."

"Yeah, that girl is dead," Augustus agreed. "She didn't have enough skin left on her to cover a chicken. And not one of those steroidal chickens, either. We're talking a Cornish game hen. Maybe a quail."

"Because no meta can survive losing some skin," I said, waving a hand in front of myself.

"Sienna," Isolde said, limping her way up. Her mouth was bloody, and her clothing torn. "You have to find her, if she's still out there." She looked me right in the eye, and for an old lady, she looked terrified. "You can't let her get away."

"What the hell did you see that was so bad?" Jamal asked, trotting up. The other three survivors of Ashleigh's torture session – four, I realized, as I saw Faith reunite with her son, hugging him madly as she swept him up in her arms – looked like absolute dog shit, stuffed in a bag and set on fire.

Isolde looked right at him. "That woman...and she's no girl, I've met girls, known girls, hung out with mere girls for a hundred plus years." She looked back at me. "She is the emptiest soul I have ever met in all that time. She's a demon from hell, with no heart, and no mercy." Isolde stepped over to me and seized me by the front of my sopping, bloody shirt. "You have to find her. Please.

"You have to stop her."

CHAPTER EIGHTY-FIVE

"Where the hell would she go?" I asked, thumping my way over to the fallen form of Lucille. I had questions, and maybe she had answers, but she looked about two steps above being comatose. I leaned over and gave her a good shake, but she did not so much as stir.

"My first thought is 'away,'" Reed said with his practiced dry wit. "Assuming she survived that, how do we catch her?"

"I have ideas," I said, and looked at Jamal. "Can you hit up the police scanner app on your phone?"

"Sure," Jamal said. "What am I listening for?"

"You'll know it when you hear it," I said, taking a knee next to Lucille. She was already bruising, rather badly, and I had a feeling it was only going to get worse from here. Not much I could do about that, but I needed some insight, right now, that only she could provide.

"You going to tap her?" Reed asked, kneeling next to me on the dusty ground. "For motive?"

"I think I know the motive," I said, putting a hand on Lucille's cheek. "Ashleigh strikes me as a sociopath, without an ounce of empathy or concern for others. She'd just as soon flay you as look at you, and some idiot gave her a drug that allows her to do just that. Still," I said, "it would be nice to know for sure, so yes, I'm diving in to get confirmation."

Reed nodded. "Try not to lose yourself in there." He had a worried look in his eye.

"Save your concern for when we really need it," I said, as my power started to work.

Seconds later...I was in Lucille's memories.

CHAPTER EIGHTY-SIX

Ashleigh and Lucille sat around the bedroom, white, lacy pillows and frilly curtains putting a definite style on the place. I found myself in among them, the sickeningly sweet smell of a perfume on the air as I stood in a sunbeam partially obscured by draperies over the window, casting long shadows across the room. Lucille was staring at her history homework, absently, chewing on the edge of her eraser. She glanced at Ashleigh, who was in the chair in the corner, and I got the feeling she had been for about an hour. It was sudden, unexpected, when she announced, "Greta sucks, doesn't she?"

That caught Lucille off guard. Not only because Ashleigh broke the silence, but because she hadn't said anything about Greta, at all, today. "She's just needy," Lucille said, with a couple of her trademark giggles.

Ashleigh's eyes were flinty, cold. "No. No, she's not. She's dangerous to us. You know?"

Lucille giggled again. "Dangerous? How...?"

"You told her about how we took the meta drug at that party," Ashleigh said, watching Lucille for reaction with those cold eyes. I got the feeling she got like this sometimes, when she was doing some deep thinking. She didn't feel very warm at all. Lucille was not a fan of these times. "She knows. She could get us in trouble with our parents. And if this law ever passes, with the cops."

"She's not going to say anything," Lucille scoffed. She looked up from her work hesitantly. "Are you really just mad at her because Mr. Berry likes her better than you?"

Ooh, that was interesting. Did Aaron Berry actually play favorites?

Ashleigh's eyes got colder, and she stood, gathering her things and shoving them swiftly into her black backpack. "I can tell you're not listening. You don't believe me."

"Wait, don't go," Lucille said, sitting up on the bed. "I – I believe you. Don't go."

That struck a quivering nerve; the alarm and thought that Ashleigh might leave hit Lucille all the way down to her core. I glanced around; an absent, probably philandering father and a mother who cared more about the way her ass looked in her yoga pants gave me the full read. The only affection Lucille felt in her life, the only relationship she had, was with Ashleigh.

The glimmer of triumph in Ashleigh's eye as she held her backpack in hand, the threat to leave hanging over their conversation, was obvious to me, but not Lucille. I had to give credit where it was due; Ashleigh's emotional manipulation was subtle enough that Lucille – so naïve – thought it was genuine. "You believe me, Lucille? Greta's a threat to us."

"She's not – I don't – okay!" Lucille said quickly once Ashleigh shouldered the backpack. "She's a threat. What do you want to do about it?" Lucille looked around her bedroom as if a cop would come jumping out of the closet at any moment.

Ashleigh's eyes showed far more calculation than Lucille picked up on. I had to appreciate it as an observer after the fact. A very tiny smile turning up the corner of her mouth was the sign that she knew she'd won this round. "She could rat us out any time," Ashleigh said, quite convincingly – to a teenage girl desperate for her affection. Less so to a twenty-something metahuman enforcer who'd dealt with the worst humanity had to offer for about a decade now. "We have to...deal with her."

"How?" Lucille asked. She had no idea.

Ashleigh, to her sociopathic credit, did not smile, though I could tell by her eyes she wanted to. "You know how."

Slow realization dawned on Lucille. "What...?"

"Yeah." The flat affect on Ashleigh's face was quite breathtaking to behold. She truly gave no damns about Greta; she was determined to kill her, probably before she'd even come in the room here. Her time spent thinking just now, I suspected, was her plotting how she was going to get Lucille to become her accomplice.

"We'll get caught," Lucille said nervously. Which was interesting. Being inside Lucille's mind, I could tell that this bothered her more than the actual idea of killing Greta. She really was a perfect match for Ashleigh. Whether she'd started out this selfishly malicious or had just come to it over her time associated with Ashleigh, they were now a well-matched pair.

"No, we won't," Ashleigh said, a little too quickly. "I watch the true crime shows. I know how these things go. We just have to make sure that everything doesn't point to us, that it points to someone else. Think about it. We have an advantage nobody suspects. We can do this with no fingerprints. Without even being close to the crime scene. And," she smiled, "we can make sure someone else *is* there."

"Who?" Lucille asked, her blood chilling a little. Then she smoothed it out. It'd be fine, she told herself, and I cringed to watch.

Ashleigh just smiled a little wider.

And that was the moment that their scheme was born.

CHAPTER EIGHTY-SEVEN

I pulled my hand away from Lucille's cheek, my questions answered in the main. Suddenly I was back under a sunny sky in Stillwater rather than a dim bedroom, fit perfectly for vicious plotting. I straightened as I stood, and said, "Well, that answered some questions."

"Like where your enemy is going?" Lethe asked, slipping up behind me.

"No," I said, flinching against the sudden, invasive light. I closed my eyes for a moment, let the darkness settle back in. "But I did get the why and the how of the plot unfolding." I'd also skimmed Lucille's memories leading up to the murder and following. "Ashleigh is definitely a sociopath. I think this might have been a 'test' murder for her, to see if she could get away with it."

"Why pick Greta Oliver?" Reed asked.

"Convenience," I said, the answers solidifying in my mind. "I think she actually had the idea of how to commit the perfect murder via frame-up before she picked the victim. And that led her to Greta." I looked into Reed's eyes. "She knew Berry was vulnerable because of his drunkenness, and maybe even because of Faith. And Greta was Berry's favorite student, at least in their grade."

Reed shuddered. "That's some damned cold-blooded shit right there."

I nodded. "You should have heard Ashleigh's casual discussion with Lucille about collecting the DNA evidence from Berry. It was funny to her." It had been damned creepy for me to hear a girl that age talk so uncaringly about Berry as she'd kept him hovering over Greta's corpse and exploited his unconscious body to produce the necessary evidence to create this whole frame-up. I felt more than a little revolted on his behalf. I'd barely dared to dwell on that memory, one that had made even pliable Lucille walk deeper into the woods while Ashleigh had done the deed. "She had a theory about how men only want one thing and how triggered society would be by the thought of Aaron Berry choosing to get that thing from a student."

"Not a wrong theory," Olivia said, cringing slightly. "I mean...everyone was so busy being horrified at Berry that they didn't dig too deep on the mountain of evidence your gal there planted."

"Yes," Augustus said dryly, "and those kids would have gotten away with it, too, if not for you meddlesome adults."

"Oh!" Jamal jumped, his phone clenched tight in hand. "Oh. I get it."

"It's a Scooby-Doo joke," Augustus said, "it didn't exactly take Cassidy Ellis to get that one, bro."

"No, not – well, that was funny, actually, I get it now," Jamal said. "But no! I meant – there's a call on the police scanner for Oakdale." He looked right at me. "A woman wearing a super realistic zombie Halloween costume, bones showing and all that – just hijacked a car." He held up the phone like we could see it on the blank screen; well, I could imagine it in my mind's eye, at least, and it was horrifying. "She's headed west on 36 into St. Paul."

CHAPTER EIGHTY-EIGHT

Ashleigh

She thumped onto the roof of the car quite heavily. She'd kept herself aloft for several miles, traversing over trees and rooftops wherever possible, trying to keep out of sight of the ground. It was a nearly impossible task the closer she got to St. Paul, but she hewed to the cover of the tall trees in the old neighborhoods as best she could until she couldn't keep herself up any longer. Then she'd found the onramp to Highway 36 at 694 and decided it'd be easier to push a pedal down on a car and guide the steering wheel than to keep herself flying, so down she went, onto the roof of a minivan.

Ashleigh heard the muffled confusion within as she landed, then a scream as she pushed the pedal down with her mind. She rode the top of the vehicle, clutching the luggage rack with the hand that hadn't been burned by stupid Syrena. Stupid Syrena, who'd failed to get much attention with the accusation Ashleigh had fed her, who'd gotten herself trapped by her stupid hovering helicopter parents afterward, and who'd only finally come to help them with the hostages when Ashleigh had pulled out every coercive trick in the book. And whose help had just cost Ashleigh half her face and all the muscle tissue and skin on her left shoulder. At least she'd paid for it; Ashleigh had seen Syrena's stupid face explode when she'd let loose with her powers.

Still, the cost was high. Bone and tendon stuck out of Ashleigh's shoulder, and if she had possessed the normal sense of revulsion girls her age had, she might have given a damn on that basis.

But she didn't. She wasn't like girls her age. She didn't get revolted by dead things, or by making formerly alive things dead. She'd proven that when she'd bent Greta Oliver nearly in half and felt...nothing, really. A little curiosity. Maybe a slight thrill, because it was so verboten. She'd felt more afterward, jumping through the hoops of setting up the frame for Mr. Berry. That had required more finesse than what she'd done to Greta. Greta had been simple, like smashing a cat's skull. Which was something else she'd done in the past.

She looked at her distorted reflection in the minivan's roof with a sense of irritation, and pride. She'd been fair looking before this. Maybe, if she could heal, she would be again. For now, this was an active impediment to her getting away. Damn Sienna Nealon sticking her stupid nose where it didn't belong. That was annoying.

But she needed to get away now. Ignoring the screams from within the minivan, she pushed harder on the pedal and the engine roared. The driver within jerked the wheel, but Ashleigh yanked it out of her hand. Another scream; this time from someone they passed as the minivan rolled by. They were pointing, horrified.

Ashleigh ignored it. These people were flies to her. She clutched the handhold and kept her mind on the ride. She needed to find a place to ditch this van, to hide. Somewhere even a freak like her might blend in, at least long enough to throw Nealon off the track.

And as she went deeper into the cities, the idea became obvious as the spire up ahead, hanging over the miles and miles of fairgrounds on Snelling Avenue. Crowds? People? A place to hide? Ashleigh grinned. Obvious as hell, really.

CHAPTER EIGHTY-NINE

Sienna

"Give us a vector, Jamal," I said, flying low over Oakdale, Minnesota with Reed behind me. We were heading in the general direction of the last known reporting of Ashleigh, but there was no sign of her on the horizon. The streets ahead were old neighborhoods with tall trees in the front and back yards, the sort of pleasant, older suburbs characterized by homes built in the fifties, sixties, and seventies. Smaller houses, but many nicely redone. Lots of wood paneling and stucco, the rooftops covered with fallen leaves and twigs.

"I'm trying," Jamal said. My phone was up to my ear. "We're heading your way now in the car, but we're a long way behind, I'd say. Last sighting was on Highway 36 at the 61 interchange. Going west."

"Why's she heading into the cities?" Reed asked. "You'd think she'd run for a more rural zone, hide out in a forest or something until her skin regenerated and she could slip off.

"She's wounded," I said, keeping my eyes peeled on the horizon. "Hard to think straight when you're hurting, and someone's on your tail." I looked over at my brother, who peered at me curiously, matching my pace nicely. "She's scared of me."

"You're going by what she said in the shed to form that opinion?" Reed asked. "I don't think you were listening. She was talking about dethroning you as the queen of metahuman body counts. She's not scared of you. She wants to supplant you."

"Well, she's going to have to work for it," I quipped. "Especially if she wants my body on her count. Jamal?"

"I will let you know when someone sees her!" Jamal shouted over the phone. Then, a second later. "Sorry. I just – oh, shit!" Then a pause. "She's on Snelling, heading south."

I blinked. "Isn't that close to...?"

Reed's jaw tightened. "The State Fair? Yeah. Yeah, it is. You don't think...?"

"She's running right for the State Fair?" I asked. "I guess so, though I'm hard-pressed to know why she'd make that choice."

Reed shook his head. "Same. Shall we kick it up a notch?"

I grinned at him, tightening my grip on the phone. "Let's do it." And I blasted ahead to near supersonic speed, leaving my brother behind to catch up. While in flight, I hung up on Jamal and made another call real quick. Just in case.

CHAPTER NINETY

Ashleigh

She let go of the minivan as it rolled jerkily along Como Avenue past the fence around the fairgrounds. With a little assist from her powers, she managed to clear the fence and landed just inside the perimeter on the grass.

Ashleigh was in.

And there was one place for sure within these walls where she knew she could go and almost certainly not be found out while she waited to heal – and then, eventually, escape.

CHAPTER NINETY-ONE

Sienna

"Keep in mind, we need to not be seen," Reed said as he caught me just shy of the sprawling State Fairgrounds. I could see the wheeled spoke of the Ag building, with its central tower jutting up. Across the street was the tall Sky Tower, with its commanding view of the Twin Cities. I patted my phone, which sat snugly in my pocket, just to make sure it was still there. I was expecting two callbacks, and was waiting to see which came first.

"I know what I'm doing," I said, lurking only so long in the empty air. The skies were clear and blue, the day warm and bright. Zero chance we weren't going to be seen.

"Man, I could go for some fried cheese curds right about now," Reed muttered, pointing down at the food building.

"I'm partial to the Australian potatoes, myself." I paused, looking over the grounds. "Now...if I were a sociopathic murderer looking for a placc to hide, where would I go?"

"Aww, don't be so hard on yourself," Reed deadpanned, "you're not a sociopathic murderer. You've got at least 2% of the empathy a normal person has."

I flipped him the bird, but kept my eye on the ground below, watching people walking along Dan Patch Avenue. The corn booth enticed me, as did Sweet Martha's Cookie Jar. I was getting hungry just thinking about it all.

Someone was screaming, and their voice caught on the wind. I peered down, trying to figure out where it was coming from as my phone buzzed in a frenzy with an emergency alert.

"Haunted house," Reed said, and we dove for the deck, trying to get to Ashleigh before she hurt anyone else.

CHAPTER NINETY-TWO

Ashleigh

The haunted house was right there, and she recognized it from where she, Lucille, and the others had gone through last year. There was an emergency exit along the side, and right as she reached it, she heard talking from within.

"I don't like it, Daddy, I want to leave, I want to get out." Muffled sobs accompanied the whining of the child.

"I know, sweetie, right this way."

The door to the haunted house emergency exit swung open in a way Ashleigh hadn't anticipated, leaving her standing on the side of the building with her bone-ridden arm and face exposed. The father with his scared, sobbing daughter was halfway out the door before he saw her there, and nearly jumped back when he did.

What the daughter did...was worse.

She screamed, and loudly.

Ashleigh thought about striking her down with a twist of her hand, but there was no point. The damage was done.

A loud buzzing from the stunned father's pocket harmonized with the tweeting of alerts from every other phone in the immediate area. Ashleigh didn't have to guess what that meant.

They knew she was here.

"Give me that," she snapped, using her powers to snatch the phone out of the dad's hand as he went for it, too stunned to get his ass out of the doorway but conditioned by that moronic device to automatically reach for it when it twittered at him. If she'd had more time, she might have killed them both for the inconvenience, but she didn't have it, so she settled for mentally shoving them again as she went past. This time they both went over, and more tears were shed.

The phone just confirmed what she already knew. An alert in big letters: <<<METAHUMAN ALERT: A DANGEROUS METAHUMAN HAS BEEN REPORTED IN YOUR AREA. POLICE ARE ALREADY ON THE WAY. SHELTER IN PLACE.>>>

"Pffft, like they're gonna stop me," Ashleigh said as the door closed behind her, leaving her in the dark of the haunted house.

The door flew open a moment later, and she turned, momentarily blinded by the light flooding in. A dark silhouette stood poised in the entry with the outline of a gun in hand, and a moment later, shouted, "Police! Freeze!"

Ashleigh smiled, reaching her hand out. The gun flew from his hand to hers, and with a hearty mental shove, she sent him flying into the wall of the building across the street. The crack was unmistakable, and she felt it through her powers even as the door closed.

She brought the gun closer and looked at it carefully in

the waning light as the emergency exit door shuddered closed.

A dart gun.

Suppressant.

Ashleigh smiled, tucking it into her waistband at the back as she plunged through the haunted house in search of another exit. If Sienna Nealon came looking for her, she'd have another surprise waiting.

CHAPTER NINETY-THREE

Sienna

The screaming by the haunted house was a little girl and her dad, both worked into a frenzy of nearly not being able to speak. At first I thought maybe they were just terrified by something they'd seen within, but a quick look around to see a cop smashed against the next building proved that nope, that wasn't it.

"Her face..." the little girl whispered as Reed and I hovered overhead, unnoticed by them, "...did you see her face?"

"Shhhh," the dad said, then screamed, "somebody hellllllllllp!"

"Oh, yeah, Ashleigh's super dead," I said, floating with Reed over the top of the haunted house. Just across the street, crowded with people, stood the octagonal cylinder of the Ag building. Just past it, up the looping road, was the 300-foot-tall blue candy cane of the sky tower. The ride itself, a disk that slowly climbed up the blue and white center support, gave riders a pretty magnificent view of the twin cities. I remembered riding it with Reed and Scott when they brought me here for the first time...

Yeah. That was a top five memory. Didn't really have time to reminisce about it now, but it definitely made the cut.

The tower's cylindrical disk that held the riders was about halfway up and crawling slowly toward the sky. I gave them a brisk wave, mostly because there was zero chance someone inside wasn't filming me.

A scream below caught my attention, and through the crowd down on the street, I saw them giving way as something – someone – cut through, running.

Ashleigh.

CHAPTER NINETY-FOUR

Ashleigh

She ran, hearing the screams around her. There was no doubt she was seen, and no doubt that she'd draw attention. Hiding in the haunted house was no option anymore, because now they knew she was there. Coldly calculating, but feeling the adrenaline pump in her blood, she ran ahead, looking for cover and–

Something slammed into her from behind, something she only felt at the last second, and Ashleigh rolled, bones cracking as she went down in a heap. She lashed out with her mind, and the thing that hit her went flying. She rolled, too, getting back to her feet, and saw her left arm dangling, broken solidly, the exposed bone hanging by shards.

She didn't dare take the time to stare at it. She kept a grip on what had hit her and pulled it forward.

"Damn you," she gasped. Not unexpected, just too soon.

"Damn me?" Nealon asked, and her eyes lit up again,

hitting Ashleigh like a kick to the ribs. The non-exposed ones, in this case. "You're the one who looks like she just escaped hell."

Ashleigh whipped around, doubling over and sprinting even as she cast Sienna Nealon away. She wanted to crush her, to smash her damned bones, but it'd require time and grip and mental effort, and none of those were easily at hand right now. Instead she ran, huffing and feeling the pain of all her accumulated wounds. Ahead was the blue and white Sky Tower, and she felt drawn to it for some reason as the crowds parted and made way for her, and she sprinted toward it like it was salvation.

CHAPTER NINETY-FIVE

Sienna

She looked even worse than I thought she would when I finally saw her. Our little exchange, that ended after she threw me twice and I eyeball-beamed her (Brance voice was out because busting the eardrums of the surrounding pedestrians would likely bring Minnesota down on me with an insane number of charges).

I got thrown. She flew, at a much slower pace than I could have made on my worst day, and her plan became very clear in the next seconds.

"Shit," Reed said, dipping down next to me and trying to throw wind in her path. It did nothing, and up Ashleigh went, smashing her way into the slowly climbing Sky Tower. My brother gritted his teeth and spoke through them. "Now she's got hostages."

CHAPTER NINETY-SIX

Ashleigh

Now she had hostages.

Ashleigh smiled in the midst of the small crowd that circled the Sky Tower's rising capsule. Screams greeted her appearance as she flew into the window she'd shattered with the force of her will, and then she slid in behind a family, anchoring them in place with her powers, using them as a shield. The acidic scent hanging over her soured in her nose as she pushed close to the family, and she heard one of them gag.

"Shhhhh," she said, because their screaming was irritating her. She locked in on a girl in front of her, only a year or two younger than she was. Just the perfect age for a member of her entourage. Like Greta, only this one had chubbier cheeks. Ugh. "Be quiet. Something magical is about to happen." And Ashleigh tuned out the screams, focusing her attention on the windows and watching, wondering where the attack was going to come from. She lifted the gun out of the back of her waistband with her powers, and sent it sideways, away from her.

Then, when she needed it most...boom. It'd be a great surprise.

CHAPTER NINETY-SEVEN

Sienna

I lurked just beneath the Sky Tower's slowly climbing apparatus, Reed hanging next to me. We were listening to the screams within, the silence of Ashleigh, and coming to our own conclusions about what was about to happen.

"So..." Reed said, meta-low. "Trap?"

"For sure," I agreed. "But the problem is–"

"I know you're out there!" Ashleigh screamed, sounding just a bit unhinged. Extremely worrying from a conscience-free sociopath. "Come up slowly...I want to talk to you." There was just enough relish in her voice to tell me that our assessment was dead on. "Maybe we can work this out."

I looked at Reed; he looked back at me and shook his head. "Minnesota is asking for this, you know," he whispered.

"I draw a distinction between the people of Minnesota and their dumbass governor and representatives," I said.

"They literally elected them," Reed said. "As Mencken put

it, they knew what they wanted when they voted for these morons, and they deserve to get it good and hard."

"Nobody put this issue on the ballot," I said. "Shipley dove on it like a starving fat kid on a loose Oreo when she realized the suburban Karens loved it. Whether the majority of people agree or not, we'll see come November. But whatever the case, these people didn't ask for some teenage sociopath with powers to come ripping into their day at the fair." I girded myself. "Come on, bro. Let's go be heroes in this town."

Reed sighed, and I knew he was with me. Again. "One last time," he agreed.

CHAPTER NINETY-EIGHT

I did not do as Ashleigh asked.

Following the commands of a lunatic leading you into a trap was a formula, in my estimation, for getting yourself and others killed.

Instead I circled around the far side of the Sky Tower, melted a Sienna-size hole through the glass windows in about half a second, and then, before the screams of people on this side of the ride could get too loud, I zipped up and came in high, figuring maybe I could surprise Ashleigh. I slipped around the edge of the center column, not touching anything, and hoping the screaming crowds would keep the secret until I could get the drop on her.

I edged around and found her sitting with her back to the pillar, focused intently on the hole in the glass she'd made when she came bursting in. The tower was slowly spinning its way up, the skyline out there turning bit by bit as it rose into the sky.

"Come on!" Ashleigh shouted, apparently not noticing the change in modulation of the crowd behind her, who knew I was here. She was intently focused on the hole she'd made, as if that was the only entrance. She was huddled behind a family of four, and they alone were doing just as much crying and screaming as the rest of the car combined.

Except for one girl, sitting just in front of Ashleigh. She was about the same age, maybe a little younger. She was sitting there quietly, her eyes a little glassy, wide. She was looking around, as if for something.

Then she looked right at me, and I held my finger to my lips as her eyes widened. She didn't say anything, though, and I readied myself to plunge at Ashleigh–

"Gotcha."

Ashleigh turned, looking up at me with a smile.

Too late, I saw the gun to my left, the barrel pointed right at me, no finger on the trigger.

Because she didn't need one.

Then it fired.

CHAPTER NINETY-NINE

I flung a hand out, thinking swiftly of Chad Goodwin and his magnetic powers. The gun flew back five feet, and something emerged from the barrel with a hiss, angling toward me–

A dart. With a metal tip, and metal nothing else.

Shit.

I pushed back against it, and Ashleigh shoved it forward at me. I knew a suppressant dart when I saw one, and this one was heading straight for me as fast as she could push it. My minimal Magneto powers were up against her full-on telekinesis; my grip was on the tip, the rest of the thing was synthetic, and there was zero chance I was holding back the tide on this forever.

And as soon as it hit...

...I'd be at her mercy.

The dart moved toward me again, infinitesimally closing the distance. It was only a few feet away now, and I was fighting back against it but pushed against the wall. The world was slowly turning around us, but for me the only thing I could see was the tip of that needle, slow death inching toward me with precision as I fought a tug of war I was bound to lose.

"Shhhhh," Ashleigh said, sweat beads popping out on her forehead as she grinned at me through gritted teeth. "Just let it happen."

"Bitch, I'm not Aaron Berry, don't say that shit to me." I strained, trying to pop the tip off the dart, rendering it useless. It didn't budge; she had a grip on it with her whole, monstrous force powers. I was not rendering it useless with my tiny, baby, metal-only one.

Ashleigh cackled, as befit her villainous role. "Fine. Don't. I'll win anyway. Soon I'll have you dosed full of that shit, and you'll be like Syrena – in pieces." She leered at me from below. "I guess it's true what they say about home – you never get out alive."

My hand wavered; I was losing this fight. Another few inches and she'd bury that thing in me. I was trying to ice up beneath my clothes but it was slow going. My attention was fully on this battle of wills in which I was plainly outmatched, and the moment I tried to shift it into another power, I was going to lose. Fast.

I was screwed, no matter what.

Something blurred between us with a rush of wind. It took me a second to realize what – who – it was, and by then...

...The dart was already buried in him up to the needle.

Reed turned in midair, dart protruding from his chest, as he sagged, and started to drift down to the ride.

"No!" I shouted. "No!"

He smiled. "I believe in you."

Then his feet hit the deck below as Ashleigh let out a cackle of pure pleasure.

My brother was powerless.

And at her mercy.

CHAPTER ONE HUNDRED

But I...

...Wasn't.

I shot across the ten feet of distance between Ashleigh and myself so hard that a sonic boom went off in the Sky Tower, sending up a fresh round of screams as the glass surrounding the ride rattled and cracked.

But when I stopped – and I did – it was inches from Ashleigh, who held up her good hand, straining, sweat pouring down her face, keeping me from rocketing into her.

I could feel my power still working, my body pushing at the invisible barrier holding me back. It was a futile effort, gauging by all my successes so far. My mind was scattered, pained, and my body was pushing against the impossible, invisible force with which she was holding me back.

"I told you, Nealon, you just don't have it anymore," Ashleigh crowed, the half of her face that was still capable of sweat absolutely drenched with it. Her other half was bone and hints of tissue; her left arm was hanging, broken, the humerus obviously fractured. She showed little reaction to a condition I was familiar with intimately, and knew came with extreme pain. All that shit, and she was still grinning at me. "You're no Slay Queen. Look at you." She gritted that hideous half smile that showed all her teeth on the left side of her face. She made Harvey Dent, post-acid, look amazing by comparison. "I would have killed to have your powers."

"Have 'em," I said, and blasted away at her with the eyebeams again. They hit an invisible barrier and bounced back, absorbed into my flesh like they'd never even existed. Weird.

"Fool me once, right?" She laughed, and it was a rattling, hoarse noise pushed through a damaged vocal box. "Now I'm going to kill you without needing a single one of them." She leaned a little closer. "And I know all of them."

"I think..." I squinted at her, the G-forces intense as I pressed forward without making progress, going the equivalent of several hundred miles an hour and not moving an inch. As if I had the rocketship equivalent of the emergency brake on. "...You might have forgotten one or two."

She cocked her skeleton head at me. "Oh? Which one?"

I just smiled.

And I hit her with the Warmind.

Never considered one of my great powers, most people tended to forget about it. It was a distractionary power at best, one that would buy me a second or two of delay against a strong meta. Like Ashleigh.

But with her...a second or two was all I needed.

The warmind hit her, filling her mind with images of crows and horror. I let them loose, picking at her mental flesh like she was a scarecrow, giving the power a little extra fear to work with and feeding it a dose of my Harmon telepathy. Carefully; that one was dangerous to me.

Ashleigh screeched and yanked her hand back like she'd been burned. The hand, by itself, meant nothing; she could have waved it around all day and it wouldn't have done a thing to take away the barrier she'd placed between us. If she was focused and paying attention.

For a rookie meta like her, though, her hand was the focusing mechanism she used to will her powers. And when it moved, it was a good sign she'd lost focus, mostly because in her head crows were attacking her psyche, a thing for which few who experienced it had any defense.

The moment she moved her hand the barrier between us dissolved.

And I burst toward her with four hundred miles per hour of built-up power.

Slamming into her ribs on the excoriated side meant I got to feel them all break beneath my strike. I smashed into Ashleigh and carried her into the window beyond, which shattered completely as we smashed through it.

Carrying her out, I debated letting her die right then and there. A three-hundred-foot drop would kill most people, after all. Even meta ones.

But probably not her.

Instead, I turned my course down, picking out a stray piece of concrete, empty of any pedestrians, and rocketed us toward it at the speed of sound.

I expected her to kick in with her powers, to regain her presence of mind at any second.

She did. About five feet before we were set to hit the ground.

Ashleigh screamed, and put a hand out. She stopped about two feet from slamming into concrete, twisted in my grasp so she could see the ground in order to stop us from plunging into it at hundreds of miles per hour.

She did not, however, see the donkey punch that I was preparing to lay on her as soon as we stopped, and that hit her so damned hard that her skull fractured in the back, and clear fluid leaked out from the bone.

Ashleigh sagged, and we dropped the last two feet to the ground as I landed on her, heavily, her ribs sounding like Rice Krispies with milk poured on them. I gave her another punch for good measure, but her head just lolled when it hit.

She was out. I checked her pulse; still there. But she was unconscious.

Sirens were echoing through the fair, and people were crowding around with cell phones, shouting questions, shouting other things. Once I was sure Ashleigh was down for the count, and when the cops were close, I vaulted up into the air again and back toward the Sky Tower. I sailed inside just as I saw the police arrive on the scene, dart guns at the ready. They aimed at me, but I was already out of range.

I heard them give Ashleigh a round. I tried not to contemplate too deeply how that was going to go for her, given she was missing ten to fifteen percent of her skin. Her metahuman healing and natural heartiness was keeping her alive. Without that...

Well, I hadn't darted her, and I hadn't skinned her. Hopefully the authorities here would see it my way on that one.

Reed was standing against the glass with the others, staring out at my battleground. As soon as I was in, he hurried over to me; everyone else pretty much edged away. I hugged him. "You didn't have to do that," I said, burying my head in his chest.

"Someone had to take it out of play," he said, smiling tightly. "Figured it should be the one of us less likely to beat her."

I looked him in the eyes. "You still believe in me, huh?"

"When you're sober, absolutely," he said, patting me on the back as he planted a kiss on my forehead. Light, pleasant.

I nodded, feeling a little choked up, then surveyed the Sky Tower riders while gently dabbing at one of my eyes. "Uh...everyone okay up here?" I didn't see any blood. A whole lot of cell phones recording me, but no blood. Except on me, of course.

The girl who'd been Ashleigh's hostage was right up front, her eyes locked on mine. As I watched, she grabbed my sleeve and tugged on it. "I saw your head sculpted in butter," she said, staring at me blankly. She pointed to one of the other fair buildings in the distance. "Next to the Princess Kay of the Milky Way one. Kind of a novelty tribute or something, I guess, since you're getting kicked out."

"Oh." I flushed a little, honestly humbled by the tribute. My head in butter? That was kind of a big deal at the Minnesota State Fair. "That was nice of them. How'd it compare to the real deal?" I asked, sticking out my chin.

She shrugged. "Pretty close. More yellow, though, I guess."

"As it should be." I looked over at Reed. He was staring out the window; lots of lights, lots of sirens. And the Sky Tower was starting to circle back around, heading down. "What?"

"We need to get out of here if we're running," Reed said. A chopper flared its belly just outside the window, slowing after a rapid approach. Another did the same a moment later, behind us, both with POLICE written on the sides, and he cringed. "Never mind. I guess we're not getting out of here that way."

"We weren't anyway," I said softly as the ride continued to rotate slowly back to earth. "Just chill. Let me handle it."

He pursed his lips. "I don't think there's a way to 'handle' your way through this one, Sienna."

I eased up to the window, making sure to keep my hands visibly raised. Among all the cop cars, marked and unmarked, I searched for unmarked SUVs. There was no shortage crowding the State Fair streets, probably from BCA and other agencies summoned by all the ruckus here.

The Sky Tower docked, and Reed and I were waiting by the exit when it did, hands raised and prepared for what was to come. "I surrender!" I shouted, trying to shuffle out without getting shot. The nearest cop was thirty feet away, and I certainly saw plenty of dart guns out there.

"FBI!" Someone shouted from off to the side. "Federal agents, don't move!"

I followed the command. Seconds later I was being swarmed and cuffed by a guy in a suit and tie. Gently.

"Hey, what the hell?" some local cop shouted. "This ain't your jurisdiction!"

"She just violated FAA sovereignty and she's wanted for questioning in regards to an imminent terrorist threat," the FBI agent at my back said, then whispered, "which will be resolved the second you're across the Wisconsin State Line. President Gondry called us after he got your message. We'll get you out of here. I'm Agent Jordan." He raised his voice again. "Back off, State. She's our prisoner."

The local cop seemed genuinely cowed. "Okay. But – we want her after you're done!"

"Sure thing, hoss," the agent behind me said, parading me and Reed toward a couple agency SUVs as St. Paul's SWAT team stood down and started moving past us to secure the ride. Job done, at least on my end.

"I don't know about you," Reed said, next to me in the back of the FBI SUV, "but what I'm really looking forward to in our next home is that maybe we can stop getting arrested."

I shrugged, and tried to hide the impish smile threatening to break out across my face. "For a while, anyway." I didn't manage it, and my brother dissolved into chuckles.

CHAPTER ONE HUNDRED ONE

On our way to the Cube, Agent Jordan let me out of the cuffs, and I called our friends. "Head for the Wisconsin line," I said. "We're making a stop at the Cube to present our evidence for Berry, then we're heading out, too."

"Hurry," Lethe said, a little muffled on the other end, since I was talking to Jamal.

"Yeah, your window is getting short," Jamal said. "It's after noon now, you know?"

"Doesn't matter," I said. "Soon as we wrap up at the Cube, we're out. BCA is not playing games, they want us and they want us now. We'll be running for the border, I promise."

"See you there, Sienna," Jamal said. "Know where we're going after?"

"To bed for a day, probably," I said, then looked at Reed. He didn't meet my eyes on that. "After that...we'll talk about it."

"We'll wait up for you," Jamal said. And then he hung up.

"We'll escort you across to Wisconsin, Ms. Nealon," Agent Jordan said with a smile. "The president ordered it. They won't get you today."

"Then they'll get us never," Reed said. "Unless they can convince some other state to extradite us."

"President Gondry thinks that's unlikely," Jordan said. "Odds are good any charges from this will be dropped within thirty days. He's got the AG already looking into whatever they can bring as a civil rights violation."

"What about the metahuman law?" I asked. "Will it stand?"

He shrugged, but I could tell by the way he said it where we stood. "Above my pay grade."

We pulled into the Cube about forty-five minutes later, after passing through downtown Minneapolis. I kept my head down for most of the ride, afraid I might be seen. Buildings passed, then trees and sunlit fields, and as we pulled into the Cube's parking lot I felt a familiar swell of...well, familiarity.

But I ignored it, and plunged ahead into the admin building, where Guard Kennebec was waiting for us, the most jaded damned look on his face. "You again?"

"Me again," I said. "Gonna need to swear an affidavit on behalf of one of your prisoners."

His eyes narrowed. "Berry?"

"Yeah."

He shrugged. "All right." And he led me down.

I talked into a recorder for an hour, laying out every single thing that Reed and I had learned in our investigation. I honestly had my doubts that it'd make any kind of impression or even a dent in the case, but I did it anyway, covering every single witness, every piece of evidence...

When I was done, Kennebec shrugged again. "Okay."

I felt drained. Not just from the fight, but from covering all that. Reed hadn't been in the room with me; he was telling his own version of the story in a different interrogation room. "Anyone going to actually listen to that?" I glanced at the double-sided mirror.

A light clicked on within, and I could see Stillwater Detective Mattie Greene almost up at the glass. "Yeah, maybe," she said over the speaker. "I mean, I'm gonna have to go back and listen to the first part, which I missed because I didn't know I was going to need to be here today, but...the part I caught? Wow. Quite the story."

"Did you get Lucille?" I asked.

"We did," she said, leaning forward on a console. "And you know what she did? Squealed like a...something...and without legal representation. Not sure how that's going to hold up, since she's a minor, but it's enough to convince me that Ashleigh Simone was the real problem all along." She shuddered. "The things they did to Greta, to Berry..."

"Yeah," I said.

"The DA is on her way," Greene said. "I'll be talking with her, and we'll see what we come up with." She clicked off the light, and I was left alone with Kennebec.

"Come on," he said. "I gotta get you out of here. You can wait in the lobby, if you need to."

"Actually," I said, "can I wait in the cafeteria? I haven't had anything but a Moons Over My Hammy today, and I am *starving.*"

CHAPTER ONE HUNDRED TWO

Reed and I waited in the lobby with our FBI handler while whatever gears needed to be spun were spinning below. I munched on some snacks straight out of a vending machine, because Kennebec wouldn't let me go to the cafeteria, or eat lunch with the inmates. Pffft. Like I hadn't before.

My brother was checking his phone every few minutes, as though that would make some difference. It was getting toward six in the evening, and I knew what he was thinking: in spite of the arbitrary nature of the deadline, and our federal protection, it would still be best if we got the hell out of Minnesota by midnight.

Detective Greene emerged from security a little before eight, a satisfied look on her face. "The DA's going to allow Lucille's statement to stand, for now. Combined with evidence we found in her room and Ashleigh's, we've got enough to charge the girls with Greta Oliver's murder."

I clenched my fist in triumph. "Are they going to be in any kind of shape to stand trial?"

Greene's expression got tighter. "Lucille, yes. Ashleigh...well..." She shook her head. "...She's in rough shape. They're letting the suppressant run its course, and they're pretty sure she'll survive because they've been giving her blood to keep her going, and once her metahuman healing factor kicks in...well, she'll survive."

"But she's going to look like she escaped from an episode of *The Walking Dead* forever more, isn't she?" I asked.

"Don't know," Greene said. "Don't care, either, so long as she stands trial. They're doing wonders with skin grafts these days, anyway."

The doors to outside opened, and in walked Paula Cunningham, followed by Faith Holloway, who was clutching the hand of her little boy. Paula caught sight of me, and came right on over.

She didn't look like a hugger, I thought. I was wrong.

She almost lifted me out of my seat. Not because she was a meta. She was just strong.

"Thank you," she whispered. "Thank you...so much."

"Hey," I said, "kinda nice to spend a case proving someone was innocent for once. Usually I do the opposite."

Thankfully, Faith did not hug me. Because there was only so much I could stand.

At ten fifteen Aaron Berry himself walked out of the security checkpoint, looking ruffled as hell and seriously the worse for the wear. He had tears in his eyes, and he caught a hug from Paula in stride. Then one from his little boy, and, well...

My eyes got a little blurry at that point. Misty, maybe. Because it was humid in there, surely.

"Thank you," he said, right there in front of me when I looked up from gently dabbing at the moisture problem I was experiencing.

"What? Oh. Yes," I said. His little boy was in his arms, hanging on his neck. "You could have made it easier on me by making less controversial life choices, you know. Or just being more honest." With this, I fixed Paula with a look, too. "All of you."

He looked only mildly contrite. "I know. I've been sober for, like, three weeks now. Made some rough choices when I wasn't. Some...I really regret. Some..." He went in for a peck on his son's cheek. "...Not so much. But now that I am sober...maybe we'll just keep that up."

Reed cleared his throat from behind me and gestured to his phone.

"Oh," I said, and started shuffling my feet toward the exit. "Hey, glad to see you got out. I have to go."

"Thank you!" he called, as I headed for the door.

I didn't answer, just waved as I headed for the parking lot.

And then I was gone.

CHAPTER ONE HUNDRED THREE

"If we drive flat out from here, we'll make it back to Hudson well before midnight," Reed said, hustling across the parking lot. I could tell he'd gotten his powers back at some point during our interminable wait by the crisp movements he made with every step. Agent Jordan was already waiting by the car; Reed must have sent him ahead.

I stopped in the middle of the parking lot and turned. The Cube's property was pretty rustic, with zero effort going into maintaining the lawns past about fifty or so yards beyond the main building. Still, in the distance, by the spotlights mounted on the corners of building, I could see the bones of another structure.

"Sienna?" Reed called. He was almost to the car already.

"Hey, Agent Jordan," I said, "can we have like...five, ten minutes?"

Jordan shrugged. "I'll get you across to Wisconsin before midnight...as long you don't take forever."

"Thanks," I said, and beckoned for Reed. He hesitated only a moment before joining me.

I walked across the poorly maintained fields of the Cube

facility, looking at the woods in the distance. "You remember when that was the science building?" I asked, pointing to a pad of concrete that had been demolished down to its foundation.

"Only if forced to," Reed grumbled.

I trudged along, toward the building in the distance. Or at least, the remains of it.

"Why are we going here?" Reed asked. There was a note of dread about him.

I held my fire until we were there, at the fallen remains of the old building. It didn't look like it once had, before it had been destroyed in an (artificial) earthquake, then mostly cleared by the government so as not to be a hazard. Still, there were a few beams left standing, the framework of what had once been the living quarters of the Directorate.

"Because this was home," I said softly, over the soft chirp of crickets in the background. I looked at my brother. "I know it never really was for you. That it was just a place you lived. But when I left my house that first time...this became home."

He bowed his head. "You went through some rough times here."

"I did." I looked into the darkness surrounding us on all sides. "But I don't think about those much. You know what I do remember?"

He looked at me attentively, but didn't speak.

I remembered it right then, clear as the day it happened. "We were packing our things, salvaging the last from the wreckage, and then...we were gone. Never to live here anymore. Opening a new chapter in our lives."

"You moved back into your house," Reed said. "With Ariadne. And I moved in with..." He smiled.

"Yeah, her," I said with a smirk. "But the point is...this was a place of graduation. I never went to school. Only ever had one house I remembered. Only ever knew my mom." I looked around again. "Here I had friends for the first time. Here I got to know family outside of her. This was really the place where I grew up." A solemn feeling traced its way over me. "But it's time to leave again."

Reed hesitated, but when he spoke, it was warm. "I know it's tough. To leave everything you've known as home. I mean, even when you were gone, it must have felt like eventually, hopefully you'd make it back here–"

"You don't understand," I said, looking him right in the eye. "The memory I'm thinking of – number one in my top five, with a bullet – has nothing to do with being in Minnesota."

And I was there on that day, three years ago, when we stood in a cramped, dusty office building in Eden Prairie, Minnesota.

"...rent is due on the first of the month," the realtor, a stuffy woman in tweed, said.

Reed had sidled closer to me. "You sure you want to do this?" He looked a little pained. "Breaking off from the government...it's not going to make our jobs any easier."

"We've got contacts," I said. "State and local is the way to go. Trust me – we don't want to work for the Harmon administration."

He sighed. "On this we agree. I'm just worried...y'-know...we're breaking out on our own. No net but this mysterious backer, who we know nothing about. Doesn't that worry you?"

I could barely contain my smile. The mysterious backer, of course, was me, and we weren't going out on anything but our own. "No," I said. "Because as long as we're together, and a team...I know we'll be fine."

"That," I said to Reed, the crickets alive in the woods around me, "is my happiest memory. When we broke free of the damned government. So – am I sad about leaving Minnesota? Yes. But Minnesota is exactly like the feds were to us back then: radioactive ground. I'm ready to cut ties with the past and face the future – so long as you're with me." And I offered him my hand.

He looked at it for a moment, and just for a second, I felt a gut check, afraid he was going to diss me. But he took it, patting me on the hand, then looped his arm in mine, where we wouldn't touch skin but I could still feel his warmth and reassurance. "I'm with you," he said, as we started walking back to the car. "All the way."

CHAPTER ONE HUNDRED FOUR

The road Agent Jordan took was not the one I expected; instead of looping 494 South through Bloomington, he ran us right through downtown Minneapolis. I watched the IDS Tower go past, lights glittering up its tall length as we blazed by on Interstate 94. The Witch's Tower up on the hill at the University of Minnesota stood out in the dark of night; down the road a bit, the new Allianz Stadium glittered a pretty white under the summer moon.

Soon we were passing through St. Paul, and then it was gone. I turned, looking out the window as it receded into the distance as we hit the 494/694/94 exchange in Woodbury.

Eyes were misty again. Damned summer humidity.

Woodbury went by, its little strip malls and shopping centers all ablaze with neon signs, and then, suddenly, it was empty fields. Wisconsin was miles ahead, and it was only 11:45. Time enough to make it.

"So..." Reed said, eyes flashing in the dark of the back seat. "...Nashville?"

"We can go anywhere," I said, feeling a tug in my heart. I knew where I wanted to be, where I was actually wanted...and it felt like the first time I'd felt that in forever. "Wherever you go, I go."

He kept his eyes on the dark road, ahead but his answer came a second later. "Nashville it is."

I felt my eyes water up, and I reached over, clenching his arm just above the sleeve, where I could hold it. He reached over and clenched my wrist just above my sleeve, and held it snugly in his. I could feel the love and affirmation through it. He really was with me. They all were.

"Look," he said softly, a few moments later, as we passed into the last mile of Minnesota before the great bridge over the St. Croix River.

Thanks for Visiting Minnesota – it was written on a stone sign, with the state's name inscribed in elaborate script. I could barely read it through wet, blurry eyes.

Less than a minute later we reached the St. Croix, and the big bridge waiting to carry us across to Hudson, Wisconsin.

My eyes were cloudy streaks of intense light matching the lamps above as the river, and the future, and Wisconsin stretched out in front of me. I didn't dare look back at the past, or Minnesota, as our tires thumped over the seams of the bridge like a steady drumbeat, marching me away from the place I'd always thought of as home, and now could never return to again.

Sienna Nealon Will Return in

SOUTHERN COMFORT

The Girl in the Box, Book 44

Coming March 31, 2021!

(Or maybe before. We'll see.)

Pre-order here!

AUTHOR'S NOTE

Thanks for reading! If you want to know immediately when future books become available, take sixty seconds and sign up for my NEW RELEASE EMAIL ALERTS by CLICKING HERE. I don't sell your information and I only send out emails when I have a new book out. The reason you should sign up for this is because I don't always set release dates, and even if you're following me on Facebook (robertJcrane (Author)) or Twitter (@robertJcrane), or part of my Facebook fan page (Team RJC), it's easy to miss my book announcements because ... well, because social media is an imprecise thing.

Find listings for all my books plus some more behind-the-scenes info on my website: http://www.robertjcrane.com!

Cheers,
Robert J. Crane

Other Works by Robert J. Crane

The Girl in the Box
(and Out of the Box)
Contemporary Urban Fantasy

1. Alone
2. Untouched
3. Soulless
4. Family
5. Omega
6. Broken
7. Enemies
8. Legacy
9. Destiny
10. Power
11. Limitless
12. In the Wind
13. Ruthless
14. Grounded
15. Tormented
16. Vengeful
17. Sea Change
18. Painkiller
19. Masks
20. Prisoners
21. Unyielding
22. Hollow
23. Toxicity

24. Small Things
25. Hunters
26. Badder
27. Nemesis
28. Apex
29. Time
30. Driven
31. Remember
32. Hero
33. Flashback
34. Cold
35. Blood Ties
36. Music
37. Dragon
38. Control
39. Second Guess
40. Powerless
41. Meltdown
42. True North
43. Innocence
44. Southern Comfort*

World of Sanctuary
Epic Fantasy
(in best reading order)

1. Defender (Volume 1)
2. Avenger (Volume 2)
3. Champion (Volume 3)
4. Crusader (Volume 4)
5. Sanctuary Tales (Volume 4.25)
6. Thy Father's Shadow (Volume 4.5)
7. Master (Volume 5)
8. Fated in Darkness (Volume 5.5)

9. Warlord (Volume 6)
10. Heretic (Volume 7)
11. Legend (Volume 8)
12. Ghosts of Sanctuary (Volume 9)
13. Call of the Hero (Volume 10)
14. The Scourge of Despair (Volume 11)* Coming in 2021!

Ashes of Luukessia
A Sanctuary Trilogy
(with Michael Winstone)
(Trilogy Complete)

1. A Haven in Ash (Ashes of Luukessia #1)
2. A Respite From Storms (Ashes of Luukessia #2)
3. A Home in the Hills (Ashes of Luukessia #3)

Liars and Vampires
YA Urban Fantasy
(with Lauren Harper)

1. No One Will Believe You
2. Someone Should Save Her
3. You Can't Go Home Again
4. Lies in the Dark
5. Her Lying Days Are Done
6. Heir of the Dog
7. Hit You Where You Live
8. Her Endless Night*
9. Burned Me*
10. Something In That Vein*

Southern Watch
Dark Contemporary Fantasy/Horror

1. Called
2. Depths
3. Corrupted
4. Unearthed
5. Legion
6. Starling
7. Forsaken
8. Hallowed*
9. Enflamed*

The Mira Brand Adventures
YA Modern Fantasy
(Series Complete)

1. The World Beneath
2. The Tide of Ages
3. The City of Lies
4. The King of the Skies
5. The Best of Us
6. We Aimless Few
7. The Gang of Legend
8. The Antecessor Conundrum

*Forthcoming, title subject to change

ACKNOWLEDGMENTS

As usual, thanks to Lewis Moore for the edits, Jeff Bryan, for the proofing, and Lillie of https://lilliesls.wordpress.com for her work proofing and compiling my series bible.

Thanks also to Karri Klawiter of artbykarri.com for the cover.

Thanks, too, to my family for making this all possible.

Printed in Great Britain
by Amazon

74615622R00271